P9-CQC-806

F Thayer
Thayer, James.
White Star
Simon & Schuster,
c1995.

F Thayer
Thayer, James.
White Star
Simon & Schuster,
c1995.

NOVELS BY JAMES THAYER

White Star
S-Day: A Memoir of the Invasion of England
Ringer
Pursuit
The Earhart Betrayal
The Stettin Secret
The Hess Cross

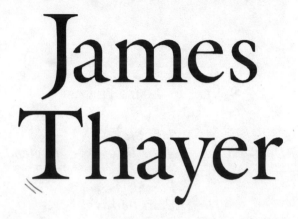

James Thayer

White Star

A Novel

SIMON & SCHUSTER
New York London Toronto
Sydney Tokyo Singapore

SIMON & SCHUSTER
Rockefeller Center
1230 Avenue of the Americas
New York, New York 10020

Designed by Deirdre C. Amthor

Manufactured in the United States of America

1 3 5 7 9 10 8 6 4 2

Library of Congress Cataloging-in-Publication Data
Thayer, James Stewart.
White Star : a novel / James Stewart Thayer.
p.   cm.
I. Title.
PS3570.H347W45   1995
813'.54—dc20   94-19678
CIP
ISBN: 0-671-79814-6

To my daughter
Annemarie Patricia Thayer

Thanks to
Peter Crow, C. James Frush, Sally A. Martin, John D. Reagh III,
Jay McM. Thayer, John L. Thayer, M.D., Laurie Dinnison
Thayer, Dexter A. Washburn, Mark A. Washburn, Robert O.
Wells, Jr., and my wonderful and remarkable wife,
Patricia Wallace Thayer.

There is no hunting like the hunting of man, and those who have hunted armed men long enough and like it never care for anything else thereafter.

—Ernest Hemingway

PART ONE
LIVING
SAPPHIRES

If you fear the wolves, don't go near the forest.
—Russian proverb

1

THE STAR APPEARED in the void where none had been before, flickering as it struggled to life, sending forth delicate tendrils of light that lanced the eternal darkness. Then the star burst to full radiance, filling the vault of heaven with opalescent rays.

"Are you kidding me?" Anna Renthal whispered. "Origami?"

Owen Gray looked down at his hand. The star rested in his palm. Startled, he flicked his fingers and it fell to the table where it lay lifeless and tiny.

She leaned slightly along the prosecutors' table toward him, looking at the jury as it filed into the courtroom. "It's a pissant hobby for a grown man, if you ask me." She spoke almost without moving her lips, her eyes following the jurors as they took their seats.

"Goddamnit." Pete Coates was also whispering. "None of the jurors is looking at us. We've lost."

"Number eight just smiled at Owen," Anna Renthal insisted.

Coates said out of the side of his mouth, "Number eight sat there for sixteen weeks and wet her pants every time Owen took the stand. She's in love with him. Sure she's going to grin."

Anna Renthal asked, "You okay, Owen?"

Gray looked again at the paper star. He had no recollection of folding it. The star often appeared at times of stress, emerging from whatever piece of paper was in front of him.

Gray shook his head. "Three years work on the Chinaman all boils down to whether a juror smiles at me."

He ran a finger along his nose. Even this small motion required an effort. Eighty-hour weeks had worn him shiny. He had caught himself in a mirror that morning. He seemed to have aged five years during the trial. The new lines around his eyes looked permanent. His black hair still had the tight waves, only there was less above his temples. He had seen so little sun during the trial that his skin had faded to a prison pallor. Gray had a thin dagger of a nose and slate-gray eyes. A grin would have softened the sharp angles of his face, but in front of a jury his expression was always carefully deadpan.

The jurors moved more slowly than in days and months past, taking their time, enjoying their portentous arrival. Gray glanced over his shoulder at the courtroom's gallery.

There was not a seat to be had, not a square foot of the back aisle unoccupied, and there was not one sound or movement from the spectators. All the throat clearing, fingernail clipping, tooth sucking, knuckle cracking, and butt scratching were at last quelled. Even the pencil hands of the media sketch artists were motionless.

Carmine "Chinaman" De Sallo had been charged with thirty-eight counts, everything from money laundering to hijacking to racketeering to conspiracy. The jury had deliberated eight days. De Sallo faced eighty-eight years in prison. "He deserves life in the electric chair," Anna Renthal had said.

The spectators were arranged as if at a wedding. Wiseguys were shoulder to shoulder in the gallery on the defendant's side of the courtroom. Federal agents and New York City police sat on the other side, behind the prosecutors' table.

De Sallo had packed the courtroom day after day with his soldiers. They were referred to as "our friends" and "nice guys" on the three hundred hours of tapes Owen Gray had listened to preparing for the trial. Pete Coates had once said that if a computer could eliminate the profanity from the tapes, there'd only be six hours left.

Detective Coates was the NYPD case officer, allowed to sit at the prosecutors' table. He had tiny features—pinprick eyes and a splinter of a nose, so small that his head appeared to have swollen

16

around his face. His hair was a dun color and was as short as a drill instructor's. His chest had the dimensions of an oil drum, and his coat sleeves were two inches too short. He wore a sagging gray suit. His blue-rimmed spectacles were surprisingly stylish, given the sprung and faded look to the rest of him.

Also at the table, for the first time since the trial began, was Gray's boss, Frank Luca, the United States Attorney for the Southern District of New York. He had said nothing since the judge had reconvened the court to hear the verdict. Newspaper columnists judged that Luca's senatorial ambitions depended on De Sallo's fate.

But this was Owen Gray's case. He was an assistant U.S. Attorney and the chief prosecutor, the mastermind of the government's massive effort to put Carmine De Sallo into prison. Anna Renthal was his able co-prosecutor. She had postponed her wedding and honeymoon because of this trial. Her walnut-colored hair was pulled back in a severe bun at the nape of her neck. She wore a gray suit with a white cotton blouse buttoned to the neck. Her lip gloss was neutral, no color. At the beginning of the trial Gray had told her, "You want this guy to do time, don't let the jury see you looking like a Bergdorf mannequin."

As the last of the jurors filed into the box, Gray said in a low voice, "I'm going to indict Pots next. Jesus, that guy sets me off."

Joseph "Pots" Asperanti was in his usual position directly behind De Sallo. He wore glasses with amber lenses and a silk handkerchief in his suit pocket. Once a month he hosted a poker game, and when he had lost everything in his wallet he would put his wife into the pot. The winner disappeared into the bedroom for twenty minutes, collecting the wager from Pots's wife. At trial, every time he found Owen Gray looking in his direction Pots mouthed a kiss.

Next to Pots was Danny Garbanto, known as the Boatman because it was thought he piloted the De Sallo runabout that dumped bodies into Jamaica Bay off Howard Beach. FBI agents called the bay the Jamaica Cemetery. Also in the room were Luigi Massarli, a De Sallo soldier said to have a collection of four thousand handguns, and Dominick "Four Nines" Rompuni, a *spallone* (a money mover, from the Italian for smuggler), who performed countless transactions involving $9,999, one dollar less than the amount federal law required banks to report.

A dozen other wiseguys had visited the gallery every day, but

17

the star was Chinaman De Sallo, and he never let the limelight drift from him. Each day his measured gait, imperious nod, and sanguine smile told his audience and jury that he fully expected an acquittal. He would not be inconvenienced, as Vito Genovese and Anthony Salerno had been, forced to run their organizations from prisons.

The source of De Sallo's nickname had been a matter of endless speculation among the prosecutors, police, and agents. Finally, informer BQ 6675-TE (BQ for the FBI's Brooklyn-Queens office, and TE for top echelon, the highest rank the FBI assigned an informer) revealed the solution. The informer was now almost eighty years old and had made his bones the same year as De Sallo's father. In 1966, the father and the informer visited Carmine at St. Luke's Hospital, where Carmine had just had a cancerous testicle removed. The first words out of his father's mouth on seeing Carmine were "Well, kid, we'll just have to call you the Chinaman. Won Hung Lo. Get it? One hung low." The name stuck.

Each of De Sallo's suits cost more than Gray made in a month, and the gangster never wore shoes unless they were made from some endangered species. His only jewelry was a pinkie ring. An NYPD telephoto showed it to be a Harvard class ring, unusual for a man who had left school forever after two and a half years in sixth grade at Brooklyn's P.S. 209.

The NYPD claimed De Sallo had four toupees, each with slightly different length hair. He rotated the wigs once a week so it appeared his hair was getting longer between alleged visits to his hairstylist. A plastic surgeon had strengthened his chin and added a slight cleft. His eyes were feminine, with long lashes. His eyebrows appeared plucked. De Sallo's delicate eyes had occasionally emboldened his underworld enemies to make mistakes, usually fatal.

Chinaman was six feet four and weighed somewhere between three hundred and three fifty pounds. The U.S. Attorney's office had a pool on what his prison weigh-in would be. Gray had paid his five dollars, and if De Sallo flattened the scales at 342 at the penitentiary strip search and medical, Gray would be five hundred dollars to the good.

On the other side of the courtroom aisle were the feds and cops —the operations supervisors of the Drug Enforcement Agency and

Customs Service and many of their agents, deputies from the U.S. Marshal's office, the chief of the Southern District Organized Crime Strike Force, and at least two dozen agents from the Manhattan and Queens-Brooklyn FBI offices. Ninety FBI agents had worked on the investigation, fully a quarter of the agents in the Bureau's New York criminal division. Twenty New York City police detectives had joined them, and most were in the courtroom. Also in the spectator section were representatives of the Italian Treasury Police and the Italian Anti-Mafia Commission. Reporters filled every spare corner of the courtroom, ready to lift cellular phones from their pockets to call their newsrooms.

The judge said, "Mr. Foreman, I understand you've reached a verdict."

Gray turned back to the jury. His breath was shallow, and he felt as if he were wearing a jacket three sizes too small. He whispered, "Here we go, Anna."

The foreman, juror number three, replied, "We have, Your Honor."

This criminal trial had been the longest ever in the Southern District of New York. Judge Robert Kennelly had withered and grown smaller as the trial played itself out in front of him. The bags under his eyes had lately come to resemble black oysters. "Please hand your verdict to the clerk."

The clerk stepped toward the jury box.

"Please, God," Anna Renthal breathed, her eyes closed in prayer. "Call my beloved parents to your kingdom today if you must, but convict this bastard. Mom and Dad live at 1441 Harrison Street, East Orange, dear Lord."

All FBI and DEA and NYPD eyes were on De Sallo. The mobster's expression as he realized he'd never again terrorize his beloved Brooklyn streets would be the agents' and officers' reward for their years of work.

The clerk took the slip from the foreman, then stepped to the elevated dais. Judge Kennelly reached across the bench for the paper. With his face professionally impassive he opened the slip to read it.

Count one was conspiracy, the easiest of the prosecution's burdens. If De Sallo walked on the conspiracy count, he'd walk on them all. Everyone in the courtroom knew it.

The accused and his attorneys rose from their chairs. De Sallo

19

stood with his back as rigid as a fireplace poker. His expression was one of sublime confidence, as if he owned the jury, the judge, the building, and all of Foley Square outside. De Sallo's battery of lawyers, arrayed at the table across the courtroom from Gray, each had an impeccably British name and a clock running at three hundred dollars an hour.

"Ah, goddamnit," Coates muttered. "Number ten just winked at that piece of dirt Chinaman."

"Contact lens problems," Gray whispered hopefully. "She's had trouble before."

The judge passed the slip back to the clerk. "You may read the verdict."

Gray glanced at his superior, Frank Luca. The U.S. Attorney dipped his chin. Christ, Gray thought, he's watching me, not De Sallo. Three years' work, and it's come down to this second.

"In the matter of the United States versus Carmine De Sallo," the clerk intoned. "On count one, we the jury find the defendant . . ."

Frank Luca inhaled sharply, the first sound he had made since arriving at the prosecutors' table.

". . . not guilty."

Gasps filled the courtroom. Then dazed silence. Then the room erupted. The wiseguys hooted and whistled and applauded. A defense lawyer raised his arms into the air like a sprinter first to break the finish-line tape. Journalists reached for their phones. Another lawyer hugged De Sallo, carefully. Several spectators began a rhythmic "Chinaman, Chinaman, Chinaman," clapping their hands in time to their chant. Some jurors grinned. Others wept.

Owen Gray's face flushed so rapidly that it felt bloated. He sagged back into his chair.

Boatman Garbanto called out, "Attaway, boss."

Luigi Massarli hollered, "You banged them, boss."

Pots Asperanti blew a particularly juicy kiss at Gray.

That is, half the courtroom erupted. The agents and cops slumped as if in unison. Some leaned forward, arms on the seat back ahead of them, hands limp. Some closed their eyes.

"I'll be go to hell," Pete Coates said. "The puke is going to walk."

The judge pounded his desk with a gavel. After a moment a semblance of order settled on the courtroom.

Next was a related RICO charge. The court clerk read, "On count two, we the find the defendant not guilty."

Another smattering of applause. De Sallo brought his arm up to check his wristwatch as if he had other plans, an impressive display of impertinence.

Next was the kidnapping charge. "On count three, we find the defendant not guilty."

A line of sweat formed on Gray's forehead, and a hum of humiliation sounded in his ears, muting the rest of the clerk's recital. Anna Renthal involuntarily leaned into him. Too weak to offer support, he leaned with her.

The clerk's voice seemed far away. "Not guilty . . . not guilty . . ."

"Jesus," Anna said miserably. Her face had gained a yellow malarial hue. "I think I'm going to vomit."

Ignoring the clerk, Carmine De Sallo pulled a photo of his daughter from his wallet to show one of his lawyers.

Judge Kennelly angrily twirled his gavel. When the acquittal on the last count was read, the judge said, "I'm going to poll the jury on my own motion. Juror number one, is that your verdict and the verdict of the jury?"

"Yes, your honor."

Kennelly went through the list of jurors. Each affirmed the verdict.

One of De Sallo's lawyers then said, "Your Honor, I move to exonerate bail."

"Granted. Mr. De Sallo, you are released." The judge thanked the jury, then asked, "Is there anything else to come before the court today?"

"Yeah, Your Worship," Pots Asperanti said. "I move that the chief prosecutor, Mr. Gray here, take a vacation, maybe to Fantasyland down in Florida."

That passed as high humor in half the courtroom. The laughter raised more color in Gray's face.

The judge dismissed court on his way to the door and disappeared into his chambers before the bailiff could call out, "All rise."

21

Gray squeezed Anna Renthal's hand. He put his notes into his leather accordion briefcase. He ventured a look sideways at the chair where his boss had been sitting. Frank Luca had already slipped out of the courtroom.

Pete Coates had followed Gray's eyes. "Luca wants to avoid the reporters. Smart guy."

The detective patted one of Gray's shoulders, then joined the other cops and agents as they left the courtroom. Gray and Anna trailed after them. The paper star was left on the prosecutors' table.

The crowd was slowed by reporters who shoved their microphones into De Sallo's face the moment he reached the hallway. Camera flashes came as steadily as a strobe light. De Sallo pushed ahead, his troupe in tow.

With reporters shouting questions, the crowd passed down the marble hallway. De Sallo remained silent but waved his hand like a Rose Parade queen. On the ceiling intricate flowers were patterned on squares of green and red and were bordered with painted gray mazes, and to Gray seemed suffocating. He and Anna Renthal shuffled along at the end of the throng.

"We'll wait two years, then indict him again," Anna said with false cheer. "We'll get him next time, Owen."

"Yeah, you bet we will." His voice was doubtful.

They passed the metal detector. The guard, from a private security company, thrust a notepad and pen at De Sallo, who paused to sign it.

The guard beamed. "My kids'll be thrilled."

A bottleneck developed at the revolving door. Gray and Anna Renthal were the last to push through. Outside they passed between two of the fourteen columns fronting the building. Topping the columns were Corinthian capitals, each with rows of acanthus leaves appearing to have wilted in the summer heat. Above the columns, carved on the entablature in block letters, was "United States Court House."

Gray saw a bank of microphones set up near the sidewalk. The reporters had known they would get an interview irrespective of the verdict, because had the jury convicted De Sallo, bail pending appeal would have been immediately posted.

Anna shaded her eyes against the glaucous midday light. "A world record, I swear. Must be forty mikes."

WHITE STAR

A mob of reporters was gathered around the microphones. A dozen videotape cameras on tripods surrounded the mikes. Furiously working their cameras, photographers flanked De Sallo as he descended the steps.

"This way, Chinaman," some shouted. "Just a few more."

"He's usually camera shy," Anna said, descending the stairs next to Gray. She carried her briefcase in one hand and three volumes of the U.S. Code under her other arm.

Gray replied, "This is his chance to make you and me and especially Frank look like dunces. He won't pass it up."

Behind them, the thirty-two stories of the United States Court House rose to the gold-leafed pyramid roof. The building had been designed to blend with the neoclassic structures on both sides. Foley Square was a collection of traffic islands, each with ragged hedges and a few uneven trees. Across the square was the United States Court for International Trade. The cabbies had stopped their vehicles to gawk at the commotion.

De Sallo stepped down to the microphones. Many reporters pushed their hand-held recorders toward him. Questions were shouted until he held up both hands.

"I just got a couple of things to let you guys in on," he said in his street accent.

When Gray and Anna started away, a reporter from the swarm yelled, "You're next, Owen. Stick around, will you?"

Gray knew better than to duck the press. Part of his job at times like this was damage control. He gripped his briefcase handle with both hands and waited his turn.

The Chinaman's soldiers gathered around their boss. A short distance from the microphones Pete Coates also waited. He would give the NYPD's version of the verdict.

Wind tugged at strands of De Sallo's wig. He patted them down with a hand. He began, "Let me first say that America is a great country."

A flock of pigeons lifted from Foley Square, passing over the Chambers Street subway station, then toward Federal Plaza. To the south was the Municipal Building.

De Sallo held forth magnificently, "I would like to thank my beloved father, whose memory I carry with me like a wallet. And my mother, still alive but on the brink, who gave me the courage to be—"

At that instant the Chinaman's head ruptured. Brains and bone blew out the back of his head in a spray of crimson and gray gore. Slivers of De Sallo's skull and brain and shreds of his toupee rained on his soldiers.

The body, its face now a mask with nothing behind it, fell heavily to the steps. It rolled against the microphone stand, the flap of face dragging after it, streaking the steps in red.

Screams and oaths filled the square. A dozen handguns and one Uzi abruptly appeared in the hands of the agents and detectives. Pots Asperanti pulled out a .38 snubnose, having somehow snuck it in and out of the courthouse. Pots waved his pistol at imaginary targets, then quickly slid it back into his coat, nervously scanning the FBI agents.

Spectators ran for cover, some up the steps into the courthouse, others toward the subway station. Several taxis drove onto the sidewalk trying to flee the scene. One yellow bounced into a *USA Today* dispenser, crumpling the box.

The agents scanned the crowd, then the rooftops and windows, looking for the killer. They had heard nothing, no shot. And now they saw nothing.

Asperanti rolled De Sallo's body over. A hole the size of a dime had been punched between his eyes. Detritus from De Sallo's head oozed down the steps.

Asperanti said softly, "Son of bitch, Boatman, we better—" He turned to find Garbanto.

Garbanto had also collapsed to the steps, where he sat with his hand over his suit's wide lapel. Blood oozed between his fingers. The bullet that had ended De Sallo's life had also clipped Garbanto's shoulder. He blinked rapidly but made no sound. He was splattered with his boss's blood and brains.

"Goddamn, Boatman, I've seen you look better." Asperanti tried to lift Garbanto to his feet, but the wounded man swayed, then sank back to the steps. Asperanti sat next to him to wait for help.

Anna Renthal dropped to the steps, books falling from her arm. Her mouth fished open. Her breath whistled. "This time I mean it. I'm going to be sick."

Holding his revolver near his ear, Pete Coates said with ill-disguised glee, "I'll take that over a guilty verdict any day."

Owen Gray bent to help Anna, but his gaze remained on the

24

growing congregation around the body. He said quietly, "I'm going to bring up Pots on a weapons charge. He's got no license for that pistol."

Her eyes wide, Anna looked up at him. "Owen, a man just died. Murdered. And you're worried about a weapons charge on a two-bit hood?"

Gray's face was as cold as a carving. His eyes were shadowed and remote. His impassiveness, his refusal to register the slightest emotion, had abruptly given Gray an aura of uncontrolled violence.

He said, "Pots blew me a kiss once too often."

She touched his sleeve. "Owen, goddamnit. We've just witnessed a killing."

She yanked her hand back from a particle of De Sallo's head that had landed on Gray's jacket.

Anna swallowed repeatedly, fighting sickness. Then her voice rose. "I'm shaking from head to toe. Doesn't this get to you?"

Gray looked down at his sleeve, then casually brushed the scrap away. "Pots has a sheet, so he's looking at two years."

"Owen, listen to me," she cried out. "You . . . you're frightening me."

"Anna, I'm not going to get misty-eyed over some mafioso getting shot, probably by some other hoodlum." He gathered her books and helped her to her feet. "Come on. We deserve a couple of beers."

The wail of bubbletops and an ambulance trying to enter Foley Square resonated between the buildings. Down the block cabdrivers honked angrily at the delay.

"Owen . . ."

Gray moved down the steps toward Pearl Street, leaving the baffled assembly behind. Anna unsteadily hurried after him.

2

THE HAND-PRINTED SIGN on Owen Gray's apartment door read "U.N. Security Council" and was stuck there by two Sesame Street Band-Aids, one of Big Bird and the other of the Count. Gray could hear the sparkling notes of a piano through the door.

He had spent that entire day at his desk replaying the Chinaman's trial in his mind, re-introducing the evidence and re-questioning the witnesses, trying to alter yesterday's acquittal. He had been unable to leave his frustration at the office and had worn it home on the subway like a yoke, but at the piano's bright sounds it suddenly lifted.

He twisted a key in the dead bolt. Pushing open the door, he called out, "I'm home and, no, we aren't having a Security Council meeting."

The twins slid off the piano bench and rushed to greet him. Gray dropped his briefcase and hugged one in each arm.

Carolyn giggled. "We already had a vote."

Julie added, "And you lost three to one."

They kissed him, Julie always on the right cheek, Carolyn always on the left.

"I want a recount," he said. "I'll bet I can change the tally."

"You lost fair and square," Carolyn countered. "We get the new piano."

This lobbying had been going on a month. One piano apparently was not enough for four hands. The twins, twelve years old, practiced with adult stamina on the old Clarendon upright, encouraging and competing with each other. Gray was tone deaf, but even he could hear they were talented.

The twins were Korean, adopted by Gray eight years ago. They had lately begun to revel in their heritage, frequently pointing out to Gray the advantages of Asian ancestry ("We're better looking and there's more of us"), and naming the doorway to their bedroom the DMZ.

When Gray had challenged Julie and Carolyn to find a place in the apartment where another piano would fit, they proposed putting one on rollers across the doorway to the bathroom and moving it aside whenever anyone needed to pee. Occasionally during this campaign they would taunt him by switching to Korean and wagging their fingers. He suspected they didn't remember a word of Korean and were inventing it on the spot, but he couldn't prove otherwise.

The twins were identical and blossoming. Gray knew that in a few years he would be sweeping neighborhood boys out of the apartment with a broom. The girls had wide cheekbones, teardrop eyes, and sculpted lips. Their teeth were as white and even as the keys on their piano, and their smiles were glorious.

His son John always got the third hug. The boy never charged his father, always waiting until the girls were done. John smiled shyly from the kitchen doorway, half an Oreo in his good hand.

Gray crossed the small room to him. He lifted the boy so their noses touched and accused, "Did your sisters buy your Security Council vote with that cookie?"

John laughed wildly and held the Oreo away from his father. "Three cookies," he crowed. "I already ate two."

"Does Mrs. Orlando know you've been pigging out on Oreos?"

The boy looked with transparent guilt toward the kitchen, then crammed the cookie into his mouth. He shook his head and laughed again, showing a mouth full of mashed cookie.

John was nine years old and of Vietnamese ancestry. Like his sisters he had been an orphan. When he was three he had found a shell in a pasture near the foundling home in the Dong Nai province and had hammered it with a stone. The explosion had ripped his hand from his arm. He had been brought to the United States by a Greenwich Village couple who somehow had not known that John's arm ended three inches below his elbow and who had changed their minds once they saw him.

Gray had been successful adopting John when he persuaded his landlord to temporarily switch apartments for the adoption-agency interview. The landlord's place had three bedrooms. Gray's had only two. The ruse worked. Now the girls occupied one bedroom, John the other, and Gray used a hide-a-bed in the living room. Unfolding the bed every evening had proven too much trouble, so he slept on it as a couch. His back ached every morning.

One day half a year ago John came home from school inconsolably bawling. Playmates had made fun of his arm, with its clamp prosthesis where a hand should have been. Gray had visited a friend, a sergeant who was an armorer at the 42nd Infantry Division at its armory on West Fourteenth Street. The sergeant had rigged a new prosthesis, a one-pound ball bearing on a short iron shaft. Next day when the teasing began again at school, John smashed the steel ball into his desktop, splintering the wood. The harassing stopped instantly. John wore the daunting battering ram only once a month now as a reminder.

Gray kissed the boy's forehead. John had ebony hair. Gray had given him haircuts in the kitchen until the twins said John was looking like Moe Howard of the Three Stooges. Now John went to the same barber Gray did. His son had gaps between his front teeth, so Gray had just started writing checks in startling amounts to an orthodontist. With John's braces and prosthesis, the twins called him their Man of Steel. He loved it.

Julie began again: "John's vote counts. Three to one."

"This family is a monarchy." Gray lowered the boy and removed his jacket. "I'm the cruel king. You three are serfs. The king scoffs at voting."

"Aw, Dad," Carolyn said.

John lifted the briefcase with his hook. He showed his braces in a smile and swung the case back and forth like a pendulum.

"Do you not hear the king scoffing at you serfs' impertinence?" Gray snorted, "Scoff, scoff, scoff."

Mrs. Orlando emerged from the kitchen and handed him a glass of iced tea. "You must choose, Mr. Gray. Me or the kimchi. Make your choice."

"Three more days, Mrs. Orlando," Gray said. "If I can stand it, so can you."

"The smell." She waved her hand in front of her face. "It is killing me."

For most of a week the apartment has smelled of kimchi. The twins had coaxed Mrs. Orlando into buying a jar of it. They both gagged at their first taste of the fermented fish, cabbage, onions, garlic, and horseradish; but in an attempt to savor Korean culture, the girls were determined to last a week of kimchi breakfasts. Julie and Carolyn had been singularly unsuccessful in getting their father to taste the dish. John had also refused to try kimchi, saying it would give him a case of the zacklies. When his father had blithely asked what the zacklies were, John had hooted, "It's when your mouth smells zackly like your butt." He had been sentenced to a night without the Nickelodeon channel.

The apartment was normally redolent of Mrs. Orlando's Caribbean cooking. She was from Haiti. When Gray interviewed her for the job, he had asked to see her green card so he could fill out the I-9 form. She had produced a photograph of her neighborhood in Cap Haiten on Haiti's north shore showing a row of destitute tar-paper shacks on a dusty road, an abandoned wringer clothes washer on its side near a mound of rubbish, and two ragged chickens. She had said in her melodic accent, "That's all the paper I've got." It was enough for Gray.

Mrs. Orlando was wearing her usual riotous colors. For Christmas, Gray had given her an ornate silver necklace with a dozen tiny bells hung among stylized fish and shells, and she had not taken it off since. The necklace made her jangle like a belled cat when she walked. Her skin was bronze and her eyes were set at a laughing cant. The children adored her but were wary of the voodoo curses she threatened them with when they watched too much television. She was generous with her singing talent, and Gray credited her with instilling musical ability in the twins. She was patient and loving with John when the boy cried out against his missing hand. If she had a fault it was that she would occasionally miss an afternoon of work, always because she had met a new boyfriend, and would later claim with heavy invention that she had come down with Haitian pox, a little-known disease whose most distressing symptoms were an inability to work and a fuzziness of mind that precluded calling in sick. Gray suspected she devoured and tossed aside these boyfriends, leaving them nothing but husks.

"Are you feeling better, Dad?" Carolyn asked.

Gray removed Julie's Discman from an overstuffed chair next to the piano, then sank into the chair. He had been unable to hide from them his bitter disappointment over the De Sallo verdict. He balanced his glass of tea on the torn armrest.

"I feel great," he said, more a sigh. He yanked on his tie, loosening it, revealing an unnatural ridge of purple skin on his neck. He leaned to the floor to pick up a schoolbook about the solar system. He laid it on the stand at the end of the couch. "Pete Coates, the lead NYPD detective on the case, is coming over in a few minutes. Will you kids pick up this place?"

"Are you going to talk about how you blew the case?" Julie asked.

"You are too kind." Gray sipped the tea. "We didn't exactly blow it."

"The *New York Times* said you did," Carolyn teased. "You and your boss blew it, the editorial said."

"John, stop swinging your father's briefcase," Mrs. Orlando ordered as she returned to the kitchen. "You'll break something."

The apartment was in Bay Ridge, a Brooklyn neighborhood of Italians and Greeks, pizza joints and Optimos, fifty minutes by subway from Gray's office in lower Manhattan. The living room was about the width of John's swing. The television, a twenty-five-inch monster purchased as the result of an earlier lobbying effort by the twins, was the only item in the living room not careworn, dented, or frayed with age. The couch was sprung. The coffee table wore the marks of John's experiments with a hammer several years ago. The living-room rug was an old and fine Sarouk that belonged to Gray's ex-wife Cathryn. In a puerile fit, he had changed the lock before she remembered she had left the rug behind. She had also forgotten their framed wedding photo, and it remained on the end table. His family had never met Cathryn.

He said, "John, the briefcase goes—"

The door buzzer interrupted him. Gray rose from the chair and crossed to the intercom. When Pete Coates identified himself, Gray pressed the lobby door button.

Gray had no idea why Coates would visit his apartment, unprecedented in all the years of preparation and trial in the De Sallo case.

"Better warn Mrs. Orlando," Carolyn exclaimed, glancing into the kitchen. "It's a cop."

Julie laughed. "Maybe she can make it down the fire escape."

Gray waved them to silence. He tightened his tie and opened the door. Pete Coates climbed the last few stairs to the third floor. He was a large man, but his bulk was in his chest, not his belly. He moved with a lively gait despite years on the beat before earning his gold badge. He was breathing easily, a man in shape.

Coates said, "I'd have been here earlier, but I stopped at Junior's for a couple slices of cheesecake. Too bad you weren't along to pick up the tab."

Gray laughed as Coates entered the room. The detective had not once paid a check in the years he and Gray had worked on the De Sallo investigation. It seemed a point of honor with him. He had once told Gray, "I've never taken a nickel under the table on this job, so I've got to make up for it by stiffing people for food."

The twins were wide-eyed. A real police detective in their apartment. John stepped quickly to his special corner beside Gray's chair.

"Nice-looking bunch of kids," Coates said as he helped himself to the couch. A fleck of cheesecake clung to the corner of his mouth. "Looks like you got your own Third World country here."

Early in the De Sallo probe, Gray had learned that the trade-off for Coates's legendary tenacity was his relentless unrefinement. At first Gray thought the crassness was an act, part of the detective's tough-cop routine. But Coates was so persistent in his boorishness that Gray concluded he had brought it into the world with him like a birthmark.

Coates had proved himself again and again on the De Sallo investigation. The detective had once dug in a Staten Island garbage landfill searching for Pots Asperanti's numbers receipts for forty-eight hours without stopping, bringing in klieg lights so he could work at night. On another occasion, when his car stalled, Coates commandeered a Number 16 bus on Second Avenue and ordered it to follow De Sallo's Cadillac across the Manhattan Bridge into Brooklyn, the passengers on the verge of a riot. On one January night Coates had posted himself down the block from De Sallo's

31

Jamaica Bay Club while the thermometer dipped below five degrees and stayed there for the entire ten hours Coates was on duty. The next day a surgeon removed the tip of Coates's frostbitten small toe.

Coates had another quality Gray valued. He detested gangsters. The detective's loathing of organized crime brought an unbending moral principle to his police work. He hated the mob so much that he could not bring himself to call them hoodlums or gangsters or any other label imparting even a modicum of dignity. Instead Coates usually used the term pukes, and had done so while testifying against Carmine De Sallo, causing defense attorneys to move for a mistrial, which was denied. So Gray gladly put up with Coates and had even become fond of him.

The detective kicked off a loafer and rubbed the ball of his left foot. "It's good to get off my goddamn feet."

John gasped at the profanity. The twins tittered and looked knowingly at each other. They were convinced they knew words their father had missed all his life. The kitchen door opened slightly. Mrs. Orlando peered out.

Coates began, "Owen, you're a cool customer, I got to admit. After the Chinaman went down, you left the scene like you had ice in your veins."

Gray opened his hands in a vague gesture. Looking back on the scene later that evening, Gray had been vexed and angered at his own dispassion, at his own callousness at the gruesome event at Foley Square. His long journey back to normalcy—for years a day-to-day harrowing struggle that had exhausted and confused him and had cost him dearly—might not have succeeded. A healthy person would have reacted differently, more like Anna Renthal, sick at the abrupt and gory passage from life to death.

"Owen, you've got a lot of scars, those ones on your arms and legs," Coates said. "But remember that first day when you went to the gym with me and I saw your neck and asked about the scar there? You said you choked on a piece of ham in your dormitory at college and had to have a tracheotomy. Well, I recently was talking to a surgeon friend of mine and he said tracheotomies shouldn't leave much of a scar, not these days. So I got a little curious and did a little digging."

The children were quiet, peering at the detective.

"If I showed initiative like this all the time I'd be mayor by now,

32

I'll guarantee you that," Coates said. "Owen, everybody at NYPD thinks you are just a run-of-the-mill prosecutor, a damn good one, but just your average PA making life miserable for us police."

The twins inched closer.

Julie needled, "You aren't a run-of-the-mill prosecutor, Dad?"

Carolyn joined in, "We thought you were."

Gray cautioned, "I'm good enough to put you two girls in juvie for ragging your father."

The detective asked, "You got a beer?"

Gray shook his head.

John called from his spot, "We got Yoo Hoos in the 'frigerator."

"Who'd have figured it?" Coates asked. "I read about that scar in your service file an FBI friend sent me. Made me queasy. No beer?"

"Pete, why were you interested in my service file?"

Carolyn asked, "Why'd the scar make you queasy? It's not too bad."

"Just some blue and red and purple skin," Julie chimed in.

The detective asked, "Your old man ever tell you how he got that scar?"

"A leech," Julie replied. "Big deal. We Koreans eat them for breakfast."

"You want that Yoo Hoo, mister?" John asked from his spot.

Gray said, "My kids know I had an accident."

"I'll say." Coates put his shoe back on. "One day out in the jungle you picked up your canteen and took a big gulp of water. And you swallowed a leech that had gotten inside your canteen when you were filling it."

Carolyn made a production of shrugging. "Wouldn't have bothered me."

"And the damned thing got stuck in your throat where it grabbed on with its little teeth. The leech started swelling with your blood, right there while it was in your throat. Your air was cut off and you started turning blue. Your spotter wasn't nearby, so he was no help."

"What's a spotter?" Carolyn asked.

"So you took out your service knife and punched a hole in your own throat, a big ragged hole. Then you cut off a short piece of bamboo and used it as a tube for air."

John moved quickly from his corner. "I'm going to ask Mrs. Orlando for Yoo Hoos."

"You got your color back but you couldn't dig out the leech. You were deep behind enemy lines and it took two days to get to an aid station and the leech was in your throat all that time getting fatter and happier."

The twins beamed.

Coates turned to the twins. "Girls, I don't know about you, but a leech stuck in my craw could take some of the luster off an otherwise fine day."

John marched back into the room carrying Yoo Hoos and straws. He handed a carton to the detective and lectured, "You open the flap and stick the straw in."

Coates did as told. He sipped on the chocolate drink. "It ain't a Guinness, but not bad. What'd you do to your hand, kid?"

John glanced at his clamp. "I don't remember." He expertly punched a hole into the carton with the tip of the clamp.

"What's a spotter?" Carolyn asked again.

"Your dad was with the 1st Battalion, 4th Marines, in a sniper-scout platoon."

Gray quickly turned to his children. "Girls, John, I need to talk to Detective Coates privately. Go to your rooms, please."

They could tell he meant business. They disappeared into their rooms without dawdling or argument.

The detective emptied the carton with a loud gurgle. "You know, I'd be proud as hell if a rifle range down at Quantico was named after me."

Gray replied tonelessly, "I don't think you would, actually."

The detective persisted. "I made a phone call to a gunnery sergeant down there this afternoon. Sergeant Arlen Able, an old friend of yours, turns out. They still talk about you. The sergeant called you a legend."

Gray rubbed his chin. "Yeah, well, I've left all that behind."

"After talking to the sergeant, I was hoping to see the Wimbledon Cup on your mantel." The detective scanned the apartment. "But you don't have a mantel. Or even a decent table to put it on."

He looked back at Gray. "I asked the Marine sergeant over the phone, I says, 'Sergeant, you mean Wimbledon like in tennis?' And he laughs like I'm a pussy and says the Wimbledon Cup is the

WHITE STAR

Thousand-Yard National High-Power Rifle Championship held at Camp Perry, Ohio, and that you won it three years running."

"I don't talk about it much."

"You know what my nickname was in the Marines?" Coates asked.

"I can only imagine."

"Pogey. That's what Marines working in an office are called. I was a typing instructor for the quartermaster at the Marine Corps Air Station at Cherry Point. Fifteen words a minute and they make me a typing teacher, for Christ sake. I should've had a name like White Star. The chicks loved that nickname, I'll bet?"

When Gray said nothing, the detective continued, "The sergeant at Quantico told me the Viet Cong and NVA called you White Star due to the little paper star you always left behind."

In fact, the name had come first, then the paper star. The enemy began calling Gray White Star early in Gray's tour because of the sniper's penchant for using twilight. All Marine snipers knew the sailors' rhyme, altered slightly: Red sky at night, sniper's delight. A lingering pink and red and purple dusk prompts the hunted to leave the safety of the trees or hedges too early. First darkness is an illusion where the near foreground seems darker to the target than it is to a marksman viewing from a distance. During a red twilight the hunted may not suspect he can still be seen in the shooter's crosshairs. Gray's name came from the first heavenly body visible in the sky at twilight, Venus, which westerners call the evening star but which Vietnamese know as the white star.

Then one day in Vietnam in his blind, waiting, it turned out, thirty-six hours for the shot, Gray had idly begun folding a small piece of paper torn from his sniper's log. He folded, unfolded, and refolded, experimenting with an intricate but random design. Eventually his spotter, Corporal Allen Berkowitz, said, "You've made a star, looks like. Just like your nickname." After the kill, Gray left the star behind. From then on, he left a paper star behind at every firing site or, if he could get there, on the corpse.

Many of history's snipers left a calling card of some sort, Gray discovered later. John Paudash, the Chippewa Indian who fought in the 21st Battalion of the Canadian Expeditionary Force in World War One and who was famous for working alone, left a bird feather at his kills. In the Civil War, Corporal Ben Burton of the 18th North Carolina Regiment was known as the Choirboy because he

35

claimed the pitch of a bullet passing overhead could tell him the precise distance to the enemy rifleman. The Choirboy always left a squirrel's tail. The Viet Minh sniper Vo Li Giap, renowned for firing through airplane windscreens at French pilots trying to take off from the Dien Bien Phu airfield, left braided pieces of twine. One of history's first recorded snipers, Leonardo da Vinci, shot several enemy soldiers while standing on the walls of besieged Florence using a rifle he had designed himself. Whether Leonardo felt compelled to leave a calling card is unknown.

"And the Viet Cong had a reward for your head, the equivalent of five years' pay for a soldier." Coates gurgled the dregs of the Yoo Hoo again. "The VC blanketed Vietnam with a drawing of your face on a wanted poster. Where'd they get the drawing?"

Gray was becoming resigned to the conversation. "From a photo of me run in *Sea Tiger,* the III Marine Amphibious Force's weekly newspaper, is my guess."

"So how many of the enemy did you whack?"

Gray glanced at the wall over Coates's head. Several of John's crayon drawings had been taped there. He always painted the sky red. "A few."

"Christ, I'll say." Coates laughed, a peculiar clatter, like a stick dragged along a picket fence. "Ninety-six is quite a few. It's hard to believe, zotzing ninety-six people. More kills than any other sniper in American military history, the sergeant at Quantico told me. I asked the sergeant why you left the service, but he didn't know or more probably he wouldn't say, and your file wasn't too clear on the subject."

Gray replied, "Well, my tour was up—"

"Not quite," the detective cut in. "Your second tour was two months from being up when you flew back to San Diego on a medevac plane."

John's door opened and the boy walked out, straight for the detective. He had taken a liking to the brusque policeman.

The boy asked, "Want another Yoo Hoo?"

"Sure. And add a shot of vodka while you're at it."

"Yum. I love vodka." John grinned widely. He turned for the kitchen.

Gray rose from the chair to intercept his son. He gently grabbed the boy's shoulders and turned him. "You better tell me you've never tasted vodka once in your whole life."

"I put it in my Yoo Hoos all the time just like the detective does."

"Back to your room with you, you big fibber."

John laughed in his tinkling way. He hadn't expected his mission to be a success.

"Nice kid you got there. I see the family resemblance."

"Why are we honored with your visit tonight, Pete?" Gray asked.

"We need your expertise," Coates said, crumpling the carton. "De Sallo's killer was an ace with a rifle. And you know more about using a rifle than anyone else we can find. Maybe more than anybody else in history."

Gray knew it to be true.

Coates went on: "Carmine De Sallo was killed thirty hours ago and we have only one hard piece of evidence—the bullet that passed through his head and then through Boatman Garbanto's shoulder. And by the way, that puke Boatman will be all right, to my regret. We dug the slug out of the courthouse steps."

Gray nodded.

"The lab is looking at its contours and weight," Coates said, "and trying to figure out the number, size, and design of any cannelures. We'll hear from them shortly. And, of course, we also know the bullet came from a westerly direction. The complete absence of other evidence also means something, but we're not sure what."

Coates leaned forward, putting his elbows on his knees. "I mean, we've found utterly nothing other than that slug. My people have talked to thirty-five witnesses to the De Sallo killing. Nobody saw anything. And more puzzling, nobody heard anything. Even in Manhattan's perpetual din the sound of a gunshot should have been noticed. We thought of a silencer." Coates dipped his chin at Gray as if testing him.

"Silencers louse up the aim," Gray answered. "A rifleman wouldn't use one if he was shooting from any distance."

"That's what we thought, too."

"There were television news cameras there," Gray said. "What's on their tapes?"

"We've got the tapes from all the TV stations. They don't show anything other than a third eye opening up in the Chinaman's head. A fast-thinking WABC cameraman turned his camera around to

Foley Square just after the shooting. He did a slow sweep of the buildings. We've studied that tape, looking at all the windows in the Fidelity Building, the U.S. Court for International Trade, Federal Plaza, the State Office Building, every window where a rifleman could have hidden. The tape showed quite a few open windows, and we checked them out. Nothing.''

Owen Gray reached around to an end-table drawer to pull out a map of Manhattan. He unfolded it carefully. Scotch tape held the map together.

Coates emphasized, ''We checked every likely firing position. We came up with zip.''

''You did all this checking since yesterday?'' Gray examined the map, first looking at the scale. ''That's a lot of potential firing sites.''

''We're damn thorough,'' Coates said defensively. ''You've worked with us long enough to know that.''

''So you looked at every building with a view of the courthouse steps''—Gray traced a circle on the map—''all the way west to Battery City and the Hudson River?''

Coates ran his tongue along his teeth. ''You think we didn't go out from the courthouse far enough?''

''A talented sniper could have fired from thirteen hundred yards.''

Coates corrected, ''Thirteen hundred feet, you mean.''

''Yards. Almost three-quarters of a mile.''

The detective grinned. ''I'll bet you've done that yourself to some poor bastard from three-quarters of a mile. Am I right? He was probably squatting there eating some rice, daydreaming of his poontang back home in Hanoi, and you tooted him from another time zone.''

Gray pursed his lips noncommittally.

''Christ.'' Coates stared intently at Gray. ''You must've been a real shooter.''

Gray studied the map.

Coates said, ''We've got another puzzle, something that's rarely happened before. We haven't heard anything on the street about the Chinaman's killing. Usually when a puke gets thumped, gossip about it gets back to us. That's usually the point of the whole exercise, one puke sending a message.''

Gray had often wondered at the NYPD's inexhaustible supply

of synonyms for *killed*. The cops borrowed from sports ("The guy was dunked," or tagged out, beaned, or called out), the fashion industry (zipped, ironed, hung out to dry), the culinary arts (cored, fried, plucked, basted), pest control (zapped, flicked, swatted), and apparently nursery school (dinked, thwacked, and boinged). There were a hundred others. Gray figured the police had a Department of Slang that issued a new word every few days.

The detective concluded, "But this time we've heard nothing. Nobody, not even some of the lums we've rolled over, has a hint about who took out De Sallo."

Lums was short for hoodlums, and rolled over meant making a lum an informer. This was worse than the twins' fake Korean, Gray reflected.

"Can you give us a hand tomorrow?" Coates asked. "If you can just find his firing station we'll take it from there."

Gray carefully folded the map. "You've got enough guys to dump on the investigation, Pete."

"Sure, but you know sniping. You'll save us days, maybe weeks."

"Yeah, well, I promised to take the kids—"

"And you might put me back in the good graces of my captain. After the De Sallo acquittal I could use a win."

Gray wearily rubbed the side of his nose with a finger. "All right, I'll go to Foley Square and look around."

Coates rose quickly. "Tomorrow, eight in the morning. I'll meet you there."

"Bring a spotting scope," Gray said. "A 20-power M49 if you've got one. And a tripod."

Coates nodded and started for the door. "Thank your boy for the Yoo Hoo. Tell him I'll buy him a beer someday. A rice beer if he wants." He laughed and started down the stairs.

Gray closed and bolted the door. Mrs. Orlando immediately appeared from the kitchen.

"You've got calluses on your ear from the door, Mrs. Orlando," Gray chided.

"You told me you were trying to leave all that behind you," she whispered, glancing at a bedroom door, expecting the children to appear. Faint Nintendo sounds came from John's room.

Except for his ex-wife and his psychiatrists, Mrs. Orlando was the only person in two decades Gray had spoken to about his

Vietnam tours. More a confession. She had been a steady and devoted source of strength.

"Now you're going to bring it all back," she scolded. "All those bad memories." She opened the door to John's room.

"Just helping out a friend for a few hours." Gray pulled his tie out and unbuttoned the top of his shirt. The skin below his Adam's apple was discolored and misshapen, resembling a dried fruit. Gray knew it was useless to try to hide anything from Mrs. Orlando, but he did not want to admit that during his conversation with Pete Coates, Gray's mouth had dried up and his chest had become tight. She would know these things anyway, always able to read him as if his mental state were written in red ink on his forehead.

She clucked her tongue. "You know what we say in my country?"

"Yeah." Gray smiled at her. "You say, 'Get me the hell out of this stinking place.' "

She said over her shoulder as she went into his room, "He who lies down with dogs gets up with fleas."

Gray pulled a coffee-table book from the couch stand. The book was entitled *Manhattan On High* and contained aerial photographs of the island. He sank into the chair and began leafing through the volume, studying SoHo, Little Italy, Chinatown, and other neighborhoods near Foley Square. Again his hands started to quiver.

Ten minutes later Gray said to himself in falsely composed voice, "That guy was a passable marksman, I'll say that much for him."

3

"THE CHINAMAN'S KILLER must've been in one of those trees was our first thought." Pete Coates pointed to the scraggly elms in the Foley Square traffic divider. The trees were thirty feet high and were sagging and broken, struggling for survival in the city. "But nobody was up there. We couldn't have missed him."

He and Gray were standing on the courthouse steps on the precise spot where Carmine De Sallo had met his maker. Gray was staring across Centre Street into the trees. He was carrying a spotting scope aluminum case. Coates held a collapsible tripod.

"The killer wouldn't have been able to see through the elm leaves," the detective said, pointing west down Duane Street. He was wearing the same gray suit as the day before and it looked as if he had slept in it. "So we could rule out some of the distant buildings due west as his firing site."

"That was your first mistake," Gray replied. "The farther a rifleman is from foliage the easier he can see through it."

Coates asked, "What sense does that make?"

"I don't know the physics of it, but take my word for it. The killer probably could see through those sparse leaves to De Sallo even though we can't see in the other direction." Gray turned to the steps, running his eyes left and right. "There's his zero shot, that fracture in the riser of that step."

The stone riser had a pocket dug out of it. A few chips of stone and concrete lay along the tread below the gouge.

"What's a zero shot?" Coates asked.

"The rifleman sighted his weapon and scope by firing a practice round sometime before he let loose at the Chinaman." Gray bent to the cracked riser to stick his finger into the hole. "The bullet isn't here. Probably bounced out and was kicked away by a pedestrian or swept up by the grounds crew."

Gray led the detective away from the steps, between several parked cars, and across Centre Street toward the Court for International Trade. They walked west along Duane Street. A man wearing a black leather coat, open in front with no shirt underneath, handed Gray a leaflet that read, "Beautiful Girls, All Nationalities, A Unique Concept, No Hidden Charges Whatsoever." Gray wadded it up and pushed it into his pants pocket. He slowed his pace and looked skyward, up the side of the twelve-story Mardin Building. He narrowed his eyes, studying cornices several floors above the street. He saw nothing of interest and moved along the sidewalk.

"You looking for the sniper's window?" Coates asked. "These windows don't even face the courthouse."

Gray was silent, intent on a light pole.

The detective walked beside him, his hands jammed into his pockets. "You know, I would've made a pretty good sniper."

Still looking skyward, this time toward a lamp fixture attached to the front of the next building, Gray said, "Sure, and I could've played center field for the Mets."

He stopped at another light pole on which was a tattered poster reading "Awake! Cruelties Go Unchecked in Malawi." He stared above him at the light bracket for a moment, then walked on.

"Son of a bitch!" Coates exclaimed. Trying to follow Gray's gaze, the detective had stepped on a discarded soiled Pampers. He tried to scrape it off his shoe, but the diaper's adhesive strip clung to him and he kicked several times before he could dislodge it. He caught up with Gray. "I'm serious, Owen. I'm pretty damn good at the NYPD firing range. I could've been a sniper."

They approached Broadway and the sound of a conga band.

Gray was still peering skyward. He said absently, "You wouldn't have had a chance to become a sniper, Pete."

"Hell yes, I would have." Coates's face lengthened. "What do you mean?"

"You wear eyeglasses. The Marines don't let you become a sniper if you need spectacles."

Coates argued, "A lot of good Marine marksmen wear glasses."

"Yes, but they aren't allowed to become snipers. The reflection off the glasses makes it too dangerous in the field." Gray looked at a power pole, then at the brackets holding a sign that said "Pal's Loans."

The detective said, "Well, assuming I didn't wear glasses, I would've made a great sniper."

"Not at all." Gray's eyes were still skyward. His gaze moved in a measured grid pattern. He had done nothing like this with his eyes for over two decades. A steady clicking—right, right, right, then back again, right, right, right, like a typewriter carriage, and shifting focus near to far, near to far. The small skill had not been forgotten. "You are left-handed. Lefties aren't allowed to become snipers because the additional movement required to operate the bolt over the top of the scope escalates the risk of detection."

At the corner of Broadway and Duane they stepped around a band of street musicians playing a maraca, a cowbell, a conga drum, and a percussion instrument made of four crushed beer cans. Their only audience was a transient with a full white beard and a red cap, eerily resembling Santa Claus, carrying a bottle of cheap port and sticking out his tongue through blackened teeth at the conga player. The hat on the ground in front of the band contained two dimes.

Gray's eyes scanned iron mounts attached to a building on the corner, perhaps once used to hold flowerpots. They crossed Broadway. A vendor had spread out several dozen wigs on a blanket on the sidewalk. The hairpieces were neon red, steel blue, and shock white. He was haggling with a woman in five-inch heels whose skirt had less fabric than most belts. Gray stepped around the display, veered through the stream of people walking along Broadway, and continued west along Duane Street, the detective in tow.

Gray's eyes were again turned skyward. He almost bumped into a woman in a Burberry plaid skirt who was stooped over trying to shove a newspaper under her squatting poodle. The dog preferred the cement and kept inching forward, so the woman had to scoot the newspaper after the poodle, saying again and again, "Do your duty, Pumpkin. Do your duty."

Coates tried again. "Well, if I didn't wear glasses and wasn't left-handed, I would've made a great sniper."

"Not even then, Pete." Gray stopped abruptly at the Winlox Building, a gray fifteen-story 1940s structure notable only for its refusal to leave an impression. Six stories up the side of the building a flagpole was attached to a column between windows.

Eyeing the pole, Gray said, "You need to have been a hunter or a tracker or a wilderness guide to get into the sniper program. You've only left New York City a couple of times in your entire life, and couldn't follow a bleeding coyote across fresh snow."

"Well, hell—"

"And even if you weren't a nearsighted citified leftie, you couldn't have become a sniper because they don't allow horses' butts into the program."

Coates laughed. "That last qualification would have sunk me for sure."

Gray pointed to the flagpole. "Your killer left some tracks. Take a look."

"I don't see anything."

"About halfway out the pole, there's a red streamer, cloth of some sort."

"So?"

"It's his wind telltale, like on a sailboat. A sniper usually uses a strip of red cloth two feet long."

"That could be just a piece of trash hanging there. Lots of crap hangs from flagpoles and signposts and power poles in this city."

Gray opened the spotting scope case. "I know a telltale when I see one. Set up the tripod, will you?"

"How'd he get it out there?"

"The window near the pole is probably in a lavatory or an empty office that he got into."

An elderly woman wearing a coat and a hand-knitted scarf despite the day's heat paused to say, "If you're looking for a peregrine falcon, there's a nest on the Wexler Building. Saw him snatch a pigeon right out of the air."

"Thank you, ma'am." Gray smiled. "We'll go there next."

"I'd have to be pretty hungry to eat a pigeon," she added as she shuffled on.

When the detective fumbled with the tripod, Gray tugged it out of his hands. The tripod was a government-issue M15. Gray pulled it open and locked the leg nuts, then withdrew the scope from its case. He attached the scope to the stand and removed the eyepiece cover and objective lens cover. The scope's lenses were coated with a hard film of magnesium fluoride to enhance light transmission. Bending over the eyepiece, he altered the focusing sleeve. Without looking up, he adjusted the azimuth with the screw clamps on the tripod shaft, and the elevating thumbscrew on the lens cradle.

He said, "If the sniper could see that telltale we might be able to see his firing site from here."

For twenty minutes Gray leaned over the scope, frequently looking up to relieve eyestrain. During that time Coates kept a running count of the passersby he chased away. "Eight palmers, six jackets, five prunes, and one mattress," meaning panhandlers, mental cases, senior citizens, and a hooker.

Finally Gray straightened himself to stare at an apartment building, two blocks in the distance. He blinked deliberately several times, then lowered himself again to the scope. "I've found it."

Coates excitedly nudged Gray away from the scope, but after a moment of squinting into the eyepiece, he said, "Goddamnit, what am I looking for?"

"A hole in that window. On the twenty-fifth or twenty-sixth floor."

"I see it."

"Your sniper was up there."

Coates raised himself. He pulled back his jacket and appeared to be reaching for his pistol. For an instant Gray thought the detective was going to crazily fire his handgun at the distant window.

Instead, Coates pulled out a cellular phone. "I'm going to call the crime-scene people." He hesitated, scratching his chin. He looked skeptically at Gray. "You positive that's his firing site?"

"It's where I would have fired from."

✧   ✧   ✧

"We searched our asses off and missed this place," Pete Coates said as he followed the building superintendent down the hallway. The detective was moving quickly, almost running up the super's legs. "Makes us look like morons, I'll guarantee you that."

Gray was carrying the spotting scope and the compressed tripod.

As they hurried down the hall, Coates jabbed the super's shoulder with a finger. "You're telling me you thought this guy was into orgies?"

"Yes, sir." The super wore a blue blazer, washed-out jeans, and ankle-top Reeboks. His hair was tied with a rubber band in a short ponytail. He carried fifty or so keys on a ring. He ran his tongue over his lips. "What else was I to think? He had those mattresses delivered two and three at a time. Too many to sleep on, so I figure he's having a bunch of people over to get naked."

"You ever see the guy?" Coates asked.

"It was just a month sublease. I handled the paperwork. Did it through the mail. He paid up front."

Coates brushed by the superintendent and drew a .38 Smith and Wesson revolver from inside his jacket as they neared the end of the hall.

The superintendent found the right keys. "I'm paid to keep the halls clean and the furnace running. Guy wants to have a Crisco party with all his friends, it's all right by me."

Coates stepped to the other side of the door frame, under the exit sign.

Owen Gray stayed well back. "The chance of this guy being in there is nil."

"Then you stand with your belly in front of the door. Not me."

The detective held his revolver near his chin. He reached across to the door and hammered on it. After a moment he tried again.

"I don't hear anything." Coates jerked a thumb at the superintendent. "You open the door."

"I don't plan on dying in a burst of gunfire." The super tried to give the key ring to Gray.

Gray refused to take it. "That's one of my main principles, too."

The detective took the keys, gingerly inserted one into the dead bolt, and turned it. Then the doorknob key.

Coates lunged against the door. His bulk should have snapped it open. It gave only a few inches and he rebounded back into the hall. He charged again. The door moved slightly, grudgingly.

46

"What in hell? He got some furniture against the door?" The detective called, "Open up. Police."

He shoved again. With a soft scraping the door slowly opened.

Both hands on his revolver, Coates rushed into the apartment. The room was dim, with little daylight entering. The detective flicked on an overhead light.

"I'll be damned," Coates said. "Place looks like a drunk tank." His pistol still in front of him, he walked through a door into a bedroom.

As he stepped into the apartment, Gray almost tripped on the first mattress. The room's floor was covered with them, as were the walls. A mattress had also been secured to the inside of the door. The only furniture in the room was a cane chair and a folding table. Stacked on the table were several bulky books next to a Sony television set with a five-inch screen.

Coates returned from the bedroom, moving unsteadily over the mattresses. "Smell anything?"

Gray looked at him.

"Got to get the smell first," Coates said. "It dissipates fast once the doors are open. CSI will ask us about it. Put your hands in your pockets, will you, Owen."

"I'm not going to muck up your crime scene."

"Not on purpose. But you might pick your nose, get a dried flake of mucus under your fingernail, and later it might fall to the floor. Then CSI would find it, pick it up with tweezers, put it into a Baggie, and take it to the lab for analysis. They don't get the kick out of that you might imagine."

Gray lowered his scope and tripod to a mattress, then shoved his hands into his pockets.

The detective added, "Don't flush the toilet. Don't run water into a sink. Don't breathe on any surface. Don't pick your teeth. Don't scratch your head. Don't do anything."

Gray glanced above him. "He's even got mattresses on the ceiling." A bulb on a wire hung between two mattresses. "Twelve-inch screws, right through the mattresses into the ceiling. Probably had to use plaster screw casings."

The living-room windows looked east down Duane Street. Mattresses leaned against the windows, blocking out the light. Only one window in the room had any exposed glass, an aperture a foot square, bordered on all sides by mattresses.

47

Coates asked, "Why did he bother with the mattresses? He could've fired, then raced out of the building."

"Yes, if he was only going to fire once. But he wanted the zero shot, which he probably did an hour or two before the reporters arrived, maybe a day or two. He didn't want a lot of sound because he was going to hang around after the first shot."

A circular hole had been cut into the glass. The opening was ten inches in diameter.

"The killer traced a pattern, maybe around a plate, with a glass cutter," Coates explained. "He used masking or duct tape to make sure the circle of glass didn't fall outside. He was here awhile and kept himself company with that television set."

Gray shook his head. "The TV means he was probably working alone and didn't have a spotter."

Coates looked at him.

"A rifleman can seldom see whether he hits his target," Gray went on. "The rifle kicks up and he can't quickly find the bull again. Sometimes dirt blows up at the target and other times there's a lot of confusion in the target area like there was on the courthouse steps."

"So what about the TV?"

"One of a spotter's jobs is to see if the target went down. The De Sallo courthouse steps interview was run live on the local TV stations, and the sniper would have known it. He fired the shot, then watched the results on his TV. Let me cross the room to the window to set up the tripod."

The detective nodded at Gray. "Watch your feet."

Gray gingerly moved to the window, sinking into the mattresses with each step. The opening in the window between mattresses was at Gray's chest level.

As he set up the tripod and attached the scope, Gray said, "He sat at the table and balanced the rifle on the books. He fired with the rifle's barrel well inside the room. The mattresses muffled the noise of the shot in all directions. Very little sound would have escaped out this hole in the glass. And we're on the twenty-fifth floor. No sound got down to the street."

"How do you know the barrel was inside the room?" Coates asked.

"There are powder particles on the window around the hole. Those crusty specks. You can see them without a microscope."

Coates ordered, "Don't touch the GSR." When Gray looked at him, he added, "Gunshot residue particles." He high-stepped over a mattress to the spotting scope. "So you can see De Sallo's position on the courthouse steps through the scope?"

"Take a look."

Coates lowered his head to the eyepiece. "I see mostly green. A lot of leaves."

"When the wind moves the leaves, you'll see the steps right where De Sallo stood."

"He was firing between moving leaves?" the detective asked. "You're right. I can see the steps."

Gray resumed his position behind the spotting scope. He loosened the clamping screw and rotated the telescope a fraction of an inch. After a moment he said, "Take another look. Don't jostle the scope."

The detective again replaced Gray behind the telescope. "I don't see anything interesting. A fire escape." Coates raised his head to peer out the window. He scratched his cheek. "The fire escape is on the Atonio Building three blocks toward Foley Square. What am I looking for?"

"Another piece of red cloth."

He went back to the eyepiece. "Yeah, I see it."

"De Sallo's killer tied the cloth strip to the fire escape to judge windage, same as he did on that flagpole. There are probably a few more telltales along the twelve hundred fifty yards of Duane Street between here and the courthouse. And he also had the Foley Square trees as a telltale. Let me see the printout we looked at earlier."

Coates lifted from his suit pocket a folded fax from the National Weather Service and passed it to Gray.

As he looked down a column of dot-matrix numbers, Gray said, "At noon that day the wind was blowing a fairly steady twelve miles an hour out of the south."

"And the telltales told him that," the detective concluded.

"Them and this scope. Take another look."

Coates bent over the scope.

Gray said, "By focusing the scope on the target and rotating the eyepiece a quarter to a half turn counterclockwise, a mirage will appear short of the target."

"What kind of a mirage?" Coates asked.

"It's the shimmer, the ascending waves you see over a hot road in the summer. Wind bends those waves in the direction of the air flow. On a clear day, like it was when De Sallo was killed, the mirage would have been pronounced."

Coates fiddled with the eyepiece.

Gray went on: "If the mirage is flowing from the right, which it would have been that day, the wind is coming from either one, two, three, four, or five o'clock. The rifleman would have turned the scope slowly to the right. As the scope turns the mirage will boil. When it does, the direction in which the scope is pointing is the direction from which the wind is blowing."

"So the wind was coming from the rifleman's three o'clock, out of the south," Coates said. "And then how does he estimate how fast it's blowing?"

"The flatter the mirage waves, the faster the wind. That day there would've been some undulation to the mirage, but not much, not with a twelve-mile-an-hour wind."

Gray looked again at the NWS printout. "The humidity that day was close to one hundred percent. The rifleman would have also known that from the mirage waves. The thicker the waves, the more humid it is."

"Why was the killer worried about humidity?" Coates asked.

"As humidity increases, air density increases, which slows the bullet and lowers its point of impact. The marksman would have had to raise the rifle to compensate for the sticky weather."

"So the rifleman would have made adjustments to his scope to account for the wind and humidity?"

"There were undoubtedly elevation and windage turrets in the scope assembly. He would have presighted on the spot directly behind the microphones, but he wouldn't have had time to tune them when the target appeared. So he would have compensated for the breeze and humidity by aligning the barrel to his right."

"How much off-target did he sight?" Coates asked.

"In a twelve-mile-an-hour wind over twelve hundred fifty feet, about thirteen feet."

Coates's chin came up. "Thirteen feet? I was standing about that distance to De Sallo's left when he was killed. And I was up six or eight courthouse steps from him."

"That's right." Gray smiled thinly. "The killer probably had your head in his sights when he pulled the trigger."

The detective was aghast. "What if the wind had suddenly calmed?"

"Then you'd have been . . ." Gray paused. "What's the word I'm looking for?"

"Tattooed."

"That's it," Gray said.

Coates blurted, "Maybe the killer was after me. I mean, maybe he knew nothing about wind and humidity. He just got my face in his crosshairs and pulled the trigger, hoping I'd go down."

"He had no interest in you," Gray calmed him. "Just De Sallo. From everything we've seen—the setup of his firing position, the telltales, the shot—the guy was an artist."

Coates laughed sharply. "Is that how you snipers think of yourselves? Artists?"

"I don't think about it at all anymore," Gray said.

"You shipped ninety-six guys to the big pachinko game in the sky and you don't think about it?" Coates cackled. "I can die happy now because I've heard everything."

Coates padded around the room. After a moment he said with glee, "Well, lookee here." He pointed to the edge of the mattress covering the main window. A spent cartridge was balanced there.

Gray bent for a closer look. "That's not the fatal bullet's cartridge."

"We'll run a neutron activation analysis on it," Coates said.

"You can tell by looking at it," Gray replied.

"And we'll do an atomic absorption spectrophotometry on it. And we'll do a scanning electron microscopy/energy dispersive X-ray analysis on it."

"Maybe you'll find the red paint on it by then." With a finger, Gray indicated a narrow ring of red just above the cartridge's extractor recess.

Coates peered closely at the shell. "Looks like fingernail polish to me. What's it doing on a shell?"

"It's the rifleman's sign. He carries an empty red shell and leaves it behind as a signature."

"Like your paper star? Any chance you know the rifleman? A sniper who leaves a painted cartridge?"

"Never heard of him," Gray answered. "But I've been out of the business awhile." Gray looked at his watch. "I'm going back to my kids. Maybe we'll get to the zoo yet today."

51

Gray followed the police detective toward the door. Two crime-scene investigators entered the apartment. One wore a salt-and-pepper goatee and had a jeweler's loupe attached to his spectacles. He carried two carpenter's toolboxes. The second CSI detective had a bunched face and a leprous complexion. A camcorder hung from his shoulder.

The bearded detective asked as he passed, "Smell anything, Coates?"

"Not until just now." Coates pointed to the empty cartridge, and the investigator opened a box to pull a plastic sack from a roll.

Detective Coates started down the hall. Gray followed. The superintendent had disappeared.

Coates said, "Christ, a paper star and a red shell. Cases for an insane asylum somewhere. And from what I read in your service file, you came close."

"Not that close," Gray said.

"You got pretty damn close to the loony bin," Coates insisted.

"Not that close." Gray felt like he was arguing with his son, John. "Give me a piece of paper from your notebook, will you, Pete?"

The detective lifted a small spiral binder from his coat pocket, tore out a page, and passed it to Gray.

Coates said, "Speaking professionally as a policeman, I can understand how giving the doughnut to ninety-six guys could put you on Valium by the truckload."

Gray's hands worked rapidly. The slip of paper seemed to leap into life.

When they reached the elevator, Gray handed the paper back to Coates. "A little souvenir."

An instant passed before the detective recognized the white star in his palm. He recoiled and his hand flew to his side. The star fluttered to the floor.

The elevator opened.

"That scared the crap out of me, Owen," he said huskily.

"I'm a sensitive type." Gray smiled thinly. "I don't like talk about the loony bin."

4

FACES FLASHED IN THE CIRCLE quickly, one after another like cards dealt onto a pile. Children's faces, laughing and whooping at the end of the school day, a cascade of faces as boys and girls walked down the school building's steps, faces falling into the ring, then out again, each face just a fleeting glimpse, inside the circle an instant, then out. To the top of the site post, then down and away.

Red Army sniper scopes use a pointed aiming post rather than crosshairs. As the children descended the steps, one face after another slid down the aiming post, beaming smiles, gap-tooth grins, ponytails and ribbons, innocent eyes, shirts and pants and skirts of wild colors, all in animation, spilling into and out of the circular frame, all flowing down the aiming post.

Hazel flecks on a green iris surrounding a flat black pupil. Frozen and unchanging, neither blinking nor altering distance to the front lens, the eye behind the telescope might have been part of the scope's optics. Even the pupil was still, neither expanding nor contracting. The eye was locked in position as firmly as the scope was fixed to the rifle. Colors and smiles flickered before it.

Then a long swath of gray rippled down the circle. A pant leg belonging to an adult. Owen Gray's face dropped into the circle. And now the scope moved fractionally, keeping Gray's face atop the aiming post. Owen Gray. White Star. Only then did the eye blink, and only once. Tight black curls, a few lines around the eyes, pale skin, a wise smile, then lips moving soundlessly, Gray's face turned to speak to someone, the aiming post just under his nose, following him smoothly. White Star. Once more the eye blinked.

The circle slowed, and Owen Gray slid out of the ring. Next came a kaleidoscope of colors—green and red and yellow and blue, an exotic scarf wrapped around a woman's head. The aiming post came to rest below her nose. Her skin was brown and burnished. Her eyes were narrowed as she laughed. Bits of metal—a necklace —danced in the sunlight, tossing back shards of light. The circle lingered on her a moment, an image of whirling colors and glittering light. Then the ring found the boy with one arm accompanying Gray and the black woman as they moved east along the sidewalk.

The aiming post returned to Gray, his head in profile as he walked east. Owen Gray.

The circle went to black when the eyelid behind the scope slowly lowered and stayed closed. White Star.

❖   ❖   ❖

Gray met Pete Coates at the Columbus Park Gym at the edge of Chinatown. They had begun their workout skipping rope and had moved to a heavy bag. Gray wore lead-lined bag gloves. The detective held the bag from behind while Gray jabbed and crossed.

Coates asked, "What's Frank Luca got you working on?"

"He wasted little time," Gray answered from behind his fists. He was breathing heavily. "On returning to work Monday, he handed me sixteen files, all of them thin. A Mann Act, an interstate flight, an illegal pen-register, and the like."

The bag bounced against Coates as he said, "Real piddlers."

"The De Sallo prosecution took forty file cabinets and eight hundred megabytes of our mainframe. All my new cases wouldn't take a single cabinet drawer and a hand-held calculator."

Early in the De Sallo investigation the detective had suggested that Gray join him at his gym for a workout. Gray had never heard of the place, and had expected the usual Nautilus equipment, stationary bicycles, Precor step machines, tiny chrome dumbbells, and all those unnaturally happy, muscled, spotless youths paid to urge him on.

The Columbus Park Gym was over the Three Musketeers pawnshop, up a narrow, squeaking flight of stairs to an ill-lit space that at the turn of the century had been a shirtwaist plant. A boxing ring filled most of the room. Everlast speed bags and heavy bags hung from frames on one wall and an assortment of Olympic free weights were along another.

The gym was owned by Sam Owl, who was in his seventies. Owl opened and closed the gym every day and spent the entire time in between teaching boxing. He referred to himself as a fistic scientist. Owl had trained welterweight champion Marco Genaro and the lightweight champ Kid Raynes, and the old man knew more about boxing than any man in New York.

The gym was last painted when Eisenhower was president. Paint chips and plaster regularly fell to the hardwood floor. All the equipment, from the bags to the ring ropes, was faded and frayed. The only bright spot was one wall decorated with a reproduction of Lord Byron's screen depicting battles for the English championship between Tom Johnson and Big Ben Brain in 1791, between Johnson and Daniel Mendoza in 1788, and many others. The floor-to-ceiling reproduction was painted by an artist in exchange for membership in the gym.

Most of Sam Owl's clientele were club fighters with ring talents far superior to Gray's or Coates's. That first day in the gym Gray had been ensnared by the rhythms of the workouts—the loud tattoos from the speed bags and jumping ropes, the scuffing of black shoes on the ring mats, and Sam Owl's incessant jabber at the boxers. Gray grew to love the scents of leather and sweat and the body ache after a workout with ropes and bags, followed by a three-round match. Gray began appearing at the club almost every noon with Coates. The prosecutor and the detective had invariably briefed each other on the De Sallo investigation during their workouts, talking through their mouthguards.

Coates released the heavy bag and stepped up to a speed bag. Both men wore running trunks but no shirts. Coates's white terry-cloth band on his forehead was dark with perspiration.

Gray followed him to a nearby bag.

The detective nodded at Gray's fists. "New gloves?"

55

Gray's gloves were bright red Surefits rather than the brown Everlasts he usually wore. "Borrowed them from Sam. I misplaced mine. Or John took them to school. So tell me about the lab report."

"You've got to admit," the detective said over the pounding of the bag, "there're some mighty interesting things in your personnel files. Coming to New York City after being raised in Nowhere, Idaho, for one." He pronounced it "Eye-Day-Ho."

"Actually it was Hobart, Idaho." Gray's pattern on the bag included fists and elbows, all moving in a circular whir.

"How'd you end up out here?"

"After the service I got into NYU law school and met my wife there. She was from New York and loathed everywhere else, so I stayed. What about the lab report on the cartridges?"

"You said a sniper has to have hunting or tracking experience." Coates's voice boomed over the staccato of the speed bags. "Where'd you pick up yours?"

"My father owned a lodge north of Ketchum, a hunting lodge. He'd take hunters into the mountains to find deer and goats and, in the early days, cougars. I learned from him."

"You a good tracker?"

Gray paused in his workout to wipe his forehead with a towel that hung from the waistband of his shorts. "I was leading four-man parties into the mountains when I was thirteen years old. I'd be out there for a week, and we'd usually come back with game strapped to our mules. So you could say I was pretty good."

"You had a tough couple of years after you got out of the Marines."

Nearby old Sam Owl barked at a black middleweight who repeatedly threw left crosses at a heavy bag. Sam Owl's bifocals rested high on his head, and every time the fighter brought back his hook Owl tapped his elbow, reminding the fighter to keep his arm tight to protect his ribs.

Gray began a new pattern on the bag, using fists and backhands. "I'm not the only person in history to have a little clinical depression. Abraham Lincoln and Winston Churchill, for example."

"But they both died, so maybe you're in worse shape than you thought." Coates chuckled, but Gray wouldn't join in. "The doctors didn't jolt you with electricity, did they?"

"My therapy consisted of counseling and a few modest medications."

The detective left the speed bag and walked to a rack of equipment on a wall. He donned a headguard and shoved his hands into sixteen-ounce gloves, brushing the Velcro straps across the wrists. Gray did the same. Coates left his spectacles on the wood bench. They bent through the ropes into the ring. They sparred lightly, bobbing and ducking, blocking most blows with their fists. Gray once determined that during the De Sallo investigation he and the detective had boxed over fifteen hundred rounds with each other. Their sparring had become choreography.

"Your file said you tried to zonk yourself," Coates said, breathing heavily. He launched a right jab that grazed the pad over Gray's ear. "How long did that urge last?"

Gray gestured, a nonresponse, letting Coates snap his head with another jab. "It never entered my drugged-up mind after that one time."

"You think it was your sniping that caused the depression?" The detective stepped back to wipe sweat off his forehead with the back of a glove.

"Hell, no." Gray's voice was too adamant. He sent a smooth combination at Coates, the left cross catching the detective in the ear. "I was a soldier."

"Ever been back to the hospital?"

"Not in ten years." Gray grinned baitingly, showing his mouthguard. "But—the strangest thing—all my dreams are still seen through crosshairs." Good effort, Gray thought. Making a small joke of the horror. He sounded fairly normal.

Coates came straight at Gray, throwing four jabs, then a right straight, finding Gray's nose. "One of your victims was a woman, I read."

"She was a Viet Cong major who had cut off the testicles of two Marines." Gray backstepped, his breath coming in gulps. "You could have done her, too, believe me. You know, Pete, you are out of character this morning, what with all this polite chat. No cracks about the loony bin."

"Not from this lovable guy."

"And this pleasant chat has a professional scent. You on the job right now?"

Coates jabbed, but Gray slipped it and found Coates's chin with a right. The big gloves resembled pillows, and the blows had little effect.

The detective said, "I'm trying to learn how a sniper thinks. You're the only one I've ever met. Thank God."

Sam Owl and the middleweight stepped to the ring. The fighter said, "Look at those two white pussies, Sam. For Christ sake, looks like the Michelin Man versus the Pillsbury Doughboy."

Without taking his eyes off Gray, Coates called, "I'll take care of you, Joe, once I'm done with this victim."

The middleweight chortled. His name was Joe Leonard, one of Sam Owl's promising youngsters. He had eighteen professional wins, twelve by KO, and no losses, and was ranked eighth in the country by *Ring* magazine.

Sam Owl said, "You two guys hurry up with your patty-cake. Bennie'll be here in a minute for Joe's workout and I want the ring free."

Bennie Jones, Brooklyn Golden Gloves welterweight champion for three years, had won his first six pro fights and was Leonard's regular sparring partner.

Owl led Leonard to a mat and lectured him about his crouch.

Gray jabbed and said, "I've got a plea-change hearing this afternoon and I want to hear the results of the lab work. Are you done interrogating me?"

Coates was huffing and dropping his guard, tiring. "Is our killer married, you think?"

Gray spread his gloves. "How would I know?"

"Is it possible for a woman to be married to a sniper?"

"It wasn't possible for Cathryn to be married to me." Gray jabbed lightly, catching Coates's forehead. Perspiration gathered in the folds of Gray's tracheotomy scar and pooled in the other shallow scars on his arms. Other puncture scars—purple and deep —stitched both of Gray's legs.

Leonard called, "Two marshmallows fighting, looks like."

"Shut the hell up, Joe, or I'll arrest you for impersonating a fighter," Coates called, backpedaling. Sweat ran down his face in steady rivulets. "So what happened?"

Gray moved in again, jabbing, finding Coates's chin twice with light jabs. "I was carrying too much freight. That was her term. Too much freight."

"From your sniping days?"

The telephone rang in Sam Owl's office, a cubbyhole near the locker room. Curled photographs of Owl and his fighters covered the office's walls. Owl walked across a mat toward the phone.

"I was up and down, a little wild maybe," Gray replied. "She thought it was an echo from the sniping. But she wasn't a psychiatrist, I told her."

"You've been divorced ten years, but it doesn't sound like you've worked her out of your system."

"Pete, if I want counseling I'll go back to the Veterans Hospital."

"I quit," Coates said, lowering his gloves. He slipped through the ropes. "Looks like I win again. Do you still love her?"

Gray smiled wanly, stepping through the ropes. "They don't teach questions like that at the NYPD detective school."

"One friend asking another."

"I did when she left, but that didn't stop her from leaving. Couple years ago Cathryn married a pediatrician and lives in the East Eighties. Has a maid. Probably belongs to a couple nice clubs. Has a weekend house in the Hamptons."

"Ever hear from her?"

"Not in years."

Gray pulled off his gloves and grabbed a towel from a table. He wiped his face. Coates pushed his glasses onto his face. They sat on a bench watching Joe Leonard shadowbox.

Gray draped the towel over his shoulder, then added, "I haven't even bumped into her on the street. But I've worked it out now. I've got a family. Three kids and Mrs. Orlando."

Coates laughed. "I'll bet those kids scare off your girlfriends."

"Yeah, something like that."

"You got a girlfriend?" Coates asked bluntly. He took out his mouthguard.

Gray raised an eyebrow. "You're not going to try to set me up with your sister, are you? I've met her and she looks too much like Casey Stengel for my tastes."

Coates went on. "I never heard you talk about anybody, no woman anxiously waiting for you while we were putting in those late nights on the Chinaman's case."

"I'll go out and find somebody today if that'll make you happy."

"Just trying to fill in my file on you." Coates stared at Gray a moment before changing the subject. "The lab report. The color on the red cartridge was indeed fingernail polish, manufactured by Maybelline. No help there."

Gray wiped his face again.

"And no fingerprints on the television or in the john or anywhere else." Coates pulled off his training shoes and rubbed his feet. "But the CSI guys found another shell in the sniper's apartment, the killer cartridge. It was against a seam of the mattress nearest the north wall, and was identical to the red shell but without the paint. Why would someone as talented as our sniper do something as stupid as leaving his spent cartridge behind?"

"Don't know."

"You leave yours, Owen?"

"When I didn't have time to look for them. Otherwise I always cleaned up."

"The spent cartridge was informative," Coates said. "In its computers the lab has the characteristic markings from over three thousand makes and models of firearms, markings from the mechanical action of loading, chambering, and firing the round and from extracting and ejecting the casing."

"And?"

"The lab looked at the number and direction of twist and the measurements of land and groove markings."

"Out with it," Gray demanded. "What kind of weapon?"

"An M1891/30 Moisin-Nagant."

"A Soviet sniper rifle." Gray moved his mouth as if tasting the information. "Why would the sniper use an inferior rifle when he could buy better equipment in any American gun shop?"

"Maybe he's a Russian and he likes his old rifle."

"Why would a Russian kill an American gangster?" Gray asked.

"Maybe with Afghanistan and the Cold War over, he's freelancing. I've got no better guess, but I've been charged with finding out."

"Keep me posted," Gray said. "And during your investigation don't get your sniper pissed off at you. It wouldn't be too healthy."

Sam Owl called from his office, "Bennie can't make it today. Some problem with his mother getting a chicken bone stuck in her throat, or so he says, the lazy bum."

Joe Leonard climbed into the ring and pointed a glove at Gray and Coates. "One of you pasty guys want to spar?"

Gray answered, "You must think Dalton and Ruth Gray raised a complete idiot, Joe."

"I'll take it easy. Pull my punches."

"No way," Coates said.

Leonard leaned against the ropes. "Owen, someday you'll be able to tell your boy—what's his name? John?—that you were in the ring with the future middleweight champ."

Gray stared balefully at the fighter.

"You'll be able to tell him you actually got in a few pops at the legendary fighter. And you need a boxing lesson, I'll swear to that."

Gray jumped up from the seat and shoved his hands back into the gloves.

"That nice tie you been wearing lately, Owen?" the detective asked. "The blue with the red birds in it? Will you leave that to me?"

Leonard laughed evilly. The bridge of his nose had a lump the size of a marble. Scar tissue had begun closing his left ear. He shaved his head every morning. He looked as hard as a fireplug. He widely gestured Gray into the ring like he was gathering sheaves.

Gray slipped through the ropes, raised his hands, and squared himself to the middleweight.

Leonard lowered himself to a stance and danced toward Gray, lecturing importantly, "Now the first lesson to learn about boxing is not to get hit."

His left hand exploded forward, landing like a hammer on Gray's nose. Gray staggered, then collapsed to a sitting position, his legs splayed out. He held a glove over his nose, which began squirting blood.

"Goddamnit, Joe, that hurt." Gray's voice wavered. "That really hurt."

"Hey, man don't want to be hit, he takes up bobsledding."

Gray struggled to his feet. Blood dribbled around his mouth and dropped from his chin.

"And that was just my pretend punch," the middleweight said. "That's the punch I give my kid brother to thank him for bringing me a Pepsi from the refrigerator."

Gray gamely held up his hands again.

Coates yelled from the bench, "Owen, you're a slower learner than I thought."

61

Leonard came on, speaking from behind his gloves. "Now the second lesson is, Don't ever forget the first lesson, the one about not getting hit."

Leonard feinted with his left and threw his right, a rocket that landed on Gray's nose and blew him off his feet to bounce against the ropes. Again he slid to a sitting position. He shook his head and leaned almost to the mat.

Coates stepped to the ring. "You okay, Owen?"

Gray managed to focus his eyes. He blinked and nodded.

"Your face has lost that little bit of color it had," Leonard said as he helped Gray up. He passed him through the ropes to Coates.

Gray spit out his mouthpiece and wiped away blood with a towel Sam Owl handed him. Owl clucked with disapproval at the spectacle.

"Goddamnit." A moment passed before Gray could pluck another thought from the cotton in his head. "I'm going to sue your ass for something, Joe, as soon as I figure out what."

Leonard laughed again and resumed his shadowboxing. "Pete's going to arrest me. You're going to sue me. I'm in a world of trouble now."

Weaving slightly, Gray followed the detective toward the shower.

Coates said over his shoulder, "You looked goofy in that ring, to put it charitably."

Gray managed, "Not as goofy as you're going to look, you don't find the Chinaman's killer."

✧   ✧   ✧

Forty minutes later Gray met defense attorney Phil Hampton at the federal courthouse's alley door where prisoners brought from Manhattan jails entered the building for court dates.

Hampton's first words were "Frank Luca didn't waste any time, did he?"

Gray gave him a pained expression, not far from how he felt. His nose still smarted.

"One day you've got the hottest case in America and the next day you're prosecuting one of my grubby clients." Hampton laughed. "The mighty have done some serious falling."

"Speculating on my career is something I can handle without your help, Phil."

"What happened to your nose? Looks like your girlfriend crossed her legs."

"Let's do some business, Phil."

"My guy is just so much chaff for your office, Owen. You don't need to stick him, do you?"

Phil Hampton rarely practiced before the federal bar. Most of his clients were B&Es, car thieves, snatch-and-grabs, and muggers, all brought up on state charges. Hampton's brother owned Bob's Bonds near the Tombs. On Bob's window: "Let Bob Be Your Ace in the Hole." The brothers fed each other clients.

Hampton resembled a pile of dirty laundry. His coat was askew on his shoulders. His tie was pulled to one side and had a splat of mustard near the knot. His shoes had been scuffed to the leather. His mustache was a haphazard collection of stray hairs. Eager to cut someone off, he worked his mouth even when not speaking.

"I haven't studied the record yet, Phil." Gray had not even looked at the file. He opened it. "Donald Bledsoe. A counterfeiter, it seems."

"Nothing of the sort." Hampton was carrying a battered briefcase. "He's just an alleged passer. Hell, the cops found four bad bills on my guy. Just four bad hundreds."

"We've got the change of plea in five minutes. I need a proffer."

At a change-of-plea hearing the accused usually switched his plea from not guilty to guilty under the terms of a deal with the prosecutor.

"What can I tell you, Owen? Mike Olander is my client's brother-in-law. Bledsoe can't really turn on him."

Olander was a co-defendant. He owned the suspect copy machine.

Gray flipped to the second page—the last page—of the file. "Detective Ames says Bledsoe is going to clam up. I'm not going to do a plea unless I get a proffer."

A Dodge van turned into the alley and approached slowly. A marshal was visible through the windshield and behind him a cage. Buildings on both sides of the alley blocked the daylight.

Hampton said, "My client is afraid of a snitch-jacket."

"I hear that every day. I want the proffer before we get to the

63

change of plea. Tell me all he knows about Olander or I'm going to recommend the charts.''

The van stopped in front of Gray. A deputy U.S. marshal climbed down from the passenger side. He wore a ring made of an unmilled nugget of gold, a brown suit with a bulge under his arm, and bell-bottom pants. He was chewing a toothpick. His nose was bent twenty degrees out of alignment, making him look as if he were about to walk off in another direction. He nodded to Gray and stepped toward the rear of the van.

''Can you get him protective custody?'' Hampton asked.

''For a lousy paper passer? I'll consider asking the court for something below the sentencing guidelines but only after I've heard what he has to say.''

''Jesus, can't you give me anything up front?''

''Phil, you're whining. Give me the proffer first.''

The deputy marshal opened the van's rear door and pulled Donald Bledsoe from the cage, then righted him and pushed him toward the alley door.

Bledsoe had spent fifteen of his forty years on this earth in assorted jails and prisons. He stole a car low on fuel. He burgled the house of a man who kept a pistol collection in his bedroom. He robbed a bank, then attempted his escape by running through the bank's closed glass door, knocking himself senseless. And now, hundred-dollar bills that felt like fax paper. He had not once in his entire life as a criminal gotten anything right.

Bledsoe ducked his head as if a flock of photographers had descended on him. Then he braved a look. He appeared only slightly relieved to see his attorney. His hands were cuffed and secured to a chain belt around his waist. Bledsoe had stopped shaving at his arrest and now wore a dark shadow across his face. His hair was tossed and oily.

''What'm I going to do, Phil?'' The prisoner's voice was fogged with self-pity.

Hampton put a hand on his client's shoulder. ''We don't know yet.''

Bledsoe glanced at Owen Gray, then back at his lawyer. ''What'd this guy say, Phil? You cut a deal?''

Hampton stepped toward the door, moving his client along with him. The marshal had one of Bledsoe's elbows.

Two steps from the door, the marshal said, "Goddamn rain. Goddamn New York weather."

There was not a cloud in the sky. Holding Donald Bledsoe by the arm, the deputy was abruptly pulled off balance as the paper passer collapsed to the concrete. The deputy had been dappled with Bledsoe's blood and brains, not rainwater. The side of Bledsoe's head was a mash of gray and red pulp.

Owen Gray ducked behind the van, pulling the defense attorney after him. The marshal lunged for the protection of the courthouse door, drawing his pistol.

"What in hell happened?" the deputy yelled around his toothpick. He was breathing stertorously as if someone had yanked his tie tight. "You see anybody?"

A still moment passed. The distant babel of traffic reached them.

"Son of a bitch," the deputy cried, brushing the pith of Bledsoe's head from his jacket. "Look at my new suit."

Holding the van's door handle, Gray rose unsteadily. He levered his head left and right. The streets on both ends of the alley were artificially bright in contrast to the shaded alley. Delivery trucks and taxis passed at the ends of the alley. The chirp of an auto alarm sounded from somewhere. He stepped into the alley and pushed Bledsoe's shoulder with his foot to roll him over. A hole had been punched into an ear.

The deputy made a show of calmly squaring his coat. "He looks a little late for CPR, don't you think, Counselor?"

Gray was silent, so the deputy added, "Who'd want to gun down a zero like Donald Bledsoe?" The marshal spat out his toothpick and pulled another from his coat pocket. "Stupid errand boy was all he was."

Phil Hampton had crawled under the front axle and showed no inclination to reappear. Bledsoe's blood snaked across the cement toward the defense attorney. Hampton's briefcase was lying in a pile of unidentifiable brown sludge at the edge of the alley.

The deputy said, "Man, the paperwork on this is going to kill me."

Gray rubbed his temple, staring down the alley. There would be a window in a building—a sniper's hide—in the deep distance amid many other buildings and among the countless windows, but the day was too brilliant and the window too far to guess where. Gray's hand on his head was trembling and he lowered it quickly. He had to work to swallow.

He whispered to that distant window, to whoever might be peering back through a scope, "Tell me who you are."

5

FROM ANY DISTANCE the shooter resembled a clump of dried weeds, nothing but a mound of dusty vegetation wilting in the Virginia heat, attended only by two dragonflies who flashed iridescence as they darted among the leaves. But from the weeds protruded a rifle barrel, its unyielding horizontal plane at odds with the wafting thistle and burr and crabgrass from which the barrel seemed to have grown. A gust of wind tossed the weeds, rolling them flat in a wave. Then the breeze stilled.

The rifle barked, a flat crack that dissipated quickly across the terrain. A handkerchief-sized piece of canvas on the ground below the muzzle prevented a dust signature. A smoking brass casing was ejected.

"It's a flyer." The voice came from another cluster of weeds, this one nudged up against a tripod-mounted spotting scope.

"Missed entirely?" the shooter asked. "Goddamnit. You swagging me?" Swag was short for a scientific wild-ass guess.

"This time I picked up the course of the bullet in my scope. No chance you hit target."

"My problem is I can't get my pulse rhythm," the shooter complained.

"Yeah, right." The spotter laughed. "Your problem is that your finger twitches like an old man's. You got to squeeze the trigger like you would a woman's nipple.''

"As if you know anything about a woman's nipple, Bobby."

The spotter leered. "Ask your sister what I know about nipples."

"No talking about nipples on the firing line, goddamnit," bayed Gunnery Sergeant Arlen Able from his position behind the sniper team. "How many times I got to tell you? You get a hard pecker, you won't be able to feel your pulse in your arms and neck, and you'll be shooting on the beat rather than between it."

Down-range a circular disc on a pole waved for five seconds, indicating the bullet had missed the target. The pole was held by a Marine in the concrete butt below ground level.

The marksman and his spotter were dressed in Ghilli suits, an invention of ancient Scottish gamekeepers that had been adopted by Britain's Royal Marines during World War One. Long strips of tan, olive, and brown burlap were attached to the team's uniforms and field hats. The Ghillis broke up the Marines' outlines. With their shifting, variegated suits and faces painted olive and brown, the shooter and spotter resembled earthen berms.

Sergeant Able called from behind the line, "I can see your problem from here, Paley." He spoke with an East Texas piney woods accent.

The sergeant walked to the two weed clumps, then bent to a knee. He tapped the shooter's hand and said, "Part of your trigger finger is touching the side of the stock as you pull back, causing side pressure, rather than getting a straight front-to-rear movement. You're going to bust a flyer every time."

"Okay, Gunnery Sergeant."

"You're at a thousand yards. The smallest finger juke is going to be exaggerated by the distance."

"Okay, Gunnery Sergeant."

Calling Arlen Able just "Sergeant" would have sufficed, but the students always tacked on "Gunnery" as a mark of respect for their instructor, a compliment each time they addressed him. They knew Able's record. Sergeant Able's face was tanned dirt brown and was lined like a cracked window. His eyes were canted as if always amused. He was a small man and graveyard thin, with abrupt movements that broadcast an enormous energy, a terrier of a man. He was wearing field khaki with a whistle around his neck and a two-way radio on his belt.

"Trigger control is the hardest shooting skill to master, Paley. You got a ways to go and I want you to keep at it."

The shooter nodded, wiggling the camouflage tassels hanging from his field cap. In his scope a thousand yards down-range was a twenty-inch ring target made watery by heat waves. On three poles—at the firing line, halfway down the range, and near the target butt—were red streamers, always displayed during live-fire daylight exercises.

Behind the firing line was a control tower, a glass and panel miniature replica of one at an airport. The range master in the tower had binoculars at his eyes. He wore a microphone mounted on a headset. He could speak over loudspeakers at the firing line or the four target butts, at four hundred, seven hundred, a thousand, and fifteen hundred yards. On this range—the Sergeant Owen Gray Range at the Marine Corps Scout Sniper School near Quantico, Virginia—no targets were ever placed at less than four hundred yards, because each painstakingly screened, highly trained Marine allowed into the advanced training unit could already hit perfect scores at anything under four hundred, and because snipers were taught here never to fire at less than four hundred yards because of the risk of detection.

Few Marine Corps riflemen—even a Distinguished Marksman, a coveted classification earned when the Marine has won a medal in a division rifle match and two other awards from competitive matches—have seen the Sergeant Owen Gray Range. Rather, they believe the most challenging Marine training range is Number 4 at Quantico, a thousand-yarder competitors call Death Valley. Number 4 is indeed a challenge.

It is not true that Marines on the Sergeant Owen Gray Range sniff contemptuously at Death Valley, but they have graduated from that range. Theirs is a different science. Shooting is only a fraction of sniping. At the Sergeant Owen Gray Range marksmanship is taught, but also camouflage and concealment, target detection, range estimation, holds and leads, intelligence collection, sniper employment, survival, evasion and escape. The Scout Sniper school is the first permanent facility in the United States to teach snipers, and it is the finest sniper school in the world.

The sniper school hopes to reverse a long trend in American soldiering. In the Great War, American infantrymen loosed 7,000 rounds for each enemy casualty. In World War Two the number rose to 25,000, and in the Korean War 50,000. In Vietnam the figure was a startling 300,000 rounds per casualty. Yet one Vietnam specialist, the American sniper, expended less than two shells per kill.

The spotter's eye was above the scope as he stared down range. When the breeze rolled the red pendants along the range, he lowered himself to the eyepiece and said, "Better click in a degree of windage, Paley."

"I'm dinked right already. I'm going to wing it."

The shooter inhaled, slowly let half of it out, then gently brought back the trigger, this time keeping his finger away from the side of the stock. The rifle bounced back against the Marine's shoulder. The sound chased the bullet down the range.

After a few seconds the spotter said, "I can't make out any new bangs on the bull."

The red disc appeared above the butt, waving left and right.

"Goddamnit," Paley said glumly. "Another flyer."

He was reproving himself for a difficult shot. Median range for a sniper shot is six hundred to eight hundred yards. For most snipers, firing at thousand yards is considered chancy.

"Still thinking about me and your sister, I bet," the spotter chided. "Lost your concentration."

Sergeant Able hollered, "You guys want to giggle and chat, go join the Navy."

Before 1977, sniper instruction had been haphazard in the Marine Corps. That year the Scout/Sniper Instructor School had opened when the Corps determined that each Marine infantry battalion would have a sniper team, part of a scout and sniper platoon called a Surveillance and Target Acquisition (STA) Platoon. For a decade most of their marksmanship training had occurred at the Quantico training and competition ranges. Two years ago the new range had opened, a dozen miles southeast of Quantico, hidden among gentle hills. The sniper for whom the range had been named had not responded to the invitation to the opening ceremony mailed to his New York address.

With only one firing line, the facility was small compared with other service rifle ranges. Target butts were found at the four distances. Other than the fifteen hundred yards of range ground, which resembled a wildflower meadow, the installation consisted only of the control tower, a gun shed, a small headquarters building, and a locker room. The Marine Corps also owned the surrounding fourteen hundred acres of pine and dogwood woodlands and meadows where snipers were instructed in fieldcraft. The facility was approached on a gravel road, and a parking lot was in front of the headquarters. Across from the lot was a low-rising hill spotted with pine trees, mountain laurel, and tufts of weeds, these weeds real. A few wild rhododendrons adorned the hill, their scrawny, sparse leaves in contrast with their flawless pink and crimson flowers.

"Cleared for firing, Paley," the sergeant said. "Get on with it."

"Lay it in there, partner," the spotter said.

The trigger had a three-pound pull. Knowing the target could be maintained precisely in the crosshairs for only an instant, the shooter applied pressure to the trigger until the slightest additional pull would be required to release the firing pin. He halted his exhale. He was so still that he could feel his pulse in his arms. He waited for that instant when two critical events occurred at once—when the bull was quartered in the crosshairs at the same time his heart was between pulses. Then he smoothly applied the last bit of pull.

The rifle spoke, leaving a diaphanous black cloud ten feet in front of the barrel. Snipers know that even smokeless powder leaves smoke. It dissipated quickly in the air currents.

"Can't see it," the spotter said.

A black disc waved above the butt, meaning the target had been struck.

"Finally," Paley muttered.

A thousand yards down-range, the pit officer pulled the target, a hundred-pound wood rack on glides, down into the butt. A moment later it slid back up on its frame, a yellow triangle marking the hit.

His eye at the scope, the spotter said, "A wart. Second ring, eight o'clock."

A wart was a shot on the white but only a fraction of an inch from the black.

"Cease firing," crackled the loudspeaker. "Civilian approaching the range."

71

"Christ on a crutch," the sergeant blurted, turning toward the office. "If we get any more congressmen on inspection tours I'm going to piss blood."

A man walked from around the headquarters building toward the line. The sergeant stared hard at the civilian as the visitor crossed the pebble grounds, then made his way toward the firing line. The visitor was wearing a madras shirt, casual slacks, penny loafers, and a tentative smile. Something was familiar about the stranger, maybe the way he held his head, at a slight cant as if favoring an eye, his scope eye.

Sergeant Able squinted at the tall man, then leaned forward as if being an inch closer would make the intruder more readily recognizable. Then Able's eyes widened. "Well I'll be goddamned." His face creased into a grin and his words were rough with emotion. "It's Owen Gray."

Gray returned the smile. "I thought you'd find honest work someday, Arlen. Guess I was wrong."

Sergeant Able shook Gray's hand, then must have decided that was insufficient, so he bear-hugged him, pinning Gray's hands to his side and almost lifting him off the ground.

The sergeant's voice wavered. "Man, it's good to see you, Owen. You've been hiding, seems like."

The Marines left the firing line and gathered around. The shooter carried his rifle with the barrel up. He and the spotter maintained a respectful distance. The spotter, Bobby Sims, cast his eyes at the sign above the headquarters door that read "Sergeant Owen Gray Range," then looked back at Gray. The shooter, Larry Paley, cleared his throat, prompting the sergeant to make introductions.

"Have you kept up with the science, Owen?" the sergeant asked. "Know anything about your range or our new equipment?"

"Haven't had much occasion." Gray caught the sharp scent of Hoppe's No. 9 cleaning solvent.

"The service eighty-sixed our old Winchesters." When Able held out a hand, Paley passed him his rifle. "Take a look. It's the M-40A1, developed especially for Marine snipers. This is a pressure-molded fiberglass Remington Model 700 rifle receiver. Nothing alters the stock—rain, humidity, heat, or cold."

Sergeant Able patted the rifle proudly and went on. "And remember the trouble we had keeping the camo on the wood when it rained? This stock's coloring, the green and copper here, is pigment impregnated into the stock. We've got other rifles for snow and still others for the desert.''

Able attempted to pass the rifle to Gray, who involuntarily stepped back. He wouldn't raise his hands to accept the weapon.

The sergeant retained the rifle. "Atkinson Company sends us the twenty-four-inch heavy stainless steel barrel as a blank, and our armorers cut a recessed crown, then pipe-thread it to fit the receiver. The barrel has a diameter of almost an inch and it's free-floated. The rifle is chambered for 7.62 match ammo.''

"You got a moment, Arlen?'' Gray asked. "I've got a couple questions for you.''

Able might not have heard him. He continued, "Makes our Winchesters and Springfields and Remingtons from the old days look like Model A's.''

"I'm in a bit of a hurry, Arlen." Gray tried to turn him toward the office door.

"Can I ask you a question, Mr. Gray?'' Paley asked.

Owen Gray tried to mix both courtesy and dismissal into his smile and again tried to lead Sergeant Able away. Gray knew the questions these students would ask of him.

Paley said, "We heard that one time in Vietnam you were in a hide for four days and that you crapped your pants and sat in it rather than chance giving yourself away and losing your shot. That true?''

Gray shook his head. "That was before you were born, if it occurred at all.''

"Christ yes, it occurred," Able said. "Our fire station was at Din Po, remember? I was there when you came in from the field. You smelled bad enough to gag a maggot, pants all soiled and everything.'' Able may have seen Gray's frown, so he halted the reminiscence. He said, "We take our schooling more seriously than when you and I trained, Owen. Today we are practicing in full camouflage, which we do once a week.''

This time Bobby Sims tried. "Can I ask you something, Sergeant Gray?''

"I'm no longer in the service,'' Gray answered quickly. "Nobody calls me sergeant anymore. And asking me questions about your profession won't get you much because what little I knew I forgot.''

The corporal had a beatific face even under his paint, with blue eyes under long lashes and a gentle smile. "But this is a philosophical question."

Sergeant Able scowled. "Sims, you want philosophy, go figure out why Goofy can talk and Pluto can't. That's all the goddamn philosophy I allow in this school."

Corporal Sims plunged ahead. "How do you know you'll pull the trigger that first time? Sergeant Able says the thing you notice most is the target's eyes. They jump out at you through the scope. So how do you know you'll do the deed?"

Able's face registered utter astonishment. "What else you going to do to the enemy? Give him a Tootsie Roll? You'll pull the jack when the time comes, Sims. No buck fever. Don't worry your little head about it."

The gunnery sergeant looked at Gray, who was utterly still, not willing to confirm the principle by the slightest motion.

Able lectured, "And after your first kill you'll find it easier to shoot a human than a stray dog. Am I right, Owen?"

With some force Gray grabbed Sergeant Able's elbow to lead him toward the office. They left the sniper students behind and stepped toward the headquarters building, a gray clapboard one-story portable unit indistinguishable from a thousand other Marine portables except for the thick bars over the windows. The only cosmetic touch to the structure was a wood planter near the doorstep that trailed ivy to the ground. A siren loudspeaker was attached to a corner of the building.

"You were always a kook about sniping, Arlen," Gray said in a pleasant voice.

"Sniping is my life," the sergeant replied defensively. "That and my church. I'm the choir director."

"You leading a choir? That's not an image that comes readily to mind."

"I'm catching up with you, Owen. Three kills in Beirut and six in Iraq. I'm up to forty-eight."

Gray avoided the invitation to discuss statistics. "I made a few calls. You've made an avocation of studying snipers."

"I wrote the Topps Company and suggested they issue sniper cards, like baseball cards. A natural, I told them. Big hit with the kids. I'd supply them with all the material. Biographies, photos, interesting tidbits. They sent back a nice thanks but they declined."

"I've got some trouble with one of our old friends," Gray said. "Or one of our old enemies. I can't figure out which or who."

The dead bolt on the door was unlocked. They stepped into the headquarters building. The front room was almost all government-issue, with a metal desk, a swivel chair, lockers, a bench, and a dozen clipboards hung on a wall. An alarm control pad was on the wall near the door, and an infrared sweeper hung in a corner, its red light flickering.

"Paley's mother sent us that quilt," Able said. "I was touched."

The patchwork quilt hung on a wall and was made of red and white swatches with gold lettering that spelled out "Second place is a body bag."

Two dozen framed photographs were on one wall, most showing a Marine receiving a trophy. Gray recognized the Lauchheimer Trophy, first awarded in 1921, which bore the name of Brigadier General Charles H. Lauchheimer, who as a major in 1901 captained the first Corps team to enter a rifle competition. Another Marine was shown receiving the Elliot Trophy, a loving cup named after a commandant who brought the Marines their first rifle range, at Winthrop, Maryland. Gray recognized himself, shaking the hand of Camp Perry's commandant after winning the national title.

The room was the repository of Sergeant Able's collection, the result of a thirty-year search for the odds and ends of a singular profession. Rifles, scopes, sniper logs, and other mementos. The weapons were mounted on the walls.

"Here's my latest acquisition." Able lifted a skull from the display case. The skull had a hole in both temples. "This is all that remains of Horace Wade, the seventy-three-year old veteran of the Mexican War who joined the 7th Wisconsin Volunteers, and picked off twelve Confederate soldiers at Gettysburg before one of the rebels paid him back in kind. I traded four scalps for it. But I still got five scalps left." He pulled a string of hair knots from the case. Blackened flesh rinds hung from the tufts. "Our old friend Sam Short Bear sent me these. He was an Indian but a good Indian. Only shooter we ever knew who took scalps, remember? Sent me nine of them for my collection, so I had enough to trade for Horace Wade's skull."

"Arlen, I'm not talking to a lunatic, am I?"

Able lifted a rifle from the wall. "Here is my museum's pièce de résistance. A Winchester Model 70 under an Unertl scope. Recognize it?''

"Jesus, I hope not."

"It's your old smoke pole."

Gray took an uneasy step back, as if his old rifle were infectious. He breathed heavily, unable to remove his eyes from his old weapon. His mouth felt cottony, and he moved his tongue over his lips.

"Brings back memories, I'll bet," Able prompted.

Gray wiped his hand across his mouth. He was determined not to let this weapon regain an advantage over him. He knew this rifle more intimately than he had known his wife, knew every grain in the wood, every tiny pock on the barrel, every curve and hollow. In the past three or four years, as much as sixty minutes would elapse without this rifle rising from the dark pit of his memory. And here it was again, thrust up in front of him, heartless, mindless, and soulless. The torturous memory of this rifle was his constant and faithful companion, outlasting his military service, outlasting his marriage, living with him with unswerving and appalling fidelity.

But Owen Gray had built a sanity stick by stick, layer after layer over the years, and he could beat this weapon. He had learned to suppress the memory, will it away from him, if only for short times. He could do so now with the actual weapon. Surely. He would not allow the grisly Winchester to possess him again. With an effort that seemed to snap ligaments in his neck and shoulders, he turned away from the Winchester and focused on the gunnery sergeant.

"You know about snipers." Gray lowered himself to the bench. He found he could continue. "And you know the stuff the Marine Corps doesn't tell the public, like Sam Short Bear and his scalps."

"Yeah," Able said with satisfaction, leaning against the display case. "Collecting these things has given me insights about snipers that've escaped most people."

Gray dipped his chin, encouraging Able.

"Do you know that heart attacks are almost unheard of among ex-snipers? Type A's can't last in the lonely bush, so they don't become shooters in the first place, I figure."

"What else?" Gray asked.

"Snipers prefer gold crowns to the new natural-looking ceramics."

"I wanted information, Arlen, but this isn't what I had in mind."

"Then how about this?" the gunnery sergeant asked with undampened enthusiasm. "Almost all snipers can routinely snatch mosquitoes and flies in midflight."

Gray scratched the side of his nose. "So?"

"Can you? Catch a buzzing mosquito or fly right out of the air every time?"

"Sure." He added hastily, "Not that I do it much. What of it?"

"Owen, I'll bet you don't even know that very, very few folks can do that. Catching bugs isn't something people sit around and talk about like they do bowling or fishing. It's our phenomenal eye-hand coordination that makes such feats possible. Same thing that makes us great shooters."

Gray sighed audibly, something he did not like to be heard doing. "Arlen, do you remember how I used to leave a paper star at my hides?"

"Sure. Wish I had one for my collection."

"Have you ever heard of a sniper who left a cartridge with a red ring painted around it?"

Able looked at the ceiling. "I haven't. He American?"

"Russian, maybe."

"Is he the shooter who nailed your gangster up in New York? I saw it on TV. Sounded like a pro."

Gray nodded. He told Sergeant Able the little he knew about the killings of the Chinaman and Donald Bledsoe.

"Wish I could help you, Owen, but I've never heard of red shells." He put his collection back in the case and the Winchester on the wall. "That all you want to know?"

"That's it."

"How come you flew all the way down to Quantico to ask me one question, Owen? I mean, it's great to see you and all, but don't they have telephones in New York?"

Gray risked another glimpse at his Winchester. It was apparent that the years had recast the rifle in his mind. It was smaller and less malignant than he had remembered, a piece of equipment rather than the embodiment of evil. Gray suffered the fleeting fancy that the Winchester was deliberately disguising its true lines, trying to woo him again, an old suitor returning with a soft knock on the door, a placatory smile, and smooth promises.

"Owen, you've got the Asiatic stare." Able laughed. "The twenty-yard gaze in a ten-yard room."

Gray shook off the notion. "I'm not welcome at my office in New York. Too dangerous to be around, what with holes appearing in anybody I'm standing next to. So I had some time and I drove down in a rental car rather than fly. Brought my kids and their nanny. They're at a motel swimming pool over in Quantico."

Sergeant Able led Gray from the building. The Marines were still standing ten yards behind the firing line, an invitation to Gray to rejoin them. Able gently placed his hand in the small of Gray's back lest his visitor escape to his car. The sun beat down from overhead, seeming to flatten the land under its weight and chasing away birds and insects. The air rippled with heat.

Corporal Paley held his arms out and turned a circle. "Anything wrong with my presentation, Mr. Gray? Am I ready for the field?"

Gray generated a smile. "Your sergeant knows far better than I do."

"I mean, Sergeant Able tells us to fit ourselves out for these sessions as if we were going into the field. Have I missed anything?"

"You look great," Gray said quickly. "You'll do fine. So long, Arlen." He started for the parking lot.

Corporal Paley said, "Advice from you could someday save my life, Mr. Gray."

Gray slowly turned back. "Your dog tags."

"Yeah?"

"I heard them click together when you got up from your firing position. Wrap some tape around them."

Paley nodded, then asked, "Want to show your stuff on this range, Mr. Gray? You can use my smoke pole." He held out the M-40A1.

The spotter, Corporal Sims, added, "There's five degrees of left cranked in."

"Go ahead, Owen," Able said. "Show these young pups what us old gummers can do. The firing lane is open to the thousand-yard targets."

When Able spoke into his radio, the range master bawled over the loudspeakers, "Butt officer, clear for firing. Ready on the left. Ready on the right. Ready on the firing line."

Able took the weapon from Paley and held it closer to Gray, wiggling it by way of invitation like an angler setting a jig. With his other hand, he pointed down-range at the bull's-eye over half a mile away. "You used to own the thousand-yard line. Let's see if you still do."

"Damn it, Arlen. Haven't I made myself clear? I hate to disillusion your men, but I detest weapons. I'm through with them forever."

"What in hell?" Able stared down range.

A red disc was waving above the butt. A bullet had hit the bull's-eye. The distant sound of a rifle shot finally washed over them, softened by echoes and distance.

"Who fired that?" demanded the range master, his anger magnified by the metallic resonance of the speakers. "Take that name, Sergeant Able." Then after a moment, "There's nobody on the line. Who's shooting?"

Owen Gray knew. He spun around to search the headquarters building, then the parking lot, then the hill behind the lot. There the shooter was, amid the pines and grass and wild rhododendrons, made insubstantial by the contours and foliage of the hillside. Then he was invisible, veiled by vegetation as if claimed by the wilderness as its own, merged entirely with the trees and undergrowth.

The shooter moved again, a short mechanical motion at odds with the timberland that hid him, a motion Gray sensed was designed to alert the watchers to his location.

"There he is," Paley yelled.

The form stood out against the backdrop of greenery. A human head, maybe blond, but at too great a distance to be sure. Was that a flash of teeth, a smile? And a rifle. But then he was gone, again slipping into the disguise of the vegetation, shedding his human form to become one with the landscape.

"I can't make him out," Sergeant Able said, shading his eyes with a hand. "That's eerie. He's there, then he's not."

"Your binoculars," Gray demanded.

Bobby Sims passed the Bushnells over. Gray held them up, scanning the hill, but he saw only pines and low bushes, tufts of bluegrass, and gray stone tinged by gold moss. Branches bent and released in the wind, rustling leaves and shifting shadows. Bumblebees flitted in and out of the sun. The shooter had vanished.

Gunnery Sergeant Able whistled appreciatively. "That target he hit is a good fifteen, sixteen hundred yards from his spot on that hill. And it was a center bull's-eye. A pure unconscious shot, a professional cap bust."

Gray's eyes remained at the binoculars. He saw only the lovely east Virginia terrain.

"That was your shooter, you think?" Able asked. "The one who leaves a red shell?"

Gray nodded.

"Looks like he's following you around."

Gray lowered the binoculars. "He is."

The sergeant added quietly, "Looks like you've got a big problem."

6

"MY DAD WAS AN UNDERTAKER," Pete Coates said, rubbing the ball of his right foot. His black shoe was on the path next to the bench leg. "I ever tell you that?"

Gray squinted against the sun and shook his head.

"He owned a mortuary on Atlantic over in Brooklyn. I was working up bodies when I was twelve years old. Worst thing I had to do was stitch closed the stiffs' mouths. I'd have to stuff their swollen black tongues back into their gullets, yellow dentures, dead breath, flies trying to get into their yaps. It was no lifeguard job at the country club pool, I'll guarantee you that."

"You sewed their mouths up?"

"Otherwise the jaw drops open during the memorial service. Then you end up with the beloved in the casket who is not only dead but who also looks stupid."

"My life was better before I knew that," Gray said. When a jogger passed close to the bench he pulled in his legs. The runner trailed Joy perfume behind her.

"You also sew their eyes closed. My dad would fine me half a dollar for every eyeball I punctured with the needle. I never got the hang of it, and some days I'd have no take-home at all."

A woman carrying a Saks bag walked her dachshund past the bench. The dog pulled the leash taut to sniff Coates's shoe.

Coates said, "Lady, I don't like wiener dogs smelling my wing-tips."

With an imperious lift of her nose the woman pulled her dog away.

Still rubbing his foot, the detective turned back to Gray. "But worse than all that was the sore feet. You can't work on bodies sitting down, so I had aching feet all the time. I became a cop instead of a mortician. Shows what I know about anything."

"Your father still around?"

"Gone fifteen years. Every time I see a body I think of him. How far did you run today?"

"Ten miles, give or take a hundred yards. It's quite a luxury, actually, not being allowed into my office because everyone is afraid to stand near me. I've got a lot of time on my hands."

"You don't feel nervous running along, knowing there's a rifleman out there following you?"

"I'm the safest person in New York. He's had three clear chances to nail me and he hasn't. It's everybody else who should be worried."

They were in a portion of Central Park called Cedar Hill near the mid-seventies. Gray had been jogging and wore a line of perspiration across his forehead. His T-shirt was stuck to his chest with dampness. Gray bent over to wipe his sweaty hands on his socks. Coates was wearing a narrow blue tie that was loose at the neck and a sports coat so frayed it looked as if he buffed his car with it. Their bench was in front of a granite outcropping and was surrounded by red maple, sycamore, and paper birch trees. The path fed a stream of joggers, walkers, bicyclists, and baby strollers past them. Overhead an orange and blue Japanese kite sliced through the wind. The distant sounds of a children's soccer game sounded like wind chimes.

Gray glanced over his shoulder. "This must be the only place in the park where you can't see a window or a building on Fifth or over on the West Side. We're completely enclosed by leaves and branches. Not by chance, I'd guess."

"Sitting near you out in the open might open up my mind, literally."

"You've used this bench before?"

Coates pulled a sack of Planters peanuts from his pants pocket.

"When a puke wants to talk to me, he doesn't want to do it in Brooklyn or down in Little Italy, so we meet here."

"You talk to the law-enforcement people in Virginia?"

"The Prince William County sheriff told me he had two dozen men looking for the shooter's tracks, led by a bloodhound named Old Blue."

Taking a peanut, Gray said, "They're all named Old Blue."

"They followed his trail for a quarter mile as the shooter rounded the hill, but the trail ended at a roadside where he must have gotten into a car."

Gray smiled at a parade of ten preschoolers as they slowly passed the bench, each child tightly grasping a loop in a long rope that kept them together. A young woman led the troop and another brought up the rear.

Gray's hand moved so quickly the detective started. It was an abrupt blur that ended in a fist.

Gray held his balled hand at eye level and asked, "Can you do that?"

"Do what?"

"Catch a fly in midflight like I just did?"

"You caught it just now?" Coates regarded him narrowly. "Is this one of your boy John's jokes?"

"I always thought snipers were made, not born," Gray said. "I'm not so sure now."

"What do you do with the fly now that you've caught it?"

"Maybe I was destined to be a sniper. I had no choice."

"Am I missing something?" Coates dug for another nut. "What's catching a fly have to do with being a sniper."

"My point is that I can snatch a dragonfly or a mosquito or a fly out of the air every time I try. I never realized before my talk with Arlen Able yesterday that few other people can. How could I have missed it?"

"Each and every time?" Coates stared at Gray's fist. "No way. Nobody can do that, and I've got a beer that says you can't either."

Gray smiled. He slowly opened his hand. The fly remained motionless on his palm for an instant, then shot angrily into the air toward the sun, a flicker of vanishing iridescence. But Gray was faster. He had to partly rise from the bench, his hand in the fly's wake. Gray's hand snapped shut. He lowered himself again to the bench.

He held his fist up to Coates's nose. "It's in here again. You owe me a beer."

"That's the goddamnedest thing I've ever seen."

"There is a Homeric quality to it, you have to admit," Gray said.

"Mr. Gray?" The new voice came from the south, ten yards away at a bend in the path. "Are you Owen Gray?"

Gray jerked to the voice, wincing as if he had been caught smoking in the boys' lavatory. He quickly released the insect.

A woman in a rumpled maroon business suit and carrying an attaché case stared at him. "After watching this little exhibition, I'm praying you aren't Owen Gray."

"Then I've got some bad news for you," Gray said.

"And you are Pete Coates?" She took a few tentative steps forward. "Two grown men? Playing with bugs?"

"He's a policeman." Gray pointed at Coates. "He made me do it." He smiled but she wouldn't return it.

She circled in front of the bench as if afraid to approach them. "I worked my tail off in Moscow. An emergency, I was told. I haven't slept or had a good meal in a week. Then I fly five thousand miles into JFK, call your office to locate you and Detective Coates, and race here in a cab."

"I'm honored, truly," Gray said. "Who are you?"

"And then I find you out in a park catching insects." She watched them both with cold surmise. Then for an instant it appeared she might laugh. But she mastered herself. Her hair was crow-black. Her eyes were a glacial blue. "I'm Adrian Wade."

Coates quickly rose from the bench. "You're the ace Don Shearson at the FBI told me about."

"Shearson contacted me after it was determined your sniper's shell was Russian. I work for the Security Section of the State Department in Moscow."

Rising to his feet, Gray offered his hand. A twist of distaste crossed her face.

"You don't need to look like a martyr shaking my hand," Gray said lightly. "The fly is gone."

"It's not the fly," she replied, lowering her briefcase to the path. "It's your Marine Corps file. I've read it."

Coates said hurriedly, "Don said Adrian has learned as much about the Russian criminal investigative system as has ever been allowed an American."

"Maybe you should've also learned about tact," Gray said.

Earlier in his life Gray had decided he had seen too much and done too much to tolerate ball-busters, men or women who try to dominate by their willingness to inflict their self-importance on others. His usual tactic was to remain silent, looking slightly bored, only occasionally nodding in a woolly way, contributing nothing and refusing to engage in the exercise until the ball-buster realized Gray was happily off somewhere more pleasant. Gray's boss, Frank Luca, never did get it, thinking Gray's silences a mark of understanding and agreement and therefore immense intelligence.

Gray had been slow to realize that he brought from his military service anything but torment, but his unwillingness to suffer insufferables came from that time. As was his refusal to measure himself by others' opinions. So vast was the difference in experience between Gray and almost everyone else that he distrusted others' judgments about him. They hadn't looked through the scope. They didn't know and would never know.

"Adrian is a real Moscow gumshoe," Coates forged ahead. "At Shearson's request she took a crack at our puzzle of the red shell. But we weren't expecting you to show up here."

She sat at the far end of the bench at a distance that implied Gray and Coates had bad smells. A jogger with the bouncing lope of a beginner passed by.

Adrian Wade's smile was wintry. "After reading about your military service in Vietnam, Mr. Gray, I had expected to meet a Jack the Ripper but with better technology. Instead I find a goof on a bench. I'm relieved."

Gray rose from the bench. His voice was deliberately dry and bored. "Pete, you can brief me later on whatever Ms. Wade has to say. Suddenly I feel like I can run another ten miles."

She smiled with the magnanimity of superior knowledge. "Then you'll miss hearing the name of the sniper who leaves a red shell."

Gray's mouth moved, trying to find the right words. Nothing came, so he returned to his spot on the bench, defeated.

"The name is Trusov," she announced.

"Trusov?" Gray exclaimed. "World War Two's Victor Trusov? He left a red shell? I never heard that before."

She went on, "I spent the week speaking with members of three Russian police organizations, one civilian and two military. I must have set a world record for enduring patent lies, evasive answers, and protect-your-butt responses."

"And flat-out lewd propositions, I'll bet," Coates said flatteringly.

"Thirteen by my conservative estimate." She turned to give her smile only to the detective. "Russian men view western women as both naive and generous."

Gray had no doubt about the number of propositions. Adrian Wade was a startling combination of pure colors. Her hair was so black it reflected light like obsidian. The bangs were swept to one side with apparent unconcern but the result was a stylish rake. The rest of her hair ended at her shoulders, tucked in a way that flowed alongside her head as she moved. The contrast between her sable hair and the white skin of her face was almost shocking, and made her resemble a Victorian brooch. Her eyes were so blue they seemed lit from within. Her lips were painted a blood red, a bold color that set off marble-white teeth. She used her smile, it seemed to Gray. One instant it was street smart, then it was cryptic and beguiling.

"Stop staring at me, Mr. Gray." Her words percussed like a sledge on a railroad spike.

Gray scratched his nose, feeling ridiculous. Another jogger passed, this one wearing a shirt with a print of the Jolly Green Giant and a logo, "Visualize World Peas."

Adrian Wade said, "I spent most of my time at the Red Army's Armed Forces Inspectorate, whose territory covers crimes by Russian soldiers. Their building is near the Khodinka end of Leningrad Prospekt."

"I've never been to Moscow," Coates said.

"The Khodinka is the huge expanse of land in the middle of the city. It has a little-used airstrip that is connected to the Kremlin by a once-secret Metro tunnel. Other than an occasional flight by a Russian leader, the Khodinka is used only for practice for the Red Square military parades. The Inspectorate's building is on the Prospekt within site of the Khodinka. My visit there produced amazement from a Red Army captain that I should be asking such questions. I got no higher and no further."

"But you persisted," Coates encouraged. "Don Shearson said you could be like a dog with a bone."

"That afternoon I received a call at my apartment. Then a black Zil limousine picked me up at the American compound to return me to the Inspectorate. This time I met with Major General Georgi Kulikov, chief of the Inspectorate. He and his superiors had apparently decided that if there is indeed a renegade Russian soldier shooting Americans they'd better do all they can to try to catch him. Doors began to open."

A panhandler dressed in a pea jacket, tattered black Keds, and a Navy wool watch cap encrusted with grime stopped in front of the bench. He bubbled a few vowels through black, broken teeth and held out his hand. Coates waved him away, but the beggar moved closer, pushing his open hand almost under Adrian Wade's chin. Coates flashed his gold badge. The panhandler grunted and shuffled on.

The detective slipped his badge case back into his coat pocket. "The general must've made some phone calls."

"Better than that. He brought in Colonel Gregor Rokossosky, who heads what was once called the KGB's Second Chief Directorate."

"Never heard of it."

"It investigates major crimes including homicide involving foreigners."

After what he thought was a respectable interlude, Gray again let his eyes settle on her, but guardedly, like a thief. At first glance Gray had mistaken her wild coloring for youth, but he now saw she had done some living. A fine pattern of lines—new and gentle lines—touched the corners of her eyes. A few strands of gray-white were lost in her black hair like shooting stars on a moonless night. Her voice had a knowing lilt and throatiness gained only with seasoning. And her manner—the way she easily crossed her legs and leaned against the seat back, the way she conversed with the police detective and, in particular, the way she had roughed up Gray—indicated she was no stripling. Late thirties, Gray guessed.

She was saying, "In the Red Army the left hand truly does not know what the right hand is doing. I think General Kulikov was being candid when he first said the army did not have a specialized sniper school. Colonel Rokossosky seconded him. But prodded from on high, I believe, they started to dig.''

"You speak Russian?'' Coates asked.

She hesitated, then with a glance at Gray as if he were the source of all exasperation, she asked, "Do you know anything about me?''

Coates replied, "Don Shearson recommended you highly, said you knew your way around Moscow, and that's about all.''

"I have a master's degree in police science and was an FBI special agent for ten years. Then I went to work for the Foreign Service in Moscow, where I've been for eight years. Most of my work is with the Moscow police, but I've also spent time with the police commissioners and security chiefs of the independent republics. My job is to investigate crimes against United States citizens. I can't pass as a Russian, but I speak the language well enough.''

A young couple on Rollerblades passed the bench. His arms were flapping but his girlfriend skated smoothly beside him, her hand on his hip as she cooed encouragement. Her clinging blue nylon exercise top was cut so low and her matching trunks so high that in most countries she would have been arrested.

"And the two Russians produced?'' Coates asked.

"It took them a while, and they got tired of me always prodding, always implying I'd call ever higher in the Kremlin.''

As she spoke, Adrian Wade flicked her head to rearrange her hair. The black hair jumped and rolled. Gray wondered if she was aware of the motion, one she might have been doing all her life. This shiver of her head produced a fresh angle of her chin, as if she were renewing her presence and demanding the attention due her. At some level of her consciousness she knew of her glamour and its breath-catching effect on others and was not afraid to make those conversing with her focus on it. Perhaps she traded on her appearance. With this little shake, Gray knew something about her that she had not intentionally revealed, and he was chagrined that such a trifling discovery felt like a victory.

She went on, "General Kulikov was discomfited when he called me in again to say he had found the Red Army snipers' school, something he had sworn the day before did not exist. He said the school was run by the SPETSNAZ, and nodded at me meaningfully, indicating he could not have been expected to know anything about the SPETSNAZ.''

Coates said, "General Kulikov and I have much in common in our understanding of the SPETSNAZ."

Her silvery laugh provided grace notes to cheers from the nearby children's soccer game. She seemed quite charmed by the detective. And the detective seemed polite and subdued, far from his normal whoopee-cushion self.

She said, "The Red Army consists of five armed services, one of which is the Land Services. One of the Land Services' units is the SPETSNAZ, diversionary airborne troops who are parachuted behind the enemy lines to destroy headquarters, forward command posts, and communications centers. They are a highly trained elite. Most Russian boxers, marksmen, and wrestlers who appear in the Olympics as amateurs are actually active SPETSNAZ soldiers, though if you ask a SPETSNAZ he'll say he's been trained at the Central Army Sports Club or Moscow's Dynamo Sports Club."

"The cheaters," Gray said genially. "Small wonder the Soviet Union collapsed."

She gave him the swiftest of glances. "General Kulikov and I drove sixty-five miles south of Moscow to the city of Kolomna, near the confluence of the Moskva and Oka rivers."

"Kolomna was sacked four times by the Tatars," Gray injected.

This time she turned her head slowly to Gray, as if reluctant to make the effort.

He said, "I studied Moskva River Basin history at Stanford. For a while I was thinking of majoring in it."

"I read your file," she corrected him sternly. "You never attended Stanford."

"I meant Oregon State."

He absolutely could not get her to crack a smile in his direction.

She shifted on the bench, turning more to Pete Coates, dismissing Gray once again. "The sniper school was another five miles beyond Kolomna. The 1st SPETSNAZ Long Range Reconnaissance Regiment operates the school, but shortages in army appropriations after the breakup have closed it temporarily, Kulikov and I were told by its commander, a SPETSNAZ colonel who claimed to have enough funds to run a desk but not much more."

"The colonel gave you the information?" Coates asked.

"He had never been a sniper, just a paper pusher. But a number of the school's instructors still lived nearby, too poor to move away. We spoke with three of them at their club, a clapboard hovel with a plank table in the center and a gravel floor. They were noncommissioned officers in their fifties.''

"They don't sound like they'd be a font of information," Coates said.

"General Kulikov ordered them to speak candidly to me about a sniper whose signature was a red shell. One of the instructors replied, 'The Red October plant,' as if that should mean anything to me. They seemed hurt when I drew a blank on the Red October plant.''

"It's the most famous sniper duel in history," Gray said.

"Once I apologized for my ignorance, they quickly filled me in. Victor Trusov was with the 284th Division at Stalingrad in 1942, where in a three-day duel in the no-man's-land between Mamaev Hill and the Red October plant he killed a German—''

"It was Major Erwin König," Gray interrupted.

''. . . a German who was the finest sharpshooter in the Reich and who had been brought to Stalingrad specifically to kill the Russian sniper.''

Gray added, "Trusov was named a Hero of the Soviet Union for his eighty-two kills.''

"Russian grade schoolers are taught to recite Trusov's story," she said. "But what is omitted from their lessons—and something few Russians, even Russian soldiers, know—is that Trusov left a red shell at his firing sites. Apparently''—she looked directly at Gray—"leaving something like a red shell was considered vulgar braggadocio that the masses could live without.''

"Trusov must be seventy-five or eighty years old," Coates said. "Could an old guy be our killer?''

With the angles of her face set with professional pride, she announced, "We can ask him.''

Gray and Coates leaned forward in unison as if by some signal.

"He's a mile and a half from here at the Russian consulate.''

The detective yanked the telephone from his pocket. "Christ, is he in custody?''

"He lost his leg to gangrene about ten years ago," she said. "He's in a wheelchair and he's recovering from heart surgery that he had two weeks ago. And I've just talked to the Russian Consul General. He is more than willing to help, probably on orders from the Kremlin, and has promised that Mr. Trusov won't go anywhere. We're free to interview him.''

Gray remarked, "Doesn't sound like our man, red shell or no."

"You asked me to find a Russian sniper who left a red shell," she said in a strychnine voice. "I have done so."

"What's this old fellow doing at the Russian consulate?" Coates asked.

"A Hero of the Soviet Union, or Hero of Russia as it is now called, is treated regally. Trusov came to the United States for surgery at Columbia Medical Center, then he was given a room in the consulate to recover. The consulate has even hired a nurse for him."

They rose to their feet. Two children on BMX bikes swerved around them.

Coates said, "Let's go talk to him."

"I need to check into my hotel and at least wash my contact lenses. Can I meet you there in an hour?"

Coates nodded. "Adrian, you walk south and I'll go north with Owen until the trees open up, then I'll take off in another direction. We'll meet at the consulate."

"Skulking around?" she said. "That's the kind of thing we in my Moscow office did before the Soviet Union broke up."

Coates said, "Standing next to Owen out in the open might result in your own personal breakup."

Perhaps unwilling to concede she had not thought of the danger, she only dipped her chin before starting south along the path. "I'll see you in an hour."

After she had rounded an ash tree and disappeared from sight, Gray said, "You've just seen the perfect example of why I don't like people knowing about my experience in Vietnam. They conclude I'm loathsome without getting to know me. Adrian What's-Her-Name acted like I was an ogre."

Coates smiled. "It could be your looks."

"Working with that woman is going to be like having a boil on my butt."

"You can tolerate her for a day or two, then she'll be on a plane back to Moscow."

"I don't like being called a goof on a bench." Gray started north along the path.

Coates followed. "You know, other than Anna Renthal, I've never seen you interact with a woman."

91

"So?"

"You're not very good at it."

✧　　　✧　　　✧

The Assistant Consul General pushed open a door on the Russian consulate's third floor. He was wearing a herringbone sports coat with the cuffs two inches above his wrist bones. His hair was slicked back with an oil or pomade, so his forehead seemed two-thirds of his face.

"Please go right in," the assistant said in heavily accented English, sounding as if he had a mouthful of pebbles. "I'll return in fifteen minutes."

Adrian Wade asked, "You aren't going to insist on being present for the interview?"

The assistant shrugged. "This room is bugged. I'll listen while I eat my sandwich in the radio room." He smiled. "Or I might tune in Rush Limbaugh."

She shook her head. "Sometimes I long for the good old days."

Gray followed Coates and Adrian Wade into the room. His first impression was that it was a storehouse for old furniture. Antique pieces cluttered the room, seeming to overflow the purple Kashan rug to spill into the corners and wash up against the walls. The furnishings were opulent and overbearing, too rich and florid for a single room. Along just one wall were an ebonized wood dressing table inlaid with satinwood, a burr walnut scriptor on a carved and turned stand, and a walnut cabinet inlaid with enamel plaques of birds. Crowding the rug were a Victorian papier-mâché pedestal table, several Berlin woolwork stools, and a dozen Queen Anne and Georgian chairs, not one matching another. Haphazardly placed among all the rest were assorted fern stands, a lowboy, a long horse dressing glass, a globe that showed the Ottoman Empire and other vanished entities, and a leaded glass china display case. A clock with an ormolu case sat on a walnut mantel. The fireplace was blocked by a needlework fire screen mounted on a tripod foot.

"Smells like my grandmother's attic," Gray said softly as if in the presence of the dead. He wrinkled his nose against the odors of mildew, mothballs, old dust, and, strangely, fish. Gray had showered and changed his clothes at the Westside Athletic Club, where after discovering Sam Owl's gym he had retained his membership only for shower and lunch privileges.

Amid the jumble of precious furniture was an English brass half-tester bed from the mid-nineteenth century, manufactured just after it was discovered that brass beds housed fewer bedbugs than wood. The blankets were made up in a taut four-square military manner.

"The Soviets filled their consulates and embassies with ornate furniture to impress visitors," Adrian Wade said. "It's their Potemkin complex. Notice that they are all French and English pieces with almost nothing Russian."

"I don't see anybody in here," Coates said.

Gray caught his own reflection in a wall mirror framed with gilded pinewood bellflowers. His gaze moved to a pile of yellowed rags on top of the only comfortable item in the room, a La-Z-Boy recliner. "There he is."

Rather than rags, the heap of motley ocher cloth was a man in a dowdy bathrobe and one matching slipper. His other leg ended at the edge of the chair. He was caught in a stark ray of sunlight from a window. His bald head shared the bathrobe's saffron color. His few remaining hairs hovered above him like insects. Blue veins showed under the stippled skin of his crown. His face seemed made of transparent parchment, and Gray imagined he could see through his skin to the skull. Spatulate cheekbones rose from the sunken skin of the old man's cheeks. His masterful nose was hooked and narrow, a blade that in old age had drooped almost to his lower lip. His lips were thin and bloodless and fluttered with each exhale. His eyes were closed. He was asleep.

"Did he know we were coming?" Coates asked.

The old man started and cried out, a tenor chirp. His eyes rolled open. He blinked, then chuckled, a wheeze that sounded like paper being crumpled into a wad. *"Koshmar."*

Adrian Wade translated. "A nightmare."

The old man said, *"Nu, byvaet."*

"He says, 'Well, it happens,' meaning his nightmares. Maybe he has a lot of them, given his history."

She stepped into the bath of sunlight at the foot of the recliner and introduced herself in speedy Russian. The old man's jaw sagged and the lips lifted, presenting an unsettling hollow of bad teeth. He replied in Russian and held out a bony hand that resembled a vulture's talons.

He spoke for a moment in Russian, grinning and lifting his eyebrows invitingly. She laughed and replied, also in Russian. He cackled appreciatively and rubbed his hands together.

"What'd he say?" Coates asked.

"He asked me for a date."

"And?"

"I told him a night with me would turn him into a burned-out cinder, a mere husk of his former self, and that he would spend the rest of his days drooling and weeping."

Coates looked at Gray. "Women tell me that all the time when I ask them for dates. I never tire of it."

"I was exaggerating." She smiled. "But only a little. And now Mr. Trusov and I are the best of friends."

She made introductions, switching back and forth between Russian and English. Victor Trusov's grin spread. He seemed delighted with the visit. He nodded to Gray and Coates. His eyes were milk-glass blue and quick. Gray suspected they missed nothing.

"Zakuski?" He pointed to a television table.

She translated, "Hors d'oeuvres. Someone has provided Mr. Trusov with a nice spread. This is *yobla,* a dried and salted fish, and this is *osyotr* caviar. It's not as rare as beluga, but it tastes as good. Do you like caviar, Pete?"

"Is a frog's butt watertight?" Coates dug into the tin with a blini. He sculpted the eggs onto the pancake with a finger, then jammed the entire thing into his mouth.

She lifted a blini from a plate and scooped a small portion of the black beads onto it. Gray noticed that she touched the caviar with her tongue, exploring the eggs before she bit into them as if she wanted tactile pleasure as well as the taste from the caviar. She was wearing a suit with stern lines but of a softening bachelor-button blue. On her lapel was a finely wrought silver brooch representing a bunch of grapes and curled grape leaves. A plain band of silver hung around her left wrist.

The old man spoke quickly, making small gestures with his right hand. Tiny prisms of his spit flashed in the sun on their way down to the rug.

Adrian Wade said, "He says the consulate is treating him like a *nachestvo,* one of the privileged. He's calling me *kotik,* a pussycat, a term of endearment."

Owen Gray stepped forward. "Tell Mr. Trusov that I've long known about his exploits and heroism, and that I'm honored to meet him."

After the translation, the old man dipped his head at Gray. His eyes moved back to Adrian. Gray suspected that as a Hero of the Soviet Union Trusov was accustomed to praise for accomplishments the flatterers knew nothing about.

Gray added, "Erwin König, Hans Diebnitz, Otto Franz."

The names needed no translations. The old man's eyebrows came up. He eyed Gray closely, hair to shoes, a professional casing. Then he said something directly to Gray.

Adrian interpreted, "Mr. Trusov says, 'We study each other, don't we?' "

Gray nodded.

"He asks, 'What did you learn from me?' "

"The hat trick."

For three glorious seconds on the rubble mound at Stalingrad, Wehrmacht Major Erwin König had thought his bullet had soared through Trusov's head. Then König was dead.

The old man waved his hand dismissively. Adrian translated, " 'A stupid trick. It has galled me ever since that someone of Major König's stature fell for it. It cheapens my accomplishment.' "

"And the over-tree shot," Gray said. "I learned that from you."

An appreciative expression settled on Trusov's face. He spoke with enthusiasm, staring intently into Gray's gray eyes.

Again Adrian rendered his words into English. " 'You probably read the German interrogation report.' "

"Yes."

" 'I was held by the SS for five days. I thought I was tough, but they broke me. I told them all I knew, everything under the sun about my history and sniping.' "

"But you got away," Gray prompted.

" 'Can you imagine being careless with a firearm around me?' " Adrian translated.

Trusov laughed, which turned into a gasping cough. After a moment he could continue, with Adrian translating, " 'One of the bucket-heads forgot himself. I took care of him and my two interrogators, goddamn them, then it took me three weeks to cross the lines.' "

"The notes of that interrogation were captured by Patton's Third Army. They are still in a Pentagon library. I memorized them."

"What's an over-tree shot?" Coates asked.

"The sniper fires over an intervening tree or building. The target invariably thinks the shooter's hide is in the tree or building, so they concentrate their return fire on it. Mr. Trusov invented that ruse."

Adrian translated Gray's answer into Russian for the old man's benefit. The old man bowed his head modestly.

Gray said, "But my favorite—"

"Favorite what?" she cut in. "Favorite way of killing someone? Like your favorite pizza topping?"

Gray snapped, "If I want moralizing, I'll dial Pat Robertson's eight hundred number." Then to the old man, "My favorite of yours was the pine needles."

Scowling, Adrian turned Gray's words to Russian.

"Da, da, da," the old man chortled.

Gray explained in English for Coates's benefit, "Mr. Trusov could often smell an enemy's breath at a hundred yards."

" 'It was the goddamn sauerkraut,' " Adrian translated as Trusov spoke.

"So Mr. Trusov suspected the enemy might also be able to detect his breath."

" 'Beet soup. That's all we had to eat and it has an odor that carries.' "

"So before a mission he would chew pine needles. I learned that from him. Needles will kill any breath."

Adrian Wade's Russian came so easily that she would finish her translated sentence only a second or two after the speaker did. She continued with Trusov's words, " 'And I learned it from my father.' "

"Your father?" Gray asked. "I don't know about him."

" 'Sure you do, if you are a student of the art,' " Adrian rendered it into English. " 'You just don't know his name. The Red Army never released his name.' "

The pride in the old man's words was evident to Gray even in Russian.

" 'My father was the rifleman who froze the front at Tannenberg in the Great War.' "

Gray was astonished. "August 29 and 30, 1914, General Samsonov's Russian 2nd Army. The Red Devil?"

Trusov laughed. He patted his knee and a puff of dust rose from the yellow bathrobe to swirl in the sunlight.

Adrian translated, " 'Yes, the Germans called him the Red Devil. Tannenberg was a disaster for our army, but my father and his rifle stalled a part of the German pincer for almost eighteen hours, allowing thousands of Russian soldiers to escape east. He killed thirty-four of Ludendorff's soldiers in that eighteen hours alone. The Germans didn't dare lift their heads above the road embankments. He was the first in my family to leave a red shell.' "

"Did he survive the war?" Gray asked.

" 'He later rose to the rank of colonel, but one day in 1938 he disappeared from his office along with every other officer in the Kiev Military District above the rank of major.' " Trusov leaned forward to the television table to lift a *podstakannik*, a silver-handled glass containing tea. He sipped loudly, then continued, " 'He was a good teacher, and I learned the sniper's craft from him.' "

Coates dipped into the caviar again and asked with a full mouth, "When is the last time you fired a rifle, Mr. Trusov?"

After the translation, the old man pursed his lips, then said with Adrian translating, " 'I suppose it's been two decades. The government didn't allow citizens to own firearms unless they were hunters, and I've never found any pleasure at shooting at animals. No sport to it. They can't shoot back.' "

Adrian shook her head at the last sentence.

The Russian continued: " 'I passed along the torch long ago.' "

Coates had been reaching for yet another blini, and his hand stopped abruptly. "You passed along the torch? To whom?"

More translation, then another proud beam from the old man. " 'To my boy Nikolai. He also served in the army.' "

Coates glanced at Adrian Wade. "Know anything about Mr. Trusov's son?"

"Nobody I spoke with ever mentioned him," she replied, her words quick in defense of herself. "But I wouldn't be surprised. The Red Army is like an onion, and maybe I wasn't allowed to peel it back far enough. Perhaps even the instructors at the SPETSNAZ school had never heard of him.''

"Could there be other sniper schools in Russia?'' Gray asked. "Another group with its own instructors and history?''

"Not that I know about,'' she answered. "But maybe. The Red Army is famous for redundancy. Perhaps Kulikov and Rokossosky never heard of it either.''

The old man dipped a finger into the tin and brought a dab of caviar to his lips. Several black eggs caught in the corner of his mouth, and only after a moment did he find them with his tongue. He began speaking again, and Adrian translated.

'' 'My boy walked in my footsteps in Afghanistan.' ''

"He was a sniper, Mr. Trusov?'' Gray asked.

'' 'Seventy-eight confirmed kills in Afghanistan,' '' Adrian translated. '' 'Lots of turbans got ruined, thanks to my boy. If the army had kept him there, we wouldn't have lost Afghanistan, and maybe the Soviet Union wouldn't have collapsed.' ''

He laughed heartily, which shook his frame like a leaf in a wind. '' 'He left a red shell at his firing sites, too. Three generations of red shells.' ''

With that revelation, Adrian Wade found Gray's eyes. She smiled narrowly. The sun was edging lower in the sky, and rays reflected off the room's bright work—the antique key escutcheons, the brass hinges, the gilt on the mirror, the brass iron knockers on a dresser, and Adrian's silver brooch. The sun picked up the dust in the room, and a fine sheet of it lay over everything.

The old man added, '' 'I don't have any grandchildren, so the family tradition will end with Nikolai.' '' He lifted a finger toward Owen Gray. "Nikolai is about your age. Handsome boy, too, like you. His hair is lighter, though. I don't know where he got his blond hair. When I had hair, it was brown. Same with his mother.' ''

"What's he doing now?'' Gray asked.

The Russian squinted his eyes at the mantel clock. Adrian turned his answer to English. '' 'I imagine he is getting ready for dinner.' ''

Gray smiled. "I mean, where is he now?''

'' 'I don't know,' '' Adrian translated. '' 'I haven't seen him since yesterday.' '' Then she blurted in Russian, "You mean he's here in the United States?''

Trusov replied and Adrian turned it to English, " 'He received an emergency visitor's visa and escorted me here for the surgery. He's having a good time in New York, too, from what he tells me.' "

Gray mulled over this news. Nikolai Trusov. Did the name mean anything to him? The detective was staring at Gray, doubtless wondering the same thing. Gray didn't think so.

"Does your son know me, Mr. Trusov?" Gray asked.

The old man scooped the last of the caviar onto a finger, dropping a few eggs onto his plate.

He spoke and Adrian interpreted, " 'Nikolai didn't know anybody in the United States. Either did I. But I've met a lot of nice people, though. My surgeons and nurses. You three. You people aren't as bad as Khrushchev said.' "

"When do you expect Nikolai to visit you again?" the detective asked.

He chewed the caviar. Adrian echoed his words, " 'He comes and goes. Brings me sausage and this caviar and *yobla*. He is a dutiful son.' "

When the old man hesitated, Adrian nodded encouragement. Finally Victor Trusov continued. " 'My boy, I love him very much. But' "—he paused and a few seconds passed before he went on—" 'but there is something missing from him. My father and I were snipers because of war. Nikolai is a sniper because that is all he can be. It is the center of him.' "

Coates said, "We'll swamp the streets around here with my people. Nikolai won't be coming and going anymore, not until we talk to him."

Adrian Wade thanked the old sniper. Gray said he was honored to have met him. They all moved toward the door.

Adrian turned back and asked in Russian, then in English, "Mr. Trusov, do you ever catch flies out of the air?"

The old fellow narrowed his eyes at her. He finally said, and Adrian translated, " 'Why would I do that?' "

She looked at Gray with both censure and triumph.

" 'But there was a time during the war when I caught bats. They were all I had to eat.' "

As she translated, Adrian looked back and forth between the two snipers. " 'Not many people can seize a bat right out of the air.' "

Adrian Wade's glare swept into Gray. Reassessing him or dismissing him, Gray couldn't tell which. She said her goodbye in Russian, then left the room. Coates followed.

Gray gave the sniper the thumbs-up salute. Trusov returned it.

"I know you can't understand me, Mr. Trusov"—Gray laughed as he crossed to the door—"but I owe you one for the bat story."

7

GUNNERY SERGEANT ARLEN ABLE poured two
fingers of Jim Beam into the range master's glass, then into his
own. "Can you believe I was ever that young, Bud? I look like I'm
twelve."

Sergeant Bud Blackman held up the photograph. "You and Gray
look like you should be carrying squirt guns, not real guns."

The photograph dated from 1969 and showed Arlen Able and
Owen Gray kneeling on a dusty patch of ground, each holding a
rifle, the butts resting on their thighs and the barrels pointing to the
sky. Both were wearing olive T-shirts, field pants, and boots. Their
heads were shaved to the skin along the sides and burr cut on top.
Both Marines' smiles were broad and engaging. Their eyes were
slanted with amusement and their heads were cocked at the camera
in confident angles. These were the guileless, hopeful faces of
youth, faces that belonged in a high school album.

"Don't let the dummy grins fool you, Bud." Able sipped his
drink. "We were already proven headhunters."

Sergeant Blackman had been in the range tower during Owen
Gray's visit. Blackman swirled the whiskey, staring at the snapshot. He had seen it before. Early in any friendship Arlen Able
trotted out his photograph of himself kneeling next to the legend.
Blackman had a miser's face, with a pinched mouth and suspicious

slits for eyes. He had starting going bald early in life, and rather than tolerate a horseshoe of hair he shaved his entire scalp every morning. He was wearing field khaki. His cap and binoculars were on the desk. "He must've left it all behind in Vietnam. He looked like any other lawyer."

"I ever tell you he saved my life?" Able asked.

"No, but I can't believe there isn't a story left about Owen Gray you haven't told me."

"Maybe I never mentioned it because it makes me look a little goofy," Able said. "Owen was even a better tracker than a shooter, if you can believe it."

"We're all good trackers," Blackman said, taking another small swallow of Jim Beam and breathing in a soothing draft of air through his teeth. "It's part of our training."

Able shook his head. "I don't mean like you and I can track. Owen had a sixth sense about it. Sometimes the ground and the vegetation seemed to be speaking to him. Before he joined the Marines, he and his old man would often be asked by the county sheriff in Idaho to track lost hunters and climbers. Rescued quite a few over the years. He rescued me, too. One day in October 1969 near Tu Lun hill I took a mortar blast to the face."

"That explains a lot of things." Blackman chuckled.

"You laugh because it wasn't you, goddamnit. When a shell blew me down, I got right back up, climbed out of the hole, and moseyed into the field."

"You were ordered forward?" Blackman asked.

"No, hell no. I was blacked out on my feet. Concussed. To this day I have no memory of it. I got up—shells landing all around, machine gun fire overhead—and strolled into the forest. None of my mates saw me. It wasn't until dawn, after the firefight ended, that I was reported missing."

"I gather you weren't killed by the enemy." Blackman helped himself to another shot.

"Nobody could follow me, because I had wandered into NVA territory. I could've been out there picking daisies for all I remember. But Owen Gray figures out two things: one, that I'm addled, and two, where he can find me."

"I'll bite. How'd he figure them out?"

Sergeant Able leaned back in his chair and lifted his feet to the desktop. "He knows nobody goes into the field in a firefight without a lot of equipment. Not just a sniper rifle, because a sniper rifle is as worthless as tits on a goat in a firefight. No, if I'd been going anywhere with all my senses I'd have been carrying heavy armament and a pack and kit. But my footprint tells him my hands are empty and there's nothing on my back."

"I'll bite again."

Able said with satisfaction, "A person carrying some weight rolls his foot out on the big toe side as he walks. My register didn't show that. Plus, a walker carrying equipment takes shorter strides and has light heel pressure and a deep toe pushoff. I wasn't leaving any of these signs, so Owen knew I was out there damn near naked."

"Which meant you were acting wacko."

"Concussed, not wacko." Able added a splash of Jim Beam to his glass. The desk lamp was the only illumination in the office except for the tiny infrared light in the corner, which blinked on and off irregularly, detecting the sergeants' motions. The bloody remains of sunset were visible through the bars of the west windows. "Owen knew that if I survived my stupid walk I'd wander to a certain spot in the Vietnam wilderness. He met me there."

"He must've been guessing."

Able shook his head. "He knew that I would gradually circle to the right."

"How?"

"Right-handed people take a slightly larger step with their left foot. They walk in a big clockwise loop. By my bootprints Owen determined how fast I was ambling along, how tired I was, and then determined when I'd get to the half circle point. He met me there."

Blackman protested, "He couldn't have known precisely where you'd show up."

"He listened for me. Someone wandering lost in the wilderness makes a lot of noise."

"What'd he do? Put his ear to a stump like Sacajawea?"

"He used an anti-sapper parabolic listening dish. He took the dish to where his calculations suggested I'd appear. When he heard me thrashing around in the bush from about a quarter mile away, he came and retrieved me."

Sergeant Blackman threw back the last of his Jim Beam. "If Gray's so smart, why didn't he wait until you had walked in the full circle right back to your foxhole?"

"That would've doubled the time I was out there wandering, and the place was infested with NVA."

"Gray would've saved himself a lot of trouble," Blackman said.

"And he might've missed me. It has something to do with the margin of error of the angles."

"I would've just sat on an old artillery shell, sipped some Tiger Beer, and hoped you showed up, having walked a full circle."

Sergeant Able wagged his head with resignation. "Bud, arguing with you is like wiping my butt with a hoop. It's endless."

Blackman laughed.

Able lowered the bottle into a lower drawer, then rose from his chair. "I'll see you tomorrow bright and early."

Blackman stepped toward the door. "Bright and early is what the Marine Corps is all about."

Pulling his ring of keys from a pocket, Sergeant Able snapped off the desk lamp. The room was shadowy, with only the last shards of daylight coming through the windows. He stepped toward the burglar alarm pad. The code was the last four numbers of his service serial number.

Able spun to the hollow sound of a blow, a dull and sickening report followed by a soft groan. A whirling blur swept in through the door, a man dressed in black and moving so quickly in the half light that his image would not fully form in Able's mind. The club swept down again, and Able heard Blackman's other collarbone break, sounding like a lath snapped over a knee.

Bud Blackman collapsed back into the room. He landed hard on the floor, an arm bent under his body and his legs buckled under him.

It was a baseball bat. And it soared high as the intruder rushed into the room toward Able. The dark demon under the bat was hidden behind a veil of dark clothes and dusky light and swift motion. Able's service 9-mm was in his drawer. He stumbled toward it in the dark but made only a few steps before the intruder was on him. Able reflexively raised a hand, a futile gesture against the bat that slammed into his nose.

Able was enveloped in agony. His knees swayed and he started to sag. He blacked out before he hit the floor.

104

WHITE STAR

✧　　　　　✧　　　　　✧

Owen Gray knew fifteen patterns on the speed bag, and he could blend them together in a lovely swirling and surging routine. The Everlast leather bag and his mitts were blurs producing a loud pounding rhythm as the bag struck the backboard. Knuckles, backs of his hands, palms, elbows, even his chin, all were used to whip the bag around on its universal joint. The leather mitts were designed for the work, with only a thin padding at the knuckles and with lead bars sewn into the palms to weight the fists.

He might not be much of a boxer, but Gray had mastered the subsidiary skill of bag punching. He worked on the bag with a savage precision. Perspiration slid down his arms and flipped into the air around the reeling bag.

"This is your health club?" the tittering voice asked from the gym door.

Gray lowered his fists and turned to see Mrs. Orlando escorting the twins into the gym. She rolled her eyes to the ceiling, showing an acre of white. "Looks like nothing but convicts in here."

Mrs. Orlando was wearing a flowing dress decorated with dozens of tiny red prints of Che Guevara's bearded face. She carried a string purse. Her necklace tinkled lightly as she guided Julie and Carolyn to the bench. "Don't you girls talk to anyone here except maybe your father."

Gray called his thanks to her. She retreated the way she had come, shaking her head all the while. She disappeared through the door.

The oldest twin—Carolyn by five minutes—wore a bulky sweater of a dozen colors and black tights, while Julie had on jeans and a red denim jacket. They never dressed in identical clothes. They turned to watch two boxers spar in the ring.

Gray had asked Mrs. Orlando to bring the girls to the gym because except for their apartment there were few venues where Gray could spend time with his family. With the sniper at large, there were no walks along Bay Ridge avenues, no visits to parks, no shopping trips, no escorting them to school, nothing out of doors, and nothing indoors near windows with distant views. Sam Owl's windows looked across a narrow alley to a brown brick wall. That morning at breakfast Gray had offered to show them the

105

speed bag if they would meet him at his gym, then had to explain what a speed bag was.

The twins had never been to Sam Owl's gym, and they seemed spellbound by the skipping, sparring, and bag punching.

Gray decided to show off. "Watch this, girls."

Then Adrian Wade entered. Sound seemed abruptly sucked from the room. The speed bags were silenced. The sparrers lowered their gloves. The heavy bags swung loosely. The gymnasium became as still as a photograph. Her eyes swept left and right as if her head were a turret.

Gray groaned when Adrian Wade's gaze found him. She marched around the ring in his direction. In the faded, steamy, tumbledown gymnasium she was wildly out of place, an electric flash of fierce colors. A spotlight seemed to pick her up, and the gym became even duller, with its olive and pea-green and dun shades fading away. Even the magnificent boxing mural lost its luster. All eyes were on her, ogling and appreciating as she made her way to the speed bags. Adrian seemed aware of her effect and accepted the silence as her due. The slightest of smiles—perhaps one of mild cynicism—passed across the surface of her face like a breeze.

From the ring Benny Jones said, "Thank you, God. My dating service finally came through."

She winked at him, a slow, lascivious, welder's torch of a wink. Jones returned a gratified grin.

She was wearing a tight black skirt that ended two inches above her knees and a cedar green jacket over a white silk blouse. Around her neck was a thin silver chain. Again Gray was startled by the contrast between her fire-red mouth, raven hair, and blue eyes, immaculate colors setting off her bone-white face. She was carrying a manila envelope.

"It smells like old sweat socks in here," she said to Gray.

"Yeah, it's great, isn't it?"

"I've got news, none of it good."

"That bench is my new office. Come on over."

The twins drew themselves up, awkwardly and anxiously, prepared for an introduction. But their father said briskly, "Girls, I need to talk to this lady. Will you excuse us?"

"Your daughters?" Adrian asked. "Introduce me."

The twins might have been witnessing the raising of the dead

106

from the Gospels. They seemed incapable of expression, their faces frozen by bafflement. Carolyn and Julie had never seen their father with a woman. Maybe a thank-you to a sales clerk or a quick word with a librarian. Mrs. Orlando didn't count. This was a real woman, someone their father's age, and so thoroughly attractive, a woman who belonged on a fashion magazine cover. This was a person of fluent confidence and obvious dignity, someone plainly of substance. And—could it be?—she had come to visit their father. It simply wasn't within their experience. Their eyes mirrored their wonder. Gray missed it, but Adrian rapidly searched their faces and may have understood.

She stepped close to the twins and extended her hand, first to one, then the other. Her smile might have been given to long lost loved ones. Her eyes engaged them fully and excluded all else in the gym, and certainly Gray. For a few moments it seemed all that mattered in the world were Owen Gray's daughters. They flushed with the attention and fairly stammered their replies. After a few minutes, Adrian Wade had learned much about school and piano practice and Bay Ridge and Mrs. Orlando.

Gray thought it a calculating inveiglement. She was overpowering his daughters and entrancing them, doubtless to irk him. He scanned the room. The fighters were slowly returning to their workouts. Joe Leonard smiled knowingly at Gray and mouthed, "Wow." Sam Owl was still staring at Adrian Wade as if she were an alien.

"We'd love to," both girls said as one. They were bouncing with excitement.

"Give me a few minutes with your father, then off we'll go."

Gray hadn't been listening. "Off you go? Where?"

She looked at him. "It's time for your girls to wear a little lipstick."

"Looks like you've got plenty to spare," he said, pleased with himself.

She ignored the jab. "I'm going to show them a few things at Bloomingdale's cosmetics counters."

"That place is the gate to hell. I don't want Carolyn and Julie anywhere near there."

"Well, that's settled," Adrian said, grinning at them. "We'll catch a cab uptown in a minute, girls."

The twins cheered.

"Am I just bumping my gums here?" Gray objected. "Is anybody listening?"

She took him by an elbow and turned him to the bench. The girls moved to a corner of the gym near the water fountain but could not remove their eyes from her.

Adrian lowered herself to the bench. "Your friend Sergeant Able at Quantico has been hurt. So has Sergeant Blackman."

Gray drew in a sharp breath.

She told him about the assault at the rifle range the night before, and ended with "Sergeant Blackman will be all right, a week in the hospital and then he'll need physical therapy. Sergeant Able has a broken nose, and was treated and released from the base hospital. He is back on duty already. The sergeants were hurt by someone who knew how to do it, someone with experience who was fast and competent."

"But what was he doing?"

She replied with gravity, "The only thing taken was your sniper rifle from Vietnam. Your Winchester .30–06."

Gray sank back against the chipped wall. He was wearing a blue sweatshirt that hid the scar on his neck. He peeled off the mitts to wipe sweat from his forehead. He ran his fingers through his dark hair. "I should've pitched that goddamn thing into the South China Sea when I had the chance."

She pulled a five-by-seven photograph from the manila envelope. "This is our man. Nikolai Trusov. It's his service ID photograph. General Kulikov wired it from Moscow this morning and we had it blown up. There isn't a sheriff or police department or FBI office on the east coast that doesn't have a copy by now. Kulikov also sent Trusov's fingerprints. The police agencies have them, too, and the prints have already produced results."

"Jesus." Gray stared at the photograph. "I wouldn't want to run into this guy in a dark alley."

With nothing but hard angles and sudden planes, Nikolai Trusov's face seemed chopped out of a log with an axe. The face was overfeatured, with a broad and blunt nose and a jutting long chin with a slightly off-center cleft. His cheekbones were so rocky they threw shadows on the face below. Blond eyebrows had vanished in the photographer's flash. The brows were low and sunk deeply, and under them were flat, expressionless eyes. His forehead appeared too small because curly yellow hair was brushed forward.

Hair on the sides of his head was short. His ears were button-sized and tight against his head. His mouth was crooked, and the left side might have been about to smile while the right was set in a stiff pedagogic line. It was a brawler's face, a dangerous face.

"What happened to him, do you think?" Adrian pointed at Nikolai Trusov's forehead. "A meat cleaver, looks like."

"He took a mean shot, that's for sure."

Trusov's forehead had a shallow trench in it, a furrow that ran from an inch above his right eye to disappear under the hairline. The groove was covered with puckered skin three shades darker than the rest of his face. The bone on both sides of the furrow was irregular, with chinks and facets. Skin alongside the fracture was pleated from surgeon's stitches. Gray guessed that the depression was half an inch below the curve of his forehead and crown. The trough and the corrugated skin added to the asymmetry and dissonance of Trusov's face.

"This injury would've killed most people," Gray said. "Did General Kulikov give an explanation?"

"So far he has found only Trusov's SPETSNAZ file."

"Aren't a Russian soldier's files all in one place?"

"You'd think so, but not this guy, and I don't know why." She slid out a stack of paper from the envelope. "These were also faxed to me this morning from General Kulikov. It's Trusov's Soviet Army record from 1977 when he joined the SPETSNAZ to 1988 when he left it."

"But he was in the Red Army before and after those dates, wasn't he?" Gray's wet shirt was clinging to his back, chilling him. His daughters were still staring at Adrian.

"He was already a Red Army sergeant when he entered SPETSNAZ training, according to this."

She flipped through several pages. They were copies of military forms, some with unit formation signs printed alongside the letterhead. They were in Russian and Gray could make out nothing from the mass of Cyrillic letters. General Kulikov was being cooperative, but even so a number of lines had been blacked out with a heavy pen on each page before they were faxed to the United States.

She went on. "In 1988 he was transferred from the 1st Brigade, 1st All-Arms Army of the North West Front to a SPETSNAZ training brigade in the North Caucasus military district at Rostov.

He trained for eighteen months at Rostov. He was taught explosives, hand-to-hand combat, communications, parachuting, survival, and the like. But he taught rifle marksmanship.''

"So he was already a shooter?''

She held up a page from the file, as if he could read it. "Trusov won a gold medal at the 1976 Winter Olympics at Innsbruck in the biathlon. Shooting and skiing.''

"That's an asinine sport.''

She looked up from the file. "You'd think a sniper like you would love that sport.''

"I'm talking about the skiing part of it. If God wanted man to ski He wouldn't have invented the snowmobile.''

After a moment she said, "Is that another attempt to be funny?''

"Probably.'' Gray exhaled slowly. "Where did Trusov go after his commando training in Rostov?''

"To a SPETSNAZ company in the 3rd Army of the GSFG, the Group of Soviet Forces in Germany. He was posted there until a little while after the Afghanistan invasion, when his SPETSNAZ company was transferred to the Turkestan Military District. The file shows he was in Afghanistan four years. That's where he killed the seventy-eight people.''

"They weren't people,'' Gray corrected her. "They were enemy soldiers.''

"I see now why you went to law school,'' she with a schoolteacher's inflection. "To learn to distinguish, which is what law school is all about. Not to understand, not to appreciate, not to sympathize, but to distinguish. It is one of the lesser talents.''

"Were I to give it any thought at all,'' he said with seeming indifference, "I would conclude you are a bonebrain.''

Her face turned a gratifying pink, and for a moment Adrian appeared to be chewing on her tongue. Then she said in the tone and cadence of a typewriter, "I'm not going to get into a kindergarten name-calling match with you. I know Russians and you know sniping. You and I are going to concentrate on finding Nikolai Trusov.''

"I was being childish,'' Gray said equably. "But that doesn't mean you aren't a bonebrain.''

Gray had a good nose, a trained nose. It had saved his life more than once in Vietnam. Adrian was wearing a perfume that was somehow both faint and arresting. The fragrance was not flowery but was darker and more veiled, maybe an exotic spice. It seemed to be dulling his senses. Calling her names, for Christ sake.

She gamely continued. "Here's more bad news. Nikolai Trusov has obtained a copy of your Marine Corps file, the same one I've read."

Until that revelation, a slight—admittedly an exceedingly slight—chance had remained that the Russian sniper's actions were unconnected to Gray, that the killer's plan, if indeed he had a plan, was impersonal, and that mad coincidence was playing a ghastly trick on Gray. No longer. Intelligence—knowing the enemy—was the heart of sniping. The Russian now knew more about Gray than Gray had let anyone learn in twenty-five years.

"How'd he get the file?"

"A Freedom of Information Act request, just like anybody else can get your file." She slid the photograph and file back into the envelope. "I mentioned that the fingerprints have produced results. Pete Coates and I have been wondering how Trusov is funding himself. Soviet soldiers are usually penniless, and even the Red Army sponsorship that sent his father and him here for the surgery would not have given him enough money to rent an apartment like he did and do the traveling he is doing."

Gray rubbed the back of his neck. He never used to get stiff like this, not playing high school football or in boot camp.

"Two weeks ago a cash machine near Great Neck was smashed and over ten thousand dollars was taken."

"I read about it in the paper. The robber used a backhoe."

"Instead of a hoe there was a pneumatic breaker hammer, like a big jackhammer, installed on the hydraulic arm. A Con Ed crew had been using the John Deere to tear up a concrete road to install electric lines underground. Sometime during that night he hotwired the tractor and drove it a block to a First New York cash machine. He used the breaker hammer to tear away the front panel and spring the money cartridge from the machine, then rupture the cartridge. He walked away with the money."

"Fingerprints?"

"The robber did nothing to hide his prints. They were all over the John Deere. But the FBI drew a blank when they tried to match them."

Gray said, "So when General Kulikov sent you Trusov's prints, you forwarded them to the FBI?"

"All this morning. The FBI just reported that Trusov is the cash machine robber. So we know how he bankrolled himself."

They sat for a moment watching Joe Leonard lashing into a heavy bag. Then she asked, "Have you ever been to Russia?"

"Never."

"Or Afghanistan?"

Gray shook his head.

She demanded, "Then how does this Nikolai Trusov know you?"

"I've thought of little else lately. I have no answer."

"Maybe the only connection is that he heard of your reputation, and he can't stand the idea of someone out there better at killing than he is. You had ninety-six kills, he had only seventy-eight. This town ain't big enough for the both of us, partner, that kind of macho testosterone foolishness."

Gray didn't feel like arguing with her. His workout had worn him down.

"I imagine that's why you became a sniper, isn't it?" she asked pointedly. "Testosterone?"

"You see that fellow over there?" Gray inquired obscurely. "The black fighter working the heavy bag? He's a middleweight named Joe Leonard. Why don't you ask him for a boxing lesson? I had a lesson from him and I learned a lot."

She rose from the bench. "I don't need a lesson. I'm already tougher than him. And you."

Gray prided himself on his poise and dispassion and his ability to step back from a situation to assess it critically. But her adeptness at reducing him to childish responses bordered on the bizarre. So he was delighted when he did not burst out with his first reaction: Oh yeah? Says who?

Still, he could not prevent himself from replying, "We are talking about different things here. You are tough only in an affirmative action, I Am Woman Hear Me Roar kind of way. You are not tough compared to me."

Gray finally caught himself. "Jesus, I'm arguing about who's bigger and meaner, you or me." He laughed in a brittle way and shook his head. "I apologize."

Her smile could have melted paint from a Chevrolet. "Let me show you something. Take a swing at me."

Take a swing? Alarms went off inside Gray's head. He brought his eyes up to hers, but they were unreadable. Unfathomable, maybe forever unknowable. But Christ they were blue.

"You mean hit you?" he asked. "I'm an adult, a member of society."

She laughed brightly, genuinely, Gray thought. Was this an awkward attempt at a truce?

"You don't have to actually hit me," she said. "Throw the punch but bring it up short."

Gray pushed himself up from the bench. "You know judo and I'm going to get my butt kicked. Am I right?"

"I don't know judo from jellybeans," she said.

"But I'm going to get hurt, right?" Gray asked warily.

"If we are going to work together you need to learn to trust me. Throw a jab and I'll show you something. Trust me."

Was this the siren's song that lured sailors upon the rocks?

She stepped closer, then tilted her head, presenting a target. Her hands were at her sides. Joe Leonard and Benny Jones paused in their workouts to watch. The girls were smiling widely, perhaps thinking Adrian Wade was lifting her head for a kiss.

Gray brought his hands up in good imitation of Muammad Ali, he thought. He gently—very gently—jabbed his left hand at her face, intending to stop his fist well short of her chin.

She moved with a startling rapidity. Suddenly she was standing next to him, her black scented hair in his face, her hip dug into his thigh in a manner that in any other situation would be erotic. At the same instant, Gray felt her leg sweep into the back of his legs, low on his calves. Her arms shot up. His feet left the ground and began a wide arc. He swung on the axis of her hip, and the floor suddenly seemed to be above him. Her hand was at his throat and his windpipe felt like it was collapsing. He had no contact with the world, no stable point of reference except where their bodies were joined at their hips. He spun in a helpless cartwheel.

The gym's wood floor must have been traveling fifty miles an hour up at him. The entire length of his body from nose to toes slammed into the floor with a sickening crack. His mind fluttered to whiteness, then regained itself. A surge of nausea rose from behind his breastbone. He tried to look up, but her foot was across his face, pinning his head to the floor.

Carolyn and Julie stared but did not move toward him, perhaps thinking their father had just shown their new friend Adrian some self-defense technique. Joe Leonard and Benny Jones and Sam Owl were fond of Owen Gray, and were trying not to laugh, but with only limited success.

"You do have one tiny endearing element to your personality," Adrian said from high above him.

"Get your foot off my face." Gray's words were muffled by her shoe pressed against his lips.

"You are delightfully naive."

"Get your foot off my face." He was sprawled on the floor like a rag tossed aside, one arm twisted painfully under his back, his legs splayed out.

She removed her foot. Gray found he could focus his eyes. She was wearing the same smile. The girls ventured over.

"You okay, Dad?" Carolyn asked.

"I'm fine," Gray said weakly.

"He was showing me one of his moves," Adrian deadpanned. "How to make a gymnasium floor surrender."

"You going to get up, Dad?" Julie asked.

"I want to lie here a minute." He could still taste shoe leather in his mouth. No part of his body did not ache except maybe his hair. He didn't trust his legs to get him up or keep him up. "You girls can go with Ms. Wade now. She'll take care of you."

Adrian Wade led the twins away. Both girls glanced over their shoulders at him several times until they disappeared through the gym's door.

"I've heard these things about white girls, but I never believed it till now," Joe Leonard called. "Was it good, Owen?"

Gray levered himself to standing. His legs seemed to work. Maybe nothing was broken. Ignoring Leonard, he wobbled in the direction of the locker room. He was tiring of these ignominious retreats to the shower.

8

"I DON'T LIKE IT, none of it," Pete Coates said. "But I can't talk the commissioner out of the plan. He told me he'd sign the documents and have them here within the hour. He's going to turn that Marine and you into New York's finest for a day."

Gray was sitting on a metal folding chair across from the detective's desk. "Did you talk to the commissioner, level with him?"

"I told him the police department is in the business of arresting criminals, not whacking them. But he said Nikolai Trusov is never going to let himself be arrested, and he'll kill four or five policemen before he goes down. So your plan is a go."

"And my part in it?"

"The commissioner knows your file better than I do. He says you are the only one who has a chance to beat Trusov."

Coates's office had the dimensions of a closet. His desk filled most of the space, with room left only for two folding chairs and two black file cabinets. Gray had to sit rigidly upright because his knees were pressed against the front of Coates's desk. An interior window opened to a hallway and other offices. A hum of distant conversations and typing and telephone ringing filled the area. There was no window to the outside, but even so, other detectives and policemen stayed well away from Owen Gray. The office was not air conditioned, and Coates's tie was loose around his neck and damp patches appeared on his shirt under his arms.

The desk was covered by an inch of assorted documents, and by abandoned paper coffee cups, doughnut wrappers, a telephone, a Rolodex, and a plastic cup of pens. Files were piled high on the cabinets and on the floor in two corners. An empty coat hanger occupied another tight corner. The computer's CPU was squeezed between the desk and a wall, and its fan filled the office with a low drone. A square glass case was mounted on the back wall with a sign on it reading "In Case of Emergency, Break Glass." Inside was a Thompson submachine gun.

Coates turned from the monitor to Gray. "So you think Nikolai Trusov will go for it?"

"He wants something from me."

"Or he wants you to do something," Coates amended. He had been working two shifts, and his face was wan and his eyes red-rimmed behind his spectacles. He needed a shave.

"Trusov will strike again, because I haven't gotten his message yet. I don't have the slightest idea what he wants."

Coates said, "He hasn't had any targets in three days. You haven't been in the open near anybody."

"So the Russian is probably hungry to deliver his message again. Maybe even desperate. I think he'll go for it. The super at this condo four blocks from my place reported a suspicious-looking character on the roof of the building next to his condo. The description fits Trusov. The Russian was scouting a firing site. That building's roof has a clear view to my apartment."

"We should just wait for him on that roof," Coates said. "Surround him."

Gray adamantly shook his head. "Pete, you still don't realize who you're dealing with. He'll kill a lot of your men before it's over. The only way to get this guy is from a distance, a long one."

When the telephone chirped, Coates snatched it and pressed it to his ear. He said a few words, then held the phone out for Gray. "It's Adrian Wade."

Gray made a face. He had told Coates about his free fall at Sam Owl's gym. "Tell her I'm busy. Tell her an orthopedic surgeon is putting my legs in casts, thanks to her." But he reached for the telephone anyway, adding, "At least she can't maim me over the phone."

With overwrought courtesy, he conversed a moment with Adrian, ending with "I'll be there in about three hours." He passed the phone back to Coates and said, "Mrs. Orlando, our nanny, hasn't arrived at our place yet. She's late, and has undoubtedly found one of her new boyfriends. It's more romantic to walk along the Brooklyn Heights promenade than appear for work."

"Dock her a day's pay," Coates suggested. "That'll cure absenteeism fast."

"I might, depending on the cleverness of her excuse." Gray laughed. "But Adrian kidnapped my daughters at the gym, took them uptown and had a fine old time, then escorted them to Bay Ridge in a cab. Now John has arrived home from his friend's. The girls have told Adrian a little lie, saying that their father never, never leaves them in the apartment without adult supervision. So Adrian is stuck there with a bunch of hungry, tired kids." He chortled again. "She deserves it."

"I did you a favor." Coates tempted him by lifting a sheaf of papers and wagging them at him.

"You've agreed to fund my kids' college educations?"

"Better. I asked a friend at the FBI to send me some information about Adrian Wade." He waved the paper at Gray again. "When I'm working closely with people, I like to know what makes them breathe hard. This file has got some hot stuff in it. Want to read it?"

Gray rebuked him. "Pete, I'm surprised at you, thinking I'd stoop so low as to read someone's private file."

"That's truly noble," Coates replied sardonically. "A lesson I might profit from."

"Read it to me."

"She's a widow, for one," the detective said without missing a beat. "Her husband was a pilot for Chesapeake Air Charter, and he went down in a De Haviland Beaver four years ago."

"What happened?"

"He ran out of air, I guess. The file doesn't say. She has studied judo for eight years, and was Northeast Judo Association seniors champion two years running."

Gray said dully, "That news would have been more useful to me this morning."

"Let's see." The detective skimmed the pages. "She was raised in Los Angeles. Her father and mother were both professors at

UCLA. She did her undergraduate work there. She has a BA in psychology and an advanced degree in police science. She works sixty hours a week on average, real gung ho, and appears to be in line for a transfer back to Washington and a promotion.''

Gray shifted on the seat, pushing his knees to one side. "Isn't there anything juicy in there?''

"How's this? Last November she was walking along Strelka Prospekt in Moscow and was attacked by a guy, a Russian, who shoved her against a wall and tried to yank her handbag away.''

"Poor fellow." Gray rubbed his shoulder, still sore from its collision with the gym floor. "What'd she do to him?''

"She stabbed two fingers into his left eye socket and flipped his eyeball out onto the snow. The guy ran away screaming and bleeding.''

Gray bit his lip. "Maybe I'd better try harder not to upset her.''

The door was opened by Gunnery Sergeant Arlen Able. The sergeant's nose was covered by black tape. Skin below his eyes had the texture of crepe paper, with touches of sunset purple and malaria yellow and splotches of red from burst capillaries. He was in civvies—navy blue chinos and a black sweatshirt. A cardboard case painted in olive and buff camouflage was in his hands.

Gray said, "Judging from your face, Arlen, it looks like Nikolai Trusov is hitting about .310.''

"If I laugh, my face will crack open and my brains will fall out.'' The sergeant pulled a large scope from the box.

"How's Blackman?''

"He's got casts on him that make both hands stick out, so he's going to walk around like the mummy for two months, but he'll live. Have you used a starlight scope before?''

"Some,'' Gray replied quietly.

"This is our new model, the AN/PVS-5. Battery powered. Uses starlight and moonlight for target illumination and amplifies reflected ambient light to brighten the target. Bud Blackman and I were a team in Iraq. Sometimes he'd spot, sometimes I would. No clouds or smog there, lots of starlight, and we used this equipment to hellish effect.''

The starlight scope resembled a bird watcher's spotting scope, about a foot long with an eye shield on one end and a range focus ring on the other from which hung a lens cap on a plastic tether. Above the image intensifier tube housing was a cylinder containing the battery cap, power switch, and oscillator cap. A boresight mount assembly, locking knobs, and an azimuth adjustment knob were on a frame below the central housing.

"Can I remind you of a couple of things?" Able asked.

Gray nodded.

"Keep your eye tight against the rubber eyeshield, or light from the eyepiece assembly will leak around the eyeshield and will illuminate your face, make it a target."

Gray remembered.

"You are right-eyed, Owen. The starlight scope will be offset to the left of the rifle, and it weighs five pounds, so it's tough to maintain a steady position when sighting with the right eye. Rest your cheek against the stock comb like you do when sighting with iron sights, and use your left eye to obtain the sight picture. And this might very slightly change your zero."

"What'll be the zero?"

"Eight hundred yards, the distance to that roof," Able replied. "And your eyes are out of practice. Eye fatigue with this Five will become a factor in about four minutes. So go easy." Able returned the scope to the box, then brought up his wristwatch. "The NYPD swat team is going to let us use their rifle range. It's about forty minutes from here. You ready?"

Pete Coates responded, "Give me a minute with Owen, will you, Sergeant?"

Able carried the scope from the office to disappear down the hall.

"So you are going to do this?" Coates asked. "Can you?"

"It's like riding a bicycle. You don't forget."

"How do you know you've still got the talent? You haven't been practicing."

Gray thought for a moment. "Ever since the Chinaman was killed I've been feeling the little skills coming back."

"Little skills? Like what?"

"You had fish for dinner last night. Probably a saltwater fish, salmon or tuna. Not lake trout."

"So?" A small moment passed, then Coates's features twisted. "How in hell do you know that?"

"The scent has come through your pores and is on your skin. I can smell it. Saltwater fish give off more odor than freshwater fish."

"Is that another of your weird talents?"

"I was born with a good nose but it's mostly learned. It's coming back."

"Maybe I should've changed my socks this week," Coates said.

"Another thing. This past couple of days I've been incapable of looking at a distant building or tree and not estimate its distance. Six hundred yards, eleven hundred yards, four hundred yards. My brain has been filled with an incessant flow of numbers. It took me a decade to stop doing yardage estimates, and the numbers are flooding back."

Coates sniffed his wrist, then pulled up his sleeve to smell his forearm. "It was tuna, but I can't smell it."

"And once again I've become acutely aware of motion at the periphery of my vision. I'm spinning to these vague movements to the right and left. These are little things, but they are changing me slowly and involuntarily as if I'm in the grip of some terrible potion."

"Why not just let NYPD swat team members handle it?"

"We know how good Nikolai Trusov is because we've seen him do his work. And the Russians confirm how talented he was in Afghanistan. So it has to be me." Gray took a long breath. "Pete, I've spent many years trying to forget that I'm a freak with a rifle. My talent is an aberration, a suspension of the rules of the physical world, like Michael Jordan with a basketball or Wayne Gretzky with a puck. I've known since I was seven years old that I could shoot the wings off a gnat at five hundred yards. Your swat team has damned good shooters, but on a range and in the field I'd chew them up, even after all this time."

Coates asked earnestly, "You've been sitting over there, fidgeting, licking your lip, staring at the wall. How's your mental health?"

Gray pressed two fingers against his temple. "What's worse for my mental health, knowing that anybody standing next to me may get an exploded head or me picking up a rifle again? I don't have a choice, Pete."

The detective leaned back, lifting the front legs of the chair off the floor. He tilted his head toward Gray as if he might hear his thoughts. "I don't know much about this because I was a desk jockey in the Marines, but have you ever thought that your role in Vietnam was no different than a bomber pilot's or an artilleryman's, just a little more personal? There was a war on. That was legal killing you did. You've been punishing yourself ever since for being a soldier, for doing your duty."

"You're right," Gray replied vehemently. "You don't know anything about it."

Coates asked cautiously, "Is there something about your Vietnam days—something more than your role as a sniper—that put you on the medication? There were quite a few American snipers in Vietnam. They didn't all end up as . . . as troubled as you."

Gray said nothing. He rose and walked down the hall toward the waiting Marine.

✧   ✧   ✧

At ten o'clock that evening Sixth Avenue in Brooklyn was still radiating the day's heat. Bricks and concrete seemed to shimmer. Fireplugs and fire escapes and car hoods were still warm. Pink geraniums and purple petunias hung dispiritedly in their window planters. Not a whisper of wind touched the street, and air trapped between the buildings was heavy with the brown scents of auto exhaust, garlic, and sewage.

Sounds of the street seemed muffled under the blanket of heat. Two cats yowled at each other in the distance. Couples out for evening strolls chatted, but quietly, leaning toward each other as if the oppressive air made speaking loudly too much effort. A stereo playing heavy metal rock could be faintly heard, and the sounds of television sets came through open windows.

Bay Ridge's tidy apartments and fourplexes were a blend of Greek revival and federal and Italianate styles, most three and four stories high with subdued but distinctive ornamentation. The entrance to Owen Gray's building was guarded by two fluted columns supporting a porch roof above the top step. The small porch was enclosed on the sides by utilitarian iron pickets designed to meet the code. The door was ancient and pitted oak but was bright with red paint. The intercom panel to the right of the door had a button near each of four numbers. Names were not displayed.

Wood window frames on all four stories were painted black, and many windows were open this night. Gray's apartment was on the top floor. The large window facing the street was to the twins' bedroom. The sheer curtains were closed, but in the bright bed-

121

room the shapes inside were visible—though surely nebulous—through the translucent cloth.

Gray's bathrobe was a Black Watch plaid that Mrs. Orlando had given him for Christmas. "Don't read too long tonight, girls."

The words were wasted. The bundles under the two beds were motionless. Above Julie's bed was a poster of Ken Griffey Jr. and above Carolyn's was a print of a woodcut of Frédéric Chopin. The room was a mad scramble of tossed clothing, schoolbooks, old dolls, art equipment, and a collection of Breyer horses. A copy of *Seventeen* magazine was on Carolyn's desk. Mrs. Orlando insisted that the room be orderly each night before bedtime, but she had disappeared for the afternoon, and when that happened, the room's contents spread like a stain, with everything taken out of closets and off desks and from shelves but nothing put back. Gray would complain of having to high-step across their room like a fullback through the defensive line.

"You two must have had a big day. Adrian Wade wore you both out?" A soft chuckle. "She wears me out, too."

Each form in the beds received a kiss. "Good night, my girls. Sleep tight and don't let the bedbugs bite."

The bathrobe moved toward the door to the hallway.

If that instant could be expanded through some quirk of nature, if that second could be dilated so that the swift appeared slow and the slow seemed still, the first indication of order gone awry would be the dime-sized hole appearing as if by sleight of hand in the curtain. The bullet breached the room like a beam of light, crossing the effluvia of the girls' lives, then ripping into the form in Carolyn's bed, digging an appalling trench the length of the body to punch through the headboard and bury itself in the wall.

Two seconds later another trespassing bullet entered the room through the curtain, this one plunging through the form in Julie's bed.

At the door, wearing Owen Gray's bathrobe, Pete Coates put the two-way radio to his mouth. "Now. He's done it."

On the roof of the building, only his starlight binoculars and the crown of his head visible above the cornice, Sergeant Able barked, "I just saw the flash. Zone two, point three, E.D. four. They were right, that apartment roof."

With those few words, referring to zones and reference points and distances, Able put the shooter on the target.

Owen Gray nudged the M-40A1 Marine Corps sniper rifle and mounted starlight scope an inch left.

Able said unnecessarily, "Chink it down a couple clicks."

"I have him." Gray did not have the time to wonder at the tenor of his own voice, a flat, stainless steel tone he had not heard in twenty-five years. The utter dispassion would have frightened him under other circumstances.

Through the scope Gray saw the head, low behind a roof cornice on a building four blocks away. A rifle was next to the head, pointed at the air, perhaps coming down for another shot or perhaps in retreat.

Gray inhaled, let half of it out. He had learned early in his sniping career that it was not always necessary to search for the pulse in his neck or arms, but rather that his vision—everyone's vision—blurred ever so slightly with each pump of the heart. He waited a fraction of a second for his sight of the target to clear between heartbeats. Then he brought back the trigger. Two seconds had passed since Able had given him the coordinates.

The rifle spoke and jumped back against his shoulder. His view through the scope bounced to the sky.

Arlen Able cheered, "You got him. He blew down. I saw his rifle fall over, too." He patted Gray's shoulder. "Nice work. You won't see *that* on the shopping channel."

Sergeant Able picked up the radio and pressed the send button. "Pete, we can stick a fork in Trusov. He's done. Let's go gather the carcass."

Below them, in the twins' room, Pete Coates muttered to himself, "Thank God. That son of a bitch." He stared down at the forms on the bed, forms made of artfully placed pillows. The bullets had spit up a few feathers. Julie and Carolyn and John were spending the night with Adrian Wade at her hotel.

At the roof's door, Able turned back to Gray. "You coming? Let's go dance a jig over this guy's body. I want to see you drop your paper star, just like the good old days."

Gray's rifle lay unattended on the cornice. He was slumped forward, leaning against the brick rail, blinking repeatedly and panting hoarsely. He had known he would pull the trigger. Of course he would. But the struggle to contain his disgust and confusion at his return to the profession and to suppress burning memories had exhausted him. Now it was done. With an effort, one of the most arduous in his life, he pushed himself upright, gathered the rifle.

He stared out into the darkness toward his target. He had seen a head and a rifle. His shot had been clean. He was sure of it. But he whispered to himself, "Something is wrong."

Then he followed Sergeant Able.

Shed of the bathrobe, the detective met them on the street. An unmarked police car picked them up at the curb. The sniper's lair was a five-story apartment building on Tenth Avenue. They arrived a few minutes later. According to the sign above the mail slots, the apartment building was named the Zenith.

Coates leaned against the buzzer until the landlord appeared. The detective had not alerted the landlord because of the risk of somehow spooking Trusov. The man was wearing a white T-shirt and Bermuda shorts and carried a half-empty package of Fig Newtons. The detective hung his gold badge in front of the man's eyes and pushed into the building, fairly dragging the landlord after him.

"Show us the way to the roof," Coates demanded. Gray and Able followed. The sniper rifle had been left in the police car.

"Sure, sure," the landlord cried. "Nothing up there, though. I run a clean place. No hookers, no drugs, and only one Greek couple on the third floor."

The party ran up the stairs, Coates's hand at the small of the landlord's back, prodding him along.

"It's them you're here for, ain't it?" the landlord asked, the wind loud in his throat. "Christ, I should've known. You should smell this place when they cook."

On the fourth-floor stairs to the roof Coates pushed the landlord aside and pulled his .38 from his belt holster.

"You won't need that," Able said. "I saw the spray."

Nevertheless Coates held the handgun in front of him as he climbed the last flight of stairs and opened the door to the roof, Gray and Able right behind.

Heat-softened tar clung to their shoes. They walked around the stair house to the east cornice. The body was in a tight curl three feet from the edge of the roof. Gray's eyes had not fully adjusted to the darkness after the bright hallways—he knew it took thirty minutes—but even so he could tell the body lay in a position he had never before seen, an unnaturally bent shape.

They drew close, their shoes squashing bits of brain.

"What the hell?" Coates snapped.

The body was tied to a toppled chair. Many strands of rope wound around the chest and waist and legs to secure the corpse to the chair. A duct tape gag was across the mouth.

A rifle had spilled to the roof near the body. Able lifted the weapon. "This is a Stevens .22. No sniper uses this. What's going on? A decoy?"

Pete Coates lifted a red-rimmed cartridge that had been carefully set on its end near the chair. "Here is Trusov's signature."

Owen Gray bent to the body. He grasped its shoulder to turn the face toward him. Tiny bells jingled. The top of her head was missing, leaving a gaping red and gray cleft where her lustrous hair had been.

Mrs. Orlando stared back at him in the sightless reproach of death.

PART TWO
BURNING
TAPERS

The best weapon is the one closest at hand.
—Afghan proverb

9

OWEN GRAY WAS GOING to ground. To the high country, to his old home. The land would gather him in and embrace him. Stone and sage and the summer wind would let him breathe again, and he would find his footing among the granite and grass. Or he would die in these mountains.

He had finally figured out Nikolai Trusov's message. The Russian had wanted to chase Gray from the city to the wilderness, to a proper dueling ground. Trusov would have kept on killing whomever was standing near Gray until Gray complied. And now Trusov would follow Gray to these mountains. Gray was going to prepare for him as best he could. The Russian would quickly determine where Gray was, and would be coming. Gray did not know when Trusov would arrive in the mountains, but it would be soon. Time was short.

A thicket of kinnikinnick crowded the dirt road, the shrub in full white bloom. Its oval leaves scraped the rental Jeep on both sides. Gray engaged the vehicle's four-wheel drive for the last hundred yards up the incline toward the cabin. Rocks spit from under the Jeep as the wheels found purchase. The canyon of white fir and lodgepole pine opened, allowing serviceberry and syringa to grow in patches of white sunlight. When he was twelve years old, Gray had made tobacco pipes out of syringa stems, using beetle grubs to eat through the pith to hollow the stems just as Chief Joseph had. Dogwood leaves flavored with licorice fern served as tobacco. Gray had spent his youth studying the Nez Perce and Shoshone and Kootenai.

He downshifted, then guided the Jeep around a stone outcropping to gain his first glimpse of the larch tree in the front yard. The larch was not common in the Sawtooth Range, and its grand trunk rose almost 250 feet barren of foliage until reaching a bushy top. This glorious spire had stood sentinel in front of the cabin for all of Gray's memory, and all of his father's and grandfather's.

Gray drove the vehicle around the larch to the gravel patch that served to keep mud from the front door during the spring melt. He set the parking brake. When he opened the Jeep's door he was met with the brace of mountain Idaho, the stirring redolence of red cedar and bracken and columbine blooms and damp earth, scents sharpened in the thin air, scents that always filled Gray with a longing for times past and people gone.

He stepped around the Jeep toward the porch. Birthplace of three generations of Grays, the cabin was made of lodgepole pine, used because their trunks taper so little. The building had outgrown its origins as a one-room hut with one door and one grease-paper window hastily thrown up to keep the winter of 1903 at bay. Over the decades several more rooms had been tacked on. Hardwood floors and plumbing and electricity had been added, and a porch and pantry, closets and a massive stone fireplace. Gray climbed the porch and opened the door with the key, then stepped inside.

The air was thick with dust and mold and the scent of dry pine. Gray left the door open and pulled aside window shutters to brighten the room. Memories rushed in with the light. The scene— every corner, every cranny, every worn stick of furniture—was from his youth. The three-legged stool next to the iron fireplace tools, the pole and peg coat hanger, the couch covered with a red and purple Shoshone blanket, a Sears Roebuck coffee table, the cracked leather chair with the brass brads, the rag rug in front of the fireplace, the room was as it ever had been. Gray had inherited the home and five hundred acres from his father. He had returned to Idaho for the funeral, but not since.

Gray's friend Jeff Moon, who lived in Ketchum, looked after the place with a weekly visit. In return Moon rented it to hunters during the season and kept the proceeds.

The heirloom was still in its corner. The term was Gray's father's, and it referred to a chair Gray's grandfather had made out of deer antlers in the 1930s. The seat and back were horsehair covered with tanned buckskin, but everything else on the chair— legs, arms, frame, armrests—was artfully placed white-tail and mule-deer antlers, more than two dozen of them, flowing here and there, with knotty curves and dangerous points. The result was a grotesquery so forbidding and unwelcome that Gray's mother had never been able to give it away despite earnest efforts over several decades. The heirloom was hazardous to sit in, took thirty minutes to dust, and was impossible not to stare at. As a child Gray had avoided the chair lest it snatch him up. And in all his life he had sat in it only a handful of times, simply to prove to himself he could escape. The chair still sat ominously in its corner, daring anyone to approach.

Built when wood was free and oil heating was a suspicious notion found no closer than Boise, the fireplace almost made up the entire west wall. The mantel and hearth and fireback were washed river stone. The firebox was as large as a Volkswagen. The andirons and grate were made of mule sled runners, bent into their new shape by a Ketchum blacksmith.

Antlers. It seemed his family history had been defined by antlers. The dining area was in the main room, to the rear near a pass-through to the kitchen. Above the unvarnished pine table was a moose-antler chandelier, another twisted horror lovingly fashioned by Gray's father. Three 1,400-pound moose had given their all to illuminate the Gray table, and each rack measured over fifty inches across. Six twenty-five-watt bulbs were attached to the antlers. The electric cord was skillfully hidden as it crawled up an antler to the ceiling. The slightest draft would catch the antlers' sweeping shovels, slowly swinging the chandelier. Gnarled and grasping shadows would creep across the table.

On a stand near the leather chair was a General Electric radio, a black Bakelite box with two knobs and a green frequency indicator that glowed in the dark. Gray knew from experience that the old radio could pull in stations as far away as Salt Lake City and Sacramento and Cheyenne, and Gray remembered roaming the length of the band night after night, finding dozens of faint and scratchy stations, a wondrous connection to the outside.

His parents' bedroom was off the main room, and Gray's room was behind the kitchen. He passed the kitchen's wood stove, made of cast iron and resembling the front end of a locomotive. Gray pulled the tong to open the door to his room. He had never understood why the room had bunk beds, as he had no siblings. He had always slept on the top bunk. His gray and brown Shoshone blanket still covered the thin mattress. The blanket was trimmed with purple glass beads that glinted with light. Gray's desk and chair were against a wall. The desk light was made of a miner's tin lunch growler. A 1905 reprint of *The Original Journals of the Lewis and Clark Expedition,* all eight volumes, also lined the top of the bookshelf. These books were the most influential reading of his youth, and Gray had never fully escaped them. The rifle case next to the desk was empty.

Gray moved to the back of his room, to the double-panel doors locked with a four-inch-square Master Lock padlock. Gray had reinforced this closet with two-inch planks on all interior surfaces and with quarter-inch steel hinges. Here were those items Gray didn't want the hunters who rented the cabin to take home accidentally or otherwise. He found the small key on his key ring and opened the lock and then the door. He yanked the string of the overhead light.

The history of the Gray family in the Sawtooths could be traced by the contents of this closet. Gray's great-grandfather Mason had resigned his army commission at Fort Abraham Lincoln and had rushed into Idaho in 1878 when gold was discovered on Yankee Fork. Mason's placer pan, almost three feet across and worn to a high sheen by years of hope and backbreaking work, was on a ledge in the closet. Mason had died broke, which was the prospector's usual reward. His son George—Gray's grandfather—turned to the forests and streams for his provender. In the early years of the century George Gray would often harvest a hundred salmon or redfish a day using spears. The fish were salted, smoked, or canned, and sent to Boise. George's spear heads—wickedly barbed and with edges that would slice grass—were stacked in a corner of the closet. George had then tried sheep and then cattle. In another closet corner was his branding iron, a rafter G. George and his son Dalton—Gray's father—had supplemented their income by trapping wolves and coyotes for the government bounty. A dozen foot traps hung by their anchor chains from the closet's side wall. The traps' jaws were closed and the villainous teeth were interlaced like short fingers.

All these endeavors had busted out, and it was a hardscrabble existence until Gray's father made a discovery that to his dying day he could scarcely credit: rich Californians would travel three days on a train to the Sawtooths to shoot game. In the mid-1940s, Dalton Gray began his career as a hunting guide.

Owen Gray lifted a Remington over-under shotgun from the weapons rack on the closet's south wall. He broke it open. The chambers were empty. His father would help the outlanders kill anything they might like: chukar, Chinese pheasants, blue grouse, whitetails and mulies, moose, elk, bighorn sheep, rainbow trout and salmon, and in the early days cougars and black bears and grizzlies.

A simple trick virtually guaranteed his clients would become repeat customers. During the hunts Dalton would always come across several rattlesnakes, and while the Californians watched he would grab the snake's tail, whirl the rattler around and around, then crack it like a whip, snapping the snake's head off. He'd offer the head—inch-long fangs dripping poison—as a souvenir to the gasping Californians. Every Gray for four generations had mastered this moronic stunt—Owen was no exception—but it never failed to leave the customer slack-jawed and convinced their guide was Kit Carson reincarnated.

Owen Gray returned the shotgun to the rack, placing it next to a Winchester twelve-gauge double barrel. Hanging on the back wall were a pair of whitetail rattlers—antlers with tips blunted for safety which hunters ground and clicked together to call bucks through dense undergrowth. Along the wall were a Remington 700 under a mounted scope and a bolt-action .330 Weatherby Magnum with a muzzle brake Dalton Gray had made himself. When Owen was sixteen years old, his father had promised to purchase the Weatherby for him if Owen could spend one week in the mountains. "That all I have to do?" Owen had asked. "You ain't heard all of it." His father grinned. "One week, and you can take your bowie knife. Nothing else." Gripping his knife, Owen had left the cabin that August Sunday as naked as when he came into the world. He returned seven days later, only a few pounds lighter and wearing a mulie's hide. The Weatherby and a handshake were waiting for him.

On a small shelf on the back wall were bottles of doe-in-heat scent, the labels yellowed with age. Boxes of shotgun shells and rifle cartridges crowded the shelf. An axe and wedge, a two-man crosscut saw, and a sledgehammer leaned against a wall. Other tools were in a wood box on the floor. The room also contained more than twenty-five knives wrapped in an oilcoth bundle on the shelf.

Gray lifted the axe. As a child he would leave this axe outside for the night and wait by his bedroom window to watch porcupines lick the handle for the salt. He left the closet and passed through his room. He re-entered the kitchen and was startled not to find his mother standing at the counter, his eternal picture of her, wide and solid in her print dress, usually pounding dinner to tenderness, the fleshy thump-thump filling the house as her meat hammer rose and fell, rose and fell. His mother had died of stomach cancer six years ago. His father passed away a year later. Ruth Gray was an antidote to the wilderness, and after she went, Dalton didn't last long. His death certificate listed heart failure as the cause, but Owen Gray knew it had been loneliness and grief.

After years in New York City it was difficult for Gray to imagine that at nineteen, when he joined the Marine Corps, he had never been outside the Sawtooth Range except for several trips to Boise, eighty miles southwest. His father had told him that if he wanted a journey he could go deeper into the mountains. Until he left for boot camp, Gray's horizon had always been the next jagged mountain range, and he knew all there was to know between himself and that horizon. He had learned since that it was only a short distance to those peaks.

Carrying the axe, Gray left the cabin through the kitchen door. The screen slammed behind him. Behind the house were two smaller one-room cabins for hunters, and behind them a small barn and corral. Attached to the barn was a tack shed. These outbuildings were made of clapboard weathered to a dull gray and curled. He crossed the packed ground to the woodshed, a firebreak distance of fifty feet from the house. Hidden by a wall of chokecherry and mountain maple and down a small ravine, Black Bear Creek gurgled and ran. Pink and purple mountains rose above him in all directions.

WHITE STAR

The woodshed was a peaked and shingled roof on four posts. Two-by-fours crisscrossed on three sides for lateral support. He walked around several horseweeds and a musk thistle, then stepped into the shed. Almost three cords of wood were under the roof. His father had cut the wood, which lasted years in the high elevations before beginning to rot. The splitting block was a two-foot-high wedge of Douglas fir.

Gray picked up a length of wood and put it on the block. The axe swung in a practiced arc, and the blade sank into the wood. Gray lifted the axe, the wood clinging to the blade, and brought it down again. The halves toppled to the ground. These pieces should have been a good size for the fireplace, but he picked up one, returned it to the block, and halved it again. Then he lifted the smallest piece and split it with a well-aimed swing. Now he had kindling.

But he swung again, this time at the sticks on the ground. The blade bit through them and dug into the earth, the shattered halves flipping into the air. Gray grunted as he brought the axe around again. This time the whistling blade missed wood entirely, and shot into the soft ground, sending chips skittering away. Then again and again and again. The blade chewed up the ground.

The axe changed course, slamming into one of the shed's support posts. Splinters shot away. The axe slashed at it again, and the ancient wood fractured and grasped the steel blade. Gray ferociously ripped the blade out of the wood and sent it soaring again into the post. A hollow cry escaped him. He chopped maniacally at the post, and the top portion of the post began to sag under the roof's weight.

He swung again at the toppling beam, a blind blow. The blade bounced off the wood and cut deeply into Gray's calf. The front quarter of the shed drooped slowly to the ground, braces and posts and crosspieces cracking loudly. Still he swung, into the post, into the shingles, into the ground, into the post again. A tear almost made it down to his chin, but his frantic motion flicked it off to the ground. He brought the blade around again and again, and chips burst from the wreckage. Blood flowed down his leg and filled his shoe. His brow was damp from sweat and his cheeks shiny from tears. He swung savagely, the mad hiss-and-chop cadence filling the canyon. The old shed slumped further as the axe slashed into it again and again.

Five minutes or an hour might have passed. When he finally dropped the axe his hands were bleeding from open blisters and his right pant leg was damp and sticking to his calf. His breath ragged, he stumbled away from the wreckage. He left red footprints.

Gray collapsed on the front porch. He gazed without seeing at the distant pinnacles. The lowering sun coppered his face. He wet his salty lips. And again, for the thousandth time in two days, his mind produced the image of Mrs. Orlando.

And with it came the black cloud, the unshakable agony of grief and guilt. This cabin, his family home, had always been his refuge and his cure. This time it had not been enough.

❖   ❖   ❖

Gray leaned against the trunk of a black cottonwood, his legs out in front and his feet dangling above the water of Black Bear Creek. He was sitting on a mat of blooming buttercups. The stream gurgled by, pooling and bubbling, idle at some spots and swift at others. A fine mist hung over the creek, softening the boulders that lined it and wetting the serviceberry and nettles that grew along the stream. The water's white hiss calmed him. Blisters on his hands were raw, blood showing at the surface. He was a quarter mile north of the house. The Weatherby rifle and a backpack also leaned against the tree. Bog orchids and ladies' tresses grew near the cottonwood's trunk.

He brought out a length of beef jerky, bit some off—not without a struggle—and began chewing. This wasn't minimart jerky made of leather a cobbler would reject, but beef jerked by Rose Schwartz down in Ketchum, beef with flavor that filled the head and then rushed down into the chest to seize the innards, a sensation so strong that anything else eaten the remainder of the day had no taste whatsoever. Gray chewed and chewed. He kept his fingers apart and his hands upturned on his lap. His palms and fingers stung.

A sniper was taught that when pinned down he had to move or die. Resting against the tree, Owen Gray was trying to move, to push his thoughts along quickly rather than let them rest, for when his mind halted it was on the horrific image of Mrs. Orlando, bound and gagged on the roof, dead by Gray's hand. He hoped he might be able to work the awful moment through, to leap from one rationalization to the next until he found one that alleviated his pain, and so he needed to keep his thoughts rushing forward. Move or die. A sniper also learned never to exit a hide by the same route he entered it. Maybe this lesson could also help, keeping Gray's thoughts from returning by the same route to the same grief. If he could just go through new doors, roll along to new territory.

His chin came up. He listened intently and searched the stream banks without moving his head. His father had taught Gray that it was possible to sense if someone was watching you, saying that you could feel a slight warp in the air, an eerie dissonance in the day. Gray felt it then. Still chewing, he slowly turned his head right. His hand inched toward the rifle. His gaze swept the banks and the underbrush and trees beyond.

Pale blue eyes were locked on Gray. They peered out from the shadows of a small dogwood, partially hidden behind the dark green leaves of an alpine laurel. Gray saw pink below the eyes. A tongue.

"A coyote," Gray said to nobody. "That's all I need."

The animal slipped out from under the tree and walked in a tight slink several feet closer to Gray. The coyote was on the other side of the creek, emboldened by the intervening water. It stepped into a dish of light that had made it through the overhead bough canopy. The animal was forty feet away, and its eyes never left Gray. Its coat was a dusty gray except for the buff belly. The fur on its legs was urine yellow. Its tail was bushy and handsome. The tongue hung out rudely.

"Beat it. I don't like carnivores staring at me for any length of time."

Gray lifted a small stone and chucked it at the coyote, a half-hearted toss that barely cleared the stream. The animal didn't move. Gray's hand stung from the effort.

"If you had any idea how many coyotes the Gray family has killed over the years, you wouldn't sit there so complacently."

The coyote panted.

"You'd realize I'm a very dangerous fellow." Gray chewed the jerky. A half pound of the cured beef remained in his hand.

The coyote's snout was sharp and its ears restless. Teeth gleamed like pearls.

"The reason I don't like coyotes," Gray explained to the coyote, "is that if I had a heart attack right now—hypothetically, you understand—and were to roll over dead on the ground, you'd be over here in two seconds, ripping hunks of flesh from my corpse, our new friendship be damned."

The coyote ducked its head at some sound only it heard, and in doing so appeared to be agreeing with Gray.

"My friend Pete Coates tells a joke you'd appreciate. He said that one time he dated a woman so ugly he had to do the coyote trick. I asked Pete, What's the coyote trick? Pete said that when he woke up the next morning with this woman in his arms he chewed off his arm rather than wake her up."

The coyote waited. Gray's bandaged calf ached where he had stitched the palm-sized flap of skin and muscle back to his leg with a needle and thread from his mother's sewing kit.

"I didn't think it was funny either." Gray paused, then said, "When I was on a mission in Vietnam I would be so in tune with the terrain that I would merge with it. I'd become a part of the soil and trees and bush. The enemy couldn't see me because I wasn't there to be seen. I was absorbed by the terrain. Are you listening?"

The coyote watched.

Gray glanced at the remaining beef jerky. When he held it out to one side as far as he could the animal's eyes followed it. "Just as I thought. You aren't listening. But I do admire undisguised greed. You want this meat so bad you are willing to reveal yourself to me, and that means you're mighty hungry. And this is truly superior beef jerky. Too bad for you."

Gray took another bite, gnawing it off with his teeth, smacking his lips for the coyote's benefit. "I'd go into enemy territory, entirely assimilated by the ground I was walking on. The field seemed to do my thinking for me, guiding me and warning me. I was so plugged into the bush that I lost my separate identity. I shared an awareness with the ground and all that was on it. If I were a hippie, I'd call it sharing my consciousness with the earth, but snipers generally aren't hippies. No surprise there, I suppose." Gray hesitated. "Is this too Zen for a coyote?"

The coyote ran its tongue along its black lips.

"That's what I'm out here doing now," Gray explained, his voice suddenly uneven. "I'm trying to get these goddamn trees and bushes to take over, to absorb some of what I'm feeling, to take some of it off me, goddamnit."

The animal sank to its belly, its eyes glowing like ice.

"But it's not working." Tears glistened in Gray's eyes.

Gray worked ferociously on the jerky, trying to hide his emotions from the coyote. The animal waited.

After a moment Gray could continue. "Here's another tactic I'm trying while you watch me. A sniper learns that much of what he sees is illusion." He held up his palm as if the animal was about to argue. "It's true. For example, distances are usually overestimated when the target is lying down, like you are. The same is true when the enemy can't be seen clearly against the background. And it's also true when the target is seen over broken ground. In all these instances the enemy is closer than you think, and so you generally become dead. Do you know why? Because your bullet soars over the enemy's head, alerting him to your presence, and he fires before you can get another round in the chamber."

Gray bit off a small piece of jerky. "The mind has performed a deadly slight. I'm trying to do something like that now, something more benign, and so, you'd think, more simple. An easy trick. All I want is to hide a memory, a little sleight of hand with a recollection." He chewed. "But it's not working either."

The coyote bounced up to sitting. It yipped once and bowed its head. The eyes were still fixed on Gray.

"Anguish and desperation aren't going to be fooled, are they?"

Gray rose to one knee. The animal was instantly alert, rising fully, ready to bolt, its tail down.

"This is the absolute nadir of my existence," Gray said. "Talking to a coyote."

Gray tossed the remaining beef jerky across the stream. It landed five feet from the coyote. The animal leaped high and dove at the jerky, as it does when it hears a mouse beneath the snow. The jerky was the size of a hand. The coyote seized the meat with its teeth, shook it once to make sure it was dead, then tilted its head back and swallowed it whole, rapidly shaking its entire body as it urged the meat down its throat. The coyote licked its mouth again, then without another glance at the human it loped away, disappearing in the underbrush.

Gray's hands burned as he gingerly lifted the rifle and backpack. He began walking downstream toward the cabin. "Whining to a coyote. The absolute nadir."

10

THE STOLEN STATION WAGON began to fail after three hundred miles. With all its miles and years, it could not tolerate hour after hour of freeway driving. First to go was the air conditioner. Then a left rear retread blew away and was replaced by a threadbare spare. Then the rods began to knock ominously. But only when an idiot light came on did Nikolai Trusov pull off the highway to raise the hood. The fan belt had disappeared. The car needed a replacement. He would face less risk in finding a new belt than in stealing a new car.

He drove off the freeway and passed through a worn and grimy section of Cleveland, full of warehouses and light industry and potholes. It was nearing one in the morning. Tractor trailers and delivery trucks were on their night runs, but otherwise the streets were empty. Most businesses—the metal fabricators, sand and gravel lots, and oil distributors—were closed. The few open gas stations Trusov could find had minimarts rather than service bays. Street lamps cast silver cones of light on the roads.

He turned onto Center Street. A flatbed truck carrying I-beams was parked at the side of the road. The truck's mud guard had the inscription "Show Me Your Tits." On the corner was a freight company with coils of razor wire atop its security fences. He passed Lincoln Towing, a Mayflower Moving and Storage, and the Thor Gasket Company.

At the end of the block was a service station. The sign identified it as Hal's Independent Service, and the fluorescent lights shining down on the service island announced the station was open. The two service bay doors were closed, but the office door was open and lights were on in the office. Leafing through a magazine, an attendant was sitting in a chair, his feet propped up on a desk. The station wagon drove onto Hal's lot and up to a gas pump. The bell rang in the office.

Hal's Independent had seen more prosperous days. The fuel pumps were old models, with money and gallon totalizers that rolled on a reel rather than with digital readouts. The metal skirt below the dial face was splotched with grease and dirt. The panels above the dials carried no advertising and instead were marred by bits of old adhesive that had once held brand-name placards in place. The rubber fender guards around the nozzle were tattered. The station had once been painted white, but stains and smog and sun fading had stippled the building in brown and yellow. Plywood covered the window openings of the service bay doors. A sign at the corner of the building read "Rest Rooms Closed." Two black fifty-five-gallon drums were near the bay doors.

The attendant brought his head up when the station wagon arrived but continued with the magazine, a lurid publication called *Gent, Home of the D Cup.* He had a hand in his pants pocket and a cigarette in his mouth. He wore a Penzoil hat backwards on his head and a blue zippered sweatshirt open at the front. A book of matches and his Camels were in the pocket. Underneath the sweatshirt was a T-shirt that had imprinted on it "Nixon Was Cool." His face resembled a greyhound's, narrow and knobby with a weak chin. His ears had pendulous, sagging lobes. An empty Domino's Pizza box was on the desk near a manila envelope from the state patrol. Hal's Independent was still receiving mail even though Hal hadn't been to the station since his business went belly up. The attendant had opened the envelope and glanced at its contents, but it didn't have anything to interest him. The state patrol was always sending bulletins.

The gas jockey's name was Boyd Slidell, pronounced like the town in Louisiana, as he told his probation officer the first time they met. Early in life Boyd Slidell had mastered the art of stealing and stripping automobiles. His first auto theft occurred shortly after his thirteenth birthday, a T-Bird he still remembered fondly because he stole the car and learned to drive on the same night. He had separated dozens of cars and pickups from their lawful owners over the years. He liked to think there wasn't a vehicle made that he couldn't get into with a hacksaw blade or a length of clothes hanger wire in sixty seconds. At twenty-two, Slidell had mastered his craft.

He worked for the Sundstrom brothers, Cleveland's leading auto choppers. The Sundstroms were in the business of dismantling stolen cars and selling the pieces to parts shops. A carefully torn down automobile was worth four times more than the intact car.

Boyd Slidell rose from his chair to peer out the door at the Ford and its driver. With any luck the customer would pump his own gas. His hand was still in his pocket. He returned to the chair.

Hal's Independent Service had lasted thirty years, but the business had gone the way of so many service stations, and four weeks ago the Sundstrom brothers had rented the building from a management company representing the bankruptcy court. The Sundstroms figured they had two months in any one location before the police found them, so they changed addresses more often than Boyd Slidell changed his shorts, as Bobby Sundstrom liked to say. Sundstrom also liked to brag that a hundred thousand dollars' worth of tools were in the service bays: power drills and saws, air hammers and wrenches, compressors, blowtorches and acetylene welders, electric metal saws, portable lighting units, hydraulic hoists and electric winches, and dozens of ripping and prying tools. The plywood over the bay door's windows was not due to broken glass but so nosy passersby could not peer in. An automobile ceased to exist within thirty minutes of arriving at one of Hal's service bays. Parked behind the garage were two three-quarter-ton Dodge trucks the Sundstroms used to deliver the parts. The brothers kept the gas bay operating as a cover for the chop shop. This night Boyd Slidell was expecting the delivery of a silver 1991 Pontiac Firebird just as soon as Danny Anderson found one. Slidell was going to call the brothers when the Firebird arrived, and the four of them would dismantle the car in a frenzy of hacking, tearing, yanking, cutting, and sawing. Boyd Slidell loved his work.

The asshole in the station wagon at the service island wasn't pumping his own gas, just staring out his car window waiting for help. A big fellow wearing a cap and a frown. Something was familiar about the customer. The station wagon had New Jersey plates. Shaking his head with resignation, Slidell flipped the magazine onto the desk and walked out toward the station wagon.

"Put gas in the car. And I need a fan belt." The words were said with obvious effort and a gnarled accent.

Any more Polacks in Cleveland, the place will be like Chicago. And why did the Sundstroms insist on keeping up the facade of the all-night service station? Pumping gas was beneath Slidell's dignity, a talented man like him. He stared at the foreigner a moment, considering telling him to take his piece of dirt station wagon somewhere else. Didn't see many of these old fake woody wagons anymore. Goddamnit. Bobby Sundstrom had told him to pump gas if anybody came in, and do it politely.

"With your big gas guzzler, you'd better turn the engine off while I pump gas," Slidell said. "Otherwise you'll never leave the station."

No laugh from the foreigner. Christ, how do they get into this country? The Polack looked like he'd taken a few cuffs to the head. A rough dude, looked like. Had the foreigner been into the station before? He was sort of recognizable.

"I'll go see if I have a belt that fits," Slidell said. "We don't take no credit cards."

Not that this Polack was likely to have any. Slidell shuffled back to the station's office, lighting another cigarette. He put the matches back into his pocket and exhaled. He looked down the street, hoping Danny would hurry back with the Firebird so they could get to work.

He hesitated at the desk. Something about the Polack nagged at him. His eyes fell on the state patrol manila envelope. And it came to him. A mean grin spread across the car thief's face. He pulled out the contents of the envelope. He was right. He laughed shrilly with building excitement. Fifty thousand dollars for information leading to Nikolai Trusov's arrest and conviction for murder. Christ, Slidell could do anything he wanted to with a murderer. And Slidell could be a hero. Maybe he wouldn't have to visit his goddamn probation officer twice a week anymore. Boyd Slidell, hero. He cackled again.

He returned to the service island carrying the envelope and another piece of paper in his hand, his walk a cocky pump and roll.

143

He lifted the gas nozzle from the boot and flipped the reset lever. The Polack was just sitting there behind the steering wheel. Slidell brought out his matches.

"Hey, Polack, recognize yourself?" Slidell held up a five-by-seven black-and-white photograph of Nikolai Trusov, delivered to every airport, bus station, car rental agency, and service station in every midwestern state. Pete Coates had organized the distribution with the help of the FBI offices, police departments, and state patrols.

"You came to the wrong station, pal." Slidell laughed.

He quickly held up the gas nozzle, not to the gas tank cover but to the station wagon's window, six inches from the foreigner's nose. He let the photo drop, and with the swift motion of one who had been smoking since he was nine, he struck a match. He squeezed the nozzle trigger and brought up the flaming match. He laughed crazily.

Gasoline poured into the Ford's cab, splashing onto the foreigner. Slidell ignited the stream. The gas roared as it caught fire, spewing into the station wagon's interior and filling it with orange light and ferocious heat. A wall of flame blocked Slidell's view of the foreigner. He took two steps back, away from the heat, but he held the nozzle out, still filling the cab with a surging, broiling flood of fire.

Slidell giggled in a piercing falsetto. The conflagration churned inside the cab. Roiling flames surged out the open window, almost reaching the roof of the service island. The leaping fire hid everything inside the cab.

Fifty thousand dollars. Slidell dropped the nozzle and fairly danced across the cement to the office. That's more than he'd make in two years working for the Sundstroms.

The station wagon moaned and crackled. The passenger side door was open and flame spilled onto the cement, spreading quickly to the front tires. Black smoke seethed from the burning rubber. The fuel tank exploded with a dull retort, adding its fuel to the firestorm. The old station wagon sank on its blazing tires. Fire consumed the wagon, inside and out, forming a cone of red and orange fire above the blackening vehicle.

"Fifty cool ones," Slidell exulted. He stepped inside the office to grab the phone. "Goddamnit, who do I call?"

The arm was around his neck before the telephone reached his mouth. A hard and massive form stepped up from behind, lifting Slidell off the ground by his neck and choking off a scream of fear and pain and rage. Another arm wound around his chest, holding him in a hug so powerful that Slidell heard two of his ribs break. He lashed back with his feet, finding his tormentor's legs, but the man behind him ignored the kicks as he carried Slidell through the side door into the shop. Slidell tried to yell, but his windpipe was collapsing. With his hands he tore at the arm around his throat, but it only gripped him tighter. The office smelled of burned flesh.

The Sundstroms' tools and equipment filled the shop, leaving only enough room for the stolen Firebird in the far bay that Slidell had expected at any moment. Overhead was a bank of fluorescent lights. Slidell was carried around a portable tool stand toward a drill press, a Sears Craftsman, with the motor housing and belt safety guard six feet above the floor on a column. A half-inch auger bit was in the chuck.

Nikolai Trusov had moved with the swiftness and skill of a man who had spent twenty years as a soldier. He had been almost out of the car before the first gasoline landed on the seat, and the flaming fuel had caught only a small patch of his trailing arm. He had dragged the nylon sports bag containing his rifle after him.

Trusov dropped Slidell, knocked off his cap and grabbed a fistful of his hair. Slidell shrieked as the Russian moved Slidell's head onto the press table below the auger bit. He held Slidell's head, right ear down against the table, and flicked on the engine switch. The drill press whirled. With his free hand, Trusov gripped the pilot-wheel feed and spun it. The drill's mounting collar and chuck brought the auger down.

Boyd Slidell saw it out of the corner of his eye. The giant's hand pinned Slidell's cheek and chin and temple painfully onto the table. The auger descended, whirling evilly, growing in Slidell's sight, coming down for him.

The auger's cutting edge bit into the hair of Slidell's right temple, twisting off the hair and spinning it around the shaft like spaghetti on a fork. The thief wailed, his eyes showing white all around. The bit dipped into skin. Blood rose on the auger's corkscrew blade, then fell away to soak Slidell's hair. Skin twirled up. Then came bits of gray matter, twisted up from the auger's point. Slidell screeched again. Brain worked its way out on the bit's blade. Slidell abruptly slumped, his limbs loose and his head pinned by the auger to the rigid table. His dead eyes were open. His tongue flopped out.

The Russian continued to turn the pilot-wheel feed, bringing the bit down all the way to the receiving hole in the table. Then he locked the tension knob which kept the auger in the down position. A gob of brain and bone had built up around the bit. Blood from the puncture dribbled down Slidell's face and across the table to drip to the floor.

Owen Gray would surely learn of this, of the terrible consequences of a meeting with the Russian. Trusov smiled and looked at the station's west wall, as if he could see through the wall and across the continent. He may have cared more about the drill press's effect on Gray than he did on the hapless victim pegged to the table.

Trusov glanced at his arm, at the slight burn above his wrist. He would have to get a new shirt. He turned away from the body and the drill press, slapping his hands together as if to rid them of dust.

He walked through the office and out to the service island, stepped around the blazing car, picked up his sports bag near a gas pump, and continued west into the night. He looked back at the garage, shook his head, and said to himself, "Crazy Americans."

❖   ❖   ❖

Hobart is up the valley from Ketchum about as far as an ore team can travel without collapsing in the harnesses, which is why the first white man settled there in 1891, hoping to make his fortune watering and feeding mules. The town is on the Big Wood River at the confluence of Black Bear Creek. The town has 205 people or 212 people, depending on whether one drives in from the north or south. The Green River Ordinance is enforced either direction.

Only a handful of businesses remain, and one of them is the Right to Keep and Bear Arms Saloon, shortened to the Right Saloon by its patrons. At the turn of the century the building had been a bank, and the structure was ornamented along the roof line with embrasures resembling archers' loopholes. An Olympia Beer neon sign glowed in the window to the right of the door.

Owen Gray entered the saloon, and by instinct he stepped to one side until his eyes adjusted to the darkness. The stitches in his leg felt as if they were clawing at him. The saloon's east wall was

146

dominated by a backbar of beveled mirrors and fluted walnut columns and topped by elaborate moldings. The backbar had been carved in New Orleans and brought up the Columbia and Snake rivers on a barge. On one of the backbar's shelves was a stuffed badger, its teeth bared and a claw raised. On another shelf were a cobra and a mongoose, the snake's coils wrapped tightly around the mongoose, and the mongoose's teeth sunk into the snake's neck, one of those taxidermal horrors sailors brought back from the Philippines at the end of World War Two. Trophies hung from the walls—the heads of buffalo, moose, bighorn sheep, and a mule deer. The trophies made the saloon seem crowded, even though the room was empty. The place smelled of cold cigarettes.

He steered around several tables, heading for the pay phone in the hallway to the rest rooms. The bartender emerged from the hallway wiping his hands on his apron. His doughy face first registered curiosity at a stranger having found the tavern, then surprise and pleasure.

The bartender stuck out his hand. "I'll be damned, Owen. It's you. Welcome home."

Gray tried not to wince as the bartender vigorously squeezed and pumped his hand. Blisters on his palm and fingers from the axe handle were red and leaking. Gray exchanged a few words with the bartender, a friend of his father's named Ray Miller. The bartender's weak chin was lost under his damp and wagging lower lip. His porcine eyes sparkled as he spoke. He had known Gray all Gray's life.

Miller said, "I hope you're in the Tooths for a happier reason than last time, Owen."

"A little R and R is all," Gray replied. "I stopped phone service out at the place when Dad died, Ray. I need to use yours."

Miller thumbed the pay phone behind him. "Let me post you to a beer when you're done."

Figuring the Right Saloon was not making any profit when its patrons chatted on the phone, Ray Miller had placed the phone only four feet off the floor and had shortened the cable to the handset so that a conversation of more than four minutes resulted in neck and back pain, usually requiring a beer to assuage. Gray punched in his calling card number, and a few moments later Pete Coates was on the line.

When Gray was a boy, telephone connections from the Sawtooths to the outside world were scratchy. He was still tempted to yell into the phone during any long-distance call. But satellites and fiber optics had come to the mountains. Coates sounded like he was next door.

The detective asked, "How you doing?"

"Better."

"Anna Renthal asked about you. Wants to know when you'll be back."

"Frank Luca gave me as much time off as I need," Gray said. "I don't know when I'll be back."

"Can I be blunt?"

"Anything else and I'd be startled," Gray replied.

"You didn't go back to Idaho to kill yourself, did you? Commit suicide like you tried in Vietnam?"

"No."

"Is that a promise?"

"I'm stronger now."

"Where are your kids?" Coates asked.

"I'd trust you with my life, Pete, but the fewer people who know where the twins and John are, the better I'll feel."

"But they aren't near you, are they? Now that we know what Trusov is capable of, it'd be too dangerous for your kids."

"They're safe." The children were with Jeff Moon and his wife in Ketchum, dropped off on the drive from the Boise airport. His eyes closed, Gray pinched the bridge of his nose. "I thought we had him, Pete."

"It was a slam dunk, looked like to me."

"Maybe your first reaction was right, that the police and FBI should have just swarmed the building."

"No," Coates said adamantly. "We would have spooked him for sure. And even if we could have trapped him, you were right when you said he'd kill a lot of my men before we got him. Your plan—give him a target, wait until he exposes himself, then take him out from a long distance—was the only one that would have avoided a bloodbath."

Gray's voice trembled. "Have you figured out how he got Mrs. Orlando?"

"She was last seen a block from your apartment at a laundromat called Sixth Avenue Coin Op. We have no idea how he abducted her."

"So he was onto us all along." Gray's voice was dark with sorrow.

"Looks like it. But we did discover how Trusov set up the shot on the paper passer, Donald Bledsoe. We had wondered how he would know you'd be in the courthouse alley and how he'd have time to set up his hide."

"Yes?"

"We think the Russian was following you, probably waiting for a shot. When you got to the alley to wait for Bledsoe, Trusov climbed a fire escape to the roof of the cafe at the end of the alley, across the street. He wasn't in a building twelve hundred and fifty yards away like he was with the Chinaman, but rather only a hundred yards away. We found his red shell on top of the cafe."

"So he didn't prepare anything, just took an opportunistic shot?"

"We're learning Trusov is a cunning boy."

Anger colored Gray's words. "Have you learned anything else, like why Nikolai Trusov is on my case?"

"That's Adrian Wade's department, and she's taking it seriously. She's in Kabul as we speak."

"Afghanistan?"

"You know any other Kabul? General Kulikov found the name of Trusov's Afghan spotter. And with the name, the U.S. consul in Kabul found the faction he fought for, and still fights for. His clan was aligned with Babrak Karmal and the Soviets during the war, and are now in the mountains. The spotter is from a village named Marjab about ten miles from Kabul. Adrian was on a plane ninety minutes after she got the news. Didn't even go back to her hotel. JFK to Charles De Gaulle to Riyadh and into Kabul."

"Couldn't she telephone him?"

"This fellow is in the hills. She's going to have to drive out to him, probably end up hiking in. But the consul thinks he's been given accurate information about where the spotter is."

"What's she after?"

"Anything that'll explain why Nikolai Trusov is hot for you."

Gray's voice rose. "I've got nothing to do with Afghanistan or the Soviets or with Trusov. Goddamnit, Pete, what's going on?"

"Maybe she'll find out, Owen."

"Yeah, maybe." Gray exhaled slowly. "Your people surrounding the Russian embassy haven't had any luck, I take it."

"Trusov never returned to the embassy to visit his father, and I found out why when I interviewed the old man again. Turns out the son called the father, and the old guy was delighted to tell his boy about all the policemen visiting."

"So Nikolai Trusov never showed up there."

"That's right," Coates replied. "And there's more news, Owen. We found where Trusov has been staying, a place called the Four Leaf Clover Motel in Jersey City. We broke into the place. He's got a box of Owen Gray memorabilia."

"Some of my stuff?"

"In a cardboard box in his motel room closet we found a Hobart High School annual, class of 1967. There's a photo of young Owen Gray wearing a Beatles haircut and a narrow black tie. There's also some recent photos of you—one leaving your Brooklyn apartment leading your son, John, down the steps, another showing you and me carrying gym bags into Sam Owl's place. There's one of you and your girls sitting in the window of a McDonald's. And another of Mrs. Orlando."

"Christ," Gray blurted, "he was following us around."

"And here's something spooky. We also found your bag gloves, the brown Everlasts you thought you had lost."

"So he's been inside Sam Owl's, inside my locker there?"

"Looks like it."

Gray rubbed his forehead. "Damn, Pete, what's going on?"

"This guy isn't going to get out of New York," the detective said. "Trusov's got the mayor and the police commissioner and the FBI director's full attention now. They've flooded this town with people. There isn't a bus station, train depot, airport, or hotel where he can show up and not be spotted. Even the uniforms are carrying his five-by-seven photo on the top of their clipboards. We've released some of the story to the media, and the Russian's photo has been playing big on television and in the newspapers. The whole eastern seaboard and the south and midwest are on the lookout for Trusov. It's just a matter of time."

Gray was hunched over the phone and his neck and shoulders had begun to complain. "The telephone at my place will be restored by tomorrow."

"I'll call with the latest." Coates hesitated, then added, "You weren't kidding me about your promise, were you, Owen? About plunking yourself? You wouldn't go and ruin my whole day, would you?'' Coates's lighthearted words were betrayed by his apprehensive tone.

Gray hung up. He returned to the saloon's main floor and waved at Ray Miller on his way out.

11

POLK COUNTY UNDERSHERIFF Mel Schneider
turned his white-and-black off the road and into the Cat's Meow
Cafe parking lot in the town of Mentor. He passed a few automobiles and pickups as he slowly headed for a vacant spot in front of
the cafe's large glass windows. He glanced at his wristwatch. He
was meeting Deputy Mike Dickerson for lunch at the Cat's Meow,
and Schneider was hungry. There were two open slots next to a
silver Chevrolet Caprice. He pulled in next to the Chevy, set his
parking brake, and again brought up his watch. He hoped Dickerson would be on time.

RayAnne Folger owned the Cat's Meow—Schneider could see
her startling red hair through the cafe's window, serving three
customers sitting at the counter—and she served a fine meatloaf
sandwich. Schneider turned the squawk box to low, then rolled
down his window to let the breeze in. He'd wait a few moments
for Dickerson before going into the cafe.

When Schneider's belly growled with hunger, it did so loudly
because it was a big belly, pushing against the steering wheel.
Schneider had been on the force almost twenty-five years, and the
goddamn squad cars had become less and less comfortable over
those years. Now the big man was wedged in between the wheel,
the radio and mounted computer to his right, a shotgun on a verti-

cal rack next to the computer, and the safety glass that separated front and back seats. Schneider lifted his hat from the passenger seat, forked his fingers through his hair, and placed the hat on his head. His hair had gone gray in streaks. His eyes were close together and faded blue. His thin, bloodless lips made his rare smile vulpine. Reading glasses were in his shirt pocket. He glanced at his watch. His stomach rumbled again. Damn it, Dickerson, get your lard-ass in gear and get over here.

A silver Caprice. Schneider's head jerked left. Christ in his cups, a silver Caprice. The undersheriff opened the car door, stepped five steps to the rear to read the Chevy's license plate. He quickly returned to his car to punch the license number into the computer. The screen told him to wait. He lifted his handset and without the usual radio rigmarole asked, "Where are you, Mike?"

The radio cackled with "Twenty seconds away. I see your bubble in the parking lot. Your gut must be doing the talking again."

The amber computer screen blinked with the information.

"Aw, goddamnit," the undersheriff whispered as he read the screen.

The Caprice had been stolen in Brainerd, Minnesota, three hours ago. The auto's owner had seen a large man wearing a baseball cap low on his head drive by in the car while the owner was getting a haircut. The Caprice's owner had later identified Nikolai Trusov from a photo shown him by a Brainerd police detective. The goddamn New York police had thought this man would never get out of their jurisdiction, and he was already halfway across the country. The FBI now believed Trusov was stealing a new car every hundred miles or so. Earlier that morning a Mercury Cougar had been found in Brainerd that had been stolen in Anoka, a town just north of Minneapolis. The Russian's fingerprints were all over the vehicle.

Undersheriff Schneider peered through his windshield into the cafe. A sticker on the door announced that the Cat's Meow was a member of the Mentor, Minnesota, Chamber of Commerce. A doughnut case was at one end of the counter near the cash register. He knew that six booths were ranged along the north wall. Two customers sat at the booth he could see. He counted four diners at the counter, sitting on stools, their backs to the window. Ketchup bottles and napkin dispensers were visible between their elbows. A large and gleaming stainless steel coffee urn was against the wall. The door to the kitchen was near the coffeemaker. RayAnne was putting a plate in front of the largest man at the counter. He was wearing a tan jacket and a green baseball cap. He lifted a fork and bent to the plate. It had to be Nikolai Trusov.

Schneider reached for his clipboard. On it was the bulletin given every Minnesota law officer that morning. He read again about the Russian. "Sweet Jesus, I don't want to do this."

Deputy Mike Dickerson pulled his patrol car into the slot next to Schneider, who waved him toward the passenger seat of Schneider's car. Dickerson stepped toward the cafe, but then saw that his boss was not getting out of the car. He squinted in puzzlement through the window, then opened the door and slid into the passenger seat.

"I got some bad news for our lunch plans," Schneider began. "You see that man at the counter, last one on the right?"

"Yeah," Dickerson said. "The big guy?"

"That's the Russian we were told about at lineup this morning. Same guy that's on the FBI bulletin."

Dickerson stared into the cafe. The deputy had a long face and a chin that protruded beyond his lips. He wore a burr cut with almost no hair showing under his cap. He was a veteran of twelve months in the sheriff's department. "What're we going to do?"

"We're going to do what the taxpayers pay us for. Arrest him."

The deputy asked, "Shouldn't we call in reinforcements?"

Schneider rubbed a temple. "There's two of us. He's sitting peaceably at that counter. He doesn't even know we're here yet. I'm going to walk right up to him and stick the Remington barrel into his face and tell him he's under arrest. I don't need reinforcements for that."

"He's tough." Dickerson wet his lips. "You read what he did to that gas jockey in Cleveland."

The undersheriff's eyes seemed to have moved even closer together. "He's not tougher than my shotgun. We're going in."

"The Russian is a commando. According to what I read, he's been at war for most of his life. He's probably pretty good at it."

"Probably," Schneider granted.

"I ever tell you I've got a three-year-old son?"

"For Christ sake, Mike, I've eaten dinner at your house a half dozen times, your kid sitting there oinking down his food each time. I know you've got a kid." He paused. "Hell, what's the Russian doing now?"

Nikolai Trusov was rising from the stool. He placed his napkin on the counter next to his plate. He spoke several words to Ray-Anne, who pointed over her shoulder toward the rear of the cafe. He walked behind the other counter customers, then disappeared down the aisle between the booths.

"He's going back to take a leak."

"There's no rear door back there, is there?" Dickerson asked.

"Just the bathrooms. Mike, the men's room has a window in it. As I recall, it might be big enough for a man to climb through. You go around the north side of the cafe and wait next to the window. I'm going in the front door."

Dickerson nodded and unsnapped his holster.

The undersheriff laid a hand on Dickerson's arm. "Mike, we only need to make an attempt to arrest this guy. If the son of a bitch looks sideways at you, shoot him. Don't give him a break. He won't give you one."

Dickerson yanked the door handle. He pulled his pistol from the holster as he exited the car. The deputy rounded the patrol car and the Caprice, then disappeared around the north corner of the cafe. The undersheriff clicked the pump shotgun from its mount. After he got out of the vehicle, he thumbed the safety off. He entered the cafe.

A few customers turned toward him. Acquaintances nodded, then stared at the shotgun. His eyes on the rest-room hallway, Schneider sidled up to the doughnut case. Her hand at her mouth and wide eyes on the shotgun, RayAnne Folger moved to the end of the counter.

Schneider said, "That big fellow who just went back into the hallway. What'd he just say to you?"

She had the look of a deer caught in headlights. Her voice was scratchy. "He asked for the men's toilet."

"He speak with an accent?"

She pounced at the question. "Yeah, he did. Pretty bad one, even those few words I heard."

The undersheriff slowly walked down the aisle toward the rest-room hall. The customers followed him with their eyes, their burgers and fries forgotten. He passed a high chair, two stacked

155

booster chairs, and the pay phone. He held the 12-gauge in front of him like an infantryman, expecting the Russian to emerge from the rest room at any moment. The door remained closed.

Schneider paused in front of the door. He could feel his blood pump, and his tongue seemed stitched to the top of his mouth. He whispered hoarsely, "Christ save me, I don't want to do this."

But he did. The undersheriff lurched forward, his shoulder slamming into the rest-room door, which jumped back and banged against the wall. He charged into the room.

One hand on his belt and the other on his privates as he stood in front of the urinal, Don Hansen dried up. His mouth fished open, and he backstepped, still exposed and dribbling.

Schneider ignored him. He turned to the stall and kicked in the door. He jabbed the shotgun into the space. It was empty.

"What the hell, Mel?" Don Hansen demanded. He adjusted his pants. "All I'm doing is relieving myself here. That ain't against no law I know of."

The window was closed and the sill was dusty. Nobody had used it. Schneider turned a full circle. Don Hansen, and that was it. A knot formed between the undersheriff's eyebrows. He turned back to the stall, staring at the toilet-paper dispenser, as if a man could hide somewhere in there. How had the Russian disappeared? He shook his head slowly and gestured vaguely toward Hansen.

Schneider pulled open the rest-room door to return to the hall. And across from him was the door to the women's rest room. And then he understood.

Knowing he was too late and just going through the motions, he lowered the shotgun, and bulled his way into the women's head. No one was in the room. A breeze poured through the open window, freshening the air. The window exited south, the opposite side of the building from the deputy. Nobody in the two stalls.

Schneider hurried from the room and sprinted down the aisle. Customers' eyes followed him once again. The undersheriff said aloud, "How did the bastard spot us?"

He stopped in front of the stool where the Russian had been sitting. He stared across the counter to the backbar. Reflected in the stainless steel coffee urn was the parking lot behind him, and his patrol car, clear as day, just like in a mirror. He moved by the stools and yanked the cafe's front door open. He went on his tiptoes and looked south. The Caprice was a block away and accelerating. The green baseball cap was visible through the rear window.

He yelled, "Mike, hurry up."

Undersheriff Schneider was going to give chase, but when he reached for his door handle, he had to bend slightly lower than usual. He glanced back. The rear tire had been slashed and the car had sunk to the wheel rim. Schneider stepped around to Dickerson's patrol car. It, too, was low on its rear axle. RayAnne and her customers were at the window staring at Schneider.

The deputy arrived panting, his pistol in his hand.

"He's gone. And we're stuck here." He waved a hand at the flat tires.

Dickerson looked down the road, but the Caprice had already vanished. "I can't say as I'm disappointed to miss him."

"Me, neither." Schneider slipped into his car and reached for the radio handset. Before he pressed the button, he said, "He'll soon be out of Polk County, and that's the last we'll have to think about him."

❖   ❖   ❖

"The hand of God made these mountains." Owen Gray's voice was soft with wonder at the panorama before them.

"It was glacial ice, not God." Adrian stopped beside Gray on the bluff overlooking the valley. "Those peaks are made of granite that crystallized below the earth's surface, then pushed through to create fault blocks. I read about them in a book about Idaho on the flight from New York. The granite crags are called batholiths. They were eroded by glaciers."

Gray said wearily, "And I'm telling you it was the hand of God."

Below them, filling Gray's vision and bringing forth a rush of childhood memories, were the narrow defiles of river canyons, topped with sharp ridges and peaks jutting forth at confused angles. Glacial gouges and cirques and horns gave the range an air of unyielding wildness. Douglas fir and lodgepole pine fought for purchase on the granite. The lower slopes were covered with blue bunch grass, wheatgrass, and Idaho fescue. Near the peaks, blue and yellow lichen colored the granite. When clouds passed overhead, the mountains changed hues, quickly purpling, then changing to gray, then lightening again to blue and gold as the billows passed. In the distance was Lewis Mountain.

Gray was wearing a Gortex backpack. The Weatherby rifle was over his shoulder. He pointed. "Look, there's a bird called a Clark's nutcracker. If you hold out a sandwich, it'll only take him a few minutes to get the courage to land on your hand."

The bird was perched on the low branch of a whitebark pine. Black wings rested against an ash-gray body. It peered at them intently, then hopped along its branch toward them.

Gray looked at her a moment. "I was startled when Pete Coates told me you were in Afghanistan."

"I was only gone two days. Even so, I'll bet you missed me."

"Well, I feel safer when you're around." He was deliberately cheery, not wanting to inflict his grief on Adrian. "I won't get mugged, anyway."

She smiled quickly and he generated a grin in return. Then he lowered himself to his haunches. "Look closely at the trail and tell me what you see."

Adrian squinted at the ground. "Dirt and some pebbles and a few twigs."

"See these slight depressions in the surface of the path?" Gray traced them with a finger. "They are paw prints. They tell us that an hour or two ago a yellow-bellied marmot passed by this way."

"What's a marmot?" Adrian asked.

"A big leaf-eating rodent."

"Like a rat?"

"Much cuter."

"How can you tell it's not a house cat lost up here in these mountains?"

Gray smiled. "A marmot has four toes on its front feet and five on its back. A cat has four all around. And cats walk like babies crawl, moving diagonal limbs at the same time. But a marmot moves both legs on one side of its body at the same time, like porcupines and skunks. See, you can tell by these prints that the marmot is shuffling both right legs, then both left legs at once."

"How do you know those tracks weren't made by a skunk?" she asked.

"A skunk has five toes in front. And we're too high for a skunk."

"Or a porcupine?"

"They like the woods, not the rocks."

Adrian was wearing a light blue jacket, jeans, and Eddie Bauer climbing boots. She persisted. "And how do you know the marmot came by here an hour or two ago, not yesterday?"

"The peaks of the marmot's prints have just begun to deteriorate, with grains of dirt falling into the base of the tracks. There's a five-to-ten-mile-an-hour wind today, so I know from experience that an hour or two of loose grains have fallen into the paw print." Gray could not resist showing off. "I also know that there were no hawks flying overhead when our marmot walked this way. And no coyotes around either."

Adrian pursed her lips. "I'm stuck out in the wilderness with Mr. Nature."

Gray hurried on. "And the reason I know is because the size of these tracks tells me this is an older marmot. He has survived several years of predators and is therefore smart about them. And had the marmot sensed the predators he would have been running and his stride would have been about fifteen inches instead of the seven or eight you see here."

A paintbrush plant, with its delicate orange blooms, was growing among balsamroot leaves near their feet.

She said, "I didn't come to Idaho to learn about rodents."

Gray shrugged. "So you found Nikolai Trusov's spotter?"

"Yakub Nadir was a member of the same faction, the Parcham, as Babrak Karmal, the Soviet puppet. Nadir worked as Trusov's spotter for almost two years. I found him in a tiny hill town outside Kabul, one of the villages still controlled by his tribe. He fell into the hands of Tajik mujahideen after the Soviets left, who, finding out his role, dug out both his eyeballs. Nadir is blind. He was wearing Soviet fatigue trousers, Afghan army boots, and a flat woolen cap called a *pakol*. I met him at a teahouse, then he took me to his home."

"He didn't mind talking to a westerner?" Gray asked.

"I think he enjoyed it. Nadir is an educated man. He attended the prestigious French-run Istiqlal School in Kabul and speaks French. He was studying to be an engineer when the Soviets invaded. He chose the wrong side, as he readily admits. He wears no eyepatches or dark glasses, and it's hard not to stare at the ragged holes in his head when talking with him. The mujahideen used a heated bayonet, and they weren't careful. So not only did

159

he lose his eyes, but much of his face around his eyes is livid with scars."

"They have always played for keeps over there. Tell me about the interview."

"I was his *mehman,* his guest, and he made me feel welcome. His wife served us green tea and *nan* while we spoke. His home had one room with a high ceiling. To keep out the heat a ragged white curtain was drawn across the one window, but beams of sunlight came through the holes in the curtain. I sat on a couch with old cushions, and he sat on a patch of worn carpet. The plaster walls were flaking, and on one was a poster of Karmal. There was also a sentence painted on a wall in bold calligraphic letters, but I didn't find out what it meant."

"Doesn't Nadir fear for his life? Why isn't he on the run?"

"He thinks his eyes are all the mujahideen will take from him."

"So what did he say about Trusov?"

"Nadir said the Russian was a master of his craft."

"I already knew that."

"And Trusov enjoyed it. Sometimes he would fire many shots at the same target, hitting a knee, then a hand, then a foot, and so forth, taking a lot of care to place the shots where they wouldn't kill the target immediately. Nadir claims he saw Trusov fire twelve shots at a mujahideen, all hits, before the coup de grace. Trusov told Nadir that his twelve shots before the kill must be a world record."

"For Christ sake, that's not soldiering."

"Trusov knew about you."

Gray's head came up.

"That same day, after the killing shot, the thirteenth, Trusov said to Nadir, 'Not even the great American Owen Gray could place twelve non-lethal shots.' " Adrian Wade lowered herself to a boulder. She crossed her legs. "Trusov frequently talked about you."

"Why? Did he tell his spotter he had ever met me?"

She shook her head. "I gather he knew of your Vietnam reputation. I questioned Nadir closely about this. Trusov never claimed any acquaintance with you, or said he ever met you. He knew of your reputation. He was envious of it."

"How did he get the big scar on his head?"

"Nadir didn't know. He had that groove in his skull when they first teamed up in 1985."

A bluebird on the bough of a subalpine fir chirruped noisily.

Adrian put her hand under her coat to adjust her holster, then continued, "Nadir said Nikolai Trusov was crazy."

"I already knew that, too."

"He meant that while Trusov was a superb soldier during his first years in Afghanistan, the Russian became increasingly unstable. Doing erratic things. But he was so valuable to the Soviet war effort that he was tolerated for a long while. Then he snapped."

"What happened?" Gray asked.

"There was bad blood between Trusov and his captain. Nadir didn't know how it started, but the two were always at each other. The captain didn't have the leeway to deal with Trusov like he would any other subordinate because Trusov was an Olympic hero and a brilliant sniper. Trusov detested the captain, an up-and-coming Moscow University graduate trying to make a mark. Nadir doesn't know what set Trusov off that day, but when the captain drove by in an open GAZ field car, Trusov put a bullet through both the captain's wrists as his hands gripped the steering wheel."

"Did the Afghan spotter actually see this happen?"

"Nadir was there, and he said it was a phenomenal shot. Four hundred yards at a moving vehicle, and Trusov called it before he fired, just like you'd call a pool shot, telling the Afghan he'd take out both the captain's wrists."

A nutcracker landed at the other end of the boulder and dipped its beak at Adrian, hoping for a handout.

"Trusov may have been a hero, but no soldier gets away with that." Gray opened his backpack and brought out a peanut butter sandwich wrapped in wax paper.

"He didn't," Adrian said.

Gray tore off half the sandwich and tossed it to the bird. The nutcracker squawked and leaped onto the handout. Two other nutcrackers instantly appeared to tear at the bread. They flapped and hopped and quarreled, flipping bits of bread down their gullets.

"Trusov was arrested and court-martialed," Adrian said. "He spent the next eight years at hard labor in the Red Army's First Military District prison. He was released six months ago."

"I thought the INS was supposed to keep criminals out of this

161

country." Gray tried to keep the touch of desperation from his voice. "Didn't they check him out before they gave him a visa?"

"A visa to accompany someone coming to the U.S. for surgery isn't examined closely."

Gray wiped his forehead with the back of his hand. The day was warming, and the sun was high in the pale rinsed sky.

Adrian continued. "But the people at the INS are helping our investigation. They checked with their counterparts in Europe, and the Swiss came up with something. Victor Trusov could have had his operation three months earlier in Geneva. The Swiss had given both him and his son permission to enter their country, and the Red Army had made arrangements for the operation at St. Paul's Hospital in Geneva. But the Trusovs refused, apparently waiting for the U.S. visa."

"So Nikolai intended to come here all along, and was willing to make his father wait for the surgery until things worked out. Old Victor could have died in the meantime."

Adrian nodded. "I suppose Nikolai was willing to risk that to get into the U.S."

"And to come for me," Gray said darkly.

"Yes, to come for you."

"How did Trusov get his rifle into this country?"

She replied, "Probably in a diplomatic pouch."

"A rifle in a pouch?"

"Pouch is a term of art. It can be anything from a letter to a container on a ship, as long as it has the diplomatic seal. A Hero of the Soviet Union would easily have found a Russian diplomat to help him get his rifle in." Adrian leaned forward on the boulder. She stared at him a moment before continuing, "You know that you are asking me to believe the impossible, don't you?"

"I'm not following you," Gray said. He tossed another piece of the sandwich to the birds.

"It is impossible that no connection exists between you and Nikolai Trusov."

"I never said there wasn't," Gray protested. "I just don't know what it is."

"By not telling me everything, you are asking me to believe the preposterous. I'm convinced that something in your past connects you to Trusov. You might not know it, but it does. And I won't be able to make the connection between you and the Russian unless you tell me everything.''

He nodded vaguely.

"You are hiding something from me. Level with me.''

"You already know everything important about me.''

"That's a lie.'' She smiled to take some of the sting from her words. "I've been a policewoman too long to buy that.''

"You and I are on the same side,'' Gray said rather feebly. "I'm not going to lie to you.''

Adrian leaned forward and brought her hands across her lap to fold her fingers. She gasped, then flicked her hand. Her mouth began a curl of horror but she controlled it. She leaped up from the boulder. Her voice wavered. "Have I hurt myself? There's blood all over me.''

Gray rose and hurried to her, reaching for the hand. "Show me where.''

Her voice was an unsteady whisper. "On my jacket.''

Her coat had more zippers than a flight jacket. A dark stain had spread along the right sleeve near a Velcro fastener. Gray quickly undid the Velcro and gently pushed back the fabric along Adrian's arm. None of the blood had seeped through the Gortex onto her arm.

Gray said, "The blood is from the rock you were sitting on.''

An edge of the granite slab was daubed with blood, and tinctures of the fluid darkened the silver moss on the stone.

"Where did it come from?''

"A wounded deer.'' The corners of Gray's mouth turned down. "A mule deer, probably.''

Gray rubbed a finger along the rock, bringing a smear of blood to his eyes. "It's been hit in the liver. You can tell from the dark color of the blood.''

"Wouldn't that have killed the deer?''

"A deer with a liver hit can take off at a dead run and go for a long way.'' Gray bent close to the rock. Mica flecks glittered in the sunlight. He found a tuft of hair. "This is his fur. It's black-tipped, which means it's from just above his belly.'' Gray knelt closer to look at the prints at the base of the boulder. He found a hoofprint. "The mulie staggered against the rock, then took off again, uphill into that ravine.''

"Is he going to die?" Adrian asked.

"He can't survive this wound."

"Who shot him?"

"Some poacher who didn't have the skill or the energy to follow the deer."

"A poacher?"

"Deer are out of season."

"Can we help the deer?" she asked. "We should do something."

"There's nothing we can do."

"Yes, there is." She looked directly into his eyes. "We can't let him just die."

Adrian started along the path, then veered off in a bank of bunch grass toward the ravine. The nutcrackers scattered, crying raucously. She looked back at Gray. "I'm going to find him."

"Goddamnit," Gray muttered. He lifted his rifle and pack to follow her.

The north-facing slope of the ravine was dotted with lodgepole pine. Adrian's approach flushed a covey of grouse that had been feeding on buds and leaves. She led him along a deer trail through serviceberry bushes, whose flowers resembled white lilies. They reached a fork in the trail where the ravine branched.

She slowed, then stopped. "Which way did he go?"

"Look for blood. Women are better at finding blood on the ground than men are. I don't know why, but it's true."

"There." She stabbed a finger at the ground.

Blood often looks like rust spots on leaves. Gray wet his thumb with spit and rubbed the leaf. It streaked. Blood. "He went up the left ravine."

"Why up?" she asked. "Maybe he stopped and then went back down."

Gray shook his head. "Confused, wounded deer always go uphill."

"How do you know?"

"I just know they do. And lost children usually walk uphill and lost adults go downhill. That's just how things work."

They marched through the pine, which gave way to an aspen grove. The soil was loose, almost a scree. Their toes dug into it, propelling them up the path. Cheat-grass stickers found their way onto Gray's socks, making his ankles itch. On a boulder a piping hare jerked up and down as it whistled, an outsized sound resembling a goat cry. Gray nodded a greeting to it.

A deep gurgling croak came from a ridge above Gray, followed by a roll of squawks and clacks, a riotous, unnerving sound in the high stillness. Ravens rose from behind the ridge, their enormous ebony wings beating the thin air. Several landed on the boughs of a scrubby ponderosa pine. Others disappeared again behind the outcropping of boulders and grass.

"The mule deer is behind those rocks," Gray called. "Maybe you shouldn't get any closer. It's not going to be fun to look at."

Adrian asked, "How do you know it's there?"

"The ravens are waiting for their dinner."

"Will they start tearing away at the deer before it's dead?"

"Ravens aren't known for their table manners."

They rounded the rocks. The ravens flew away, but not too far before landing on the scree to stare sullenly at the humans. Adrian looked sadly at the wounded deer. The mulie was lying on a blanket of bunch grass, its large white-patched ears moving independently of each other like a mule's. It was a doe, and it was breathing raggedly, blowing pink blood from its nostrils. A red smear ran along its flanks. The entry wound was high in front of its hindquarters. Blood trails mapped the animal's flanks and thighs, seeping onto the stones. The deer stared blankly at the humans. Its nostrils flared as it fought for breath. The ravens shrieked at the intruders.

Adrian said softly, "He's going to die, isn't he? He looks bad."

"It's a she. Yeah, she's in bad shape."

"There must be something we can do." Adrian Wade blinked back tears. "The poor animal shouldn't have to die."

Gray looked at her. Adrian had known loss, had been pushed to the brink by grief. Gray didn't want his small tour of his mountains to freshen those emotions. He said, "Maybe I can dig the bullet out. You never know about deer. She could make it." He stepped across the lichens and stones to the deer. It followed him with its black eyes, and raised one hoof, but did not have the strength to lever itself off the ground. "Too many of us around here will scare her. You head down the ravine. I'll catch up when I'm done."

A tear trailed down Adrian's face. Her gaze went between the deer and Gray, then she turned back down the mountain, down the loose stones toward the deer trail. She looked back at Gray to see him draw the bowie knife from the scabbard. Gray waited until she was out of sight before he brought the blade to the mulie's throat.

Three minutes later he caught up with Adrian.

She glanced at the bowie knife, which was back in its place on Gray's belt. "That deer might live?"

"Maybe." Gray stared down the valley. "You bet."

Gray looked over his shoulder at the ridge. The ravens had left their perch and were hidden by the crest of the ridge. It seemed to him their renewed croaking held a victorious note.

She said bitterly, "I thought you said you weren't going to lie to me."

After a moment he said, "I won't. Mostly."

✧   ✧   ✧

Andy Ellison moved on his knees among the stalks, stopping at each one to sprinkle a small handful of fertilizer onto the ground, then using a hand to scratch the granules into the dirt. His stand was thick, and the pointed leaves brushed his face, a feathery sensation he associated with freedom. He dragged the paper sack of fertilizer along with him as he went from plant to plant.

His marijuana patch was hidden in a black cottonwood glen in Jefferson County, Montana, in the low foothills of the Rocky Mountains, two dirt-road miles north of the interstate highway. The glen bordered an open field, one of many pastures where the Rocking R ranch's six thousand head of cattle grazed. Ellison's crop was protected by a barbed-wire fence. All marijuana plants favor sun, but this species, Chiang Mai Red, craved it, and it was Ellison's despair that he could offer only light dappled by the cottonwood branches overhead. Otherwise DEA planes would quickly find the crop. Ellison had tried hiding his crops among Louisiana sugarcane (his arrest netted two years probation), between rows of Washington State corn (two years at Walla Walla), and under grow lights in a California basement (four years at San Quentin). He had sworn he would never go back to prison, for those were hard years, particularly at the Walls, where Ellison was Booby Decker's girlfriend. Ellison still wore a tattoo on his buttocks that proved it. "If you reeding this, Booby kil you." Decker had pricked it onto Ellison's butt himself, smashing his fist into Ellison's ear each time Ellison howled. Booby was no artist, so the

166

blue ink letters wiggled and bled, but the message was plain enough, and nobody at the Walls bothered Ellison except Booby. The tattoo had only humiliated Ellison. The misspellings had outraged him.

No, sir, Andy Ellison wanted no more to do with prison, and the next time the DEA or some local sheriff found him tending his crop Ellison would surely face six to eight years, being a three-time loser already. So he was careful. He limited each patch to twenty stalks, spending hours determining shadow patterns on the soil beneath the cottonwood boughs before he planted. Black cottonwood leaves—shiny dark green on top and white-green with rusty veins underneath—perfectly blended with Chiang Mai Red's leaves, especially when the wind roiled and blurred the foliage. No DEA plane was going to spot his crop, Ellison believed. He had fifteen such patches at the edge of the Rocking R land. The ranch's owner, a corporation based in Missoula, rented a homesteader's shack and barn to Ellison, one of the many busted-out spreads devoured by the corporation over the years. The corporation's concern were Herefords and tax codes, and it was not too attentive to the perimeters of its grazing land.

Ellison crawled along the ground, dropping the fertilizer and mixing it in. His plants were a bit leggy for lack of full sun, but the leaves were broad and green, a lot of product. A wren trilled in a cottonwood, its flicking tail seen at the edge of Ellison's vision. And a nearby towhee flicked aside leaves and twigs on the ground looking for insects, making a pleasant racket. Ellison whistled a Loving Spoonful song, keeping himself company. A nearby grasshopper rubbed its legs, squeaking along to Ellison's tune.

A small breeze brushed the stalks, but even so it was warm. Sweat dropped from Ellison's forehead onto his spectacle lenses. He took them off and wiped the lenses on his shirt. He had worn granny glasses since the Sixties, and the spectacles and his sandals and tie-dyed T-shirts he wore whenever he was tending his crop were his personal commemoration of the Sixties, that lost time that would never come again, that apex of Andy Ellison's life, those shimmering years of innocence and incense. And babes with no bras.

The intervening years had hardened Ellison, at least his appearance. He wore a ponytail tied with a rubber band, but the hair came from the sides and back of his head because he had lost most on top. Deep lines ran from his nose to the corners of his mouth. In a jealous rage, Booby Decker had punched out one of Ellison's front teeth, and the replacement cap had yellowed and now showed a line of blackened gum above the tooth. Ellison was indifferent to food and had always been thin, but lately his rib cage had begun to show and the tendons and veins on the back of his hands looked like road maps. He made enough money growing dope to feed himself most of the time, but as harvest approached he was usually down to pocket change and he missed many meals.

Ellison scratched his wrist, maybe an ant bite. Then Ellison's head came up. He looked left and right between the stalks. Something was amiss. The towhee and wren were abruptly silent. The buzz and clatter of insects had quieted. Even the wind had stopped, and the heat was suddenly thick and choking.

The prickly rash of fear crawled up Ellison's back. He had experienced this sensation once before, in the cornfield just before he was arrested, an indefinable sense that something was awry. He was no longer alone in the cottonwood glen. Somebody was closing in on him. Surely the DEA.

Ellison rose quickly, and more sweat dropped onto his glasses. He turned south toward the house, his view blocked by the tall marijuana stalks. But surely his pursuers had come from the house. He dropped his paper bag and turned north, ducking his head to hide below the top leaves of his plants. Still he heard and saw nobody. The sweat spread on his lenses, smearing his view. He turned left toward a brace of dwarf maples, brushing by the last of his plants. Then a man appeared before him, forming out of the maple leaves, obscured by the droplets on Ellison's lenses. A huge man with a blond plug head. Moving toward him.

The old hippie turned back, willing his legs to work, sprinting through the marijuana stalks. The once friendly leaves seemed to grab for him. He missed his footing on a cottonwood root and fell to one knee. He rose, limping, pushing himself forward. His breath rattled in his throat. Dear God, he didn't want to go back to prison.

The marijuana stalks ahead of him parted, and the big man was there. Ellison jerked his eyes over his shoulder. Were there two of them? How could he have moved so quickly? Panic rose in Ellison. Six years this time, maybe eight, every day of it spent as some con's girlfriend. A wail of fear escaped his lips. He dodged right, toward a thimbleberry thicket, his feet churning the loose soil. His chest heaved. He swatted aside vegetation and braved a look over his shoulder. He had lost the intruder. He turned back toward the thimbleberry, and there the big man was again, smiling slightly and raising a hand.

Panic almost closing his throat, Ellison turned again. His legs seemed made of rope but he dug at the ground and flailed at the vegetation as if swimming, pulling himself through the underbrush. He groaned with effort and his vision blurred even more.

Then he was on the ground, his face hard against the dirt, a rough hand at the back of his neck pinning him there. Ellison inhaled deeply, drawing in bits of dirt. Helpless, he closed his eyes. Six to eight years this time.

The hand rolled Ellison over. The intruder towered over him, the details of his face lost in the sun overhead. The hand gripped Ellison's arm and easily brought him to his feet.

"It's this scar, isn't it?"

Ellison was still blowing loudly, and he thought perhaps he hadn't heard the man. "A scar?"

"It frightens people." A blocky voice, unaccustomed to the language.

"Where's my Miranda rights?" Ellison was suddenly angry. He peeled off his glasses and wiped them on his shirt sleeve. When he returned them to his nose, he wished he hadn't. Seen closely and clearly, the intruder was even more frightening. Chopped face, gash of a mouth, and a red and scaled dent above his right eye that disappeared back under the blond hair. The scar made everything on his face seem askew.

"I demand my Miranda rights, goddamnit. Where's the protocol?"

"I need a bed for the night."

"A bed?" The slightest flutter of hope. "You just want a bed?"

The stranger nodded.

The six to eight years vanished. "Thank you, God." Ellison turned toward the shack. His confidence soared. "I don't mind saying you scared the hell out of me."

"I do that a lot." The accent was strong. "Sometimes on purpose, sometimes not."

✧   ✧   ✧

The trailer was cramped and hot. Squeezed between banks of electronics, Pete Coates drummed his fingers on a tiny metal table. "Can't you hurry up?"

"I'll tell the pilot to rock back and forth in his seat to make his plane go faster," the technician replied with a Southern accent, not bothering to look at Coates.

The technician was an Air Force captain assigned to PHOTINT Tasking and was the master of the trailer, which was called a C3, for command, control, and communications. The trailer and the captain and the reconnaissance planes were on loan to Coates and the FBI. The technician had given Coates a ten-minute tour of the trailer, which consisted of both men slowly turning in their chairs as the technician pointed out one system after another, speaking mostly in unfathomable acronyms like SIGMA and MAC and TOT and DISCUS, all communications systems. The interior of the trailer glowed in soft green light from several monitors. Coates faced a wall of digital numbers, blinking red and green and yellow lights, dials and knobs and switches. The trailer was filled with a faint crackling. Three monitors were black but with the tiny power lights glowing red. On another monitor was ESPN.

After the tour of the communications equipment, Coates had asked, "You sure it's a car in there?" The captain had once again reviewed his evidence: an Army Beechcraft RC-12d—a plane notable for the dozen antennas protruding from its wings and fuselage—had with its UAS-4 infrared equipment detected heat coming from a dilapidated barn in Jefferson County, in foothill country. Within an hour Coates's team had checked the farmstead against the Jefferson County tax assessor's rolls and determined that the Allcrop Corporation, the parent company of the Rocking R Ranch, was paying property taxes on the land, and that the county assessor had dropped the structure component of the assessment on the parcel three times as the farm and barn fell into disrepair. So there should not have been a heat source in the dilapidated barn, yet there was.

"A yellow Buick Regal is what I'm looking for," Coates offered once again. "That's the last car Trusov stole, and we haven't found it abandoned anywhere, so he's still got it."

The technician nodded. "The second plane should be there by now. We'll see what shows up."

The Beechcraft had not been equipped with cameras, and in any event the plane had covered the ground too quickly to take still photographs, so another plane, a Grumman Mohawk from Fort Ord, had been sent for a second fly-by. The Mohawk was a multisensor tactical observation and reconnaissance platform equipped with an ESSWACS (electronic solid-state wide-angle camera system), a five lens assembly that focused light onto five charge-coupling devices. The five currents were sent through an on-board video processor, then through a multiplex system to turn them into a single burst of digital pulses. The plane carried a stabilized transmitter in a helmet-sized blister under its starboard wing, which would send it to an LOS (line of sight) relay station atop Moller Mountain. The signal would be instantly forwarded to the trailer, and the picture reconstructed on the monitor in front of Coates and the technician.

"Still enough light, you think?" Coates asked.

The tech glanced at his wristwatch. "It's only eight-thirty. The sun sets late this time of year. There'll be enough light."

Coates was counting on the tumbledown barn to be missing shingles. He rubbed his forehead with frustration. "I thought I had Nikolai Trusov bottled up in New York."

"Sounds like he got out."

"He went through my so-called impenetrable ring like crap through a goose, goddamn him anyway."

"You know, Detective, I've read the FBI's case report on your Russian. He's a hard man."

"He is that."

"I've never met Owen Gray, but I feel sorry for him, real sorry for him, what with this Nikolai Trusov after him."

Coates snorted. "A gunnery sergeant told me some stories about Owen Gray."

"Yeah?" His instruments instantly forgotten, the captain turned to Coates.

"Gray has a series of scars on his arms and legs. He got them in Vietnam."

"Yeah? How?"

"He fell into a tiger pit, a man trap set by the Viet Cong. The enemy disarmed him, dragged him a mile to the nearest village, and nailed him to a wall."

"Nailed?" The tech made a face. "Like Christ?"

"The VC had more nails than the Romans. They nailed Gray's

171

hands, his biceps, couple more nails in his feet and through his shin bones, nails through his shoulders. Twelve nails in all."

"How'd Gray free himself?"

"He was pinned to that wall for all of a day and some of a night." Coates said his next words slowly, one at a time for emphasis. "Then he ripped himself free."

The captain's face lengthened. "What do you mean?"

"He couldn't pull the nails from the wood, so he yanked himself off the nails. The VC were sitting around an iron pot, boiling their fish and rice, and didn't see or hear him. Gray left chunks of himself on each nail, bloody gobs of skin and muscle. But he freed himself, then walked for three days back to American lines."

"Good God."

"So while you feel sorry for Owen Gray"—Coates smiled narrowly—"I feel sorry for the Russian."

A moment passed, the captain digesting the story. Then he asked, "You hungry? I've got a top secret LAPSAT radio downlink that'll order us a pizza."

Coates shook his head. "I want to get the hell out of here as soon as—"

In front of the technician, the NEC monitor's screen turned to white, then ran through a color protocol, flickering quickly through a palette of primary colors. Then an image appeared on the screen showing approximately a square mile of Jefferson County. Visible were a small stream, rock outcroppings, patches of forest, several fence lines, and two buildings. Above the image appeared a series of menu buttons.

"Here we go," the tech said, pulling a mouse from behind the monitor. The tech clicked twice on a screen button. The image was instantly sectioned into twenty-five parts. The arrow then moved to the section containing the house and barn. Another double click, and that portion was magnified. The image was taken directly over the house and barn, and they showed clearly. A chimney throwing a long shadow, a collapsed chicken house near the barn, a wood stand that had once supported a windmill, another pile of wood that might have once been a toolshed, and a green van parked near the house, all were plainly visible on the screen. More clicks, and this image was sectioned, and the arrow found the part containing the barn. Yet more clicks, and that part was enlarged.

"Looks like you're right," the tech said. "Missing shingles. But look here, too. In front of the barn, in the grass, the double lines of an automobile track. Abandoned barns usually don't have fresh tracks on the ground in front of them.''

Coates rose from the chair to lean toward the monitor. ''And beneath the barn's roof in the gaps left by missing shingles . . .''

The captain pointed at a feature on the screen. ''Looks like there's some yellow in that barn.''

''Bright yellow, looks like,'' Coates added. ''And shiny.''

''Yeah, that's not hay bales or an old tarp or anything like that.''

Coates lifted his jacket from the back of his chair. His voice was tight with excitement. ''It's a goddamn Buick Regal is what it is. We've found that Russian son of a bitch.'' He slapped the captain on the shoulder and turned for the trailer's door.

12

"YOU CAUGHT THESE FISH?" Adrian asked, nodding at the two rainbow trout on the pan. The fish were cleaned but still had their heads and tails.

Gray moved a skillet over the heat. "In the creek."

"Did you kill the pig, too?"

Gray ignored her. He placed three strips of bacon into the frying pan. The bacon hissed and spat. He jiggled the pan to move the bacon back and forth. Gray lifted a pinch of cornmeal from a porcelain canister and dropped it onto the plate. He rolled the trout in the cornmeal. When bacon grease covered the skillet, he slid the fish from the plate to the frying pan. The trout and bacon sizzled together. On the other grill, steam rose from a stainless steel pot containing brown rice in boiling water. Gray placed a steamer over the water and rice. He lifted spring peas from a paper sack on the counter and dropped them into the steamer. He was wearing jeans and a high-neck University of Idaho Vandals sweatshirt.

Adrian leaned against the post that separated the kitchen from the main room. Her arms were crossed in front of her, and a glass of chardonnay was in one hand. Her mouth was pursed and her eyes moved back and forth. Gray thought she had the look of someone whose guard was up. He lifted a piece of wood from the iron box next to the stove, then opened the stove's front grate.

Flame cast the kitchen in flickering red light. He shoved the wood through the opening and closed the grate.

She turned her head at a distant plaintive tremolo that ended it a series of sharp barks. She raised an eyebrow at Gray.

"A coyote." He used a spatula to turn the fish in the skillet.

"I thought they only bayed at the moon." She was wearing a white wool fisherman's net sweater and jeans.

"They howl at anything. Maybe he's mad at the weather."

Living in New York, Gray had gotten away from monitoring the weather. Rain or snow or sun, by the time it reached Manhattan's walled streets it didn't make much difference to Gray. In the Saw-tooths, Gray checked the Emory and Douglas barometer on the kitchen wall several times a day, just as his father had for so many decades. That afternoon the mercury had dropped abruptly, and the storm had swarmed into the mountains as night had come. Rain lashed against the roof in wind-driven waves. Windows rattled with the gusts, and beads of rainwater were pushed horizontally along the glass. The wind bawled through the trees, filling the cabin with a deep rumble. Tossed by the wind, the trunks of young aspen trees in the grove behind the cabin clicked together in an uneven staccato. The old cabin creaked and groaned.

Gray lifted the skillet and used the spatula to slide the fish onto two plates. He opened the fish and poked gently them with a fork. "They're done."

With a spoon he retrieved the spring peas from the steamer. "The difference between perfect peas and overdone peas is about ten seconds. It's all in the timing."

He placed the peas on the plates and sprinkled them with pepper. He drained the rice in the sink and used a serving spoon to divide it onto the plates. Then he carried both plates around the dining table and into the main room to place them on the coffee table next to a wine bottle and two place settings.

"My grandfather was smart in a lot of ways." Gray pushed aside the screen on the fireplace. "One of them was this fireplace. You don't need to carefully balance your firewood on the grate, hoping it won't roll out onto the floor. This fireplace is so large you can just toss a couple of logs in and they'll be all right."

He brought two pieces of wood from the box and lobbed them onto the fire. Red sparks swirled and disappeared up the chimney. Gray closed the screen. The fire surged, engulfing the new offering.

The blaze was the size of a bonfire, and it roared and popped, filling the room with warmth and dancing light. He lowered himself to the couch, facing the fire.

Adrian Wade joined him on the couch. "You didn't take the head off this fish."

"A trout looks better whole."

"You'll eat it, but you won't disfigure it."

"Something like that."

She placed her glass on the table. "You're not having wine?"

"Even one glass takes my edge off. I can't afford that right now."

Gray glanced at her. The fire's hues played on her face and sweater. Golds and reds and blues painted her in reeling patterns, making her seem an illusion. She brought up a few flakes of the fish and touched them with her tongue before eating them. Gray watched her chew. She seemed to do it absently, with the delicacy of disinterest. She gently twirled the wine. Colors of the fire sparkled in the wine and her eyes.

"You're staring at me again," she said quietly.

"Damn it." He shifted his gaze to his plate.

"I still mind, but not so much."

They ate in silence awhile. Gray had hoped for a comment about the fish, but none came. Trout was a meal he knew he cooked superbly, and this fish was tender and buttery, suggesting the wilderness without being gamey.

She sipped her wine. Her lips left a slight red print on the glass. Gray stared at the glass a moment. He wondered why such a common sight—lipstick on a wineglass—could be so suggestive.

She said, "Your friend Pete Coates likes to look at the files of people he works with."

"He knows more about me than I do."

"Did he tell you a lot about me?"

"Nothing I'd call tantalizing," he answered.

"You know about my husband?"

"A pilot who died in a plane crash. Sad business."

"I read once in a psychology text that for any given person in the United States there are sixty thousand other people that person could fall in love with. But I knew that statistic was sheer nonsense. There was one person for me and I had the good fortune to find him. Then I lost him."

Gray brought up a forkful of rice. He wondered where the conversation was going.

"I first met Rick when I was in grade school. Then we went to the same high school, and we both went to UCLA. I don't remember when I didn't know him, and I always knew that I would one day marry him. It was just a given in my life."

She was looking fully at him, so he thought there would be little risk in turning to her to listen. She might not snap at him for staring at her. Her eyes shimmered with reflected firelight.

Adrian went on, her voice a whisper above sounds of the fire and storm. "When I heard Rick died, I died, too, everything except my pulse. I became an empty shell with nothing inside."

"It must have been hard." About as inane a comment as possible, but he could think of no other.

"I have a few seconds of happiness each day just after I wake up in the morning. Then I realize again that Rick is gone. Every morning I endure again the crushing return of his loss."

Gray nodded his understanding.

"Do you know that I haven't dated anyone since he died? I doubt that little fact was in Pete's file."

"In four years?"

She smiled and shook her head. "Four years. And you can infer all you want from that about my sex life, and you'll be right."

"It's not my province to infer anything about you. And besides, I'm too gentlemanly." He chewed several peas. "Not in four years?" He wanted to add that it was a terrible waste, but thought better of it.

She renewed her smile. "It's a terrible waste, right? I've heard that before from guys trying to put the make on me."

"But not from me."

"When I get hormonal urges, I go to my martial arts gym and use a striking bag. An hour's worth usually does it." She ate some of the rice, then said, "From what I understand, you are like me."

Gray shrugged. "I get out once in a while."

She laughed. "Yes, to the zoo or a children's museum or McDonald's for Happy Meals."

He rubbed the side of his nose. "I know what you are doing, Adrian."

"Yes?"

"You are opening up to me, confiding your deepest wound and

177

the great secret of your sex life. But you and Pete Coates are alike, always on the job.''

She again sipped her wine.

"You believe that I have something hidden in my past that will help your investigation," Gray said. "You think that if you bare your soul to me I'll reciprocate, that I'll reveal my past so you can clinically examine it like some coroner picking apart a body.''

She grinned at him. "It's working, isn't it?''

"Not at all.''

"Sure it is. The fire, this remote cabin, the storm outside, the delicious food, me. You are yearning to tell me your secret. The urge is overwhelming.''

"I don't feel any such urge." Gray turned back to the fire.

"I can outlast you.''

"Outlast me?" He tried to add a touch of scorn to his voice but failed. "You don't know anything about endurance. You don't know—''

He abruptly rose and walked into the kitchen. He returned with a wineglass. He held up the glass to fill it precisely halfway. "Half a glass and I'll still have all my reflexes.'' He took a drink of the chardonnay, then returned to the couch.

"Tell me your secret," she demanded softly. She crossed her legs and leaned back against the armrest as if expecting a long confession.

Gray swallowed more wine.

"A line of perspiration has appeared on your forehead, Owen.''

"This sofa is too close to the fire.''

She laughed lightly. "You are sweating because you are about to break. You are desperate to tell me, someone who will under-stand.''

He waved his hand in dismissal.

"You don't have a choice," she said. "Tell me.''

Gray swallowed. His throat was dry. He held the glass with both hands. The fire swayed and flashed and hooked its tongues of flame, curling around the logs and twining together and pulling apart. It was enticing him, beguiling him. Tendrils of her scent reached for him, a light gardenia. The wind coursing through the trees had gained a low musical, pulsing quality. The air had become dense. Gray was having trouble breathing.

"You've put something in my wine," he protested feebly.

"It only feels like it. You were about to tell me."

"I . . . can't."

Her voice brushed him. "Tell me."

An age passed.

"That number." The words at last escaped his mouth. "Ninety-six."

"The number of your kills in Vietnam." She was utterly still, perhaps not wanting to derail Gray by a movement.

"That's the number that brought me fame in the Marine Corps, that got a rifle range named after me at Quantico, that got the stories in the *Marine Times* about the so-called legend. And my ex-wife and the army psychiatrists thought that number was the source of all my problems. The doctors talked about the patriotism of that number, of a soldier doing his duty. My wife kept asking what it was like to look through crosshairs at ninety-six people."

She lowered her chin slightly, a delicate encouragement.

"The number wasn't ninety-six." He emptied his glass. "It was ninety-seven." He had said it. She had broken him. Gray looked at her, but her face carried no trace of a victor's smirk.

"Ninety-seven," she said, not a question.

He turned back to the fire. Blue flames purled around the bottom of the logs. "My last shot in Vietnam. In Elephant Valley, or at least that's what the Marines called it. My spotter Allen Berkowitz and I had been out for three days. We hadn't had any luck. I don't like to look back and think I was impatient and careless, but of course I was. Berkowitz didn't see them, but I did, the telltale three white dots of a human in the brush, the face and two hands. And a flash of reflected light from a scope or binoculars. We knew we were in enemy territory. No friendlies anywhere near. So I aimed and fired as fast as I could, thinking the flash might be a scope and the enemy had me in it." Gray's eyes dropped from the fire to the stone hearth.

"Go on," Adrian whispered.

A moment passed, then he said, "My kill fell out of the bush where he had been hiding." Gray placed his glass on the table. His hands were trembling, and the base of the glass rattled on the tabletop. "He was an American. A Marine sniper."

With two fingers, Adrian gently touched her chin, as if exploring a bruise. "Are you sure?"

"He was wearing a Marine Corps field uniform and he was a

179

Caucasian. And the only whites operating in the area were Marine Corps snipers. We usually stay away from each other's territories, but somehow our signals got crossed.''

"Did you recognize him? Was he someone from your unit?''

"I didn't get close to him. I couldn't. A look through Berkowitz's binoculars was enough, though. It was a good shot, a head shot, right through his nose. Blood and gore and brains were all over his face as he lay there. He was as dead as I've seen anybody, and I saw a lot of dead people. Mostly people I made dead.''

"Was it someone from your unit?''

"We all were accounted for that evening. But there were other Marine sniper companies in Elephant Valley. They suffered losses all the time. It's the nature of the profession that sometimes snipers don't come back from patrol.''

"And you didn't report this to your commander?''

Gray moved his head left and right, an almost imperceptible motion. "I didn't have the courage. I never learned who my victim was.''

"Did Allen Berkowitz have the same trouble you had coping with this?''

"Berkowitz was killed by mortar fire two days after I left Vietnam.'' Gray continued with his dinner, chewing mechanically and tasting nothing.

"What happened after the accident?'' she asked.

"The old-fashioned term for it is a mental breakdown. I had one. My captain found me sobbing, sitting on an upside-down bucket near the latrine. He hid me for several days, thinking I'd come out of it, but I didn't. So he drove me to the Fourth Marine Division Hospital at Phu Bai. They locked me up in a padded ward in a MUST. The kook cell.''

"A must?''

"Medical Unit Self-Contained Transportable, a portable hospital that looks like an immense inflated tube.''

"You attempted suicide?''

"I don't remember it very well because of the medication the doctors were giving me at the division hospital. I took a couple of stabs at my wrist with a scalpel I stole from a surgery cart.''

Adrian reached for his left wrist. She pushed back his sleeve. Pink scars were only slightly visible on the underside of his wrist. She said, "These don't look too bad.''

"After I got to New York, I had a plastic surgeon work on the wrist. So now I can pass it off as a childhood accident with a pop bottle."

She looked at his other arm. "You only took the scalpel to one wrist?"

"It hurt too much." He smiled weakly. "I quit after the first wrist."

"What about the scar on your neck Pete Coates talks about. Let me see it."

He pulled down the neck of his sweatshirt.

She said, "It looks like an egg fried over easy."

"The plastic surgeon worked on this, too. You should see the 'before' pictures."

"Any more scars?"

"Couple puncture scars on my arms and legs that don't amount to anything. And I clipped the side of my foot with a .22 bullet when I was seven years old." He tried to generate a waggish tone, but his voice wasn't cooperating. "I still wear a crease of red skin there. Want to see it?"

"I think I'll pass." She finished her wine.

He said, "You are the second person I've ever mentioned the ninety-seventh kill to. You and Mrs. Orlando. You've hypnotized me somehow."

"You didn't tell your ex-wife?"

"Cathryn couldn't handle ninety-six. No sense telling her about the last one."

"Why did she marry you if she couldn't reconcile you with your past?"

Gray spread his hands. "I lied to her about it. At first I told her I was an infantryman in Vietnam and only saw a little action, nothing much."

"When did you tell her you were a sniper?"

"Two years into our marriage I figured Cathryn knew me well enough—knew my good qualities, knew that I wasn't crazy, knew that it was behind me—that she could handle the news."

"But she couldn't."

Gray exhaled slowly. "She couldn't come to grips with me peering through a scope at ninety-six human beings and pulling the trigger. I argued. Christ, I argued. A war was on. They were the enemy. I was doing my duty. Made no difference to her." Gray wet his lower lip with his tongue. "I'm not sure I blame her. It's a hard number, ninety-six. Tough to push it around and come up with anything redeeming. It hit her hard, I guess." Gray paused, then decided to risk the confidence. "We never made love again, not once, after she learned I was a sniper."

"Have you come to grips with it?"

"The first ninety-six, yes. But the last one—the American I left dead in the Vietnam bush, and forever left his family wondering— is something . . ." Gray hesitated and again looked at Adrian Wade. He measured his words. "It's an inescapable pit of agony for me. That terrible moment is always present, every hour of the day and many hours of the night. You'd think a tough ex-Marine and federal prosecutor like me would be able to deal with it, but I never have. I make do, with my kids, with my job." His voice was barely audible. "But I know now that number ninety-seven is never going to go away."

They stared into the fire for a few moments. The fury of it had abated and now the flames leisurely worked on the blackened logs. Embers glowed at the base of the fire. Smoke twisted and rose up the chimney.

She gently patted his arm. "I'm going to turn in. You'll talk about this more tomorrow, won't you? You won't clam up?"

"Feel free to interrogate me further. It's your job, after all."

She smiled good night at him. She put her plate in the kitchen on her way to his parents' room, where he had made the bed earlier in the day. She closed the door behind her.

Owen Gray sat on the couch another two hours, utterly still, gazing at the fire. When he rose to go to his bedroom only blood-red embers remained.

❖　　　　　❖　　　　　❖

"Are you on the run?" Andy Ellison asked, bringing his cup of chamomile tea to his lips. The hands shook uncontrollably, and the tea splashed over the cup's sides. His voice was as steady as he could make it but still sounded like he was entering puberty. The rush of confidence he had felt on learning this man was not a DEA agent had quickly evaporated.

"On the run?"

"A fugitive?" Ellison had quickly determined that the stranger

knew no colloquialisms or slang, even the most common phrases.
The foreigner had learned English from a book, probably an old
book.

"Yes."

Ellison sipped the tea, wishing he could control his hands. He
was terrified of this big man with the dent in his head and the bony
face. The man's eyes were curiously flat, and they seemed to look
through things rather than at them. His large nylon bag was on the
floor near his feet.

"Who is looking for you?"

"U.S. Immigration Service."

"They want to send you back? To where?"

"To Russia." The big man plunged a cleaning rod into the barrel
of the Moisin-Nagant rifle. A scope was mounted on the rifle.

"You handle that weapon like you know what you are doing."
Ellison was determined to get this man to like him and therefore
spare him.

The Russian said nothing, working the rod in and out. Half of
the items in the farmhouse would have been recognized by the
homesteader who built the place a hundred years before—the pine
table and primitive chairs, the rocking chair, the washstand, a hur-
ricane lamp, the glass doorknobs, and the lacy curtains. The homesteader would have been clueless about Ellison's additions—the
poster of John Lennon, a wood tie-dye frame, a glass and brass
hookah, a boom box near a rack of Grateful Dead and Jimi Hendrix
and Janis Joplin CDs, a well-thumbed 1969 Volkswagen van repair
manual, an incense bowl, and a bead curtain that hung in the door
to the kitchen.

The Russian abruptly asked, "Have you ever been in prison?"

Ellison hesitated, wondering if he was being asked to incriminate
himself. Then he said, "Yes."

Trusov wrapped a new patch around the tip of the cleaning rod
and reinserted the rod into the barrel. "In the United States?"

"Yes, in California and Washington State."

"The prisons here are . . ." Trusov paused, apparently searching for the word. "Are fun."

Ellison was affronted. "Fun?"

"Not like in Russia."

"It was hardly fun," Ellison said petulantly. "And for what? I
was just trying to make a living. I'm never going back to prison."

He decided the huge stranger probably didn't want to hear any more whining, so he asked, "What were you in for?"

No answer, so Ellison tried, "Why were you sent to prison?"

"I wounded a Red Army officer."

"Accidentally?"

Trusov's mouth cranked up into what might have been a grin. "No." Then he returned his gaze to the window or perhaps he was staring at the blank wall above the window. After a moment he said, "I was in the army's First District Prison. It was called"— he glanced at Ellison as if for help with the language, then he tried —"boulder house?"

"Probably stonehouse. That's more poetic."

"Stonehouse, because its walls are made of a stone and concrete mix. It's near Podolsk, forty kilometers south of Moscow. The comforts of American prisons are not at the Stonehouse."

"Sounds like you did hard time."

"Twenty percent of Stonehouse inmates die each year. Some freeze. Some starve. Some kill themselves. Some just show up missing on the prison's papers."

"The prison's records," Ellison helped.

Trusov nodded. "Every day we would march out chained together for road work. Sometimes the snow on the sides of the road was over our heads. Sometimes ice would form on our faces and beards as we worked. If a prisoner fell, he was left on the road until night, when a truck would pick him up, pick the body up."

Ellison nodded, taking more tea. The Russian's hands were busy with his weapon, but he continued to stare at the wall.

"The cell . . . the alone cell."

"Solitary confinement."

"It was ten meters below ground, a three-meter-by-three-meter hole. No light. No toilet. No clothes."

"They took your clothes away in solitary?"

"First they beat you, then they take your clothes away." Trusov turned away from the wall to pull back his right cheek with a finger. His upper molars were missing. "A rifle butt."

"Is that also how you got that crease on your head?"

Trusov turned back to the window. "I was in the Stonehouse eight years, and I spent over five hundred days in that cell, two hundred of those days for my walk to Riga."

"You escaped?"

Trusov nodded. "I ran from the work line, ran across a field, the guards shooting, but they were poor shots, like most soldiers everywhere. I walked eight hundred kilometers west, with no papers or money, and only my prison clothes."

"But you were recaptured?

"The Riga KGB. I don't know how they found me, but they took me back. When my time was over, I was given a new suit of clothes and two hundred rubles, and I walked out the Stonehouse's gate. I weighed seventy kilograms."

Ellison's eyes widened. Like all folks in his business he was good at metric conversions. "You weighed a hundred and fifty-five pounds?" The Russian appeared to now weigh close to two-twenty, all muscle and bone. He had indeed served hard time.

"You hungry?" Ellison asked.

"I was always hungry."

"I mean now. I've got dinner on the stove. There's enough for two." He pushed aside strings of beads and disappeared into the kitchen. He returned with two soup bowls, spoons, and a loaf of bread.

Trusov carefully placed the rifle across the table to accept the bowl. He dug into it with a spoon, turning the steaming contents over. Finally he asked, "Where's the meat?"

With proud defiance Ellison replied, "I don't eat meat."

"What is this?"

"Rice and beans and corn in a tomato base. Some oregano and garlic."

Trusov ate several spoonfuls, then pronounced, "You are a hippie."

Ellison beamed. "Yes, yes I am. How do you know about hippies?"

"I read about them in Red Army school at Rostok, a political class, a class about America. But I thought all hippies were gone many years ago."

"Not many of us are still around," Ellison conceded. "Only the strong of heart and the pure of purpose."

The Russian tore off a hunk of the bread and used it to ladle the soup into his mouth.

Ellison asked tentatively, "Why are the U.S. Immigration authorities looking for you?"

"After my release from Stonehouse, I was not supposed to leave

185

the First Military District. A condition of my release. But I did. I came here. Now the Red Army has asked the U.S. police to look for me.''

That made sense to Ellison, except for one thing. ''Why did you come to the U.S.?''

The Russian chewed. ''I need to stay here tonight. I will go in the morning.''

''Sure,'' Ellison said quickly. He wasn't going to press this man for answers. But he was emboldened by the man's statement that he was journeying on after a night's sleep. His hands were calming. After several more spoonfuls of soup Ellison ventured, ''Can I ask where are you going?''

''To your state of Idaho. I'm meeting someone in Idaho.''

✧   ✧   ✧

''Three minutes,'' the pilot called over his shoulder. Bruce Taylor had flown for the U.S. Army for eight years until joining the FBI. He wore a holster strapped to the leg of his blue flight suit. He scanned his gauges, then ordered loudly, ''Check your safety harnesses.''

''You ever done this before?'' shouted the FBI agent next to Coates.

''All the time.''

''You don't look too comfortable in that flak jacket.''

Coates yelled above the scream of the General Electric free-turbine engines, ''Don't worry about me, sonny. I'll do fine. That son of a bitch'll regret the day he came here.''

The agent grinned. ''The Russian's got your goat, sounds like.''

''Something like that.'' Coates pulled his service pistol from under the jacket. He checked the load.

''Why don't you trade in that nosepicker for some pop.'' The agent's name was Ray Reardon. He held up his assault rifle. ''With this you just point and spray.''

Coates shook his head. It was hard to think in the belly of the Sikorsky Black Hawk. The engines roared and the blades pounded and the wind whipped by. The helicopter rose and fell with sickening abruptness as the pilot followed the terrain. Coates and three FBI agents sat in the waist. The agents wore bush coats over their Kevlar vests, and ''FBI'' was inked on the back of the coats, hardly noticeable amid the green and brown camouflage colors. Their faces were blackened. Coates had been so awkward applying the grease paint Reardon had finished the job for him. Between the agents' knees rested their M16s. At the rear of the compartment were two litters. They were approaching the farmhouse at 150 miles an hour.

Across from Coates was an agent named Buddy Riggs who had earlier told the detective he had earned a business degree and had become a certified public accountant, but after two years found the profession was "not meeting my needs for personal growth," so he had joined the Navy and had become a SEAL, then had gone on to the FBI. Riggs was missing an eyebrow, and it looked as if it had been burned off. Coates hadn't asked him about it. Next to Riggs was John Ward, a blunt-nosed special agent Reardon had said could do six hundred push-ups.

Reardon and Riggs and Ward were members of an FBI organization called Inter-Agency SWAT. These men were often called to assist sheriffs' departments and police forces who abruptly found themselves over their heads.

This helicopter was one prong of a three-way deployment. The Black Hawk was going to land a mile north of the farmhouse in a clearing that was close enough to the farm to walk in but far enough away so the Russian would not hear the approach. Another copter was landing two miles south of the farmhouse in a field. Yet more agents and police were hiking in from the highway and the dirt road. They would have the Russian surrounded.

"Here we go," yelled the pilot.

The helicopter sank and Coates's belly rose in his throat. The pink sky of dawn was visible through the portholes in the fuselage. Then the view turned dark green as the Black Hawk dipped into the trees. Dust and leaves blew up and the blades gained an even deeper throb. The pilot was skilled, and Coates did not know the helicopter was on the ground until Reardon slid open the hatch.

The detective popped open his harness and crouched low to approach the pilot. He tapped the pilot on the shoulder. "Keep your engines idling." He touched the radio in his pocket. "We may have to call you in."

The pilot nodded.

Coates dropped through the hatch to the ground. He squinted against the swirling dust. The turbines still shrieked. The FBI team waited for Coates to lead off. This was his show. The detective crouched low under the spinning blades even though they cleared his head by eight feet.

"You ready, boys?"

Reardon gave the stock of his assault rifle an affectionate squeeze. "We're always ready."

The detective brought up his wristwatch. "The farmhouse is a mile south. We've got eighteen minutes to get there. It's broken ground but fairly open. Let's go."

Coates led them away, the FBI agents running like infantrymen, their weapons across their chests, while Coates stumbled ahead, unused to traversing ground that wasn't paved. The sun had just begun its climb in the east.

The pilot watched them go. The detective and the agents crossed the meadow single-file, heading for the trees. Special Agent Ward brought up the rear, occasionally glancing back at the helicopter, checking the avenue of retreat in the best infantry-school fashion.

Dust blown up from the blades had coated the inside of the copter's windscreen. Taylor kept a soft cloth at his feet. He swatted the rag against the glass, brushing away the dust.

Just as the pilot's eyes refocused through the windshield, a red halo abruptly formed around Ward's head. Mist and light swirled and flickered. Ward crumpled to the ground and was still.

The pilot squinted. The distance and the sun reflecting off his windshield made Taylor unsure what he had just seen. All he could hear was the Black Hawk's turbines.

The three men ahead—ducks in a row—were unaware Ward had fallen. They had apparently heard nothing. They continued to cross the field to the pines. With Ward down, the last man in the single file was now Buddy Riggs. The pilot saw Riggs's head blur red. Riggs fell.

Coates and Reardon marched ahead, the detective in the lead. They were almost to the trees.

The pilot leaned out the hatch to scream a warning, but the sound was lost in the noise of the turbines.

Then Ray Reardon's head flew apart and he collapsed onto the cheat grass. The three shots had taken less than ten seconds.

Panting and oblivious, Coates reached the trees. He glanced at his watch, then lifted a compass from a pocket. "Due south. We've got a lot of time." He turned around to confer with the team.

And only then did he see the horror, all three down and bloodied, a ghastly trail of bodies.

Coates dropped to the ground before he fully understood what had happened. His instinct saved his life, as the fourth bullet, the one intended for him, smacked into a lodgepole pine near where his head had been an instant before. Coates crawled behind a tree.

Taylor fought with himself. He might be able to help here on the ground, but all his training told him a helicopter was useless when idle. He decided he would get airborne, he would radio for help, and he then would try to extricate Coates.

Taylor engaged the rotors. The engines began to wind up. Twigs and grass and dirt whirled up.

The pilot yelped as the hot bore of a rifle was pressed into his neck.

A voice from behind. "Go up. Go west." The words were slow and bent by an accent.

The killer had climbed into the fuselage. He must have been shooting from behind the helicopter.

Again the careful words, "Go up. Go west. Listen to me."

The Black Hawk lifted off and gained elevation quickly, then banked away from the sun. Trees and fields slipped by below.

From behind came "Pick him up."

At first Taylor didn't know what the voice was referring to, but a hand came forward and pointed out the knee hatch.

A man was running wildly across a field, all legs and arms, churning away. The man stumbled and fell. He gazed fearfully over his shoulder, then scrambled up and started off again.

"Pick him up," the man behind ordered again. "I need bait."

The pilot narrowed his eyes. Perhaps it was a trick of the dawn light, but it appeared the runner below was wearing a tie-dyed T-shirt. Taylor hadn't seen one in twenty years. He did not know what the man behind him meant by bait.

With the rifle barrel still against his neck, Taylor put the Black Hawk down in a field near the runner, who crazily veered away, running and limping and working his arms against the air, in a panic.

The gunman leaned out the hatch and beckoned once, then again, and when Andy Ellison dared to look over his shoulder again, he saw the Russian signaling him. Ellison slowed, then stopped. He gritted his teeth with indecision. Grinning, the Russian waved at him again. Ellison bolted for the helicopter, stumbling over straw and stones, looking left and right, blowing like a bellows.

Wetting his lips with his tongue, Taylor watched. The gunman helped the hippie into the copter's waist. His Moisin-Nagent on the pilot, the killer pointed skyward. The copter lifted off again.

Ellison slumped onto a jump seat. He was unable to catch his breath. He wiped his hands across his forehead. His jeans were soiled and torn. With trembling hands he removed his spectacles to straighten the wire frame.

He managed, "The DEA. They were after me. Christ, there were dozens of them, maybe hundreds."

The Russian grinned as he helped Ellison into a safety harness. "It is dangerous being around you marijuana farmers."

Ellison barked a laugh of relief. "Good God, yes. But it doesn't look like I'm going back to prison. Today, anyway. Thanks to you."

Trusov buckled himself in, the rifle still on the pilot. "No, neither of us is going to prison."

✧   ✧   ✧

Owen Gray lowered the M-40A1 sniper rifle to the apple box. He picked up a bowl of Wheaties. Also on the apple crate were a carton of milk, a box of cereal, and cleaning and oiling equipment. The rifle was fully assembled. He put the bowl under his chin and shoveled flakes into his mouth with a spoon. He was sitting on the porch, the apple box to one side. He chewed mechanically, his eyes on the big larch tree. The ground was damp from the rain, but a gray weeping dawn had given way to blue sky. An Idaho State Patrol car was parked on the other side of the tree. Two troopers leaned against the front hood. One carried an automatic shotgun. They were eating a breakfast sandwich brought up from Ketchum.

Adrian emerged from the cabin squinting at the morning light. She was wearing a white terry-cloth robe that had a red rose stitched over her heart. She was barefoot and wore no makeup. She ran her hand several times through her hair, then stepped toward one of the cane chairs Gray had moved onto the porch. Gray thought she looked alluringly undone.

She stopped near him. "Cereal? I thought you mountain men ate moose and moss for breakfast."

He chewed a moment more, then said, "I told you I caught the trout we ate last night, but actually I bought the fish down in Ketchum."

She raised a hand against the sun. "Why the fib?"

"To see if you knew anything about the outdoors. You don't."

"How could I have known you didn't catch the fish?" Her frown reflected her disapproval.

Gray dug the spoon into the cereal. "The fins of a hatchery fish are worn down and nipped. Its pectoral fins may be missing altogether."

"Why?"

"Fins wear off on the concrete runways. And during feeding time the fish in their frenzy bite each other's fins. Wild fish are prettier, with full rays to their pectorals and dorsal fins. Those trout we ate were raised on a farm down in southern Idaho, probably near Hagerman. No outdoors person would mistake wild trout for farm-raised trout."

"Well, golly," she said in broad hick's accent, "I sure am dumb and you sure are smart."

Gray wiped the corner of his mouth with a finger. "I learned quickly in Vietnam to always test my partners. I need to know what you know and use what you know and make allowances for what you don't. I'm not going to let my life depend on a stranger."

"I don't know anything about the wilderness." She walked behind him toward the south end of the porch. She gripped her bathrobe around her. "If you had simply asked, I would have admitted it. Like, if I ask if you know anything about being a dolt, you can admit that you do."

Gray mumbled around a mouthful of cereal, "Don't get yourself bitten by a rattlesnake."

"Thank you, Marlin Perkins," she replied. "I won't."

"Yes you will, if you take three more steps toward the end of the porch."

Adrian's hands came up as if someone had thrown her a basketball. Her mouth widened. She danced backwards, away from the chair and the reptile that was near it.

The rattlesnake was lying half on and half off the south edge of the porch, absorbing the early morning sun, its flat head on the wood and its rattles over the side. With the black and white diamond patterns on its back, the rattler's scales resembled bathroom tiles.

"Goddamnit, Owen, you let me get too close to that snake."

"You were perfectly safe. They crawl, they don't fly."

"What's it going to do?" Adrian's voice carried a trace of fear unsuccessfully masked.

"It's going to sit there until the sun goes behind a tree or a until a mouse comes along, whichever happens first. They don't move much on hot days."

"Get rid of it. Shoo it away. Look, it's staring at me."

Gray lowered the bowl to the apple box. He crossed the porch, passing Adrian toward the snake. The snake's tail came up as its body contracted into a loose coil.

"Rattlers are less dangerous than people think," Gray said. "Watch this."

The snake's rattles—a series of horny buttons at the end of its tail—trilled loudly, sounding more like an electric spark than a baby's toy, a throat-grabbing, relentless, sinister burr. Gray slowly moved his right hand away from his body. The snake's villainous eyes followed the hand. Its forked tongue flashed in and out and its scales glimmered in the sun. While the snake's head was turning, Gray's other hand shot out and snatched the rattler just below its head. The reptile squirmed frantically as Gray lifted it. The snake wrapped itself around Gray's wrist and forearm. Adrian had stepped back as far as the door. Her right hand was at her mouth.

"My father and I tried venom harvesting for a while. We'd catch a rattler like this, then press open its mouth with our thumb."

When Gray pressured the back of the snake's head, its mouth opened, revealing its half-inch fangs below pink fang sheaths.

"We used to collect the venom in bottles," Gray said.

Glittering liquid appeared at the tip of the fang. Several drops fell to the porch.

"I saved my father's life once," Gray said, still holding the rattlesnake's head in Adrian's direction. "We were climbing a steep embankment and my dad was reaching up for a handhold when his hand found a rattler sleeping in the sun. The snake bit him on the back of the hand. So I got out a knife, cut little Xs where the fangs had punctured the skin, and sucked the venom out. My dad said later he was lucky the snake didn't bite him on the ass, because I would have sat there and watched him die."

Gray stepped down from the porch, peeled the diamondback from around his arm, and tossed the snake toward the remnants of the woodshed. The rattler crawled quickly under a pile of shingles.

Adrian exhaled loudly. "What an incredible showoff you are."

"But you have to admit you are impressed."

After a moment, she grinned. "A little."

Gray returned to the apple crate. He poured more Wheaties and milk, wiped the spoon on his trousers, then handed her the bowl and spoon.

He lifted the sniper rifle. "Scientists should study rifles more."

Around the Wheaties in her mouth, she said, "They should study you more."

"I've never fully understood everything a rifle does, but one thing I've noticed is that the weapon slows time. The passing day has a curious dilation whenever I hold a rifle. Tell me what you hear when I fire this rifle."

Gray yelled a warning to the troopers that he was about to use the weapon, then tucked the butt into his shoulder, aimed the rifle at a tree stump off to his left, and pulled the trigger. The rifle sounded loudly. Rotted pieces of bark jumped away from the stump, leaving a small black hole in the old wood.

She looked at him quizzically. "I heard a rifle shot, then some echoing from the mountains."

"But there was much more." Gray returned the rifle to the box. "The sound began with a fierce little slap, like metal on metal. Then came a brief pause full of rushing wind. Next came a bass thump, followed by a trumpeter with a mute making a wa-wa-wa tone. After that came the roar of passing train. When that trailed away, the echoing began. The sound was full of nuances."

"You sound like one of those snooty wine critics. They say it has a nice nose and a pleasant but presumptuous fullness when all they've really got is a simple glass of wine."

"It isn't just the rifle shot I'm talking about. When I'm holding a weapon, everything seems in slow motion, like everything is moving underwater. It's an odd effect and beyond my explanation."

She smiled. "Did these Wheaties stay crisp in the milk longer?"

He stared at her. "Maybe I should be talking to that rattlesnake."

Her spoon paused over the bowl. "The victim never hears anything, does he?"

"The bullet gets to him before the sound does."

"That's eerie," she said with a subdued voice.

Gray's gaze was again on the tree. He whispered, "He never hears a thing."

13

"THE DAMNED THING is reaching for me!" Pete Coates exclaimed, kicking his right foot. "Christ, that hurts."

"Watch where you're walking," Gray said mildly. "And it's only a wild blackberry vine. It won't kill you."

"Goddamnit, it's torn my new pants. I just bought these new slacks at Moe Ginsburg's last week."

The blackberry had sharp spines on almost every part of it—the leaves and leaf stalks, and on the grasping vines, where they were curved like talons. This plant had grown over a mountain maple, smothering it, and had reached along the path for more victims. It had found Coates, or rather Coates had found it.

"Is it any wonder I hate leaving New York?" With two fingers Coates pried the blackberry vine away from his pants leg. "It's got my thumb now." He flicked his hand. Blood oozed from the meat of his thumb.

"Looks like Central Park is about all the wilderness you can handle, Pete."

Gray and the detective were walking downstream along Black Bear Creek a hundred yards from the cabin. Gray carried the Weatherby Magnum on a sling over his shoulder. He was also wearing a backpack over a duck-hunting vest. A deer path shadowed the stream, curving with it, never straying far from the bubbling, swirling water. The trail was so narrow that Gray and Coates had to walk single file. Boulders edged some of the stream, and dark pools of still water gathered behind them. The current slipped from behind rocks, cascading in white and blue to the next pool. Sword and maidenhair ferns edged the water with their pure green, a color Idahoans believe with some justification occurs only in their state. A willow trailed its branches in the water, the current tugging at its leaves. The stream's sibilant whisper was mixed with the mirthful, flutey trill of a western tanager high in an aspen above the water.

They came to a larger pool ringed with small-leafed plants growing in patches as thick as a mat. The plants were anchored in the mud, with buoyant stems and leaves above the water. Gray brought out a plastic bag from his backpack, stooped over the pool, and tore bunches of the plant away from the water. He put several handfuls into the plastic bag before returning the bag to the pack.

"What is that?" the detective asked.

"Watercress."

"It grows in streams?"

"Where did you think it came from?"

Coates shrugged. "From grocery stores."

Gray shook his head. "Don't get near those stinging nettles." He waved a hand at a five-foot-tall bank of nettles in front of them. The stem, leaf stalks, and veins on the undersurface of the leaves had stinging hairs that injected poison into skin like hypodermic needles. Gray had to turn sideways to slip between the nettles and the water, sidestepping on a narrow ledge.

"You think I'm a city slicker who doesn't know nettles when he sees them," Coates groused.

He followed Gray, scooting along sideways, hanging his hands out over the creek away from the nettle leaves. The path turned away from the creek for a few yards. They walked over goose grass and creeping buttercup. The stream flowed through a ravine filled with hemlock and mountain laurel. Leaves were still damp from the storm the night before, but the strip of sky visible above Gray, seen from the shadows of the ravine, was rinsed and smiling and lapis blue. Gray smelled the pungent treacly odor of yarrow. The Shoshone had brewed a tea from its fernlike leaves. They passed several bunches of the plant.

Gray looked over his shoulder. "You ever been out here be-fore?"

"Never."

"You'll like Idaho."

"In New York we pronounce it 'Iowa.' "

"Did you bring any outdoor clothing?"

"I wear a tie when I'm on business." Coates's gray sports coat was dappled with water spots from the leaves. He wore a red tie and white shirt. His pants cuffs were ragged from the vines. "And when you said your place was in the mountains, I sort of envi-sioned the Poconos, not this wild place. Aren't you supposed to put asphalt on these paths, and handrails?"

Gray had picked up Pete Coates at the Hailey airport two hours ago, a Horizon Air flight up from Twin Falls. During the drive, Coates had told Gray of the murder of the three FBI agents. Gray had never before seen the detective's hands tremble. Now, feeling each owed it to the other, both men were trying to generate a good humor neither felt.

"Watch the creek bank," Gray said. "It's soft here."

"Where?" As Coates asked, the bank crumbled under his feet and his left leg plunged into the water to his knee. The creek boiled around his leg and wicked up his pants to his crotch. He flailed the air wildly before his hands seized a laurel branch to lever himself out.

"There," Gray said.

He began climbing out of the ravine along a path he had known since he could walk, a trail so stitched into his memory that a growth of moss on a feldspar outcropping caught his eye as new, and a stretch of stones near the rim of the creek canyon was brighter than he remembered; and when he glanced skyward he saw that the bathtub-sized raven's nest that had been in the nearby aspen for a generation was gone, perhaps blown down in a storm, allowing more sun to reach the ground.

Pete Coates scrabbled up the path behind Gray, leaving a wet shoe print every other step. His damp trousers clung to his leg. His eyeglasses flashed on and off in the dappled sunlight below the trees. Near the rim the detective's leather brogans could not find purchase on the pebbles and loose dirt, and he churned his legs, slipping with each step. Gray grabbed his wrist and lifted him over the top.

Coates shook away Gray's hand and said with indignation that was mostly mock, "You think this gives you some sort of moral authority over me, don't you? Out here in the land time forgot, showing me the ropes, watching me cope."

"One of your shirttails is out."

Coates tucked himself in. "Just like I've been showing you the ins and outs of New York all these years."

"Correct me if I'm wrong, but you asked for the tour of the property."

"Now you get the chance to lord it over this city slicker." Coates followed Gray toward the cabin. "You are positively glowing with it, parading your knowledge. You know what the biggest difference is between you and me, Owen?"

"I'm afraid to ask."

"It's this: I know crime and criminals. I know the underside of life, the rot of the big city, the vicious and the cruel, the myriad ways to squander lives, the complexity of urban life. And you know watercress."

Gray laughed.

"What happened to this garage?"

"It was a rickety old woodshed. Wind probably blew it down."

"Pretty violent storm, must've been, to hack out wood chips from the support poles just like an axe."

"You don't miss much, do you, Pete?"

They approached the home. A panel truck was parked near the porch. The vehicle was unmarked, but Gray knew it belonged to the FBI. On the porch Adrian Wade pointed directions to two technicians who carried a fax machine and computer into the house. The technicians returned to the truck to pull out a five-foot-diameter satellite dish.

Gray muttered, "She's going to make my place look like Houston Control."

A black-and-white police car was also parked on the gravel. The blue bubble was on the dashboard, not on the cab roof. On the door was a complicated insignia featuring a braying elk, a medieval gauntlet gripping a lightning bolt, a miner's shovel, and a fleur-de-lis. The insignia had resulted from a Hobart High School art class contest in the 1940s. Above the insignia were the words "Hobart Police Department." The police officer was sitting on the car's hood watching the truck being unloaded, and watching Adrian in particular.

When he saw Owen Gray, the man's face wrinkled into a grin, and he slid to the ground and crossed the gravel, hand out in front of him. He pumped Gray's hand, and then he continued to hold it, patting it like he might a child's, smiling all the while.

"Tell me you are moving back into the Sawtooths, and that handsome woman is your bride."

Gray smiled. "Walt, I'm only here for a while."

"And that's not your wife?"

"Lord, no. She's a combination ninja assassin and Grand Inquisitor, and I'm not related to her in any way." He introduced Coates to Hobart Police Chief Walt Durant.

Walt Durant had a doughy overfeatured face. His mouth was wide and his lower lip hung an inch out of his mouth and was always damp. His nose was the size of a light bulb and was lined with burst capillaries. Acne had left pits high on his neck below his ears. With small gaps between every one of his teeth, his smile resembled a picket fence. He was bald except for a horseshoe of gray hair from temple to temple. Durant was walleyed, and Gray never knew whether the chief was looking at him or staring over Gray's shoulder at something more interesting. Durant was wearing a tan uniform shirt and slacks. Above his badge were four citation plates awarded by the city council, each representing five years of distinguished service. Gray had heard the chief complain that it was cheaper for the city to give him a medal than a raise. Durant wore a holstered revolver on a Sam Browne. Also on the belt were a handcuff case and two bullet dumps. He had left his hat on the car seat.

"You carry two shields, Chief?" Coates asked, pointing to Durant's shirt pocket.

Durant lifted the second badge from his pocket. It glittered gold in the sunlight. "I'm also the Hobart fire chief. The badge I wear depends on the nature of the emergency. I'm also in charge of the Hobart sanitary landfill." The police chief brightened. "Another job I had once was a bounty counter."

"A bounty hunter?" Coates asked.

"A counter. The federal government back in the early sixties offered a bounty for coyotes. You remember that, Owen? You and your old man brought in two hundred fifty coyotes in one month. Most ever, I'd bet. I'd pay you ten dollars for every set of coyote ears you and Dalton brung me. That's still talked about in this town, Pete, two hundred fifty coyotes in thirty-one days." Durant whistled appreciatively.

Durant had been Dalton Gray's closest friend, the first visitor to the house when Owen had been born. Decades later, as Dalton was being lowered into the ground in the Hobart cemetery, Durant had told Gray in a breaking voice, "In the future, if you need anything from a father, you ask me, Owen."

The police chief said, "You haven't mentioned what brings you out here, Pete."

While Coates told Chief Durant about Nikolai Trusov, Gray crossed the lot to enter the cabin. He returned a few minutes later carrying sandwiches piled high on a plate. He stopped at the porch to hand some out to Adrian Wade and the two techs, then returned to Coates and Durant. They helped themselves.

"What's in it?" Coates asked, lifting the top slice of bread like a flap.

"Watercress, a lot of butter, and salt."

"Where's the pastrami? It's like you've given me two bookends with nothing in between." The detective bit into it, then admitted, "Not bad."

"And what makes you think the Russian is coming to Hobart?" Durant asked.

"We put two facts together. One, Trusov is heading west. And two, Owen is here."

"How does this Trusov know where Owen is?"

"I haven't figured that out," Coates replied, glancing at Gray. "Trusov knows Owen was raised in the Sawtooths, because he had a copy of his high school annual and he's seen Owen's service record. Maybe he's just guessing Owen has returned home."

"So what are you proposing we do?" Durant asked.

"I tried to erect a series of concentric circles around Manhattan, circles of people looking for Trusov. But he got outside them all. Now I'm going to put the same circles around Hobart, hoping I can spot Trusov coming in."

"And you want my help," Durant said skeptically. "To protect Owen here? Owen can probably take care of himself."

The detective said, "My task force isn't assigned to protect Owen. Its job is to catch this murderer."

"A task force," the sheriff repeated. He looked at Owen, his eyes mirroring his mirth. "An entire task force?"

"I'm going to make it impossible for Nikolai Trusov to come to this area without being noticed, I'll guarantee you that."

From a coat pocket Coates removed a contour interval map of the area. The map had a 1/250,000 scale, with contours every hundred feet. The detective asked questions about the lay of the land, about State Highway 75, which was the only paved road in and out of Hobart, and about the smaller gravel and dirt roads that wandered in a number of directions up into the mountains, short roads because the peaks east and west of the town were close. He asked about the emergency grass airfield north of Hobart, about trails that crossed the mountains on which a hiker might approach the town, about locations for highway checkpoints.

Coates finally summed up. "It looks like I'm going to need two shifts of about eighty people each. A hundred and sixty. I suppose you know most of the sheriffs and police chiefs around here."

Durant nodded. He crammed the last quarter of his sandwich into his mouth. A stray watercress leaf escaped his jaws and floated to the ground.

"Will they loan you their people?"

"As many as they can spare." The police chief produced a can of Copenhagen from his pants pocket. He tapped the lid before opening it, then held the tin out. Gray and Coates declined. The chief inserted a wad of tobacco behind his lower lip.

They were standing thirty yards southwest of the house. A tangle of weeds was at their feet. Owen Gray lowered himself to his haunches and absently began pulling weeds from the ground, one at a time, throwing them off to his right. The police chief followed him down and also yanked the plants from the ground.

"And I need some of your resources. What's the size of your department?"

"You're looking at it."

"You? That's it?"

Durant put a backcountry drawl into his voice. "Hobart ain't Manhattan, Pete."

"How about communications equipment?"

201

"I don't have much, because when I'm out of the office there's no one to call at the office, and when I'm in the office there's no one out on the road."

Pete Coates also lowered himself. He imitated the others by yanking a weed from the ground and throwing it aside. "Does the Hobart Police Department have anything useful?"

"Twenty orange traffic cones."

"That's it, for Christ sake?"

"Four portable barricades, one police car, four assorted firearms, and a one-person jail that an imbecile could break out of."

The detective removed his eyeglasses to scratch the side of his nose where the tabs had left red marks. "Does your office have electricity?"

"Yep. And we get the mail whenever the river freezes over and the dogsleds can get in."

Gray and Durant continued with the weeds. The small pile of discarded plants was growing. Behind them toward the ravine was a thicket of taller weeds, these with sharply pointed elongated leaves of bright green with slight purple veins.

The detective asked, "Is there anything else you can do to help me, Chief?"

"I'll call everyone in Hobart and tell them to keep their eyes out. A stranger won't be able to belch in this town without me hearing of it."

"Can you tell me by tonight how many people you can borrow?"

"You bet."

Coates lifted a spiral notebook from his coat pocket and flipped through a few pages. He spoke for a moment about response times, about how his circle of men and women would collapse around the first location where Trusov was spotted. He used SWAT team jargon. Walt Durant pursed his lips and nodded.

"That's all I got right now." Coates returned the book to his pocket before saying, "I'm loath to display my city ignorance once again, but why are we pulling these weeds?"

"These are wild oats," Gray replied, tossing another aside.

"Aren't you supposed to sow wild oats, not pick them?" Coates asked.

"See these?" Gray held up one of the wild cereal stalks. "This bristlelike appendage that sticks out of the grain is called an awn. It can get stuck in an animal's throat and cause an infection. I lost a mule once that way. By the time I noticed the infection, the mule was a goner.''

Coates picked another oat stalk. "But you don't have any mules or horses around here now."

"I do it on principle." Gray flicked another weed onto the pile.

"We're both principled guys," Durant said.

The detective rose to his feet. "Yeah, well, you're both having fun at this big city guy's expense. But I'll tell you, the only thing I can see favorable about the mountains is that you can walk thirty feet in any direction and take a leak."

Coates turned to walk across the gravel into the taller weeds behind him. He brushed a few aside, and stepped further into the thicket. His back to Gray and Durant, he unzipped his pants. He was hidden from Adrian by a stand of mountain laurel. He said over his shoulder, "No need for pay toilets out in Idaho."

There were the sounds of a satisfied grunt, then of liquid falling onto the ground.

Chief Durant clucked his tongue and asked Gray, "You want to tell him or can I?"

"What's a friend for if he can't break bad news?" Gray called to the detective. "Hey, Pete. How you feeling about now?"

"Never better. Nothing like relieving pressure on the inner systems."

"Well, as they say in the song, 'You're going to need an ocean of calamine lotion.' "

It took Coates a moment, then he yelled, "Aw, goddamnit." He held his hands away from his body and shook them as if that might rid them of the poison oil. "Goddamnit."

Without turning, he looked over his shoulder at them. "What do I do now, for Christ sake?"

The police chief said, "I'd put your peter back in your pants, for a start."

"It'll be best if you can do it without touching it," Owen said, pulling out another wild oat stalk. "Otherwise the oil will spread and you'll end up looking like you got the Bangkok pox."

"And don't ask me to help you with the task," Durant said with a straight face. "I wouldn't get the kick out of it you might suppose."

"Goddamnit," Coates yelled again. He jiggled himself, then jumped up and down, and finally used the thumb and little finger of one hand to put himself back into his pants. Still holding one hand away from his body and high above the surrounding plants, he zipped up his pants.

"Son of a bitch." He turned on his heels. "What do I do now?"

"You wearing socks?" Durant asked. "Otherwise your ankles will get it."

"Of course I'm wearing socks. Goddamnit, get me out of here."

"Why don't you walk out like you walked in?" Gray advised. "Keep your hands up."

The detective tiptoed out of the bank of weeds. When he got back to them, he demanded, "Why didn't you tell me I was walking into poison ivy, for Christ sake?" He grabbed the back of one hand with the other. "Christ, my hands hurt already."

"Pete, you're a smart guy," Gray said, dropping the last of the wild oats onto the pile and rising to his feet. "Never in my wildest imagination did it ever occur to me that a smart guy like you would walk into a patch of poison ivy with his privates hanging out."

Durant laughed.

"I was speechless," Gray explained. "I couldn't warn you."

Coates frantically scratched the back of his hands. "Funny guy, Owen, goddamnit."

Chief Durant returned to his car. He said he'd be in touch, and then he backed around the larch tree and drove down the road, disappearing down the hill, dust rising from the car's passing.

Coates and Gray started back to the cottage. Adrian Wade and the FBI technicians were inside. Coates scratched and scratched.

The detective said, "Owen, you're having a lot of fun at my expense, looks like. But you'd better do some serious preparing for Nikolai Trusov. He's coming and I'm going to try my best to stop him, but I tried in New York and failed. I don't plan on it, but I might fail again, and then he'll show up here."

"I'm getting ready."

"Doesn't look like it to me," Coates said. "Goddamnit, I got some poison ivy on my third leg. I can feel it." He scratched his crotch.

"Follow me." Gray led the detective to the side of the cabin. As a firebreak, the wild grass and bushes were kept well away from the structure. They walked on clover and grass and pebbles around to the back of the house, to the main bedroom window at the back. Moss grew on the lower logs of the house.

"Are you jacking me around, Owen?" Coates scoffed. "Cow-bells and tin cans?"

Partially hidden in a stand of quaking aspen was a length of wire on which were three rusted cowbells and several empty cans. A trip wire was attached to the second log of the house and ran across the firebreak to the string of cans and bells.

"This looks like a kid designed it!" Coates exclaimed, working on his hands. "You don't think for one minute that Nikolai Trusov will fall for this, do you?"

"Nope." Gray stooped to lift a hand-sized rock. "But it'll take his attention off of more serious matters."

He lobbed the rock onto the ground two feet the other side of the bell-and-can alarm. The rock bounced on the leaves and grass.

The sound of an explosion filled the space between the brush and the building, a concussive wash of wind rushed past them. The air instantly filled with leaves and twigs, twisting and falling.

Coates jumped back, grimacing as if wounded. Smoke was gray and acrid, filling the air and making it shimmer. He reached under his armpit and pulled out his service revolver. "What in hell?"

A speckled pattern had appeared on the logs of the house. Some of the bird shot was visible in its craters, others had sunk further into the wood. A few pellets had dropped to the base of the building. Splinters had been torn away from several logs. Dust rose from the damaged mortar. The shot pattern was the size of a basketball.

"Jesus Christ, Owen. A spring gun?"

Gray nodded. "A 12-gauge hidden in the bush. I built a pressure plate out of some sticks."

Coates peered into the bush. "I don't see the shotgun."

"I hid it a little better than I hid the alarm. I've got five other weapons placed here and there, cocked and ready. I'll come back in a while and reset this one."

Coates returned his weapon to its holster and resumed scratching his hands and his groin. "All right. Maybe you are tak-ing Trusov seriously."

They moved toward the front of the house.

Coates asked, "Where'd you learn about spring guns?"

"In Vietnam. We'd usually set traps at rear approaches to our hides so nobody could sneak up on us. All snipers are taught about booby traps."

"I'm going to be bunking out here in Frontier Land with you,"

Coates said, biting the back of his hand for relief. "You sure you remember where you put all the guns?"

"I'll draw you a map, if you like." Gray led him to the porch. "I only hope you're not a sleepwalker."

❖   ❖   ❖

Montana State Trooper Ross Bowen lifted the plastic photo frame from his dashboard and grinned again at his new daughter. Eight pounds, seven ounces, twenty-one inches long, born six days ago, and if there was a God in heaven the girl would look like her mother. He gently tapped the photo, sending his love to his daughter. Bowen had been unprepared for the emotions that had overtaken him in the birthing room and that were still with him. His wife had laughed when he told her that food was tasting better since their daughter was born. So he hadn't told her that the Montana air seemed purer, that he could do more chin-ups than ever before, and that their Labrador retriever was more obedient. Everything was better. Bowen was suffused with parental joy.

Then the silver Honda Accord appeared in his mirror, growing quickly. Bowen didn't need to refer to his daily briefing memo and he didn't need to radio for confirmation. He knew the Accord had been stolen forty minutes before from the parking lot of a minimart. The State Patrol had assumed the Russian was behind the wheel.

Bowen's patrol car was parked behind a stone outcrop that hid much of his vehicle from westbound travelers yet allowed him to aim his mounted radar gun back east along the rising road. His radar was off, and the cone was against the windshield pillar. Trooper Bowen had viewed this duty as an opportunity to sit in the sun under his windshield and consider the good fortune of a new daughter.

The Accord tore by Bowen's patrol car. The trooper cranked over his ignition and slammed his foot down on the gas pedal. The patrol car fishtailed from the shoulder onto the asphalt. The photo of his baby fell to the floor.

The silver Accord wasn't speeding, only sixty miles an hour or so, Bowen determined as he closed the distance. He could see the back of the driver's head, but details were lost in the flashing reflection from the Accord's rear window. And there was a passenger in the car. Bowen flicked on his cherries and siren, then lifted his handset to notify the dispatcher that he would need assistance. He pulled within ten car lengths of the Accord.

To Bowen's surprise the Russian's car began slowing, and the rear blinker indicated the car was about to pull over. The trooper turned off the siren. He bit his lower lip. He had been hoping this Nikolai Trusov would outrun him, give him a reason to claim that further pursuit would have endangered civilians, which is when the Montana State Patrol regulations demanded the chase end. The Accord kicked up dust as it rolled onto the shoulder.

Trooper Bowen grimaced. Pulling over drunks and dopeheads and car thieves was dangerous enough, but this son of a bitch was straight out of a foxhole. Nothing in Bowen's training had addressed stopping a skilled combatant, a Soviet-manufactured fighting machine. From what Bowen had read about him and from the briefing given that morning by his lieutenant, the trooper knew Trusov was a superb killer—merciless and efficient—who apparently loved his craft. This man was perhaps the best the Russians could produce at shedding blood, and in a moment the Russian was going to turn his attention to one Ross Bowen of the Montana State Patrol. Bowen didn't like the situation at all.

The Accord came to a stop on the gravel shoulder. The trooper pulled up the patrol car forty feet behind the Russian's vehicle, then yanked back on the emergency brake. Bowen was breathing quickly. He silently ran down the procedure for arresting an armed and dangerous suspect. He unsnapped the holster strap over the hammer of his .357 magnum, a Colt Trooper. He opened the door and pulled out the revolver. He crouched behind his open door, the weapon in both hands and braced against the windshield pillar. Christ, he had forgotten his hat on the passenger seat.

His voice was more strident than he would have wished. "Put both hands out your window. Now." Bowen concentrated on the Russian. He would worry about the passenger later.

The window rolled down and both hands came out, fingers spread wide. Bowen could make out the green baseball cap above blond hair. The bile of fear rose in the trooper's throat. The procedure was to immediately control the situation and put fear into the arrestee. He barked, "With one hand, open the door using the outside handle. Do it now."

The Russian's left hand lowered to the Accord's exterior handle. The door cracked open.

Bowen's hand was shaking, and he could see his Colt's barrel wiggle back and forth. He breathed deeply to steady himself, then called, "Now keep both hands in my sight and step out of the car. Do it slowly."

The Accord's door pushed open. The Russian rose from the car, moving with a fluid confidence that was evident to Bowen in even those few seconds. And Trusov rose and rose. He seemed enormous, with a massive chest and a head cut from stone. He filled the road. His face was bony and hard and expressionless, as cold as a carving. He stood motionless next to the Accord's door. The passenger was staring out the Accord's back window, but Bowen could not risk glancing at him.

Trooper Bowen suddenly realized that in climbing out of the car Trusov had put his left hand back into the door. The Russian stood there with one hand not showing.

"Pull your other hand out of the car," Bowen yelled in his best voice. "Do it now."

The Russian remained still. He seemed to be calmly and unhurriedly studying the lawman. Bowen flushed with fear, and the fear played games with him. He heard a clock ticking away, centered in his head behind his eyes, counting down his last seconds on this earth. His life would end on a desolate road.

Nikolai Trusov spoke slowly. "Get back into your car and you will live."

The truth of the words seemed blinding, and struck Trooper Bowen with the force of Biblical revelation. Entirely at odds with the apparent situation—Bowen was holding a fearsome weapon on an unarmed man standing forty feet away—the Russian's warning offered the miraculous hope that Bowen's newborn daughter would not lose her father this day. The clock behind his eyes stopped its ominous ticking.

Moving slowly to make his intentions clear, Trooper Bowen lifted his Colt from the door frame and smoothly re-entered his car. He lowered the weapon to the passenger seat near his hat, turned the ignition, and performed a U-turn on the road. The patrol car picked up speed as it headed east. In Bowen's rearview mirror, the Russian slipped back into the Accord. Bowen lost sight of the stolen car as the road ducked behind a hill.

The trooper reached for the photo of his daughter. He pressed it back onto the dashboard. Then he brought up his radio, about to report that the Russian had somehow shaken him. He smiled. Life offers few clear choices but it had just then. Bowen had made the correct one. His wife and daughter would see him again at the end of his shift.

✧   ✧   ✧

"I usually don't eat things I can't lift." Adrian Gray poked her dinner.

Baked potatoes filled their plates, hanging over the edges. They had been opened and filled with spiced meat, cheese, olives, sour cream, and topped with a sprinkling of chopped chives. Steam still rose from them. Potatoes were the specialty of the Right to Keep and Bear Arms Saloon. The owner, Ray Miller, hovered behind the bar wearing an expectant smile, waiting for Gray and his guests to begin their meal so he could enjoy the gratification on their faces. He served the best potatoes in the Sawtooths and he knew it.

Coates didn't disappoint Miller. The detective took his first bite, then began an insistent shoveling from plate to mouth. Ray Miller's smile widened. His potatoes never failed.

The detective mumbled, "Don't get between me and this potato. It'd be too dangerous."

Adrian lifted a measure of potato. As always with the first bite of anything, she touched it quickly with her tongue before putting it into her mouth. Gray stirred in his seat. She chewed a moment, then beamed at Ray Miller, who seemed to grow three or four inches with the smile. When Gray had entered the saloon with Adrian Wade, Miller had gleefully whispered to him, "And to think I worried about you." Miller had been only slightly dampened when Pete Coates followed them. Adrian's coat hung on the back of her chair. Pete Coates was wearing a pea coat over a plaid shirt, and jeans above hiking boots. Gray had loaned him the outfit, which had belong to Gray's father. The clothes were stretched to their limit over Coates's bulk.

The detective said, "Chief Durant was as good as his word. Hobart is crawling with sheriffs' deputies and State Patrol, even some police personnel from Boise and Twin Falls. I've got their duty rosters ready. And the FBI will start arriving soon. Flights into Hailey will be full of them."

Gray cut into his potato. He had eaten dozens and dozens of Miller's famous potatoes over the years.

"Adrian, you're all set up?" Coates asked around a mouthful of potato.

"All in one corner of Owen's living room. I've got the communication capacity of the Manhattan FBI office. I'm already talking with General Kulikov and Colonel Rokossosky. And it's easier to get hold of them in Moscow from Idaho than if I were in Moscow. The telephone system there is that unreliable."

Ray Miller held up the telephone behind the counter. He called, "Detective Coates, it's for you."

Coates dropped his napkin on his seat and walked to the bar.

Gray said quietly, "I suppose you've mentioned to Pete about my ninety-seventh shot."

"He's your best friend, isn't he? He should know."

"My best friend?" Gray laughed. "I haven't thought in those terms since I was in grade school."

"Well, then you can be the last to realize it. Of course I told him, because he's your friend and because he's trying to figure out what's going on. Do you mind?"

Gray shook his head noncommittally.

Coates returned and said bleakly, "Nikolai Trusov was spotted in Butte by a policeman there an hour ago. Trusov was driving a pickup truck, a red Dodge Ram, heading the opposite direction as the cop. He had a passenger with him."

"The policeman is positive it was Trusov?"

"No question. He yanked his patrol car around and tried to give pursuit but the pickup disappeared. He alerted his department and the Montana Highway Patrol. They found the truck in the western outskirts of Butte, abandoned. They can't find Trusov anywhere, and speculate he has found another vehicle and is continuing west." Coates lifted his beer glass. "I'd like to know how Trusov determined you are in Hobart, which it sure looks like he has figured out, coming in a beeline here."

"Do you want to tell him?" Adrian asked, bringing her gaze around to Gray.

"Tell him what?"

"How Nikolai Trusov knows where you are."

"You tell me," Gray challenged.

Adrian said, "You left him a message, Owen."

The detective stared at Gray.

She went on. "I called your home telephone number in Brooklyn. On your recorder is the message 'No one is home right now. If you are looking for Owen Gray, he is at his father's place on Black Bear Creek near Hobart, Idaho.' "

"Son of a bitch." Pete Coates's voice rose and he pointed his fork at Gray. "You guessed Trusov would call your number, and you've deliberately told him where you are."

Gray was silent.

Coates fairly shouted, "Owen, you are intentionally setting up a duel between you and Trusov, is that it?"

Again Gray said nothing.

Coates put down his fork. "Trusov wants you to meet him in the field, and you've decided to oblige him. Am I right"

"I came to Idaho," Gray said lamely. "If he is following me, so be it."

"Owen, this isn't the goddamn OK Corral. Nikolai Trusov is a killer, and he is superb at it. And now you've decided to play a game with him, to go mano a mano with him? I thought you and I were working for the same thing, but I guess we no longer are."

"I guess not," Gray said quietly.

"I ought to throw you in jail for your own protection." Coates's voice was lower. He was settling down. He lifted his beer. "Goddamnit."

"Pete, you might be the most skilled detective at the NYPD," Gray said, "but I don't believe you'll be able to stop Nikolai Trusov before he finds me."

PART THREE
MYSTICAL JEWELS

Sometimes the fish devour the ants,
and sometimes the ants devour the fish.
—Vietnamese proverb

14

FEW ENTERED IDAHO'S Big Wood River Valley unnoticed and unremarked.

Big Ed Gatwick cruised in from Lewiston on his 1950 Harley panhead. The motorcycle's frame-off restoration had taken him two years, and he had installed the best: S&S rods and pistons, Sifton lifters and cam, and a Screaming Eagle carb. The fenders and frame were painted black-cherry pearl, and everything else was either black leather or gleaming chrome. Big Ed blew through Hailey and headed north toward Ketchum and Hobart in a reclining position, his gloved hands on the handlebars above the springer fork, his black boots high on rests, and his bulk low in the curved seat. Seventy-four cubic inches filled the valley with an echoing rumble, a throbbing balls-grabbing pulse that for Big Ed Gatwick was proof God existed, for only He could have created such a sound, with apologies to the Harley Davidson Company.

Gatwick's club was the Lewiston Death Deacons, and he was leading six Deacons to the Galena Lodge near Galena Summit, north of Hobart. Going to do some drinking, toking, joking, bust a head or two, it was all on the agenda. Once in a while he and the others would push around an overwhelmed small-town sheriff, and you couldn't have more fun than that. The club liked to show up in some jerkwater town unannounced and uninvited, party hard, then clear out before the law could rally its forces. The biker wore a black leather jacket with the Deacons' colors, a hooded grim reaper carrying a scythe. Gatwick's gray beard was blown over his shoulder by the rush of wind. He wore a pill helmet, and on his nose were green-tinted granny glasses.

In Gatwick's rearview mirror—a glass sliver put there only to appease hard-ass state patrolmen—Jig Lawrence piloted his Harley. The others trailed behind, weaving side to side, filling the highway and turning some heads, and that's what it was all about.

Gatwick rounded a corner and squinted through the sunglasses. A cop car was ahead on the side of the road, and some orange barricades. Gatwick slowed the Harley, drawing near to the road-block. A copse of pine trees bordered the highway, where a dirt road trailed away into the hills. The cop was an old gummer, his belly over his ammo belt and jowls over his shirt collar. A soft touch, looked like. The biker squeezed the brake. A lone old man wearing a gun, and all the hicks in this valley depending on him for law and order. Gatwick laughed as he brought the Harley to a stop in front of the cop.

"Everything's legal, Officer." The biker called, grinning contemptuously. He revved the engine once for punctuation.

Roy Durant could move faster than he looked. He took three steps and pressed the kill button on the Harley's handlebar. The motorcycle sputtered and died.

Big Ed rose over his seat. "Hey, you got no right—"

Jig Lawrence pulled up next to Gatwick. Then the others came, roaring their engines, a threatening, demanding sound, and they circled the police chief.

Durant held out his hand to Gatwick. "Your license, quick."

Big Ed insolently leaned back on his seat and was about to say something when the air was split with a hammering bellow that drowned out the motorcycles, a gut-thumping percussion that made the bikes and their riders seem puny and irrelevant, drowned in the blare.

Gatwick's head jerked to the sound.

"Sorry," Idaho National Guard Sergeant Ralph Neal yelled, smiling. "Just clearing my barrel."

The sergeant's fists were gripping the handles of an M2 heavy machine gun pintle-mounted on the back of a hummer. His thumb was on the butterfly trigger. The 100-round disintegrating-link shell belt rose from the sergeant's feet to enter the breech, and was still swaying. Slight wisps of gray smoke rose from the barrel as bits and pieces of a pine tree drifted to the ground. The sergeant's driver, Private John Goode, also grinned malevolently, the stock of an M16 resting against his thigh, the barrel poking above the windshield. Arrayed in the trees behind the jeep were a dozen other members of the Guard, all dressed in desert camouflage, all on loan to Pete Coates. They had been assigned to help man the checkpoint. A troop truck was parked farther into the trees.

Big Ed swallowed so hard his Adam's apple bounced against his leather jacket's lapel. He said nothing. It took only a moment for Chief Durant to look at each Deacon's license and stare into each face, matching it with the features of the Russian he had memorized. The Deacons were silent and docile, refusing to meet Durant's gaze.

Then Big Ed Gatwick kicked his Harley into life, leaned it over to turn south, and sped away, back down the road he had just come up. Jig Lawrence and the rest of the Deacons followed, a swift and ignoble retreat.

Chief Durant gave the sergeant a thumbs-up and hollered gleefully, "That's about as much fun as this old man is ever going to have."

❖   ❖   ❖

This was Elsa MacIntire's fifteenth round-trip from Missoula to Jackpot, and her right arm ached as it always did. In fact, everything ached on her right side: knuckles, wrist, elbow, shoulder, even her hip. She once figured that between the time the bus dropped her group off in Jackpot at five in the afternoon until she reboarded the vehicle at nine the next morning, she pulled a slot machine handle over five thousand times, and that included a slight pause every ten minutes to light a new cigarette. She stood at the machine like a sentry at her post, steady and resolute, unfailing in her duty to drop another quarter into the slot the instant the wheels stopped. Her gaze was usually on the middle distance, the cigarette smoke a veil in front of her face. She rarely bothered to look at the bars, bells, and fruit on the wheels, because the spinning red light on top of the machine would announce a win, and she would be rewarded with the nurturing sound of quarters dumping into the payout cup.

Slumped in her bus seat, Elsa MacIntire was exhausted. She came once every other month to the tiny gambling town on the Idaho-Nevada border. On the run home she was always five hundred dollars poorer, she always smelled like an old ashtray, and her right arm always pumped pain into the rest of her. She loved it. At seventy-three years of age, Elsa figured she had done everything worth doing, had had all the fun allowed a person in one life, and these coach trips to Jackpot were an extra she allowed herself, and she would continue to make them as long as her right arm could yank the handle. She didn't mind the money she lost each trip, because the smidgen of character her trollop of a daughter possessed would not be improved in any way by inheriting her money.

The bus was filled with elderly Missoula women. They had an informal club, with its nexus the bus trip to and from their Montana homes. On the way to Jackpot they laughed and told stories and gossiped. On the way back they were quiet, utterly worn out, having stayed awake the entire night to pull the arms. Elsa napped on and off, but she tried to remain awake as the bus passed through the lovely Big Wood River Valley, from Ketchum on north over the Galena Pass. The views of mountains and the river refreshed her, made her feel as if she had taken a bath.

She was hungry, having had no time to eat while playing the slots. She always packed four sandwiches, saving two for the road home. She pulled a roast beef sandwich from her large handbag and unwrapped it. The bus unexpectedly began to slow. She raised herself to her full height in the seat to peer forward over the horizon of blue-gray hair. There was nothing to be seen, so Elsa bit into her sandwich.

The door hissed and a German shepherd climbed into the bus. Behind the dog was a large man wearing a black windbreaker with "FBI" imprinted on its front. A second FBI agent, this one carrying a rifle, followed them up the stairs into the bus. Elsa MacIntire didn't know a rifle from a shotgun, and certainly didn't know that the FBI agent's weapon was a Valmet assault rifle.

The agent spoke for a few seconds with the driver, then announced to the passengers, "The FBI will be conducting a search of this vehicle, looking for a fugitive. The dog will be searching by scent.''

One of Elsa's friends shouted, ''How's the dog know what the fugitive smells like?''

The handler replied, ''We've got a few of his shirts. Found them in his hotel room. It's faster for the dog to vet all of you than for us looking at each ID and face.''

''Especially our old wrinkled faces,'' a passenger cracked.

The agent smiled at the joke. The German shepherd slowly led him down the narrow aisle. The dog's head methodically turned left and right, sniffing at sleeves and dresses and purses. A few of the ladies petted its tan and black flanks as it passed. The German shepherd seemed happy in its work.

When the dog reached Elsa MacIntire, she asked, ''Does he like roast beef?''

The FBI agent grinned again. ''He's been trained not to eat while he's on duty. And he won't take food from strangers.''

Elsa replied, ''There's not a dog alive who'll turn down roast beef.''

The agent's voice was condescendingly polite. ''Go ahead and try. His name is Dooley. He won't even sniff at it.''

She opened her sandwich and pulled out the roast beef, three palm-sized slices of Grade A with no fat at the edges. Dooley's ears lifted, and he squared his grand head fully to the old lady. The agent laughed confidently.

''Here you go, poochie.'' Elsa held out the meat.

The dog instantly grabbed the meat with its teeth, but carefully so as not to catch Elsa's fingers in its gleaming white fangs. Dooley ecstatically gulped the beef down and leaned forward on the leash for more.

Elsa asked sweetly, ''Might he like my other sandwich, too?''

The agent growled, ''Goddamn worthless cur.'' He yanked on the leash. ''Get back to work, Dooley.''

The dog began his sniffing again, looking back over its shoulder several times at Elsa. The girls laughed and laughed. When the search was done, the dog handler exited the bus, the back of his neck still red as paint

✧   ✧   ✧

Six miles northwest of the bus, high in the Sawtooths, Glen Reeves and Bob Valiquette hiked along a trail toward the base of Mount Ash where they were going to climb a crag known as Ben's Throne, a 5.11 bolted, four-pitch climb that would take them all day and would leave them twitching and stumbling and delighted as they returned at sunset to their car parked on a logging road below.

Reeves and Valiquette were laden with ropes, harnesses, cams, holds, chalk bags and lunch. They were bringing many runners rather than quickdraws for the crux pitch. A tough semi-hanging belay was near the Throne's roof. Stunning views awaited them on top.

They climbed the steep hill of loose stones at the base of the crag, then slipped off their packs to ready themselves for the assault. They donned their climbing slippers and harnesses, then hung their gear on the belts' fixed racking loops. Their climb—the vertical pocked and cracked five-hundred-foot-high face—was two-thirds up Ash Mountain. Below them was a deep valley falling away to a narrow line of aspen at the valley's seam. Then the terrain rose again to ragged granite ridges two miles across from them.

Valiquette dusted his hands with chalk. "Know how I know I'm getting old, Glen?"

"New wrinkles around your eyes?"

"That, too. But mostly it's that I increasingly prefer the safety of a bolt at my feet."

Reeves rechecked his harness buckles. "What's the farthest you've ever fallen?"

"You were there. Seventy feet."

"That's right, on Mount Borah. You fell so far I couldn't see you." Reeves laughed. "I couldn't tell if you'd tumbled into the dihedral to our right or had simply fallen free."

Valiquette was going to take the lead, and Reeves would be second. Just as Valiquette reached for his first hold and slipped his rubber-covered foot into a crack, a deep fluttering sound poured into the valley, an extraordinarily foreign noise.

Both climbers instinctively ducked. Any strange noise was at first thought to be something falling toward them. A fist-sized rock would sound like a man screaming as it rocketed past them to the floor. But nothing fell.

An ugly metallic nose edged around the face's vertical horizon, a frightening piece of brown machinery suspended in the fine air.

"A helicopter!" Valiquette exclaimed. "What the hell is it doing so close?"

"Bastard," Reeves said, prepared to ignore it. "Some rich Californians looking for vacation property. A Ketchum realtor probably hired the helicopter to impress them. They do it all the time. Let's go."

Valiquette turned to face the copter. "That's no charter helicopter. Take a look."

The machine closed on the climbers, nearer and nearer, blowing up dust from the scree.

"You were in the army," Valiquette said nervously. "What is that?"

Reeves licked his lips. "It's a Huey Cobra."

"Jesus, what're those tubes with the openings?"

"It's a 40-millimeter grenade launcher with 300 bombs."

"And the thing under its snout?"

"A 30-millimeter chain gun that fires something like a million rounds a minute."

"All for us?" Valiquette asked.

The helicopter drifted closer, its blades beating the air and the turbine engines howling. Sun reflected off the windshield, hiding the pilot. A loudspeaker attached to its nose crackled out with "Please turn fully to the helicopter and present your drivers' licenses or other identification."

Reeves quickly pulled his cloth wallet from his pack. His finger trembling, he opened it to find his Idaho driver's license. He held it up to the copter. "Do you think this is the Forest Service, and they're checking permits?"

"The Forest Service using Huey Cobras?"

"I wouldn't put it past them."

Both climbers stood motionless, their licenses in front of them. They did not know that a Nikon TRL camera attached to the fuselage next to the loudspeaker was taking a photograph of them and the licenses.

The loudspeaker squawked again, "Thank you."

The turbines wound up. The Huey lifted away from the mountainside, bringing its tail rotor around and yawing downhill. The

221

helicopter raced to the valley floor, low enough to blow up a trailing cloud of dirt all the way, then disappeared downstream just above the treetops.

The climbers turned back to the granite and lichen face, and for much of the ascent they cursed the newly officious and newly high-tech United States Forest Service.

✧   ✧   ✧

Down in Hobart, Ray Miller sadly shook his head. "I'm sorry, miss. I don't have the work."

"I've been a short order cook on and off for ten years," the woman argued. "All I need is a week's employment. I work hard and I don't steal."

"I don't doubt anything you say," the Right to Keep and Bear Arms Saloon owner said. "But take a look around. It's lunchtime, but you and I are the only people in the place. I can hear my echo in here."

The woman had walked into the saloon a few minutes before. She was in her late thirties. Her brown hair had a badger's streak of gray and was loose down her back, and a length of rawhide and ribbon was tied into it. She wore no eye shadow or lipstick. The bridge of her granny glasses had been mended with a small piece of duct tape. Her yellow and white print blouse was tucked in at her waist. A belt of braided cloth held up her jeans. Her old backpack had a grease stain along a side. Miller guessed she dressed like a hippie to hide her poverty.

"What's your name, young lady?" he asked. He had been standing behind the bar doing his paperwork. A hand-held calculator, a corporate checkbook, and a sheaf of bills were in front of him.

"Susan."

"Where you coming from, Susan?"

"Calgary. My husband left there three months ago, gone to Texas to look for work in the oil fields. I'm on my way to join him. But he couldn't send me any money."

"You hitchhiking?"

"Yeah." She brushed her hair back with a hand. "You wouldn't believe the crap I have to put up with, guys picking me up in their pickups and semis."

"How about a chili potato on the house? I make the chili from

222

scratch, and I dump it into a baked potato and grate cheese over it.''

She grinned gratefully, then slipped off her backpack and put it at her feet. She slid onto a stool.

Miller wrapped an apron around his waist. ''I like to think my potatoes are famous, but I serve less than thirty meals a week. I cook and wait tables, and then I bus and clean the plates. I wish I could offer you a job.''

''I understand.''

''I used to make a pretty good living,'' Miller added. ''But the town has dried up and is on the verge of blowing away.''

''Don't apologize.'' She smiled warmly. ''I understand.''

The Right's door swung in and four men entered single file. They had the look of tough accountants, which meant they were FBI agents. They were all in slacks and windbreakers. They took chairs together at a round table under an elk head. The first to take his seat lifted the menu which was encased in an upright plastic stand.

Ray Miller said to the hitchhiker, ''I'll get these guys' order and be right back to start on your potato, Susan.''

As Miller rounded the bar to wait on the table, five more men and two women entered the saloon. All wore Idaho State Patrol uniforms. They took the table near the stuffed Chinese pheasant.

Miller nodded at the State Patrol officers as he walked to the table of FBI agents. ''May I help you? I recommend the potatoes.''

Before any of the agents could answer, the door opened again. This time two men in sports coats entered. Miller did not know it, but they were Boise plainclothes policemen. Before the door pulled itself closed, in came five more state patrolmen, then three Idaho National Guardsmen in summer field uniforms.

His pen poised over the pad, Miller asked the FBI agents, ''You fellows looking for that Russian that Chief Durant told me about?''

''That's right.'' The agent had a preacher's quick, confiding smile.

''Lots of you folks coming to Hobart?''

''Lots.''

''How many?''

The agent asked, ''What's an Oinker Potato?''

''Strips of crisp bacon and chunks of tomato over melted cheddar cheese.''

''I'll have one of them.''

223

The door swung open again. A man and a woman entered wearing uniforms Miller did not recognize. He squinted at their arm insignia. Coeur d'Alene police.

Miller tried again. "You could do me a big favor helping me plan my kitchen by letting me know how many of you are in town."

"Couple hundred."

"Going to be here for long?"

"Four, five days, a week. Who knows? And a Diet Pepsi."

"I'll be right back," the saloon owner blurted. He hurried to the bar, weaving between the full tables. He rushed to the stool where the hitchhiker Susan had been sitting. It was empty.

"Gone," Miller breathed miserably. "Goddamnit."

But she was still in the saloon. Wearing an apron she had found on a hook on the cooler door, she was behind the bar, bent over the ice machine, ladling ice into glasses. She put one under the Diet Pepsi spigot.

She smiled again at Miller. "I take it I have a week's work."

"Looks like it'll be a long, long week. Make both of us some money."

He scurried back to the FBI agents, still smiling

So it was that Hobart and environs came to groan under the weight of law personnel. They emptied the Big Wood Grocery Store, bought all the gas at the Sinclair station, filled the Hobart Motel, and cleaned out Bud's Drug of candy bars and newspapers. But Ray Miller never ran out of potatoes, because if there is one thing Idaho has, it's potatoes, and as the state's license plate will testify, they are famous. The law officers and soldiers filled the streets with their vehicles, jammed the telephone lines, stood on the corners, swaggered and smiled, and added a sense of wonder and purpose to the lives of Hobart citizens.

✧   ✧   ✧

Owen Gray lay on his belly, the M-40A1 Marine Corps sniper rifle in front of him. His left hand was forward, with the palm against the stock ferrule swivel and the sling high on his arm. His wrist was straight and gently locked so the rifle rested on the heel of the hand. The fingers cupped the stock but did not grip it. His left elbow was under the rifle's receiver. The bones, not his muscles, supported the rifle. The wood butt was firmly in the pocket of his right shoulder. His right hand was wrapped around the checkered stock with the thumb extended over the narrow portion of the stock. Gray's left elbow was the pivot to move the barrel. His shoulders were level. His trigger finger lay alongside the guard.

The barrel was free-floated, meaning that it was secured to the chamber but did not touch the stock. The gap between the stock and barrel was the thickness of a dollar bill, and this clearance prevented the stock from distorting the barrel from one shot to the next. The barrel was heavier than on most other rifles, and this distributed heat from the powder discharge more evenly, reducing warpage. Near his elbow was a box of match ammunition, so called because each bullet in the same box and each box in the same case had the identical serial number, indicating the bullets had been manufactured with the same batch of gunpowder on the same day, thereby eliminating the vagaries in powder that might randomly change muzzle velocity.

He peered over the scope. Shepherd's Bowl was spread out before him. The bowl was misnamed, and was in fact a U-shaped valley. Fed by a small spring, Black Bear Creek originated in the valley and exited at the eastern end to wander two miles to the Gray ranch and then on to join the Big Wood River. Shepherd's Bowl was so named because a Basque shepherd—one of many who had come to Idaho in the early years—tried to raise sheep in the valley, had lasted one bitter winter, and had retreated with far fewer sheep than he had arrived with.

Gray was three-quarters up the north side of the bowl. The area was two miles long, running west-east, and a mile and a half across. The valley's center was thick with trees and undergrowth, particularly dense where Black Bear Creek formed itself and dribbled out of the valley. The creek was only a foot across at the mouth of the valley, but it provided water for hundreds of mature trees that trailed like a snake along the bottom of the valley. Also along the valley floor were a dozen patches of wild grass, each a half acre to an acre. These swaths of grass had convinced the poor shepherd he might be able to graze his flock in Shepherd's Bowl. The small meadows were covered with red-top grass, wild oats, rattlesnake grass, fireweed, and cheat grass, most growing to the height of a man's waist, with the fireweed protruding a foot or two from the soft blanket of weeds. The slightest wind pushed waves into the grasses. At this time of year the grass was yellow and dry.

Gray's hide was a small protrusion on the north slope, a cleft in the incline formed by stones and dirt sliding down the grade and building up behind a boulder over the centuries. The ledge was just large enough to lie on. By taking an indirect route, ducking through bushes and taking advantage of a few sparse trees on the north slope, it was possible to climb to the ledge without being seen from anywhere else in the bowl, but it took care and skill. Other distortions in the half-cone of the bowl's north side included more boulders, some with dogbane growing around them, banks of yellow-blooming Scotch broom, a few stunted lodgepole pines, and clusters of rolling brittle tumbleweed blown against outcroppings, but most of the north slope was open and clear. It curved around like the stands of a football stadium.

High on the bowl's north side at about Owen Gray's ledge the grade increased. He glanced over his shoulder at the surface that rose like a wave behind him. Here stones lay on each other, not cemented by soil but loose enough to sink or roll away under a footstep. Reflected sunlight flickered from quartz flakes in the granite stones. Occasional blades of cheat grass grew in the rubble. Papery yellow and red lichen topped many of the rocks. A few sego lilies dotted the scree, their blossoms resembling white butterflies. But these few living things did little to change the arid, tumbly, sun-baked nature of the north slope.

Gray looked back over the rifle to the other side of the bowl. The south side was hidden in shadows much of a summer day and all of winter, and was forested with pine and aspen and other trees. Gaps in the tree cover revealed green and flowering underbrush. So different were they that the north and south sides of Shepherd's Bowl could have been on different continents. Behind the bowl, jagged peaks were limned against the diamond-blue sky.

He lowered himself over the rifle's butt stock and grip, which snipers call the furniture. Gray checked himself again. His right cheek and right thumb—curled over the small of the stock—formed a spot weld. He could not feel where his body ended and the rifle began. This firm weld would allow Gray's head, hand, and rifle to absorb recoil as one unit. He brought his eye to a position behind the lens's eyepiece, sighting on a low knot in a pine near the valley's mouth. He kept his eye back from the lens to protect it from recoil. Too close, and the scope would cut a bloody circle to the bone around the eye. When he took a deep breath, the crosshairs moved down straight through the center of the target, indicating he was well balanced over the rifle.

Gray had always credited a rifle scope with magical qualities. He well understood the optics. He knew the objective lens at the front of the scope produced an upside-down and backward image of the target. In the middle of the scope, the erector lens magnified the image and returned it to its correct position. The eyepiece lens then magnified the image further. He knew that while the average eye can distinguish a one-inch detail at a hundred yards, a one-sixth-inch detail could be seen with a 6X scope. An object viewed from six hundred yards through a 6X telescope will have the same clarity as if viewed by the unaided eye from a hundred yards. He knew that the magnesium fluoride coating on his lens increased transmission of light from about 45 percent to 86 percent. No sorcery in any of this.

But those same optics that magnified the view and flattened the perspective also flensed away humanity. In Vietnam when Gray peered through a scope, the image quartered by the crosshairs was not a human but a target, nothing but a mathematical problem of windage and velocity and direction. The scope had a marvelous ability to eliminate sloppy moral issues and extraneous questions of commitment to the cause. If it appeared through the scope, Gray could kill it.

The scope's magic survived time and tragedies, it seemed. He had accepted the rifle with stomach-churning trepidation, but even after the decades he had felt its supernatural power of simplification on the Brooklyn roof as he found the target. Once his eye was on the crosshairs he was ready in all respects to pull the trigger. The ghastly outcome—the death of Mrs. Orlando—had sickened him, had left him exhausted with grief. Yet here he was on a perch high in a mountain bowl ready again to pull the trigger, as long as all the world's complexities were filtered out by the rifle scope.

He lifted his head to avoid eyestrain. At the mouth of the valley, several low branches of a dogwood were rattling, whipping left and right. The only animals that would make such a commotion were a bear using the tree to scratch its back or an elk or moose trying to rid its horn of felt. Gray sighted in on the dogwood, not intending to pull the trigger, but saving himself from reaching for his binoculars. He narrowed his eye slightly. The rifle was dead calm in his hands, so still that a bead of mercury placed precisely on top of the barrel would have remained there.

Adrian Wade's face popped into the crosshairs, her eyes like flares in the scope. She had emerged suddenly from under the tree, but now caught her jacket on a branch. She yanked on it and finally freed herself.

Gray jerked his eye up from the scope.

He pivoted the weapon aside. He found her with his unaided eye. Her red coat and black hair stood out like a sailor's emergency dye on a calm sea. He brought up the binoculars. She was scanning the bowl, moving her head randomly, an amateur's visual search that would miss him entirely. He stood, removed his coat, and waved it back and forth until she started in his direction. She crossed a wide clump of purple heather and ducked through a barricade of Scotch broom. She climbed the slope, coming at him from the southeast, gaining elevation as she hiked deeper into the valley.

She was hurrying. More than hurrying, she was frantically pedaling her legs. Again Gray brought up the binoculars. Sweat flowed freely down her face, and her mouth was open and panting. He used the field glasses to search the trees behind her, but she was not being chased. As he watched her ascend the bowl, he pulled an apple from his pack and ate it from the bottom up, and consumed every part of it except the stem, which the twins had told him was the weirdest thing in existence. He had learned to eat an apple that way in Vietnam because an apple core might be found by an enemy trying to follow him.

He liked watching Adrian Wade, Gray admitted to himself. She moved with the grace of an athlete, even on the unstable slope and even though she was breathing heavily in this oxygen-weak altitude. She reached the loose scree just below his hide and used her hands to climb the last yards up to him, pumping her legs as the rocks gave way.

She gasped. "I don't suppose you could have met me halfway."

"I was eating my lunch." He flicked away the apple stem.

She climbed onto the ridge and collapsed on the soft soil and gravel. Her chest heaved as she worked the thin air. She leaned back on her elbows. Her face glimmered with sweat. She dragged a sleeve across her forehead. Gray lifted a canteen from his pack and handed it to her. Her pistol was a bulge under her coat.

She drank greedily, then said, "I thought I was in good shape."

"You were running like you had turpentine on your butt. What's going on?"

After a moment her breathing eased. She smiled and said majestically, "I have your answer."

Gray scratched his neck where a deerfly had bitten him. "I have more questions than you have answers, I'll bet."

She laughed gaily and shook her head. "I'm good, you know that? Man, I'm good."

Gray couldn't help but smile along with her. "You are busting your buttons."

"Owen, you are going to grovel with thanks before me. You've spent years and years wandering around in the dark, your hand out in front of you to ward off unseen dangers, and now I'm going to lead you to the light." She tilted her head back and laughed again, a victorious chortle.

The sun played with her hair. He had not seen the flecks of red and gold in it before, but the harsh high-altitude light found tiny glints of color among the ebony. And the light made the shock-white skin of her face translucent, revealing delicate blue lines beneath. Her mouth was curved and lush and red. Perspiration made her face shine as if in the afterglow of passion.

Her mouth came together to say something but Gray beat her to it. "I know. I'm staring. I'll stop."

Her eyes were amused. "Go ahead and stare." Then another laugh. "I'm going to blow you off this ledge with my news."

"Stop crowing and tell me."

"I don't want you to think it came easily."

"You're still crowing."

Surrounded by computer and communication equipment, Adrian Wade had spent hour after hour in her corner of the cabin's living room. Last night Pete Coates and Gray sat at the table under the antler chandelier sipping coffee and watching her. She seldom rose from her seat in front of the monitor, and when she did it was to insert or retrieve a document from a fax machine. She would stare, then pound the keyboard, then stare again, gritting her teeth, drumming the table, occasionally leafing through the pages of several

229

three-ring binders. Or she would speak into the telephone, sometimes in English but usually in Russian. Gray once delivered coffee to her, but it remained untouched on the desk until it was cold. Once in a while she would say something aloud but only to herself, and Gray doubted she was aware she was speaking. Things like "Good for Captain Mason. I've got the patch through." And, "I didn't even think Donetsk had telephones." And, "His assistant owes me one, so I'll try him." Coates and Gray would look at each other and shrug, not having the slightest idea what she was talking about. Her voice and manner changed from one phone call to the next. At times she was as hard as a labor negotiator. On other calls her voice had the dulcet tones of a diplomat. Sometimes she wheedled and entreated and cajoled, then abruptly became angry, then smoothly placating. It was an entertaining performance, even though Gray and Coates could not understand most of what she said. Last night she had been at her station when Coates and Gray had turned in, and she was there when they got up in the morning. Gray did not know if she had slept.

She demanded, "Give me a date between 1947 and half a year ago."

"A game? I don't feel like playing games."

"Any date."

Gray pinched the bridge of his nose. "April 5, 1956."

"Nikolai Trusov has six weeks remaining in the third form at the Korsko Preliminary School in the village of Valosk, south of Moscow. He is wearing a cast on his forearm because of a fall from a tree."

"December 6, 1975."

"Trusov is in Olympic training at the Central Army Sports Club facility near Pervouralsk in the Ural Mountains. He is skiing forty miles a day, is on a rifle range two hours a day, and is undergoing an hour of weight training each day."

"August 12, 1987."

"Trusov is operating near Safir Chir, a town in the Panjshir Valley about seventy-five miles north by northwest of Kabul. He is attached to the 1st Recon Company, 2nd Motor-Rifle Regiment, 15th Motor-Rifle Division."

"I'm impressed," Gray admitted.

"I've known all this for two or three days. But there was a hole in my Nikolai Trusov calendar, and try as I might, I couldn't fill it in.''

"What dates?''

"July through November 1970. General Kulikov and his staff in Moscow appeared to be working hard, but they couldn't find anything. I began to wonder about the dedication Kulikov was bringing to his investigation. Armies around the world produce mountains of records, and half of any army is employed generating documents about the other half. A chronicle of those five months of Nikolai Trusov's military career had to exist somewhere.''

"So what did you do?''

"I goosed Kulikov.'' She leaned back further on her elbows, and her back touched the scree. It rattled and shifted, and a small stone slipped onto her shoulder. She flicked it aside. "At my request, FBI Assistant Director Robert Olin spoke with the Russian Republic's Vice President Felix Ogarkov, whose main job is lobbying western governments for aid for Russia. Olin spoke of how our government would view favorably in its foreign aid considerations any further and diligent assistance General Kulikov might give to the investigation of Trusov. This was yesterday morning. As I understand it, Ogarkov immediately alerted General Kulikov that should Kulikov help in procuring American aid, a diplomatic position might open up somewhere for him, maybe a consulship in the U.S. or Europe.''

"It worked?''

"Kulikov dug his heels into his horse, I think. He found what I was looking for. In the late 1960s a training brigade was formed from troops in the Moscow Military District. So secret was the new brigade that rather than being somewhere in the chain of command under General Polynin, who was head of all ground forces, the brigade was under General Bukharin, chief of the Main Political Directorate.''

"A training brigade that was secret? That's unusual, isn't it?''

She let the question hang for a few seconds before delivering the hook. "The 1st Special Training Brigade was sent to Vietnam. The Pentagon has long known that Soviet pilots trained North Vietnamese pilots. And now it seems that the Soviets were training soldiers, also. Nikolai Trusov taught marksmanship and fieldcraft. And he did some shooting, maybe in Vietnam. The general found

231

out that Trusov already had eleven kills before he went to Afghanistan. Polynin said the files weren't complete, and he doesn't know the nature of the kills, but they are recorded. So with Trusov's seventy-eight kills in Afghanistan, he's up to eighty-nine.''

A cable seemed to tighten around Gray's chest. "He was in Vietnam?"

Another smile. "He trained NVA and Viet Cong snipers. General Kulikov has now spoken to three other sniper instructors in the 1st Brigade. They all have clear memories of Nikolai Trusov, and they all remember his last day of active service in Vietnam.''

Owen Gray stopped breathing.

She said, "The 1st Brigade instructors all knew of you, Owen. White Star was famous and feared. You and the other American snipers were the reason the 1st Brigade went to Vietnam. You had shown the devastating effect of a lone man and a high-powered rifle, and the Vietnamese were determined to counter you with their own snipers. So in came the Russian instructors.''

Gray willed his lungs to work, and he asked, "Where was Trusov in Vietnam?"

"He spent most of his five months in Vietnam at an NVA camp near Chu Lai until he left the camp to travel south.''

Gray closed his eyes.

"He bragged to his 1st Brigade friends that he was the finest marksman in the world, and there was only one way to prove it. He told them he was going to hunt you down. And so one day in November 1970 he took off, knowing you were operating somewhere in Elephant Valley.''

"The man I killed was an American."

She shook her head. "Nikolai Trusov was wearing a U.S. Marine Corps field uniform and backpack. He had gotten it from the NVA, who must've taken it off a dead American. He wore it to confuse you, knowing that at the very least you would hesitate a moment. That's all Trusov thought he needed to defeat you, a moment of indecision on your part.''

Gray opened his eyes. Adrian was no longer smiling. He said, "Even if what you say is all true, I killed the man in Elephant Valley.''

"As hard as it is to admit for a sharpshooter like you, your bullet was high and wide.''

"He was dead. I saw him.''

232

"You put a trench in his head. It knocked him senseless and he bled profusely. You saw a mask of blood over his face, but you weren't looking at a fatal injury. And you've said yourself you only saw the downed target through your binoculars. You never walked to the enemy soldier to check him out."

Gray was staring at the scree behind Adrian, seeing nothing. He stammered, "You . . . you have no idea . . ."

A small wind brushed her damp hair. "I've been unable to discover who found the wounded Trusov in the valley, or when, but we can presume it was an NVA or Viet Cong patrol. But General Kulikov, rushing after a diplomatic post, connected me with the 1st Brigade medical officer who first treated Trusov after he was carried back into the Chu Lai camp. The medical officer is now a professor of medicine at Moscow University. He told me that the bullet had exposed Trusov's brain, left it open to the air. He put a dressing on it, and Trusov was returned to the Soviet Union several days later, still out cold. At some later date he regained consciousness, and later still a metal plate was put in his head."

The revelations seemed to have deboned Gray. He was limp and sagging. He whispered, "For all this time . . ."

"Your ninety-seventh kill wasn't a kill, and he wasn't an American."

Gray was still staring over her shoulder. Her news was seeping into him, impossible to absorb all at once. The central fact of his existence for most of his adult life—the anchor secured to his mind and heart and soul—had just vanished. It left a vacuum, and for the moment he was incapable of filling it with amazement or elation or gratitude.

"So you are back down to ninety-six." Her grin was back in place.

He shook his head. "Ninety-seven. Mrs. Orlando."

"I'm sorry," she said in a diminished tone. "But poor Mrs. Orlando's death was different. You were tricked by an expert. You didn't kill Mrs. Orlando. Nikolai Trusov murdered her. You only pulled the trigger. You might as well blame the rifle's manufacturer as yourself."

"I know all the rationalizations already," Gray said.

"Much of your burden has been that you ran away in Elephant Valley."

"That's so nicely put."

"But it's true," she persisted. "You've railed against yourself all these years not so much because you fired quickly and you thought an American soldier died by your hand but because you ran and never reported it to anybody and left a family wondering. It was a bit of cowardice, and it has worked inside you like a worm ever since."

Gray rubbed his temple.

"Nobody goes through life without an unflattering glimpse of himself or herself. You've had yours. You can fairly ascribe it to pressure of the field or youthful inexperience. But at the very least, the hard fact of killing the American is gone, just disappeared."

He abruptly grinned. "It has, hasn't it?"

Her news was sinking in. He felt lighter, as if gravity were exempting him. And giddy.

She smiled in recognition of her effect. "Am I good or what?"

"I never doubted it." He breathed the sweet air. "God, you have no idea . . ."

"So now all you have to worry about is Trusov."

"Why has he waited all this time to come after me, do you think?" Gray asked.

She shrugged. "Most of the time he was in the army or in a prison and couldn't come. Before that, who knows? Maybe the desire for revenge and to prove himself against you took a long time to eat away at him. Or maybe he wasn't crazy enough yet."

Gray nodded, lost in thought, his eyes on the distant rim of the bowl.

She waved at the valley below them. "What are you doing way up here?"

"I'm learning the terrain. Or relearning it, as I played a lot here as a kid."

She stood up, stepping over his legs, staying well away from the rifle. "I'm going back to the cabin." She turned for her descent. Stones skidded down the steep hill in front of her. She sidestepped down. A redtail hawk drifted over the bowl's ridge, black against the sky.

After several moments Gray put the binoculars to his eyes to watch her. Watch her move. Watch her black hair and her hips and shoulders.

She must have known he was watching her, because she suddenly turned to look back at him and smile and wave. Gray flushed.

She knew him better than he had supposed. She disappeared in the grove of trees at the mouth of the valley.

He tapped the sniper rifle's stock and said, "I'm more comfortable with you than with her."

15

"WHAT ARE YOU MAKING?" Andy Ellison asked.

"A surprise."

"For whom?"

"For the people chasing us." Trusov poured nails onto a plate in front of him.

"Are you making a bomb?" Ellison nervously chewed on a lip. He was wearing a Janis Joplin T-shirt and denim cutoffs. A string with one ceramic bead was around his neck.

"Something like that."

"Don't you think that's a little . . . a little violent?"

Trusov shrugged. He used a knife to cut a stick of dynamite in half, then snipped off a length of duct tape to close off the dynamite's open ends.

"Where'd you get all this stuff?" the hippie asked, pointing to the table and then to the green duffel bag on the floor next to Trusov's left leg.

"I find things. I'm good at finding things."

"I mean, a person just doesn't find dynamite."

"He does if he looks in a build house." Trusov inserted a Madoz detonator into the half-stick.

"Build house?" Ellison hesitated, then understood. "The phrase is 'construction shack.' "

Trusov nodded. "I have always been a good traveler. I change my clothes, I change my routes, I change my carrying bag. I pick things up as I go. I watch the ground in front of me, and every fifty paces I check over my shoulder." He placed the dynamite and detonator onto the plate, then placed several more handfuls of nails on top of them. "I'm never caught, not while I'm still moving."

They were sitting in the kitchen of a two-story house on the outskirts of Butte. The vacationing owners—the tiny placard under the doorbell identified them as the Robinsons—had stopped their newspapers, but it had taken the paperboy two days to figure it out. Trusov had found two old newspapers on the front step. He had broken in by a side window. The kitchen floor was of black-and-white tile. Pots and a strings of garlic and dried red peppers hung from a frame above the stove. Trusov had spread a newspaper below his work on the table. Near the duffel bag on the floor were several five-gallon cans of gasoline and a box of plastic garbage bags. Ellison hadn't asked him about the gasoline. The rifle leaned against the wall behind Trusov. Ellison had glimpsed several other rifles in the duffel bag. The blinds were drawn throughout the house.

Trusov explained. "In Afghanistan our airplane was hit by anti-aircraft. The pilot landed the plane in a field. I walked three hundred kilometers across that country to safety. Nobody caught me. Nobody even saw me."

"What happened to the pilot?"

"I left him at the plane."

"What happened to him?" Ellison asked.

"Sometimes it is better to travel alone. Sometimes it is not." The Russian put a second plate on top of the first and bound the two plates together with duct tape. Inside the plates were the explosive, detonator, and nails. He held the thing up to show Ellison, turning it slowly. "A mine." He picked up yet another plate and ladled handfuls of nails onto it, beginning the second mine.

"Where did you learn English?"

"In prison. From a book." Trusov's smile was turned down at the corners. His grin never touched his eyes. "Now I ask you a question."

"Shoot." Ellison peeled back the wrapper on a granola bar, feeling safer now that the stranger was taking an interest.

"Why do you grow marijuana? Why not get a work?"

Ellison was offended. "The word is 'job,' and that is my job."

"Why not get a job where you don't go to prison?"

"Growing weed is all I know how to do. And it's a matter of principle."

Trusov fiddled with the detonator.

Ellison went on: "I'm holding on to my past as a matter of principle. My girlfriend of fifteen years left me and got a license to sell real estate. My dog wandered off because I wouldn't feed him meat or meat by-products. But I'm sticking with it. Rubber-tire sandals, peace medallions, the works."

"You might not be as smart as I first thought," Trusov said, still working on the detonator.

Ellison hoped the big maul-faced man was joking. He ventured, "I've tried to stop time, stop the clock, just like the Amish in Pennsylvania and Ohio have. They stopped the clock in the last century, and I stopped it in 1968."

Trusov appeared uninterested, working on his second mine.

Ellison forged ahead. "Do you ever wish you could stop time?"

The Russian slowly lowered the plate. "I'm happy where I am. And with what I'm doing."

"Isn't there a time you wish you could return to?"

Trusov eyes were blank. "There is one day I would want to have back, yes." Then he was silent and unblinking.

A full minute passed.

Andy Ellison generated cheer in his voice. "But this'll soon be over. We'll shake them. They'll never find us."

"Yes, we will soon be released."

"The word is 'free.' "

The Russian looked at him. "Yes. Free."

✧   ✧   ✧

The monitor glowed with vibrant colors, blue and green and red and orange and yellow, all in wavy lines unreadable to Owen Gray.

Coates pointed at the blue. "That's him. Heat shows as blue. He's in an upstairs bedroom."

"What's this?" Gray raised a finger at a dot of blue on the first floor.

An FBI technician answered, "He left a light on in the kitchen, probably the same light the Robinsons left on when they went on vacation.''

The three men were in a delivery truck that read ''Big Sky Plumbing'' on the side. They were parked fifty yards from the Robinson house. The infrared's sensor was located in the passenger-side rearview mirror, and the apparatus was pointed at the Robinsons' house. The technician played with a dial. A row of blue shades appeared at the bottom of the screen, from ice-blue to dark purple, each in a small box.

The technician instructed, ''A person asleep has a different blue signature than one awake.'' He pressed a finger onto the screen below a light blue, then pointed at the wavy blue figure in the middle of the monitor. ''See? Same color. So he's asleep.''

''You sure it's Trusov?'' Gray asked. He was squatting on one side of the technician, Coates on the other. He held his rifle by the stock, butt plate on the floor. Gray's leg ached where the axe had sliced into it. The tech sat on a low milking stool, facing the monitor and keyboard.

''A mailman on his way home from a softball game spotted Trusov entering the house about nine tonight.''

Every post office in the western U.S. has a photograph of Trusov. Same with every Federal Express and UPS office and 7-Eleven and gas station. Every newspaper had run photographs of the Russian. In Montana alone three quarters of a million people knew his face.

Coates carried a flashlight in his hand. ''And the Silver Bow County sheriff's department has been watching the house since about ten. No one has come or gone since then. It's the Russian, we're pretty certain.''

''What about that dope grower Trusov forced the Black Hawk pilot to pick up?'' Gray asked. ''That could be him asleep in there.''

''We don't know where he is. He's not in the house, because the heat detector sees only this one body, and Trusov was seen going into the house.''

An hour ago Gray arrived in Butte, flown from Hobart by Bruce Taylor in the Black Hawk. After the disaster in Jefferson County, Coates had realized he was in over his head. Coates had said that had Gray been there, Gray might have sniffed out Trusov's presence in the field behind the helicopter. Gray had doubted it, but Coates had insisted Gray be present when next they cornered the Russian. Gray had the best chance of detecting a trap.

The technician asked, "Why don't you just plug the Russian right now from here. Hell, we've got rifles powerful enough that they'll send a bullet through that house's wall, through Trusov, out the far wall, and into the Pacific time zone."

Coates rubbed his chin. "There's a chance it's that hippie lying sleeping in there, not Trusov. There was an hour gap between when Trusov was seen entering the house and when the sheriff's department started the surveillance."

The tech was wearing a Pendleton shirt and climbing boots. He had a porky face, and it creased into a grin. He reached for a manila envelope. "But look at this." He pulled out an X-ray radiograph, switched on the cab's overhead light, and held the sheet up.

"You X-rayed the house?" Coates asked. "X rays will go through wood?"

"You bet, if you crank them up. They're called hard X rays. But it won't go through metal. And that person on the bed is never going to have children, but we don't care about that, do we?" He started a laugh but swallowed it when Coates and Gray would not join in. The technician pointed at the plate. "This dark figure on the X ray is the barrel, bolt, and scope of a rifle."

Coates stared at it for a moment. "No hippie carries a rifle around. That's Trusov all right."

The tech suggested again, "Let's plug him from here. Save the taxpayers some money."

Coates ordered, "You tell me over the radio if Trusov gets up from that bed. You got that?"

The tech dipped his chin, returning the X-ray photo to its envelope. Coates pulled an earplug from his shirt pocket and pushed it into his ear. The plug was in fact the entire radio, manufactured by Motorola, with receiver, antenna, battery, and speaker all in a package no larger than the tip of a finger. Coates led Gray out the van door. The night was still, the Montana night sky vast and painted. The Robinson house was a smudge in the distance, black on black. Six other law enforcement personnel waited at the back of the vehicle. The detective pulled his revolver from under his coat. "We're going in."

"Terrific." Gray's voice was flat.

Gray flipped the M-40A1's safety off. He followed the detective along the road toward the house. An FBI agent followed, carrying a set of picks on a steel ring. He clasped the picks together so they would not jingle. A quarter mile down the road was a sedan with three FBI agents standing near it, barely visible in the starlight. Other agents and sheriff's deputies were a hundred yards behind the house.

The three men neared the house. A slash of light was visible under venetian blinds at the kitchen window, the same light seen as a heat source on the monitor. At the picket fence Gray ran his free hand up and down the gate pickets and over the latch. He nodded at Coates. There were no booby traps attached to the gate. They pushed it open slowly. The gate did not squeak. They moved along a concrete walkway between planter beds of orange and red marigolds that stunk even at night.

The FBI agent took the lead and stepped onto the porch. He knelt at the door and worked his picks. Ten seconds later he nodded. Gray and Coates removed their shoes. Gray slowly twisted the knob. He nudged the door open three inches, then reached behind it to check the inside knob. He pushed the door open a fraction further, and reached inside further, checking for string triggers.

When the door was open fully, Gray led Coates inside. He moved slowly to avoid sound and to carefully survey the house. Each step was deliberated before taken. Gray's eyes searched the walls and the rugs and the furniture. The living room was dark except for light coming from the kitchen. Mrs. Robinson's collection of porcelain dolls—dozens of them—stared from a display case. A Wurlitzer organ was in one corner, with open sheet music on its stand. The room smelled of a dog, probably on vacation with the Robinsons.

Coates tapped Gray on the shoulder to stop him, then put his lips at Gray's ear. The detective whispered, "The earplug just said he's still lying on the bed. Hasn't moved."

Gray's hand ran over the riser and the first step to the second floor. He began up, checking the banister rail and pickets and the steps as he climbed. He paused on each step, listening and feeling. Gray led Coates into the second-story hallway. Gray slid his stockinged feet along soundlessly.

When they reached the closed bedroom door, the detective

tapped his earplug and gave the thumbs-up. The tech had just reported Trusov was still asleep.

Gray put his hand around the knob. As slowly as he could and still be moving, he turned the knob.

Coates lifted his thumb again, keeping his fingers around the flashlight handle. Still asleep. His pistol was at his ear. His teeth were bared.

Gray turned the knob. The bolt freed itself from the door frame. He inched the door open and slipped his hand inside to feel the interior knob. He slid his hand up and down the inside of the door as far as he could reach in up to his elbow. Nothing. No traps. He nodded at the detective.

Coates clicked on the flashlight and rushed the door. He swept into the room yelling, "Hands up, asshole. You're under arrest."

Gray followed, the bore of his rifle instantly pointing at the bed. He almost slipped on the damp floor.

The detective aimed the flashlight. "Goddamnit." He pointed the beam up and down the body. "Goddamnit to hell." The beam found the face on the pillow. "It's that hippie."

Andy Ellison lay on the bed, fully clothed, his throat laid open ear to ear. Blood was pooled on the floor in several places. Trusov had slit his throat, then dragged him to the bed.

Coates stepped to the wall to throw the light switch. Nothing happened. He pointed the flashlight at the overhead socket. The bulb was missing. He returned his flashlight's beam to the body on the bed. Blood had further dyed Ellison's tie-dyed shirt. A deer rifle leaned against the wall near the bed. A framed charcoal drawing of a bearded, severe family patriarch from the nineteenth century hung on one wall.

Gray put his hand across Ellison's forehead. It was still warm. "He's only been dead fifteen or twenty minutes."

Coates brought his gun hand to his forehead, pressing the back of his hand against his head. "That sensor didn't detect the heat of a man sleeping but of a man permanently cooling." He added sourly, "He might've been a puke dope grower, but he didn't deserve this."

Gray's nose came up. He sniffed, then suddenly pushed Coates toward the door. Too late.

Fire spilled from above the doorway to the wood floor, where it splashed into the room. The wall where the charcoal portrait hung shimmered as if liquid, then licks of fire curled through the wallpaper. An instant later the wall was a sheet of fire.

Gray pushed Coates's shoulders as they fled the bedroom. In the hallway fire gushed from a heating vent like a blowtorch, spreading quickly along the hall and slopping down the stairs, black smoke twisting away and ebbing against the ceiling. Lace curtains disappeared in a flash of fire. Above the second bedroom door the hatch to the attic had been left partly open. The sound of a dull burst came from the attic, then flames spewed down through the hatch, a red and yellow torrent of fire. The two men splashed through puddles of flame. Gray's pants legs caught, and he swatted them. When another muffled rupture sounded, the bathroom instantly filled with flames, billowing and surging, then rushing out into the hall.

Wallpaper peeled and curled, then caught on fire. The ceiling was abruptly made of flame rather than wood, a dome of fire above them. The old house popped and hissed and groaned. The fire sounded like a locomotive.

They reached the stairs. The steps crawled with flames. Gray fought for breath, and his throat and lungs seemed parboiling. The air was black with acrid smoke. Gray blindly led Coates down the stairs, feeling the fire work on his pants legs. Flames swirled and coiled, reaching for them. They tumbled down the stairs, a huge hand of fire reaching down after them.

Gray and Coates sprinted through the main room and out the door, leaving the blaze behind. Gray sucked the cool air into his lungs and swatted at his pants legs.

Coates bent over, hands on his knees, gulping air. He wiped his face with his sleeve. He formed the words slowly. "Christ, that was nasty."

Gray squeezed his eyes closed. His pants and shirt radiated heat as if just taken from a clothes dryer. Behind him the second story of the Robinson house was fully on fire with flames pouring out of windows that had been shattered by heat. The FBI locksmith was running toward them, and several law-enforcement cars were speeding along the road toward the house.

"We could've been killed," Coates said. He swatted embers from his jacket sleeve.

Gray shook his head. "Trusov was toying with us."

"He was playing a game? Why?"

243

"Trusov is a predator. A cat. And a cat plays with its mouse before it kills it."

❖   ❖   ❖

Owen Gray sat under the antlers in the dining room. The Marine Corps sniper rifle was on the table. He was installing an Army-issue MILE—a multiple integrated laser engagement system—on the barrel. The MILE was slightly larger than a cigarette pack, and it fit on the front of the barrel just behind the sight. Also on the table was a scope mount extension that would raise the scope an inch to allow the shooter to peer over the MILE. The installation and instruction booklet was held open by a Crescent wrench placed across its pages. Gray worked slowly, occasionally turning pages in the booklet. He was unfamiliar with the laser system designed to put a dime-size red dot on the target's forehead.

Coates returned from the telephone. "The FBI has determined how Trusov booby-trapped the house in Butte."

Gray looked up from the weapon.

"He removed light bulbs from their sockets, then connected the electrical wires above the bulbs. He did so for all the lights on that fuse, essentially making one long filament from the fuse box. When I threw the light switch on in the bedroom the fuse should have blown."

"So why didn't it?"

"Because Trusov had removed the fuse and stuck a penny in the fuse box. With no fuse to blow, the electrical wires overheated in just a few seconds. Trusov had also been in the attic, where he placed eight or nine plastic containers of gasoline right on the exposed wires. When the wires caught fire so did the gasoline. Our Russian is a smart boy."

Coates sat across from Gray and lifted the bottle of beer he had been nursing. He resumed peeling the label off with his thumbnail. His half-filled glass was near his elbow. A tray of cold cuts and a dish of apples were also on the table. He sipped the beer.

"The FBI has learned that his name was Andy Ellison, the one Trusov killed in the booby-trapped house," the detective said. "Why do you suppose the Russian went to all the trouble to pick him up in the helicopter and take him along for the ride, when all

Trusov was going to do was slit his throat. Any warm body would've worked to draw us into that house.''

Gray replied, "A sniper works anonymously, seldom with an audience, except his spotter. Maybe Trusov needed an audience for his cleverness, even some poor fellow he was going to murder.''

Coates nodded. "Yeah, maybe.''

"Or perhaps the Russian just wanted to talk, to unburden himself a little.''

"He doesn't strike me as the talky type.''

Gray said quietly, "We all need someone we can let go a little with, even snipers.''

Behind Coates, Adrian Wade tapped at her computer keyboard. Lights in the room were low, but her hands and documents and notes were under an orb of illumination from a nightstand light. The fire on the grate was crackling.

Coates looked across the table at his friend. "You can let go with me, Owen. Are you holding up all right?''

Gray lowered the rifle to the table near several tubes of camouflage grease paint. He glanced over at Adrian, then back to the detective. "No, I'm not.''

"You getting any sleep?''

"Not much.'' Gray's voice was the ghost of a whisper. "And I'm not keeping my food down.'' He wiped his upper lip with a finger. "A couple of times out in the woods I've found myself bent over, heaving away. My stomach feels like some farmer is turning it over with a mule and plow. I look back now, Pete, and I don't know how I did two tours in Vietnam.''

"We older guys can't take it.''

"I'm terrified.'' Gray let out a long breath. "My children have been orphans once and I'm afraid of leaving them orphans again. And I'm afraid for myself. I don't want a bullet to find me. I'm so frightened I'm having trouble swallowing.''

Adrian Wade flicked off her light and rose from her desk. She walked over, her hands at the small of her back as she twisted out a kink in her muscles. She sat next to Coates, then lifted an apple from the basket.

She must have been listening, because she said, "You don't need to be afraid yet, Owen.''

"The mad Russian isn't after you, so perhaps you aren't the best judge of whether I should be afraid." He smiled quickly to take offense from his words.

She brought the apple to her mouth, but instead of biting into it, she said, "Nikolai Trusov wants one thing in this life, and that is to re-create the day you shot him. Brick by brick, board by board, he is reconstructing that day."

"Do you think he wanted Owen to return to Idaho?" Coates asked. "Was that part of his plan?"

"He had Owen's high school yearbook, and so he knew Owen came from Hobart. So Trusov might have guessed Owen would return to Idaho. But I suspect that the precise location where Owen went after Trusov chased him from Manhattan didn't matter to the Russian as long as it was wilderness. Trusov needs wilderness as part of his plan."

She took a tiny bite of the apple, more a gesture, and went on. "Look at what he has done so far." She brought up her other hand to count off with her fingers. "First, he has chased you from the city into the wilderness. Idaho isn't Elephant Valley but it's still bush and forest. Second, he has forced you to return to your old profession of sniping. Third, he has stolen your Vietnam weapon, and he is going to insist you use it, not some other rifle."

"What's he going to do with my old Winchester?" Gray asked.

"He is going to somehow present it to you. And that's what I mean when I say you don't need to be afraid yet. That day in November 1970 won't be fully re-created and he won't begin the duel until you are using your Marine Corps sniper rifle. That's why he stole it from the museum. And fifth, we know that he is carrying with him a Moisin-Nagant sniper rifle, the one he used in Vietnam, or one identical to it."

Gray stared at the sniper rifle.

"Trusov would import tropical birds and bamboo and potted palms if he could. But he is going to settle for what he can get."

"Does Trusov have any more rules I ought to know about?" Gray asked.

Adrian pointed at the MILE. "He isn't going to allow you to use technology you didn't use in Elephant Valley. No lasers, no parabolic listening devices, no night vision goggles."

"What if we don't follow his rules?" Coates asked.

"He'll continue to kill anybody standing next to Owen until Owen understands his message and agrees to his rules."

Coates stepped to the couch in front of the fire and sank into one end of it. Adrian followed him, tucking herself into the other corner of the couch, leaning against the armrest. She kicked off her shoes and tucked her legs under her. Her blue-striped shirt was open to the second button. Her light-blue jeans were tight at her ankles. After a moment, Gray followed. He lifted a log from the box and threw it onto the fire before sitting between Adrian and the detective. Gray spread his legs, hooking a foot under the coffee table leg. Adrian was watching Gray.

"I think Nikolai Trusov has been telegraphing his movements." She spoke between bites of the apple.

"Wanting us to know his progress toward Idaho?" Coates asked.

"Sure. He is keeping ahead of the law but not particularly hiding his progress. He has left fingerprints everywhere. He has let himself be spotted a couple of times. For example, he didn't have to eat in that cafe in Mentor. His picture had been in the papers throughout Minnesota. He must've known he'd be spotted."

Coates agreed by nodding.

"And more than that," she continued. "The violence he inflicted on that gas station attendant in Cleveland was a message to us. He didn't need to do that. He could have flicked that fellow aside with the back of his hand. Trusov is too steady and professional to get carried away in trying to fend off some kid. He was telling us what we can expect if we don't go along with him."

"A long-distance message," Coates agreed.

The flames worked noisily at the wood. A charred log fell onto the embers, sending sparks up the chimney. The air was crowded with scents—fire smoke, old cedar, garlic from their pasta dinner, and Adrian's distinctive aroma, an eerily arresting and confounding fragrance.

When the telephone rang, the detective rose to cross the room to Adrian's desk. He carried his beer glass with him. After a moment he dropped the handset onto the receiver and walked back to the couch. "A sporting goods store near Butte has been broken into. A smash-and-grab. Trusov left his prints again."

"What'd he get?" Adrian asked.

"A .30-30 deer rifle and a .22, two shotguns, ammunition, three dozen hunting and fish-cleaning knives, some climbing rope, baling wire, and some cold-weather clothing. A cap, a pair of boots, that sort of thing. What's he want with the knives and rope and wire? And so many weapons?"

"Traps," Gray answered. "Protecting his hide and his routes with nasty surprises. Same thing I've done around here."

The detective rubbed the back of his neck. "Owen, I had hoped we wouldn't have to get to this because I thought we'd catch Trusov before he got here, but tomorrow you'd better start teaching me the lay of the land so I can help you when the time comes." He headed toward Gray's childhood bedroom. "I've got the bottom bunk. I'll be asleep in ten seconds." He disappeared through the door.

When Gray started to rise from his chair, Adrian's hand on his shoulder stopped him.

She asked, "Do you want to talk?"

"I'm out of talk." Gray's voice was so soft it mixed with the sounds of the fire. "Nikolai Trusov is reducing me to a rifle. Rifles don't have much to say."

Her hand was still on his shoulder. "We could talk about your plans after this is all over."

He looked at her a long moment. Then he gently shook his head. "For a number of days I haven't been able to think of any future beyond Trusov."

"You have a future, Owen. I'm interested in it."

He lifted himself from the couch. He stepped to the bedroom door, then glanced back at her. Searching for something to say, he found only "I'm interested in your future, too." He looked at her another moment, then continued into the bedroom.

16

THE CIVILIAN CONSERVATION CORPS built the fire tower in the late 1930s, and it had been repaired and upgraded over the years, until the mid-1980s, when it was abandoned, a victim of Forest Service cutbacks and satellite technology. The tower was on Fellows Mountain, a granite peak that offered a thirty-mile view yet was accessible almost to its peak in a four-wheel-drive vehicle. So many mountains formed this long spine of central Idaho that many of them, even those over nine thousand feet, were unnamed. Fellows Mountain owed the distinction of a name because the Forest Service spotter who had worked there for twenty-two summers carried the name.

The tower offered a 360-degree view of the crests and cliffs and ridges and chimneys of the surrounding mountains. The distance in all directions was filled with powerful cut-tooth shapes. Below the jagged granite formations were the forested foothills and alpine cirque lakes. From the tower's height, man's feeble inroads into the wilderness—a few ranches, the stunted town of Hobart, the occasional hunter's shack, the winding roads—were entirely hidden.

The tower was five miles east of Owen Gray's cabin. It straddled a sharp ridge, two of its four support posts on the south slope and two on the north. Valleys fell away in both directions, steep walls of fractured granite that plunged with dizzying abruptness to avalanche gullies below. Beyond the valleys were more ridges and peaks, some with sparse coverings of pine trees. The rim of Shepherd's Bowl was visible, the basin out of sight. Daisies and thistles and tarweeds tried their best but made little headway on gray stone.

Gray and Coates parked the Jeep fifty yards from the tower, where the Forest Service road ended. They traveled over the broken ground, following a trail that wound to the south side of the ridge. Even after years of footsteps from rangers and hunters the path was hardly a path, noticeable only because some of the sharper stones had been turned aside by boots over the years. The sun was a flat plate high overhead. The rocks radiated heat. The air was light and scentless.

"So you know where Trusov is?" Gray asked between deep breaths.

"You think I've been picking my nose all this time?"

"It means he crossed some hard country on foot."

The detective said, "The man is a machine. We learned a long time ago he could jog forty miles with a full pack over rough country. And he's done just that." Coates turned his head halfway to Gray. "But he's still twenty miles away. He hasn't made it over the Galena Pass yet. We're sure of that."

The trail narrowed and curved around a boulder formation that brought Gray and Coates near the precipice. They carefully stepped around stones and continued up the ridge. Gray was carrying the Marine Corps sniper rifle on a sling and the backpack. In his hand was a rolled-up map.

They drew near to the tower, which loomed above them on the ridge. A shaky ladder was attached to one post and was connected to a closed trapdoor. Wood planks framed all four sides, above which were picture windows on all sides. The roof was pitched sharply to allow snow to slide off. A stovepipe breached the roof, its conical metal cap tilted.

Coates bent over, his hands helping him scramble up the incline. They reached the cool shadow under the tower. A few milkweed plants grew at the base of the poles. Gray tested a rung with his weight. Then he began to climb. He pushed open the trapdoor with the palm of his hand. Its hinge was made of leather. The door fell back onto the floor with a loud slap. He pulled himself up and through the hole. Coates climbed after him, his feet disappearing through the hatch.

The tower contained one room. The furniture and equipment had been removed long ago. The roof leaked when it rained, and spots on the wood floor were brown from dry rot. Several nails were on a corner post where the rangers had hung their coats. Two-by-tens laid over sawhorses had served as a table and were still in the tower.

Gray spread out the map on planks near a window. "We are here." He drew a finger across the map. "My house is here. This is north."

"I know north," Coates said testily.

"Your people shouldn't come anywhere inside this area." Gray's finger traced a large circle around his house.

"I'm going to catch that bastard before he gets anywhere near your place." Coates stabbed the map. "Owen, I've now got three hundred law-enforcement personnel in the field, a wall of people. Trusov isn't going to get near your place."

Gray might not have heard him. "Once Trusov is loose inside this area, keep your people away."

"So you can duel with him? That's not what I'm here for."

"It'll be too dangerous for your people to follow the Russian into the forest."

"Three hundred people—"

"They'll be ducks in a shooting gallery, Pete. Entirely outgunned and outwitted."

"These are skilled people."

"Trusov will kill as many of them as he wants to. A dozen, two dozen." Gray's voice rose a fraction. "I'm telling you, it'll be a slaughter. Keep your people away from him and me once this has begun."

Coates stared at him.

"I'll have too much else to think about. I won't be able to keep them alive." Gray pointed out the window. "That's Bighorn Ridge." He located it on the map. "Over there is Sallick Mountain." Again back to the map to draw a circle. "I want you to promise me your folks won't get inside this circle."

"Well . . ."

Gray spit out, "Anybody in this circle is going to be a target. For Trusov and for me. I won't have the luxury of analyzing targets. I'm going to fire at any human I see."

Coates finally nodded. "Okay, nobody inside the circle."

✧   ✧   ✧

Fine optics can make even clear air have a grain. The blue of the sky seems to ripple and bubble, giving substance to nothing. Those optics seem to enhance color, and the small circle of pallid blue sky inside the metal band was sparkling blue. Inside the little disc of sky was a pointed post, a needle-sized metal twig sharpened at the top. The sky, made viscous like a stream by the lenses, floated toward the top of the circle as the scope slowly lowered.

Rising from the bottom of the blue ring of sky was the stovepipe lid, then the pipe, then the tower roof's shingles. Then came the window, the sun's reflection harshly magnified by the scope's lenses.

Nikolai Trusov smoothly moved his finger from the trigger to the eyepiece lens to turn it two degrees. The window frame sharpened. He lowered the rifle, and rising in the scope was more of the tower window. The Russian could make out slight warps in the glass as wind brushed the tower. With steady motion, as if the weapon were on rails, the barrel and scope glided lower. Owen Gray's head rose in the circle. Black hair, pale skin, a tall man. Gray's nose came to rest just above the point of the scope's aiming post. The American's image was shivered by heat currents. Owen Gray. White Star.

Then the scene in the eyepiece lens drifted smoothly to the left. The shorter form slid into view. Barrel-chested, sandy hair, small features in a melon head. The aiming post came to rest on his nose, just below a pair of spectacles. Then it sidled down his neck to the man's right arm. Eight hundred yards south and a hundred yards below the tower, Trusov brought his trigger finger back. Slowly and slowly and slowly.

The Moisin-Nagant bucked back against his shoulder. Most snipers will remain in position after a shot, letting their barrel return to the firing plane. Thinking about another task to be accomplished immediately after the shot makes the attention wander. Trusov had more skill than most and more concentration than most. He instantly lowered the rifle to the boulder he hid behind and brought up his binoculars. He had practiced the maneuver, and the binoculars immediately found the tower glass.

A black slash in the flat scene visible in the binocular lenses was Trusov's bullet, flickering through the air, then disappearing with distance. The tower window shimmered as a hole was punched into it.

✧   ✧   ✧

Blood and bone and shards of glass filled the air and lashed against the tower's far window like windblown rain. Pete Coates spun and then collapsed. Blood and bits of flesh slid down the far window. Trusov lowered the binoculars.

Snipers are taught that if they are captured or if they are surrounded, the time to break out is now, not later when the enemy has had time to regroup. All glass and plywood, the fire tower offered no protection from bullets. Coates groaned, blood spreading on the floor under his shattered elbow. Gray pushed him toward the hatch and without a word shoved him through. Coates landed heavily on the ground. The rifle in one hand, Owen Gray followed the detective through the hatch to the rocks below.

He landed hard on the incline and rolled involuntarily downhill, almost to the support post. Behind him, blood dripped from the hatch to splatter the stones. His shoes pushing against the loose rocks, Gray scrambled up the incline to push Coates behind a boulder. The detective moaned and his eyes opened. His elbow was frayed and bleeding, his jacket wicking away blood.

"Stay down," Gray ordered.

A bullet slammed into the rock supporting Gray's right foot. His leg collapsed, and he slid further down the incline. He tried to reach for the eight-by-eight, but he slid past, out into the blinding sun. He tightly gripped the rifle.

Hoping to find a foothold, he jammed a leg against the mountainside, but the loose stones slid away beneath him, rolling and bouncing down the slope. He clawed at the rocks and managed to slow himself. His slide stopped when his foot found a brace against a stone.

Blasting up a cloud of granite grit, another bullet kicked away that stone. Gray fell again. The side of the mountain gained in pitch, and he slipped more quickly, his body bouncing painfully as he skidded over the rocks. He tried to jam the stock of his gun against a boulder to stop himself, but he was sliding too quickly and the boulder ripped the weapon out of his hand.

Feet downward he slid, crashing down the incline. With his left hand he frantically grabbed at a Scotch broom, a tawny, strong plant that would hold him. His fingers caught a branch. He stopped, perched precariously against the side of the mountain. Blood flowed from his legs where pants and skin had been abraded.

A bullet coursed into his left arm, digging a half-inch trench in his triceps. His arm jerked spastically and he lost his grip. Yet another bullet struck the heel of his boot, tearing off the leather and burning the bottom of his foot. His leg collapsed, again sending him helplessly down the steep hill. When his leg caught on a rock, his momentum flipped him to one side and he began to roll lengthwise down the gully side, stones smashing into him as he tumbled. The world whirled madly around him. Blue sky and gray stone spun over and over. His head banged into a rock, then another.

He came to rest at the bottom of the gully. Scraped and shot and bleeding, he crawled behind a boulder that hid him from the south slope. His rifle was somewhere up the slope.

Gray heard several more shots and the shattering of glass. Trusov was disabling the Jeep.

Five minutes passed before his vision lost the fuzziness at the edges and Gray admitted to himself that he could think clearly again. The Russian hadn't been out to kill him or he would have. All the pieces of that day in Vietnam weren't yet in place. Gray was safe, the Russian probably gone.

Gray rose from behind the boulder. Limping and bleeding and aching, he crawled back up the slope.

✧   ✧   ✧

The computer monitor displayed the photographs one after another, all with the clarity of 35-millimeter slides. Owen Gray at twelve months, a scant halo of dark hair, pudgy cheeks, an open smile revealing four baby teeth. Owen Gray, eighth grade, shy grin, eyes a little to the left as if a friend off-camera is razzing him. Owen Gray wearing a narrow black tie and a full grin, his hair over his forehead in the new fashion imported from Liverpool, his high school yearbook photo. Owen Gray's Marine Corps boot camp ID photo, shaved head, stunned look. Another Marine photo of Gray, this time receiving the Honor Man citation from a colonel, Gray wearing a white dress cap and a single chevron.

Next was a snapshot of Gray sitting in front of sandbags wearing a small mustache, a rifle with a starlight scope just visible at the edge of the frame. Next was a college yearbook photo, then one from law school, then a photo from his first year as a prosecutor. Gray was aging as the photos rolled by, a few wrinkles at the corner of his eyes, a slight rise in his hairline above the temples. The last, from six months ago, was taken at a federal prosecutors' dinner, showing Gray in black suit and a floral tie, wearing a confident but tired grin.

For a moment, Adrian stared at the screen, at the most recent photo, then she stroked the keyboard several times and Gray's baby photo appeared again on the monitor. Distant laughter from the troopers at their car on the other side of the big larch tree did not distract her. She went through the photos of Gray, this time more rapidly, watching him grow and stabilize and age. The photos revealed little, only what Gray was prepared to show the camera, but still, for a student of human nature as Adrian Wade was, there was much to be seen. Some scoffed at the notion of intuiting personality traits from photographs of a face. It smacked of the fakery of phrenology. But a camera could peek behind the surface of the skin, could betray confidences and convictions to the careful viewer.

She leaned back in her chair studying Owen Gray's face. Her work in the mountains was finished, her investigating and computer skills no longer needed. She should have been packing her few things, readying for the journey east, but her clothes remained on pegs in the bedroom. She idly tapped her fingers on the base of the keyboard. She wore her Gortex jacket, only slightly askew on her shoulders because of the handgun under the fabric. To her left, the antler chandelier swung slowly in a draft. Sunlight streamed through the windows, making the room dark by contrast. Outside, a song sparrow let loose with its three piping cheerful notes, followed by a rapid slur of a smaller trill. Adrian lifted her wallet from the desk and pulled out her driver's license. She held it up alongside the monitor. She stared at the small colored photograph of herself, then her eyes shifted to the image of Owen Gray on the screen.

She smiled knowingly and said to the screen, "I know your future better than you do."

The cabin's front door burst inward, the sound of the blow and the splintering of wood seeming to have a physical impact on Adrian. She flinched, then spun out of her chair. The door wagged left and right, its top hinge dangling loose and the knob hanging by a few wood shreds. Sunlight poured through the door. The room was alive with new light. Her hand went inside her jacket.

Holding a deer rifle, Nikolai Trusov stepped to the door. He filled the frame and was backlit with rays of sun streaming off the black silhouette of his body like tiny searchlights. He was magnified by the harsh light, but his stony features were made murky by the shadows. Adrian hissed through her teeth at the sight of him.

He held out the rifle. His voice was guttural and entirely foreign. "Give Gray his rifle. And give him this message—"

"Not likely," she cut in.

The Russian must have been astonished at her speed. She had told Gray she was qualified with a pistol. More than that, she was good with one. Her Smith and Wesson Model 459 weighed only twenty-eight ounces and had a four-inch barrel. It was small, yet it was a semi-automatic 9-mm Parabellum with a fourteen-shot staggered clip. So it was also fast. It whipped out from under her jacket, its nickel finish gleaming like evil. She was pulling the trigger before the Russian was in the sights. Thoughtful aiming was not this weapon's purpose, but rather it was designed to fill the air with projectiles. She fired six times, as rapidly as she could pull the trigger. The gun climbed a ladder rung with each shot. The flat crack of the shots rattled the cabin's walls. Dust drifted down from the chandelier.

She lifted her finger from the trigger, the pistol still up and ready. Where she had expected to see a body there was nothing, just sunlight filling the doorway. The room screamed with the absence of the body that should have been there. The air smelled of burnt powder. She glanced through the door. One state patrolman was lying on the ground in front of the car, a slash of blood under an ear. The other officer was in the front seat slumped forward, his jaw open in mortal surprise. Trusov had killed them both a moment ago.

Adrian kicked the door shut and stepped quickly to the wall near her desk. She held the gun up with both hands, her back against the log wall. The room had too many windows, too many places where the Russian could peer inside. She would be safer in the back bedroom. She bent low to pass under the window that looked out onto the destroyed woodshed.

Trusov's arm lashed through the window, through windowpanes and sash bars. Glass chips and shards followed the swinging arm into the cabin. The arm seemed covered with sparkling scales that blinked and glimmered. The fracturing glass sounded like a harsh laugh. The hand seized Adrian around the neck, yanked her upright, then backwards through the shattered window, dragging her over slivers of glass. Glass fragments resembled teeth, and she seemed to be sucked back into the jaws of a dragon. A shard bit into her hand and she dropped her pistol.

Glass hung from her jacket and hair. A necklace of blood appeared on her neck. Nikolai Trusov held her upright from behind, one hand on her neck, the other clutching her upper arm. His hands secured her like steel bands. His breath was on her neck.

The Russian growled, "Give him the rifle and this message—"

Adrian Wade had trained for years for this moment. All the falls on the mat at the dojo, all the tournament rounds. She fiercely jerked her head back, cracking her skull into his nose. He grunted with pain. His grip lessened.

She abruptly shifted her weight to one side and launched her elbow back at his groin. She caught his genitals with full force, the point of her elbow sinking inches into his pants.

He should have buckled over. He should have collapsed to the ground and lain their vomiting and gasping. Instead he lifted her fully off the ground and marched her to the next window. He caught a fistful of her black hair, then rammed her face through a windowpane. Glass shattered and shimmered. A cascade of flashing prisms surrounded her, a sea of glittering refractions. Cuts opened on her forehead, sending a wash of blood over her eyes. When he brought her head back out, glass splinters dug into her skin behind her ears, spilling more blood.

"Why do you Americans never listen to anything?" he asked

levelly, his voice a study in reason and courtesy. Again he had her by the neck and arm. "Will you listen this time?" He moved her head back and forth, as if she were nodding. "Good. I'm going to let you live because you are to give Gray the rifle and give him this message. I will be within eight kilometers of this house. He is to come into the field alone and with his rifle. Do you understand?"

Again he tugged her head back and forth, forcing her to nod. He tossed her against the logs of the cabin wall, a casual offhand motion, but her head hit the wall. She fell onto glass pieces and lay motionless, her face a bloody mask. He retrieved the rifle from the porch. It was Owen Gray's Winchester 70 with the mounted Unertl scope. He treated it more gently than he had Adrian, propping it up next to her, carefully so as to maintain the scope's alignment, the butt on the ground.

"I will be waiting for him." The Russian disappeared around a corner of the cabin.

Only after several moments could Adrian push herself to a sitting position and dab at the blood on her eyes. She winced as her fingers pushed needles of glass further into her forehead. She tried to rise but could not. She blinked, and her eyelashes flicked away droplets of blood. She was too dizzy to move, so there she waited for Owen Gray.

17

STEALTH OR SPEED. The dilemma had been an endless source of debate among Gray and his sniper friends in Vietnam. Hurry but risk detection? Or proceed carefully and risk losing the target? No satisfactory answer was ever produced, but now Gray settled on speed. He moved up Black Bear Creek Valley at a brisk walk, the rifle in both hands.

He was dead tracking, moving faster than the man who had left the sign. Gray glanced at several fresh footprints near the stream. Then came a rough patch of boulders, then bent stems of marsh cudweeds, then the prints again. Trusov's register indicated he had walked rather than trotted up the valley. Trusov was doing nothing to hide his direction or speed. Gray knew that at some point ahead, when Trusov decided it was time, the footprints would simply vanish.

Noise is the exception in the wilderness. Silence is standard. Gray moved along the creek with unearthly quiet. A watcher might have concluded Gray was floating along the path. He was imitating a fox's walk, moving his feet in line, one directly in front of the other with each step coming down on the outside of the foot before rolling to the inside. The gait reduced the number of branches the legs might rasp loudly against, and the rolling footfall crushed fewer twigs and leaves.

As Gray walked up the valley he also traveled into a new state of consciousness. His old skills had been slowly coming back to him since that day on the federal courthouse steps, but now he was enveloped in the armor of his Vietnam mind. The wound in his arm from Trusov's bullet should have been flooding him with pain, but Gray felt nothing. The scrapes and bruises—and he was nothing but grainy red scrapes and purple bruises from his mad slide—should have frozen him with pain, but he hardly felt them. He had the right to be propelled by revenge, but he knew that in the field hate kills the wrong person. Here, too, he felt nothing. And he should have been frightened, but he was dead to fear. He was a coyote, with no ability to ruminate, with no thoughts of the future or past, considering nothing but the ground that carried him and the flora that hid him. He had entered a fog of indifference where he would be distracted by nothing and would address only the puzzle in front of him.

And that was all it was, a puzzle, no more complicated or monumental than a dime-store toy. Gray had to center a man in his crosshairs and pull the trigger, the irreducible act. He simply had to find those clues in the field that would allow him to move his finger back a half an inch before Trusov moved his own finger. Then the puzzle would be solved.

Gray moved up the valley, passing aspen and cottonwood and pines. Black Bear Creek was a carillon to his right. He looked at nothing and at everything, using a technique known as splatter vision, where he let his vision spread out. Rather than focus on any one object, he softened his eyes to gather in all in front of him. His field of vision was of half the compass points ahead.

His face and hands were covered with brown and olive and green greasepaint. Some of his cohorts in Vietnam had worn loose clothing like the duelists of the last century, thinking an opponent would be deceived as to the location of the heart. But with bullets fired from a modern sniper rifle the precise spot the bullet entered the trunk was usually irrelevant. Gray wore a field uniform provided by Arlen Able that Gray had brought with him to the Sawtooths. Rawhide was tied around his pants legs at the ankles to keep the trousers from flapping. Several leafy twigs were stuck into buttonholes. On his feet were a pair of his father's buckskin moccasins that were almost as quiet as bare feet. He wore a regulation-issue Marine Corps utility cap. Gray had put several short syringa branches into the webbing, and the leaves bobbed against his head as he walked. He had cut flaps from the cap's sides, so pieces of cloth hung down on his ears and hair, breaking up the cap's lines along his temples. He had left his belt and wristwatch behind because of the danger of reflection. A length of rope secured his trousers. He wouldn't need to know the time.

A Marine sniper in Vietnam entered the field traveling light, but even so his pack outfitted for a three-day mission contained over forty items, including tactical maps, washcloths, C-4 plastic explosives, wire cutters, extra boot laces, water-purification tablets, BFI blood coagulant, toilet paper, a strobe light, foot powder, a transistor radio, Kool-Aid, a Turkish battle-axe, and more. Gray carried far less. In addition to the rifle and what snipers called the basic load—eighty-four rounds in a pouch—Gray had with him only a pair of binoculars, a Swiss Army knife with screwdrivers for adjustments to the scope, a canteen, a pen, and matchbooks. In his pocket was a small spiral notebook in which he hoped to record his kill. Gray would sanctify the Russian's death by entering it in his notebook just as he had done for ninety-six other kills. Gray had no doubt Trusov also carried pen and paper. And a red shell.

Gray suspected Nikolai Trusov had outfitted himself with almost the same load. The two men were now distillations of all that was known about the craft of the sniper, and this reduction made them identical. Everything Gray knew—every small stratagem, every trace of wisdom about fieldcraft—Trusov also knew. Their destinies had been intertwined since the day Gray fired at Trusov in Elephant Valley. Gray had been fated for this march along Black Bear Creek toward Shepherd's Bowl since then.

Gray pushed through spikes of elephant grass, the Russian's tracks still plain. He ducked under pine boughs. The stream narrowed as it neared its source, and to avoid impenetrable brush thickets Gray jumped across the creek and back several times. As he neared the bowl, he began using a technique his sniper school instructors had called scanning, moving the eyes in abrupt and irregular movements, stopping the eye for only an instant on any one thing. Scanning is unnatural. The eyes demand a rest. But the technique allows the viewer to review and catalogue the immense amount of information the wilderness offered. Scanning seeks not animals or men but disturbances.

He had suspected Trusov would head to Shepherd's Bowl. It

was four o'clock in the afternoon. A sniper's instinct is to get the sun behind him, and the bowl was west of the cabin. Trusov would want Gray staring into the setting sun not just because it would impair Gray at the instant of the shot but also because gazing toward the sun is highly fatiguing, and with weariness come mistakes.

Shepherd's Bowl offered something else to the Russian—a closed horizon, a self-contained dueling field. The bowl would fit Trusov's sense of order and his fervent desire to play the game. The bowl would also limit the area Trusov had to scout.

Because Trusov had sent several shots into the Jeep, putting it out of action, Gray had used his belt as a tourniquet around Coates's shattered arm, and had left him at the fire tower. Gray had then taken two hours to hobble back to the cabin to find Adrian, and another hour had passed before an ambulance arrived for her, before he could leave her. A helicopter was on its way to the tower for Coates. So the Russian had been in the bowl several hours before Gray could get there, and in that time Trusov would have learned all there was to know about the area. Trusov might also have had maps of the area.

Gray jumped the creek again. The sky was narrowed by the valley walls and darkened by tall trees, but it was opening up ahead. Another five hundred yards would put Gray at the mouth of Shepherd's Bowl. His options now were to travel faster or slower, but not at a walking pace. Nothing in the wilderness—not a deer or a wolf or a snake or a bear—moves at a human's pace, and anything traveling four miles an hour is always a target. He slowed, coasting over the ground. His feet melted to the earth's contours. Gray let the wilderness soak him up. He might have been invisible.

The memory of Adrian tried to push itself into his mind, and only with effort could he dismiss it, his eyes scanning and scanning. He had left her in the care of a physician and ambulance attendants. She had worn on her face most of the blood she had spilled, and so looked worse than she was. She wouldn't need to stay overnight at the clinic in Ketchum. Still, she would require stitches near her shoulders and behind her ears. Butterfly bandages would be sufficient for her forehead. The doctor said she might have a slight concussion, but she had been asking Gray questions, as always. Gray had gently chided her. He was relieved when she laughed.

Gray had peeled her hand from his, then taken up the rifle to begin his journey to Shepherd's Bowl.

Gray rushed up in shadows cast by the trees in front of him. He ducked left and right, left and right, to new shadows, always nearer to the bowl's mouth. Nikolai Trusov was within two miles of him, of that Gray was certain. The most dangerous thing in the field for a sniper is another sniper, because he knows what to look for. Those tactics of travel and camouflage that made Gray blend with the wilderness worked only up to a point with another sniper, who would see what others could not and expect what others would not. Gray stepped around a chokecherry. Through the trees he could see the bowl's west wall. The sun was lowering in the afternoon sky, sending out spokes of gold light that turned like a wagon wheel.

Black Bear Creek dwindled to rivulets winding between stones. Not far into the bowl was the small pool where the stream originated. As Gray moved forward, the valley grew in front of him until it filled his vision. He stood behind a lodgepole pine and pulled his binoculars from the pack. He held his hand above the objective lenses to guard against reflection.

Shepherd's Bowl was a study in shifting greens and browns. On Gray's right the north slope resembled a desert. Lower on the north slope were the muted dusty greens of sagebrush and bitterbrush and mountain heath and Scotch broom, with green leaves shading to yellow. Higher on the slope, brown and gray boulders were spotted by stonecrop with its tiny, waxy green pods.

Gray shifted the binoculars. The bowl's center was a mix of grasses that had dried to yellow. Lodgepole and yellow pine, mountain hemlock and mountain laurel, dotted the patches of grass. The trees were dense along the bowl's east-west crease.

On Gray's left was the south slope, the darker wall where the green of lodgepole pine was touched with the blue and black of shadows.

Gray moved the binoculars right to left again, looking for agitation in the underbrush, looking for a too-straight line, looking for the slightest of reflections, looking for color that was too lively, looking for anything white or black, looking for perturbed crows or jays, never focusing on one thing for too long. All he found was more green and brown.

Trusov's footprints went due west, entering the long swath of trees on the seam of the bowl along the creek. Following this long dell was the only way to enter the bowl unseen by anyone on the bowl's slopes, and this was the route of Trusov's prints. To follow the Russian's path would most likely mean walking into a trap.

Gray moved west through the trees into the bowl, then took a dogleg route, south a few paces, then west again. He walked with exceeding care, slowly and with patience, following Trusov's westerly route but by a parallel course a hundred feet from Trusov's trail. He watched the ground, avoiding dried foliage that might crackle underfoot. He moved so silently he could not hear his own footfalls. The Winchester was across his chest.

He approached a dell, a hundred-yard expanse spotted by only a few trees. The spring and pool were to Gray's left. The odor of tarweed carried to Gray. The dell was also filled with sow thistle and yarrow and knapweed. Gray lowered himself to his knees and elbows and crawled forward to survey the dell. He shimmied along the ground around a pine tree to two rotted logs. One tree had fallen over the other several years after the first came down. Gray crawled into the vee formed by the logs. The fallen trees were so old that dandelions were growing from their decomposed bark. Gray flinched when a goldfinch flashed by. The bird trilled as it flew, the notes sounding like "potato chips, potato chips."

Gray checked over his shoulder. From behind he was protected by an upright pine. His hide was almost fully enclosed. He was satisfied he was in a position a bullet could not reach. Gray rose to kneeling, brought his backpack around, and reached for his binoculars. Moving half an inch at a time, he rose to peer over the log.

Sound and the pain rushed over him at the same instant. An explosion from above lanced his back from shoulder to the base of his spine. Ferocious jets of pain. Gray toppled sideways onto dry cheat grass. His back felt as if a surgeon had opened it with a scalpel. He gasped with pain, then scrambled closer to a log, trying to tuck himself under it. He didn't know where the danger lay. Blood was left on the ground. He squeezed his eyes against the racking pain, then opened them to stare skyward.

Around the tree above him, about fifteen feet off the ground, was a circle of baling wire. Something had been attached to the tree. Gray's hand found several fragments of pottery, portions of a plate. Then he saw a littering of nails.

Gray knew then the trap he had fallen for. The Russian had placed an impact mine above a likely hide. Trusov had somehow glimpsed Gray but had been unable to get Gray in his scope. Trusov had set off the explosive with a bullet fired from a long distance, causing the nails to blast down at Gray. In effect the mine allowed Trusov to reach around corners. The Russian would have more mines in the bowl. The mine had not been meant to kill him. Trusov would want the purity of a bullet for that task.

Gray slowly brought a hand around to his buttocks. Teeth clamped together, he pulled out a protruding nail, then another. He ran his hand along his shirt and found several more nails in his back, gingerly pulling them out. His back was damp but there was less blood on the ground than he had feared. Gray decided he wasn't badly hurt. Nothing vital had been cut. Several nails were still embedded in his flesh where he couldn't reach, and when he crawled away from the logs the skin and muscles of his back shrieked. But this wasn't going to kill him. Trusov had failed with his first attempt. Gray was almost cheered by the thought.

Then he realized he had been entirely surprised. Not once, not in months and months in the Vietnam bush, had Gray been caught utterly unaware. Now it had happened.

He stilled those thoughts. He checked his canteen. No leaks. His binoculars were scratched, but the lenses were intact. His pack had holes in it but would carry his equipment. The Russian's mine had failed.

Gray concentrated on the best way to make it back to the thicket of trees near the bowl's mouth. He could not cross the glade, not with Trusov out in front of him—at least, that's where Gray thought the bullet had come from, although the blast from the plate mine had masked the sound of Trusov's rifle.

Trusov had been in the bowl at least three hours. Time to prepare many other surprises.

Gray returned east the way he had come, this time even more slowly, his head moving left and right. Moments later he had returned to the mouth of the bowl.

He wanted to circle around Trusov, who Gray presumed was somewhere in the middle of the bowl in the dense trees. Because the north slope was mostly barren, Gray would have to do his circling on the south slope. But between him and that incline were tracts of grass, open killing ground, an artilleryman's dream and an infantryman's nightmare, almost impossible to cross without being observed. The grass began under the trees where Gray stood, and ran toward the south slope.

Gray slid his backpack around so that it hung on his left side, hugged the rifle to his stomach with his left hand, then lowered himself to the ground. His back and buttocks yelped with pain.

Because lying on his belly would flatten more grass Gray stretched out on his right side. A nail in his back ripped his flesh as he stretched out. Leaving the cover of the trees, he began a side crawl into the thick grass. He used his right hand to part the grass in front of him, pushing the grass stems to either side, careful not to snap the stalks. He moved slowly, nothing like the pace of an infantryman crawling under barbed wire but more like a worm where every part of his body was in contact with the earth and was used to push himself along. His motion resembled a swimmer's sidestroke but more constricted and much slower. He traveled only a few inches a minute through the grass and by the occasional blue-blooming larkspur and yellow paintbrush. With his toes he righted stems that did not spring back on their own. This would prevent shining, which occurs when the sun bounces off vegetation that has been pushed down, leaving a bright trail. And the grass was dry from the day's heat, so Gray knew he was not leaving a trail of dulling, a highly visible path where rain or dew has been knocked away.

His passage through the field of grass would have been invisible to anyone standing ten feet away. In Vietnam, Gray had used grass fields many times, not only to move unseen but also as a hide. Grass is a sniper's safest shooting position because there is nothing —no rocks or trees—that an enemy can use to sight or range his gun.

The crest of the grass was a foot above Gray's head. His nose was in the dirt. Had he allowed himself the luxury, he would have reeled from the sensations. The raw scent of the earth, the hot puffs of an idle wind that pushed through the grass, the insistent drone of yellow jackets and bees, and the taste of his own sweat as it slid from his cheek into his mouth were all magnified by his tiny horizon. Twenty feet away, also hidden in the grass, several chukars let loose with their strident chuk-karr, chuk-karr, unaware of Gray's presence. But he had not gone entirely unnoticed. The sunlight flickered, and Gray moved his eyes skyward to see a vulture passing between him and the sun. The bird wheeled over Gray, its oddly tipsy flight distinguishing it from its raptor cousins, then it soared away, apparently deciding Gray was too far from death to be of interest. A tick hopped onto Gray's leading wrist. Gray could not risk the extra motion of swatting it away. The insect burrowed into the skin and its spotted body swelled with Gray's blood. Gray inched along.

There had been no choice between the M-40A1 sniper rifle and his old Winchester 70 that had been delivered by Nikolai Trusov. After he had tended to Adrian and the ambulance had carried her away, Gray approached both weapons, both on the porch leaning upright against the log wall. The Winchester had seemed to leap into Gray's hands like a lost dog. And the instant the Winchester found Gray's hands it seemed to vanish. Over the past several days he had become accustomed to the M-40A1 and was confident with it. But that rifle was still a stranger. Even after all these years the Winchester felt like an extension of Gray's body. His arteries and nerves and sinews continued into the wood and all the way up to the bore. And now, rather than being inert wood and metal, the rifle helped Gray worm his way through the grass, bending and pushing. Gray had not had the chance to zero the weapon, but he trusted it to be accurate. His old friend the Winchester would not allow itself to fall out of zero. And Trusov would want Gray's old rifle to be accurate. It would fit the Russian's notion of fairness.

Gray and his rifle pushed through several tufts of fleabane, and then rather than change direction he let a bull thistle scratch his face as he passed. He pressed himself against the ground as he moved. Dirt and twigs kept finding their way into his mouth, and he quietly spit the bits out as if he were a Pall Mall smoker.

Gray could do nothing better in this world than to move invisibly across terrain. Each small and silent motion was an art, his art. When the rhythm of the crawl came back to him after a while, he found he could pick up his pace a few more feet an hour. The slightest mischance with an errant stalk of grass might send a bullet his way, so Gray constantly reined himself in. He desperately wanted the shelter of the trees. His clothes were sodden with perspiration. He was still leaking blood. Stray pieces of dried grass clung to him, and he began to resemble a scarecrow.

Two hours passed, all the while Gray knowing Trusov was in a hide somewhere in the bowl, searching with his binoculars, occasionally raising his rifle to use the more powerful mounted scope.

Then the sound of a shot rushed over the grass. Gray bit into the ground, flattening himself. The noise echoed around the bowl, washing over Gray several more times. Gray did not hear the bullet passing overhead or through the grass. He allowed himself the slightest smile of satisfaction. Trusov must be nervous. He had fired at a shadow or a bird or a wind-blown branch. When a nail in his back brushed a nerve the smile vanished.

Gray dug his leading hand into the ground and pulled forward, parting the grass, sliding over the ground, rearranging the grass behind him, a smooth mechanical motion impeded only slightly by the spikes of pain in his back. He could smell pine sap and knew he was drawing close to the trees. Maybe another sixty or seventy yards.

Then he smelled something else, a scent entirely foreign in the bowl. For an instant all his nose could detect was some sort of chemical. And then he knew it was gasoline. Next he smelled fire.

Gray could not risk raising his head above the grass, but he could hear the fire ahead of him, spreading rapidly left and right, probably along a line of gasoline Trusov had poured. The Russian had probably left behind a partly filled can of gas, and had ignited the gas by firing into the can. Trusov must have suspected Gray was in the grass but could not know precisely where.

The fire quickly consumed the dry grass. The wind was easterly but indifferent, only haphazardly pushing the flames, but the cheat grass and bunch grass and nipplewort were hay-dry, and the fire briskly ate into the field, quickly working east toward Gray. Smoke reached him, then tossing embers. Grasshoppers flicked by, fleeing the flames, then mice, one after another, a few crawling along Gray's arm, too frightened to care about the human.

A wind-tossed bit of burning grass landed on Gray's back, but to swat at it would ruffle the grass that hid him. Trusov was surely scanning the field, hoping to flush Gray and put a bullet into him as he tried to escape the fire. The fire was meant not to kill Gray but to flush him. Only a bullet would do for the killing.

The heat reached for Gray, the first blushes of it rolling over him, then subsiding with a quirk of the wind. Then more insistently, a pulse of heat that made him suck air. He looked forward through the grass. Orange licks were blackening and twisting the grass and sending waves of black smoke skyward. Not enough smoke was over him to cover him for a sprint. Gray had no choice but to lie there. From Gray's point of view—his eyes two inches above the dirt—the fire seemed to be sprinting toward him. Bits of flaming grass rose and swirled as smoke billowed. Grass snapped and hissed. A new gust of wind sped the flames. The fire roared as it closed in on Gray.

18

BITE DOWN. NO TREMBLING, no thinking, no equivocating. If he rose to flee he would die. If he made a sound or if he made any quick move he would die. He could feel the sweep of Trusov's binoculars, feel the Russian's eyes searching and searching.

To protect his weapon and prevent ammunition in the pack from detonating in the heat, he slowly brought his backpack and rifle to his stomach. He tucked the pack and Winchester under his belly. Walls of heat rushed at him. He crammed his hands under him, squeezing the Winchester's stock, knowing he would need a grip on something.

Embers landed on Gray's shirt and pants, burning through the cloth and into his skin. The fire sounded like an animal tramping through the brush, closer and closer, cracking and bursting, homing in on Gray. Curls of flame came for his cap. The odor of burning fabric filled him. The blaze came on louder, now the sound of an engine.

He clamped his eyes shut and ground his mouth into the soil, filling it with dirt to dampen any scream. The first licks of fire found his face, caressing him then eating into his skin. The cap was on fire and his hair with it. Gray tried to dig his face deeper, deeper into the cool soil. His head felt as if razors were being dragged across it, temple to temple.

An ear caught fire. The fire stitched its way down his neck to his shoulders. It felt as if he were being flayed, as if his skin was being peeled back to reveal his skull and bones. His shirt caught with hissing flame, and the sensation of flaying continued down his back. The fire line advanced past his shoulders and to his back, then along his back, baking his skin, bubbling it with heat. But the quickened wind pushed the flames. The fire ate but did not tarry. A cloud of smoke covered him and he gasped for breath, and in the smoke was his salvation. The smoke was above him now. He had cover.

Marine snipers know that the fastest way to travel from one position to another is the rush. Gray slowly drew his arms to his body with his elbows on the ground, and pulled his right leg forward. He rose by straightening his arms as if doing a push-up. Keeping his grip on the rifle, he dug his left foot into the soil and leaped up, rising in the flame. Gray willed his knees to work. He ran low to the ground.

The blaze leapt and twisted around him. Fire stuck to him, consuming more of his skin. He bolted along the fire line, the only place the smoke was thick enough to hide him, keeping a shroud of black around him. His burns were a straitjacket of pain, and every step squeezed him with agony. He ran along the fire, right along the fire line, running for his life. He could see nothing but roiling smoke.

Then the south slope and its trees appeared before him, blurred by the smoke. His burned skin wrapped him in an agony he could not outrun. A pant leg trailed fire, and Gray could feel the flames chewing into his thigh and knee. He sprinted out of the fire, and carried smoke along with him as he ran uphill, then finally out of the smoke and into the woods. He passed several trees deeper into cover before he dropped the pack and rifle and collapsed at the base of a pine tree. He rolled on the ground, trying to extinguish the flames. He scooped pine needles onto his head, dampening whatever fire remained.

His cap was gone, and so was most of his hair. His mouth gaped open with the pain. When he sagged back against the tree trunk, a thousand needles of pain sank into his skin. He lurched away from the tree, and fell slowly to one side. Behind him, the fire continued across the field. Smoke churned up, then collected in a mushroom before drifting slowly east toward the bowl's mouth. The back of his shirt had burned away, but the sleeves and front were held on by a stretch of fabric at his collar. One leg of his pants was gone.

Gray breathed deeply against the pain. He brought his feet up and bent over into a fetal curl. He shook uncontrollably. His skull was a universe of suffering, the pain blocking other senses, blinding him and deafening him, making him useless in the field. His thoughts were dim pulses. He was safe in the trees, he knew, but he would have to move out, and he had to gather himself. He had to push aside the agony from his back and head and shoulders and leg.

He closed his eyes. Isolate the pain. Move into myself. Cut out every sensation that would not work to defeat the Russian. Concentrate. Push it away. Survive this day.

He opened his eyes. He drew himself upright. He surveyed himself. His left arm was burned from the shoulder to the elbow, resembling bacon. His belly had protected the skin below the elbow. The back of his shirt was gone, burned away, and Gray knew the skin there was scorched, leaving pink and red blotches. Same with his shoulders. His left pant leg had burned away, and the skin below was blistered and red and pink and already leaking. When he gently touched his scalp his head was jolted with pain. A little hair remained in clumps, but most of his scalp was exposed and raw with burns. His left ear was curled by a burn.

He brought his hands up to his face. He curled his trigger finger. Gray's hands were fine, and he now found he could focus his eyes. And he could run. He was still alive and could still work his rifle.

He whispered, "I'm not done yet, you son of a bitch."

But his camouflage had gone up in smoke. He was as pink as a pig. His back and leg and arm and shoulders were a vibrantly colorful target. In the green and brown and gray bowl Gray's raw skin would stand out like a flare.

He had to camouflage himself, and he knew he would have to improvise and he knew it would test him to his limit. Gray opened his pack to retrieve his canteen. He twisted off the cap and allowed himself two swallows. Then he crawled several feet from the tree to a flat patch of ground. The soil had a thin mat of needles and dried leaves and wild straw. Gray poured the water from his canteen onto the ground, shaking the last drops from it. Then with his hands he worked the ground, kneading it like a child making mud cakes. He spread the mud out, making a bed of it.

Gray sat down at the edge of his mud bed, locked air in his lungs, and leaned back onto the mud. The pain was as if a knife was sinking into his back again and again, a red wash of agony. But Gray squirmed on the ground, rubbing his back into the mud and leaves and sticks and straw. And when he thought he might pass out from pain, he forced himself to go on, to continue to writhe until the mud had caked his back.

He sat up shivering with agony, but before his resolve melted with pain, he scooped up handfuls of the remaining mud and dabbed it onto his leg, pressing it onto the oozing red burns up and down his leg. His hand shook with suffering. He pressed more mud onto his shoulders, then onto his face. His teeth were clamped so tightly together his jaw ached. And finally he lifted the last of the leaf and straw and mud mix and crushed it onto his skull. He bucked with agony and his hands faltered. But he pressed scoop after scoop of it on, caking his head with the mud mix.

He gasped with the pain, and he had to will himself upright. He breathed against the suffering, and again focused. He looked at his leg and hands and shoulders. He resembled a bog monster. After a moment he could bend down for his rifle and pack. He put the empty canteen back into the backpack. With the Winchester in one hand and the pack in the other, Gray slowly surveyed his position. The trees offered cover in all directions. He walked unsteadily up the gradual hill into the deeper cover of the forested south slope.

✧　　　　　✧　　　　　✧

Nikolai Trusov lowered his binoculars and rubbed his eyes. From his hide he had been scanning the grass. He crossed his brow with a hand, bringing away dampness. He had patted mud onto his face and hands, and had stuck small branches into his clothing. His hide was behind a fallen and decayed pine trunk. His arms rested on a sunken portion of the trunk where hooves had chipped away at it over the years, as the tree had fallen across a deer path. His Moisin-Nagant rifle was at an elbow and his pack was near his feet. On his head was a brown wool watch cap. He had camouflaged the cap by pressing fistfuls of pine needles onto the fabric. He wore the cap high, above the caked mud on his forehead. His scar resembled the flat plates on a lizard's back. Only four inches of Trusov's head showed above the log.

He brought up the binoculars again, pressing them against his eyes. Again he stared at the wild grass near the mouth of the bowl, the same carpets of grass he had been looking at for hours. He knew his mine had forced Gray to enter the bowl in the grass. But the grass field was broad, and he had not seen any movement in the field, no twitching grass. Trusov nodded, an acknowledgment of the skill required to move unnoticed through grass. But Trusov had known of Owen Gray's skills for decades.

The blaze was reaching the east end of the field. Fire was almost done with the grass. Yet he hadn't flushed Gray. Gray hadn't bolted. Where was he? Trusov lifted the rifle to use the scope for a closer view of the charred field. Burned clumps of grass, not much else. Impossible to hide in the field because the fire had burned away the grass cover. Where was Gray?

Trusov needed a closer look. He crawled away from the hide, rose to a crouch and sped fifty yards east down the gradual incline toward the blackened field. He dropped to a crawl, his rifle in his right hand. A perfect hide was ahead, a log topped with brush. He moved toward it, then along the log, secure behind it.

Then he stalled. An animal was ahead of him, digging with a paw at the fallen tree, then moving several steps toward Trusov. The creature walked with a rolling sailor's gait, its toes in and its heavy tail brushing the ground behind it, obscuring its trail. Its blunt nose and button eyes were followed by a mass of tan and black quills that shifted left and right as it walked. The porcupine waddled toward him, unhurried and unconcerned, safe beneath its mantle of needle-sharp barbs. Its snout was to the ground, its thirty thousand quills quivering and shifting. It did not see or did not care about the Russian. The animal stopped below the brush growing on top of the log.

Trusov may never have seen anything like it. But the Russian was in a hurry and had no time to wonder about the strange animal. The creature was in his way, occupying Trusov's perfect hide. He brought out the knife from his belt and moved toward the animal. When he reached the porcupine he slashed down once, then again, the knife cutting into the animal, blood pouring instantly. The porcupine shivered its quills and caterwauled, then trotted away, leaving a trail of blood. Trusov wiped the blade on his pant leg and returned it to his belt. He crawled into the cover of a thimbleberry bush.

He brought up his binoculars, but before he could place them against his eyes his nose came up. He had a scent. It was faint, there and gone. He sniffed the air hungrily. And the scent was there again.

He allowed himself a small smile, a terrible grin where the corners of his mouth were turned down. He had, after all, caught Gray in the grass. He smelled burned meat. Gray's burned flesh. Gray was either dead or injured. The Russian's victory was closer. Still wearing the rictus smile of a cadaver, Trusov peered through the binoculars and began scanning the blackened grass field.

✧   ✧   ✧

Gray had to keep moving. He began a low crawl, keeping his body flat against the ground. He gripped the sling at the upper swivel with the rifle resting on his forearm and the butt dragging on the ground. He moved his arms forward and brought up his right leg, then pulled with his arms and pushed with the right leg. It was slow, but nothing of Gray or his weapon rose more than fourteen inches above the ground. His burns made it feel as if the ground was clawing at him with sharp talons. He crawled through mountain heath, its pointed leaves raking his face.

Gray flinched and dug his head into the ground at the sound of a projectile soaring in at him and passing a few inches from his ear. He cursed himself. It was a hummingbird, curious and fearless, then bored and gone as quickly as it came.

He rose behind a pine, his back to the tree. He swung his gaze along the protective trees uphill from him on the south slope. Nothing visible amid all the trees and brush. Because he never looked around a tree unless his head was close to the ground, he lowered himself again. He turned toward the tree, pressing his cheek and temple against the coarse bark, then brought an eye around.

His view was of much of the bowl, from the mouth off to his right to the high banks of the north wall. He again brought out the binoculars. Nothing. Gray's mouth pulled down. The sound of a woodpecker's rapping came from the thick wedge of trees downhill at the bowl's center. The fire was burning itself out near the mouth of the bowl. The wind was slowly clearing the bowl of smoke.

Huckleberry and heath and sorrel offered low cover. Gray crawled from tree to tree, traveling a hundred yards, then another hundred, moving west farther into the bowl. Its snout forward, the Winchester urged him on.

Early in his sniper career Gray would stay up most of the night before a mission because it was thought that being tired reduced pressure. But on the mission Gray had found his concentration wandering, perhaps in search of sleep. Instead, as he learned more and more about his craft and recognized the nuances of the wilderness, he discovered that the sheer volume of information pushed aside the pressure and fear. Now it was the same. Leaning into the tree trunk, critical intelligence poured into Gray. The sun's position, humidity, wind, temperature, ground cover, sights and sounds, all were ever changing. Every few feet he journeyed he had to assess entirely new conditions. He looked for unusual movement, he searched for possible hides, he searched for untoward reflections, he listened for peculiar sounds. Gray knew that whoever could best marshal his mental resources and keep them honed the longest would leave Shepherd's Bowl that day. All Gray needed to do was concentrate.

He crawled over a mat of moss campion then through a spread of wheatgrass. Lodgepole pines marked his way on both sides. The tick was along for the ride. Gray could not pinch off its swollen body because its head would remain below the skin and might become infected. Later he would put a lighted match close to the tick's behind, and the insect would back out of Gray's skin on its own volition. This presumed there was a later for Gray.

He moved over the ground quickly and quietly. He should have been as comfortable crawling on all fours as a weasel, but his skin howled with every motion. He was thirsty and had no water, and he knew that thirst, magnified by pain, would alter his judgment. He would need water soon.

He brushed by gumweed that left a sticky resin on his arms and cocklebur that deposited green burrs on his pants. He crawled forward between a pine and a tree stump that was bracketed by gorse, a thick bush with vicious spikes on its stems. He could see through trees to the bowl's center. When he reached into his pack for the binoculars, his back and shoulders sent electric jolts of pain deeply into Gray. His hand trembled when he brought out the field glasses.

When he pressed the binoculars against his face, his hand jumped. He swatted at his face, knocking a paper wasp away from the corner of his eye. He had been stung at the lines near the corner of his left eye. Had his back and shoulders and leg not been in agony, Gray would have laughed. Fate had decided Gray just wasn't suffering enough yet, so it added a wasp sting and a tick bite to the mix. Gray touched the corner of his eye. The skin was already swelling. It should have smarted, but the pain was lost in the suffering of the burns. He looked skyward to find a nest the size of a basketball in the tree eight feet above the ground. A dozen wasps angrily patrolled near the nest's mouth. A wasp flitted down toward him. Gray resisted the instinct to swat at it because a sudden movement would alert Trusov if the Russian was surveying the area with field glasses. The wasp moved away. Gray returned the binoculars to his eyes.

Not for long. Pain altered perception, but Gray still trusted his ears, and they picked up a delicate sound, a wispy press of a leaf against another leaf. Other sounds reached Gray—the last crackling of the fire at the base of the bowl behind and below Gray, the brush of wind-tossed needles in the trees, the drone of the wasps overhead. But this slight crackle from the other side of Gray's pine tree was against the grain of the bowl's sounds. It stood out, however trifling. And Gray knew that whoever had made the little sound had not intended it to escape.

It came again, just barely penetrating the threshold of Gray's perception. A tiny crackle, there and gone, but closer, coming from the other side of the pine and gorse. A stalker, someone good at it, someone intent on Gray, coming to kill him, believing Gray was living his last seconds on this earth.

With a calm and slow and utterly quiet motion, Gray brought the rifle up so that its bore was above his head, aimed at the gorse to the left of the tree. He flicked off the safety and put his finger on the trigger.

This time the sound was so quiet, so professional, that Gray could only suspect he heard it. Coming from behind the tree, a little to its left. The nudging of a pine needle.

Gray shut down his systems. No breathing or blinking. He willed his heart to slow. So intent was he on the predator coming toward him that the pain from his burns subsided. The world and all that was in it was on the other side of the brush, coming for him.

Gray felt himself switch onto automatic. All discretion was gone. Gray's instincts and training would tell him when to move without Gray consciously making the decision.

A branch of the gorse wiggled unnaturally, a small flicker. The predator was four feet away with only a tree trunk intervening.

Gray waited three beats, then another and another.

He suddenly pushed himself left with his knees, a leap from behind the tree that took him left to the edge of the gorse for a view of the stalker, Gray's rifle ahead of him, the trigger beginning its short and lethal motion.

Gray was as startled as the bobcat.

The animal's stubby black-barred tail shot up. The bobcat seemed to inflate as the fur on its back and chest rose. It showed its fangs and hissed, a searing noise like steam escaping a locomotive. The bobcat's legs were striped, and its face was decorated with black lines that fanned out to its wide cheek ruff. The cat leaped straight up in fright, and landed in a dead run, back the way it had come, leaving Gray's breath in his throat.

"Goddamnit," he mouthed after a moment. "When this is done I'm coming back here and making mittens out of you."

Gray slowly rose to his feet and started west through the trees. So fearsome was the pain from his back and shoulders that they felt they were still on fire. With each step his skin pulled at itself, washing him with agony. His left leg from thigh to moccasin was burned down to the muscle, and was raw and seeping, and caked in mud and leaves. It rocked Gray with pain with each step.

He slowed, then slowed again. He was not gathering information like he should. The pain was diverting his attention, not letting him gather and filter all the bowl was offering. The pain was numbing his senses. In this arena the slightest disadvantage might be lethal.

An ancient tree stump—so old it was losing its shape as the wood rotted away—offered a spot where Gray could try to recoup. His life depended on pushing the pain away. When he neared the stump he saw a porcupine to one side, rocking back and forth. The animal was gurgling pitiably, and not until Gray reached the stump did he notice the trail of blood the porcupine had been leaving. The animal seemed indifferent to Gray, not moving away, only mewling terribly. Gray quickly surveyed the view of the north slope from the stump, saw nothing, then looked more closely at the porcupine.

Blood was bubbling up from the creature's shoulder and back. Nothing in the wilderness made those wounds. To Gray's knowledge, the only way a wilderness carnivore—usually the fisher, a large and rare and ferocious marten—attacks a porcupine is to flip it to get to the unprotected wiry hairs on the porcupine's belly. These wounds were made by a man with a knife. Trusov.

The porcupine's blood trail showed the animal had come from the west. Trusov was to the west.

The animal was suffering, grunting and panting and swaying, and was clearly going to die, but perhaps not for an hour or two. The porcupine has an Achilles' heel, a lethally vulnerable spot—its snout. Gray whispered, "Sorry, friend," then brought his rifle barrel down sharply across the animal's nose. It collapsed instantly, dead, a pile of sharp points.

Gray pushed himself up the rotting tree trunk. He was facing north, with the mouth of the bowl to his right and the high ridges all around. The view was only partial, with much of the bowl obscured by trees on the lower south slope. Some of the charred field was visible, and across was the parched north slope. Hundreds of trees interrupted Gray's view, and the Russian might be behind any one of them. Or behind fallen logs or thick brush or boulders or clumps of grass.

Just as he was about to crawl on, a glint of light held him to the stump. The metallic shimmer had been distant and faint; and just as he had felt with the bobcat's footfalls, Gray knew the fleeting light had been a mistake. Something was below him, fifteen compass clicks west, a quarter mile away. The view was through a veil of vegetation, and Gray could make out no forms other than trees and undergrowth. Yet there was the tiny flash again. He moved his head slowly a foot left, then back. The speck of light returned at the center of this motion, and when Gray held himself still, the silver pink light remained. It had been his motion that had made it flicker, and when Gray was still it was constant, but only an infinitesimal leak of light, a thin beam, the smallest of offerings. Gray lifted his binoculars.

✧   ✧   ✧

Two hours later, in the failing light of evening, Gray's binoculars were still at his eyes. He had lowered them and brought them up again and again to avoid eyestrain as he stared at the dot of light. All he knew was that the source of the light was out of place in the wilderness. It was man-made, and it came from a backpack buckle tongue, a boot's metal eyelet ring, a jacket button, a telescope lens, or a piece of litter.

Two hours studying, all the while growing weaker and more thirsty. Although his stomach and chest and right leg and face had been spared by the fire, every square inch of his skin seemed to emit pulses of pain. The burns frequently pried Gray's mind from the task at hand and allowed it to wander dangerously. Toward the end of those hours, the binoculars were almost too heavy to lift, and Gray slipped lower and lower against the stump. His tongue felt as if it had swollen and he could no longer swallow. He was so thirsty he caught himself daydreaming about a water fountain.

And as he stared at the glint and tried to imagine something recognizable from the surrounding brush, his mind started to play, throwing shadows across the bowl's floor, creating phantoms around the puny light. Ruses of the mind, Gray knew, but the pain carried along his thoughts. If only he could send a bullet at the light and end the waiting, but he could not. A wasted shot would alert the Russian to Gray's location.

The sinking sun was turning the little flash purple. The base of the bowl was in deep shadow and was losing its features. The south wall was a deepening smudge of rock against the dark blue sky.

The pinpoint of light had remained as motionless as a stone for two hours. No human could do that. He needed to decide, and so he decided the light was the reflection off a piece of litter, probably a chewing gum wrapper. It was a fuzzy decision, and a terrible disappointment. He had tapped deeply into his mental and physical reserves to study the tiny light, and it had come to nothing. He was now desperately thirsty and exhausted beyond his ability to make clear judgments. His binoculars came down despite his best effort to hold them in place.

He had to find the strength to move. The sky was as red as blood. Soon darkness would cloak him. But that maddening glimmer was worth one more look. With an effort that fogged his vision from exhaustion, he brought up the binoculars again.

✧   ✧   ✧

At that moment Trusov caught Gray's scent again, the gratifying odor of badly burned flesh. The wind had been shifting and irresolute for much of the afternoon, but for several hours it had been steady from the south, bringing Trusov reliable information about his enemy. Earlier in the afternoon the Russian had moved out of the scent, but the smell had found Trusov again. Gray was alive, was south of the Russian in the trees somewhere, and had slowly moved west. The odor of cooked skin had traveled.

Trusov would move toward the still-pink sky in the west. His and the American's paths would converge at the western end of the bowl. Because daylight was fading quickly, he would not be able to watch his feet and would have to walk more slowly and softly.

When Trusov lifted his rifle the jaws of the earth seemed to open up, seize him, and take him down its black throat. Trusov fell into the void, vaulting down into the wicked murk. He spent an age falling into the black pool, and then he slammed against the bottom of the pit.

He found himself on his knees on the ground. He had only fallen a few feet, but had been blacked out for the two seconds of the fall.

Then a red sheet fell across his eyes, a veil of blood that blocked his view of the ground. He grabbed at himself until he found the wound, a crease across his forehead a quarter inch deep and pouring blood.

Gray had shot him.

Blood spilled through his fingers onto the ground, a torrent of it that filled his vision with cascading red. On his hands and knees he scrambled blindly, dragging his rifle, downhill until he felt the resistance of a bush of some sort. He let himself fall to the ground and burrowed under the bush.

Again he felt his head. The slash was to the bone, into the bone. He could feel his skull, not for the first time.

Trusov's mouth contorted in rage and pain. Owen Gray's Vietnam shot had marred Trusov, and now the second had crossed the scar of the first. The Russian's head was marked by an X.

281

Blood splashed to the ground. He pulled off his pack and pressed it against his forehead, trying to stem the river of blood, all the while his face screwed up in rage. Moments passed. The blood ebbed. He returned the sopping pack to his back. Night had come. He could see little in the black basin. Shaking with rage and revelation, he lifted his rifle and moved west, slowly and silently and skillfully.

✧   ✧   ✧

The bowl was lost in darkness. Owen Gray had tried to find his target again, but Trusov had moved quickly, and the gathering darkness prevented Gray from spotting him. Gray had missed. Sheer luck had given Gray a shot, and he had missed. The shard of light he had stared at had indeed been a piece of litter, probably a gum wrapper. Just as Gray had given up on that target, the Russian had walked into Gray's field of vision. None of Gray's tracking skills had been involved. Happenstance had offered him the target. The Russian just happened to travel over the glint of light, and it had blinked out. Gray had lifted his rifle and fired, quickly, before Trusov was lost in the surrounding vegetation. Too quickly. Gray's rifle had bucked up, and by the time he found the spot again in the scope, Trusov was gone. A miss.

Darkness providing cover, Gray walked downhill. Every yard of ground was an effort. The burns were rapidly sapping his strength. His thirst was an all-consuming craving. His mouth and throat were sawdust. He could not generate saliva and could not swallow. Thirst was deadening him to all else in the bowl. If he could not quench his thirst, Gray's judgment—the only thing keeping him alive—would be impaired, and he would soon begin acting irrationally and dangerously.

He moved around boulders and trees, the rifle now a burden. No longer did it lead him and encourage him. He staggered but caught himself against a lodgepole pine. When his moccasin kicked a rock downhill he paused, listening, but could hear only the scrape of his throat as it tried to swallow. He knew he might be making many sounds that would signal the Russian, but the pain and thirst were dampening his hearing. He stumbled on, turning more east toward the mouth of the bowl.

The shallow pool was there, the small spring that was Black

Bear Creek's headwater. Gray made his way toward it, brushing the undergrowth too loudly, walking in too straight a line, letting his footfalls sound, all careless. Gray felt in himself the beginning of apathy, an indifference and impassivity brought about by his burns and thirst. If he let this new and unbidden pulse from his brain go unchecked, he would die in the bowl. But these were all weak thoughts. He needed water.

He moved toward the pool, through a patch of field mustard and balsam root, and then in a giddy rush of sensation he could smell the water, almost feel the cool liquid on his lips and tongue. He heard the ripple of a thin stream of water rolling over rocks. Predators from frogs to cougars know to lie in wait at a pool of water, and Trusov was nothing if not a predator. Forty yards from the pool, Gray lowered himself to the ground and once again tried to push aside the pain and thirst to focus on the pool and the surrounding brush and grass.

He waited, searching and listening, the pool all the while enticing him with the scent and sound of water to come forward. He waited, smothered by pain, fighting to fasten his attention on the pool.

He whispered, "It's okay, Dad."

He clamped his jaw. His father's voice had just asked about the south fence. Was it in good repair after the storm? A voice Gray had not heard in years had spoken to him, as clear as if his father had been sitting beside him. Gray clamped his eyes shut for a moment. He had begun hallucinating. He was now fighting the Russian and his own mind.

He waited thirty minutes. He could no longer be certain of his own conclusions, but he did not think anyone was near the pool. He gripped his rifle and crawled forward, across the pine needles, then onto moss at the pool's edge. He could see only vague black outlines of a tree or two, and the inky black water.

He planted his hands on the edge of the pool, and one hand pressed onto a small, soft form. He jerked his hand away, then felt for it again. He brought up a dead salamander. Gray held it close to his eyes to try to determine what had killed it, but then tossed it aside.

He lowered his head to the water, about to drink when he saw another dead salamander, this one floating on the surface of the pool.

Gray carefully touched the water, and it was cool and promising.

But when he rubbed his finger and thumb together, his skin felt soapy. His jaw opened involuntarily. Despair made him sag, and his head almost went into the water before he could fight it back. To be sure, he dipped a finger into the water and brought several drops to his mouth. The water stung his tongue, and he spit it out.

He knew what Trusov had done. Lye and fat are combined to make soap. Trusov had dumped lye into the pool, and the slick, soapy feeling on Gray's fingers had resulted from the lye quickly working on the skin there. The water was poison, not meant to kill Gray but to deprive him of water, to weaken him.

Gray gripped his rifle and backed away from the pool. Dampness clouded his vision, and he paused to wipe at his eye. He was losing. His father spoke again. Owen Gray ignored him this time. He did not need his father to tell him he was not going to make it out alive.

19

NIKOLAI TRUSOV STALKED all night, traveling counterclockwise in the bowl, making no more than fifty yards an hour, trying again to find Gray's scent. But he did not. Several times he had to blot away blood from his forehead with a sleeve. The shock of the wound was gone. His strength had returned. He used the night to try to cross Gray's trail.

He succeeded. He came to a stump that had dense spiked bushes on both sides and was protected uphill by a tree. The Russian knelt to peer at the ground. Even in the black of night he could see that the needles and leaves and grass had recently been ruffled. Trusov felt the ground and brought up a leaf stained with dried blood. Gray's blood. The American had been here, had used this tree and these bushes as a hide. A good place to begin the stalk again at first light. He leaned against the stump to wait. A bat flitted by.

✧   ✧   ✧

During those same hours Gray was lying on his belly near the pool. He had gathered handfuls of the damp moss and had held it above his mouth and had squeezed out drops of water. He had spent two hours extracting precious water, in all not more than half a cup, and if it had restored him to any degree he could not feel it. Then he lay on the stream bank and waited for the night to pass. Nights in the Sawtooths are cold, even in summer. Gray spent the dark hours shuddering with cold and pain, his thoughts meandering. He gripped his rifle fiercely as if that might compensate for his slipping mind.

He might have slept. He could not be sure. The first purple light of false dawn found Gray on the moss and dirt, his eyes and his mouth open. He tried to rise, but his body refused. He argued with his body, demanding it rise, and at the first motion the pain from his shoulders and leg and back erupted anew. He gripped his gun. He was so weak he felt nailed to the ground. He crawled forward, away from the dead pool.

He heard a rough scrape. At first he thought it was his father again, clearing his throat for some new pronouncement. He heard it again, carried in the soft wind. He thought it was real, not a trick of his mind, but he could not be sure.

Dawn had begun, streaking the high rim of the bowl in faint purple but leaving the basin in blacks and grays. Gray turned to the south slope to face the sound. He could see nothing. He wrestled his gun to his shoulder anyway and put his eye to the scope.

❖   ❖   ❖

Trusov had coughed in his sleep, and the ragged sound had brought him out of it. He hugged the ground. In the still bowl, a cough was the equivalent of a foghorn blast. He lay utterly still. His position between the uphill tree and the stump he was leaning against was well protected. Any shot fired his way from the center or the opposite side of the bowl would sail over the stump, and he was below the stump.

Trusov recoiled when the sound of a shot reached him. Gray had fired. At what? Trusov looked left and right. The Russian was well hidden. What had the American fired at?

A full-throated roar suddenly came from above Trusov. He looked skyward, to the uphill pine tree. A wasp nest had a ragged hole through it, and bits of the nest were floating to the ground. And a black ball of wasps was growing in the air next to the nest.

The nest blew apart as the second bullet sailed through it. The sound of the shot followed. Patches of brown paper fluttered to the ground. As wasps streamed out of their fractured nest the black ball of insects floating in the air grew and grew. Then the wasps found their enemy, the alien on the ground below their ruined home.

Within five seconds of the second shot, fifty wasps were on Trusov, and within fifteen seconds three hundred more. Then five hundred and more.

Gray knew where he was. The Russian dared not move from that spot. The wasps covered Trusov's face in a wriggling black and brown mask, working their stingers repeatedly. His shirt and hands were also soon covered with the insects. So many wasps crawled angrily over Trusov that his form seemed molten.

His face was bunched against the pain, but he could do nothing against the wasps lest Gray's third bullet find him. So he lay there, and he lay there. His eyelids were stung, and his lips and ears, every square millimeter of his forehead, stung and stung again. Wasps crawled partway into his nostrils to sting him there. All along his neck, all over his face. After several moments the wasps began to calm and to lift away from him. The mask dissolved and the squirming shirt dissipated. Trusov had been stung hundreds of times. The inhuman effort not to move or to scream seemed to have stilled Trusov, because when it was time to search for a safe way out from under Gray's rifle, the Russian did not move. A moment passed before he opened his eyes.

Or he tried to. His face had begun to swell. His eyelids and nose puffed up. His bony face began to lose its contours and the skin bloated with the wasps' poison. His hands inflated to resemble mittens.

✧   ✧   ✧

Four hundred yards down the slope and east, Owen Gray was exhausted, desperate, and pain-racked. But he grinned.

Then he moved out, this little encouragement helping him walk in the direction of the wasps' nest, under brush and alongside pine, carrying his rifle, trying not to let it drag on the ground. Progress was slow. Each yard was marked by pain, but he traveled toward Trusov, one tree at a time, keeping himself covered. He came to the shattered wasps' nest. The insects still patrolled, but they paid no attention to Gray.

He lowered himself to his knees and began following Trusov's trail. Perhaps the Russian had been in too much pain to disguise his obvious trail. But after fifty yards it became less so, as if Trusov was slowly gaining control of himself. Then even less so.

Gray had noticed in Vietnam that when he was on a mission—stalking, low to the earth, rapt with the danger—he was incapable of contemplation that took him more than eight inches above the ground. He might lie on his belly for two days waiting for the mark, and in all that time he would be unable to think of his parents or the Sawtooths or the nurse he had met at the division hospital. No daydreaming, no escape. His mental horizon was the dirt two inches in front of his nose, but it was a focused horizon. He missed nothing, absorbing every tiny crease in the land and every minuscule facet of the flora. The smallest irregularity—a drop of blood, a shallow footprint, a shell casing, a few grains of spilled rice, the scent of human urine—was made plain and portentous by his closeness to the ground. Now, despite his wounds, and revived by his small success with the wasps, he believed he was missing nothing.

So it was that when Gray had gone a hundred yards from the wasps' nest he was brought up by a slight resistance, a negligible increase in friction of the ground. He froze, at first unaware where the irregularity was, then determined it was from his left arm, his wrist, maybe a finger. He did not breathe, he did not swallow, he did not incline his head even a fraction of an inch. He moved only his eyeballs, and even them slowly. His gaze coursed along his arm to his left wrist, which was ahead of him on the ground, partly hidden by grass. He could see nothing wrong. Sweat trickled into his eyes. He was utterly motionless, and he could hear and see and feel nothing irregular, yet he was certain that at the end of his left arm was a vast peril.

The rifle was in his right hand. He let it slip slowly from his grip, its stock and trigger guard and swivel pin settling on the ground with no more force than a tuft of airborne thistledown. He moved his right hand slowly forward, sliding up the rifle barrel so he could see his right hand in front of him. With the tip of one finger of his right hand he parted grass stalks. The finger worked its way into the grass, nudging aside the brittle stems until he saw a glint of reflected green light, a slight foreign spark three inches above the ground.

A length of fishing line. The little finger of Gray's left hand had caught it and pulled it an inch out of its taut north-south line. It was the trip wire of a spring gun hidden to Gray's left or right. Set by Trusov. Gray willed his mind to work. Some lethal devices, such as the Claymore mine, relied not on pressure but on the release of that pressure. As long as the infantryman stood on the mine he was safe. Gray tried to recall snare techniques that used back pressure. He knew of none. He pressed his cheek against the ground and slowly pulled back his left hand from the fishing line. The spring gun was silent.

When his hand was under his chin, he brought his head up. He looked left up the slope. At first he saw only horseweed and cheat grass among the pine trees. Then he detected the two menacing black holes eight feet to his left, the dark eyes of a double-barrel shotgun. To his right the line was tied to the branch of a Scotch broom. The weapon had been placed here to cut down anyone on Gray's route. Which meant that Nikolai Trusov felt he could not cover this approach.

Gray quelled a rising sense of triumph, fought it back as useless and premature. This trap was not a warning or a feint. The shotgun was well hidden and the trip wire detectable virtually only by intuition. His right hand found his Winchester. He rose to his knees and crossed over the trip wire one limb at a time, moving like a cloud on a calm day, soundless, his eyes ever on the fishing line. When his trailing foot slipped over the line, Gray again lowered himself to his stomach. He slithered forward again.

He came to a short whitebark pine, more a shrub than a tree, with a twisted and irregular trunk. On the ground beneath it was a blanket of thick scales from the tree's cones that had been torn apart by chipmunks and nutcrackers for the seeds. The whitebark offered a rising cover. Gray lifted his head, ducking branches, twisting his body to insert it up between the boughs without jiggling them. He brought up the binoculars. Nothing ahead. Yet Trusov had to be there. The spring gun meant Trusov was protecting this passage to his hide.

Just as he was about to return to the ground, the slightest of motions, as insignificant as it was out of place in the high country, caught the corner of his eye. Gray trusted his peripheral vision. Its best use was at dusk when objects that couldn't be seen directly might be observed at the edge of the eye. In daylight, side vision would pick up an oddity, some angle or motion that did not fit into the wilderness pattern that might be missed if viewed straight on. Gray slowly brought his head around to face the irregularity.

A moment passed before he located it. A rifle barrel. Even at a hundred and fifty yards, the barrel, so true and purposeful, seemed a violation of the mountains. Only eighteen inches of the barrel appeared above a fallen log, but when the bush behind it, perhaps a grouseberry, wafted gently in the slight breeze, the barrel stayed fixed in position. Then the barrel moved on its own, stark against the soft grouseberry background. He could not tell if Trusov was facing him or another direction. He could not see the Russian's head. Moving as slowly as if in a barrel of molasses, Gray lifted the Winchester.

He found the Russian's rifle barrel through the Unertl scope. He could see its blued front sight and bore. Gray lowered his rifle a hair. In the scope now was a brown wool cap. Only the top few inches of the cap, but enough.

Gray was acutely aware he might be pulling down on a dummy position, an artful trap left by the enemy that would cause the shooter to reveal his position. Nikolai Trusov's father had used this ruse at Stalingrad. But Gray could not wait. He was at the end of his resources.

Deep breath. Let half out. Hold. Crosshair once. Crosshair twice, softly, ever so softly, squeeze.

The Winchester bellowed and leaped back into Gray's shoulder. He lost the target in his sights but he quickly brought the rifle back down, searching through the scope for the target.

Gray's left hand vanished in a spray of blood and gristle that filled the air in front of him. He cried out and yanked himself down to the ground, his head bouncing against two whitebark limbs. His face plowed into the ground and he rolled onto his belly to flatten himself. Only then did he hear the distant roar of a rifle shot as it chased the bullet. The echo raced around the bowl's walls, washing over Gray again and again.

Gray frantically grabbed the Winchester and rolled to his right, out from under the pine and across a bed of needles and through bunches of cheat grass, turning over and over like a child down a hill. He left a trail of blood. But a second shot did not come. Gray bumped into a tree. Only then did he look at his arm.

Trusov's bullet had blown out a third of Gray's left palm. Several bones lay bare and others might have been missing. Much of the carpus was gone. Flaps of skin and shattered tendons dangled in the breeze. The little finger and ring finger seemed only nominally attached to his hand. Blood spurted from the wound with each of Gray's heartbeats, shooting out three feet as if from a squirt gun. Gray had brought no twine or a thong to use as a tourniquet.

He fought the churning white clouds of shock that dipped down at him from above. He had felt no pain, just a dead tingling somewhere near his left elbow. But then his mouth was pried open by a spear of agony that flew up his arm and neck and landed behind his eyes. Gray's head snapped into the ground, jolted by the pain. The entire left side of his body was spiked by it. He desperately wanted to run away, to leave behind the maimed part of himself and all the suffering it was dispensing.

The day seemed to fade. Tiny dots of neon colors blinked on and off in front of Gray's eyes. He was growing faint with the loss of blood. Holding his breath, Gray reached into his pack. Even this small motion amplified the pain. He breathed deeply, but this acted like a bellows on the pain. His body shook. Blood splattered the tree trunk and rifle. He guessed he had only a minute or two before the heart would have no more blood to pump.

With his right hand he brought out one of the matchbooks. He bit off a match, then dropped the matchbook to the ground. He scraped the match against the score several times before his trembling hand could press down hard enough. When the match head sputtered to life he held the flame to the matchbook. It flared. Gray pinched the matchbook at the staple and held the flame under his wounded left hand.

The fire cooked his hand, turning the ragged gash brown, then black. Flesh crackled and hissed. The air was filled with a nauseating scent. Pain was an acid coursing back and forth in his body. Gray's teeth sank deeply into his tongue, and blood squirted from between his teeth and down his chin.

The hanging flaps of skin curled and shrank. Grease dripped from the cooking flesh. And still Gray held the matchbook in place. His trigger finger and thumb burned as flames consumed the matchbook down to the staple and score. Finally blood from the exposed radial artery stopped spurting. Gray dropped the matchbook and lowered a knee over it to extinguish it before pine needles and dry

291

grass caught fire. He did not have the mental capacity to pray that Trusov had not seen the smoke from the matches. Gray coughed with agony. Every limb shook with suffering.

His thoughts careened to Pete Coates. Then to Mrs. Orlando. He owed them.

He reached for his rifle and began crawling again. His mind was gone. He did not have the capacity to order his body to continue. It acted on its own. He came to the cap and rifle that had fooled him. The hat was on a stick, and the weapon was balanced on a log with a length of twine between the stock and a nearby maple trunk. When the wind moved the maple, the trunk swayed and so did the rifle, just a little, not as much as the background foliage, making the rifle appear to move independently of the foliage. A good ruse, he decided dimly.

❖   ❖   ❖

When hunting for animals it is always assumed the target has been hit, but when hunting for men that assumption is never made. Trusov grimaced as he ejected the smoking brass casing. The distance had been only four hundred yards, but Trusov had seen human movement, so he had snap fired. He had fired too quickly. After the shot he had seen a fine mist of blood in the air, so he had hit something. But he dared not waltz over to find out. Now he could see nothing but underbrush through his telescope. He brought out binoculars for a wider view. Nothing. But then he detected again the smell of burned flesh.

There was a chance Owen Gray still lived, but it would be foolish for the Russian to remain in one place to speculate on it further. Tree to tree, Trusov moved downhill toward the bowl's center. Either Gray was dead, in which case the vultures and ravens would soon alert Trusov, or Gray was alive but soon dead, and the birds would have to wait awhile. The Russian moved softly across the ground, a specter flowing along silently and smoothly, closing in on the American.

❖   ❖   ❖

The Winchester pulled Gray along. Down the slope, toward the seam of the bowl, crawling, one hand on the wood stock, the other uselessly waving in the air. His head was downhill, and gravity seemed to pull the pain into Gray's head. Even blinking hurt. His arm and ruined hand were lost in agony somewhere beyond his left shoulder. He scrabbled over stones and through barricades of thistle and wild raspberry. Because his ears rang with pain to the exclusion of all other sounds, Gray could not judge his own sound. He guessed he was making as much noise as a belled cow. But his thoughts were few and growing fewer. He did not have long. His body and mind were moments from surrendering.

Gray glimpsed a patch of skin—maybe a cheek, maybe a wrist or forearm—off to his left four hundred yards. Too little and too fast to dope it in before it disappeared in the kaleidoscope of leaves and boughs. That fleeting patch was moving closer, yet in a roundabout way. Trusov was following his nose, Gray vaguely suspected. Gray could no longer care.

Gray came to the porcupine he had killed. A bird or rat had eaten out its eyes, but otherwise it was intact, its quills dully reflecting the morning sun. Each time Gray exhaled, his lungs paused, as if wanting to be stilled forever. He tried to rise to his feet, but his legs gave out and he toppled sideways into the dry cheat grass, his hand brushing the porcupine's quills. Gray's vision misted, then began to go dark. A quill stabbed at him insistently.

✧   ✧   ✧

The tantalizing scent of cooked flesh had lingered in the bowl all night and now again in the new morning. Gray was shackled to the odor like a ball and chain. The smell was an inescapable telltale.

Trusov moved south and then back north until he had centered the odor. He moved toward it, through a thick stand of pine, the smell growing stronger. Owen Gray, Trusov's great tormentor, had to be within four hundred meters, dead ahead.

The Russian dropped to his knees. The trees offered thick cover. Because he was low, he could see only thirty or forty meters in any direction, and that also meant that he was not presenting a target for a distant shot. The scent was like a homing beacon. Owen Gray was ahead, now perhaps only three hundred meters. Trusov pushed himself through the underbrush as silently as a shrew.

Then at two hundred fifty meters the woods opened slightly, and there on the ground was a body, partially obscured by trees and brush and just visible above bunches of wild grass. Gray's olive pant leg and his khaki shirt, dappled by intervening syringa leaves. The clothes were charred. Here was the source of the odor that had been beckoning Trusov.

His moment of victory was upon him, but Trusov frowned bitterly. Gray might already be dead. The body lay still. Then it appeared to move. Trusov squinted. The movement might have been an illusion, caused by the sway of leaves. The body moved again.

Prone on the ground, Trusov positioned his Moisin-Nagant in front of him. His fingers were swollen from the wasp stings, and his trigger finger barely fit into the guard. He found the khaki shirt in his scope, then it was hidden by waving leaves, then visible again. A sure shot even through the brush.

Trusov's exquisite moment was at hand. Decades in the making. He nudged the rifle down the shirt for the pant leg.

His finger smoothly came back. A hair's width at a time, the trigger giving lovely resistance. The trigger came back and back.

The rifle fired and snapped back into Trusov's shoulder. The sound of the shot burst away and then echoed in the bowl. He worked the bolt, sighted in, and squeezed again, this time sending the projectile into the thigh. The body bounced as the bullet ripped into it.

The third shot was aimed at Gray's chest, but the target was mostly obscured by underbrush. The bullet flew true and the body jumped. Gray's head was not visible through the scope, hidden behind brush, but Trusov sent two more bullets where he estimated Gray's head to be.

Nikolai Trusov rose to his feet. He touched the fresh wound on his forehead, then the older wound, the deep gouge that had been with him since his first encounter with White Star. Now it was over. He walked toward the corpse of his enemy. Trusov had always been the careful soldier, so he moved slowly, a fresh shell in the breech. He pushed aside thimbleberry and syringa as he approached. Fifty meters to Gray's body, to his vindication, to his rapture.

The body lay still. As he drew near, Trusov could see two of his bullet holes, torn red gaps in the cloth. He could see burns on the cloth. Not much blood, though, so perhaps the burns and Trusov's earlier hit had killed Gray a while ago after all. The smell of seared flesh was now strong. He walked with more confidence, pushing aside syringa branches and stepping over bunches of cheat grass. Closer to the body, to the ineffable pleasure, to the capstone of his years of dreaming.

Five meters from the body, Trusov's mouth twisted with antici-pation. And then he saw it was wrong. Everything was wrong. The Russian was allowed three seconds of astonishment. The pant leg was filled with grass. The burned shirt covered not a human body but the body of that quilled animal Trusov had hacked at with his knife the day before. Just behind the porcupine, a small fire had been ignited, using the dry grass, and the fire had scorched the porcupine's body, providing the fresh scent of burned flesh, Tru-sov's homing beacon. It was all wrong, shockingly wrong.

Trusov only had time to bring up his rifle a few inches.

His left foot danced when a bullet tore through his ankle. The Russian instinctively shifted his weight to save himself from falling. He desperately looked around for the source of his torment and tried again to bring up his rifle.

Then his leg buckled, shot through at the knee. A rifle's bellow came from uphill, from somewhere in the pines. Trusov kept him-self upright with his good leg, and twisted around looking for a target but found only pieces of his shattered knee and splashes of blood on the ground behind him.

Trusov stabbed the ground with his rifle trying to catch himself, but a second bullet streaked through his left elbow, almost severing his forearm from his body. Trusov screamed and began sliding to the ground, losing his grip on his rifle.

Another shot, this one tearing apart his right arm. Trusov's arms were nothing but useless flails, hanging by strips of flesh from smashed elbows.

Toppling and twisting, Trusov cried out, a shriek of rage and perhaps of sorrow. But the sound was lost in yet another shot. A bullet flew through the meat of both thighs, spraying a nearby tree with fragments of the Russian.

Trusov landed on the ground near the porcupine. He tried to squirm toward his rifle, but neither his legs nor arms worked, and he lay still, his eyes open. Waiting.

✧   ✧   ✧

Not for long. Owen Gray emerged from the trees, his reloaded Winchester on Trusov. Gray was almost naked, with mud and pine needles and seeping burns covering his body. His mouth was open and his breath was a rasp. He weaved as he came for the Russian, and fifteen feet away Gray had to stop. He tottered, then found his footing again and stepped ahead. Even Gray's rifle waggled unprofessionally, as if a bough in the wind. He held the weapon in his good hand.

Gray had only a meager recollection of having surfaced from the blackout a few moments ago, prompted by the porcupine's quills stabbing his hand. From somewhere—from the depth of his training or from the desperate need to beat the Russian—he had found the strength to take off his pants and stuff a few handfuls of grass into the remaining pant leg. Then with a match he had ignited a handful of dry cheat grass and had burned some of the porcupine's belly flesh, leaving a trail of scent for the Russian. Then he had draped his shirt over the animal and had crawled away to wait.

Now Gray stepped across pine needles and loose pebbles to the Russian. Gray's steps were small and uncertain, and he had to balance himself after each new step. He fought the blackness that wanted to take him.

The Russian stared back at him. He coughed, inhaled raggedly, and whispered, "That was good. Burning that animal's body, letting me think the smell was from you, drawing me to your trap."

"I don't feel like chatting." With difficulty Gray bent to the porcupine, to his pants. He pulled the spiral notebook from the pocket and ripped out a sheet. He fumbled with the paper but after a few seconds the fabled white star emerged.

Breathing shallowly and gurgling, the Russian stared at him. The red shell he had hoped to leave at Gray's body had fallen from his shirt pocket and lay beside him, insignificant in the grass.

"This is from me." Gray let the white star float down to the Russian's chest. Trusov followed it with his eyes. It landed on his bloodstained shirt.

"You and I are even now." Gray's voice was crabbed with pain. "Our accounts are balanced. I'm done with you." He took a few steps away from Trusov.

Trusov might have sensed a reprieve. He asked weakly, "You are done with me?"

A long moment passed, Gray weaving as if from a strong wind.

Gray turned back, as if with an afterthought. "But then there's Mrs. Orlando. Her account is still owing."

Gray lowered the rifle, put its snout against Trusov's forehead, and pulled the trigger. The Russian's head came apart.

"That was from her."

Gray managed only two steps away from Trusov's body until he sagged to the ground. There he lay, wondering for a few seconds if he would be found, then able to wonder no more.

20

THE TWO-MAN crosscut saw creased the log, gliding across the pine, but it was a feeble effort, and the saw did more sliding than biting. A twin was on each end of the tool. Their usual smooth teamwork had abandoned them. They pulled and pushed against each other, the saw teetered and wobbled, and the log remained largely unscathed.

"Can we quit now?" Julie asked.

"You didn't give it much of a try," Gray replied.

"Maybe you could spell us." Carolyn wiped her brow with histrionic embellishment.

"Can't. Doctor's orders. The surgeon said specifically, 'No two-man crosscut sawing.'"

Julie pulled again on the saw, to no effect, as her sister also pulled at the same time.

The woodshed's four new corner posts were now set in concrete. Adrian had leveled the concrete with a trowel. Tools from the closet were spread around the construction site.

The girls tried to balance the crosscut saw in the groove, but they hadn't cut far enough into the log, so they laid the saw on the ground.

Gray was sitting on a stump. He lifted a canteen from his lap and took a long drink.

"The girls and I have a pretty good start on your woodshed," Adrian said. "Are you going to be able to finish it after I'm gone?"

"One way or another."

"Will you have enough return in your hand?" She sat next to Gray, taking the proffered canteen.

"Viable but flail. That's the surgeon's term."

"What's that mean?"

"I'll keep all my fingers, but the smallest two—the little finger and ring finger—aren't going to be of much use. I won't be able to flex or open them. In their charming terminology, the surgeons call such useless fingers flails."

Gray's hand was wrapped in gauze over which was an ulnar gutter splint held in place by an Ace wrap. The two fingers were covered, but three showed. The gutter splint reached a point four inches above his wrist.

Two weeks had passed since the showdown with Trusov. Gray had been in a Boise hospital all that time, and had just returned to the Sawtooths. Under his loose shirt, his back and shoulders were dressed with gauze. Same with his leg under his pants. The hair on his head was starting to grow back, but still looked ragged. The healing burns on his scalp were scabbed and pink. His ear was also healing. Stitches had closed the first wound Trusov had inflicted, on Gray's arm. He would be returning to the hospital for skin grafts. Gray's old tracheotomy scar was the only part of him that didn't hurt.

Adrian had taken care of the children at the cabin for those days. But now Gray was back. Her bag was packed and on the porch.

"They took bone from my hip, a spare tendon called a palmaris from my right wrist, and a sural nerve from my leg, then put all of those assorted parts into my hand. I'll also need skin grafts, and that's the part that bugs me."

The girls had heard it before but they listened intently, adoration and worry written large on their faces.

"How so?" Adrian drank from the canteen.

"Trusov's bullet took out my ulnar artery. I was spraying blood all over like the stuff was free, so I cauterized the wound with a matchbook, as you know. But the surgeons tell me there was no need to do that. That artery would have closed itself off in what they call a vasospasm. I just added to the injury by burning the hell out of myself."

"But you thought you were bleeding to death. It was a good choice under the circumstances."

Gray shrugged.

The twins stepped up to the porch. Shards from the shattered window lay on the ground. A glass repairman from Ketchum had already visited. Adrian had set the door back on its hinges. It would work until a more permanent repair could be made.

Hobart's only police car pulled into the yard, stopping next to the larch tree. Chief Durant was behind the wheel and Pete Coates was in the passenger seat. Durant had found Gray unconscious in Shepherd's Bowl that day, had brought him out, and had spent days at the Boise hospital looking after him. He waved at them, then looked at his watch. Time to get Adrian and Pete to the airport was growing short. She was scheduled to be back in Moscow in two days.

Adrian's forehead and neck were patched with small bandages. Her skin was so white the bandages seemed to blend in. She was wearing washed-out jeans and a denim shirt. She and Gray were silent a moment, watching the twins furtively observe them and speculate about them.

"Got it," John yelled, pumping his arm. He was sitting on a patch of grass near his father. "New record." He beamed with Game Boy success. Gray gave him a thumbs-up and the boy immediately returned to the game.

Pete climbed out of the car and walked toward them. His right arm was in a sling. He had been in the hospital bed next to Gray's for most of a week.

Adrian watched him approach. His face was gray, and he had not figured out how to shave with his left hand, so his chin and a cheek were nicked.

She asked, "Why did Trusov have to shoot at Pete?"

"He knew we were partners. Maybe Trusov wanted to make sure Pete wouldn't help me in the field. Or maybe the Russian just couldn't help firing at him. He was like a crow that eats robin chicks. It was his nature, no more to be denied than a crow's nature."

"How did Trusov know you and Pete would be at the fire tower?"

"He couldn't have. Trusov was traveling to the fire tower for

300

the same reason we were, for a look at the land from a high point. We just happened onto him.''

"But I thought you and Pete knew Trusov to still be twenty miles away at the time.''

Gray closed his eyes a moment. "He fooled us, didn't he? Not for the first time.''

On the porch the twins watched them, speculating.

Coates stopped in front of Gray. "Owen, when are you coming back to Manhattan?''

"I don't know.''

Coates glanced at Adrian, then back to Gray. "Are you coming back, Owen?''

"Most likely.''

"I mean, we're a good team—me arresting the pukes and you blowing the prosecution. At least they spend some time in jail between arrest and acquittal.''

"I'll be back most likely, Pete.''

"You proved to me you know sniping, but it's clear there's lots you don't know, I'll guarantee you that.'' Coates smiled. "Come back to Manhattan and I'll teach you the rest.''

He threw a kiss to the twins and patted John on the shoulder as he walked back to the police car.

Adrian dabbed at a bandage on her neck. "Let me ask you something, Owen. Give me a straight answer.''

"I always do.''

"You always do eventually, after I've spent a good deal of time prying it from you. Why didn't you just call in a squadron of those Air National Guard helicopter gunships and have them spray all of Shepherd's Bowl. There was an easier way to rid the world of Nikolai Trusov, but you chose not to do it the easy way.''

After a moment Gray brought his eyes around to hers. "I wanted him.'' His voice was compelling. "Me, not some helicopter.''

Chief Durant tapped his horn, and held up his wristwatch, pointing to it with a finger.

Julie and Carolyn walked quickly toward them, looking at each other as they always did, silently scheming, communicating with each other with the slightest of expressions.

The girls stood in front of Gray a moment without saying anything. Adrian smiled at them. They appeared to be working up their courage.

Carolyn licked her lips and finally said, "Have you asked Adrian, Dad?"

"Pardon? Asked her what?"

"You were going to ask her not to go back to Moscow, but to stay with us here in the Sawtooths. At least for a while."

Julie was never one to let her sister carry all the load. "At least to see if things worked out between you two."

Gray protested, "I never told you anything like that."

"But we could tell you were going to," Carolyn said.

"We could tell by the way you always look at her," Julie added.

Gray glanced at Adrian. She grinned at him and raised her eyebrows.

"I'm not that obvious," he said.

Both girls said at once, "Yes, you are."

Carolyn raced on, "And now Chief Durant is waiting to take Detective Coates and Adrian to the airport. You've got to ask her now."

Gray spread his hands in a gesture of reasonableness. "Girls, Adrian and I haven't talked about anything like that. You're making presumptions, and it's sweet of you but—"

"Ask her, Dad," Carolyn demanded.

"Adrian will say yes if you ask her to stay," Julie insisted. "She told us she's got three weeks of vacation coming, and after that, who knows what might happen?"

"You're already hurt enough," Carolyn added with an impish grin. "If Adrian walks away, you'll have a broken heart, too."

Gray's face warmed. He looked out of the corner of his eye at Adrian. She was still smiling, but there was a touch of color to her cheeks.

He drew a hand along his mouth. He turned fully to Adrian. "We haven't talked about these things."

"Looks like we are now," she said.

He cleared his throat. "I don't like being brazen and forward, and I know—"

"Be brave, Owen," she said, widening her grin. "Show me some of the stuff you showed the Russian."

He asked quickly, "Will you stay, Adrian? For a while."

"Yes. For a while." Then she added, "At least."

The girls whooped and leaped and ran toward Chief Durant and Detective Coates to tell them Adrian wouldn't be going with them to the airport.

As the twins ran past their brother, Carolyn yelled at him, "Adrian is staying. She and Dad are together now."

John didn't look up from his Game Boy. "Cool."

Adrian reached for Gray. They sat there holding hands and leaning toward each other while the twins danced and pointed back at them and happily speculated with the police chief and Pete Coates about the Gray family's future.